LITHIUM
Part I

Anna Lurex

Publishing Services provided by Paper Raven Books LLC

Printed in the United States of America

First Printing, 2023

Paperback ISBN: 979-8-9881058-0-0
Hardback ISBN: 979-8-9881058-1-7

Chapter 1

I let out a heavy sigh, exhaling all of the darkness from my lungs as I rested my head against the airplane window and watched the workers dressed in yellow scurry around the maze of suitcases and cones. Tapping my feet, I peeked my head over the seat in front of me, trying to gauge how long I had to sit there before takeoff. I was impatient to get in the air and didn't want to spend another second in Minnesota. I buckled my seat belt, ready to fly across the country. I glanced down at my boarding pass, the one-way ticket to my new life. I nodded to myself, feeling confident in my decision, and tucked it into the seat pouch in front of me. I craned my neck forward so I could see what was going on ahead of economy class. I rolled my eyes as I looked through the blue curtains into first class and watched the smiling flight attendants offer mimosas. I relaxed against my seat and fiddled with my AirPods, mulling over the important decision of which band I was going to listen to during the long flight. I felt a little prickle of awkwardness when I noticed that the passenger next to me was staring at my shaking hands, so I pulled them into my lap and hid my tremors under my sweater.

"Good morning, ladies and gentlemen, this is your captain speaking, and I would like to welcome you to Delta Air Lines. This is a nonstop service trip from Minneapolis to San Francisco. Our flight time is four hours and two minutes. Please be sure that you are seated and your seat belts are fastened."

Finally, the pilot announced our departure over the speakers as the flight attendants scanned the aisles for any unbuckled passengers, reclined seats, or bags in the aisle. My body jostled in the chair as we sped down the runway, and my stomach dropped once the plane lifted into the air. I let out another heavy sigh, then an inhale of excitement as I looked down and watched Minneapolis get smaller and smaller and my past get farther and farther away as we continued our climb into the sky.

I was leaving behind twenty-four years in Minnesota. Saying goodbye to my family was difficult, but ridding myself of my traumatic past was not. It was liberating. Those towns, buildings, streets, faces….memories—they haunted me. Every breath I took was toxic. It had become harder and harder to breathe as the years passed, not easier. "Time heals all wounds," my ass. I wasn't healing, and I suddenly realized that I was suffocating. The memories held me down, restricted my growth, and crippled any hope I had of healing. That was why I was on this plane en route to San Francisco. No one knew Amelia Bell in San Francisco. Better yet, I didn't know myself, and there would be no person, place, or thing that would remind me. A tear of gratitude, or two or three, slid down my cheek as the plane broke through the blanket of clouds and the life I hated disappeared from sight.

I wanted to believe that I wasn't afraid—it couldn't get much worse than the suicidal doldrum of a life I was leaving behind. Still, I was terrified. I was making a leap toward happiness that I craved so much, but I also feared failure. If this new life couldn't save me, then nothing would. It would mean that the miserable life I'd been leading was it—no more hope, just darkness. Back home, I was sheltered and surrounded by my family, but making this move, this leap of hope, held the answer to the question—did happiness exist for me? Me, the defective, lonely, and scared woman who yearned to love and be loved, to feel more than the acute pain that depression and rejection had made me so familiar with, and to slay the fears that festered deep inside me.

"Hey. Why ya goin' to San Fran?" The man seated next to me nudged me out of my melancholy and foreboding thoughts, and I decided to humor him with friendly conversation. Unfortunately, that friendly conversation lasted an hour until I finally put my AirPods in and looked out the window at the blue sky, not caring if I was rude or not.

Being bipolar had sucked away four years of my life. Four years of my early twenties that most people spent partying, getting degrees, establishing jobs, and building relationships. I spent my early twenties in inpatient and outpatient care, experimenting with a whole pharmacy of medications to handle my massive mood swings, being a reject, dropping out of every college class that I signed up for, and piling more trauma onto the trauma I already had with men.

There was one exception from everything that dragged me down— my best friend, Ozzie. He was older than me, but that never mattered. Our parents had been best friends since our moms met each other in the Mommy and Me class where they'd taken him and my older sister. He had two sisters, and I had two sisters—he was the oldest, and I was the middle child. The six of us had always been close. Ozzie and I grew closer over the years, as we both loved art and understood each other. Which was why when he called me up with an invitation to visit San Francisco, I accepted without a second thought. He'd invited me to stay indefinitely and work with him and a group of artists. An informal phone "interview" with his team, a review of my portfolio, and I was hired—all thanks to Ozzie. His colleagues trusted him, and so did I. I knew that I would have to prove myself once I was there, which was intimidating, but I wasn't worried. I knew I was a good artist with a plethora of creative ideas dying to escape my head and get onto paper. My mom had been telling me since I was sixteen that "it'll get better" for me, and this time, I tried to believe her.

I turned off my mind for the remainder of the flight and turned on Queen's *Jazz* album.

———

"Mia!" Ozzie called from his SUV in the arrivals lane. He put his Range Rover in park and ran to greet me.

"Oz!"

He picked me up in a big, heartwarming hug and helped me load my two massive suitcases into the back of his car. He asked me how my flight went, and we caught up on the few things that had happened since the last time we'd talked, which was only a day ago.

"Do you have Tylenol?" I winced as I situated myself in the passenger seat and shifted my shoulders. He shook his head. "Ibuprofen?"

"No, sorry. Robo-back?" he asked as he kept his eyes on the road and merged into traffic.

"Yeah, those plane seats are torture," I grumbled as I continued to try to find a comfortable position. I gave up and shrugged it off. I'd had a spinal fusion when I was a teen, which had some disadvantages, like not being able to move my entire thoracic spine. "Ah, well." I sighed, then turned in my seat to face him. "You're lookin' good," I observed, since I hadn't seen him in person since Christmas and it was now the beginning of April.

"Why, thank you." Ozzie was four years older than me and had been working as an artist in San Francisco for the past five years. He was a handsome guy, very sweet and fun, but we'd never had any feelings for each other past friendship. He had a full head of thick, wavy brown hair that was longer on top and was always clean-shaven. I teased him that he had an Owen Wilson nose, but it really wasn't *that* crooked. About six feet tall, with a body like a swimmer—yep, basically his dating app bio. "You've looked better." He smirked and looked over at me, then back at the road.

"Hey! I was just in an airplane for four hours," I defended myself but didn't take offense. "You know how airplanes are—makes your hair flat and your skin feel grimy."

"I'm just messing. So…let's go to your new apartment." I did a little bounce in my seat and let myself bask in my excitement over my new reality. I'd be subletting his old apartment, since he'd recently moved into a nicer one—same with his old car, which I'd be borrowing, as he'd recently gotten a new Range Rover. Apparently, the job paid well. Really, he couldn't have made the move any easier for me.

We pulled up to a tall apartment building, and Ozzie put his truck in park. To spare my back, I let him carry my two suitcases for me as I followed him into the building.

"Alright, this is how you get in—here's your keys—and up to the fourth floor." As I followed him into the elevator, I noticed that it was still a very nice place to live. When he'd lived there, he'd made it sound like a dump. We wheeled my suitcases inside, and Ozzie showed me around. There wasn't a lot of furniture, but all the simple necessities were present. The place was roomy—including a full kitchen with a center island and a large living room with a couch, loveseat, coffee table, and TV. It was all hardwood floors and white walls, with big windows that let light pour in to brighten the rooms.

"Damn. This is awesome. You said it was shitty!" I slowly twirled in the middle of the living room, soaking in my new home.

"Well…I guess it's not shitty, but it's really old." He shrugged, and I checked out the bedroom and en suite bathroom. "Yeah, it has two bathrooms, which is nice if you have friends over. Hey, you'll finally make friends!" I rejoined him in the living room, giving him a funny look, but I couldn't blame him for the comment. It was true—except for Ozzie, I hadn't had friends since going through a lot of horrendous bullying in high school. Yes, that was six years with no friends. "Well, now you have me, Jax, Nick, and Steven as automatic friends," Ozzie said.

"Ah, yes. I'm going to need full reports on them." He promised to fill me in on the members of his artist team, who were also his close friends. "Okay. Let's go shopping. I need a record player. I should be getting a few boxes delivered here tomorrow, including my vinyl collection."

"You got it." Ozzie clapped, and we didn't waste any time. He showed me around the city a little, pointing out anything relevant to him, and me, as we drove around trying to find the best record player—something that I didn't mind splurging on. After we'd found the perfect record player, my stomach growled, reminding me that I hadn't eaten anything all day and it was already five o'clock, so he took me to an Irish pub down the street from my new apartment.

We settled into a small booth, and I took in my surroundings. The dark wood and dim lighting felt cozy, and the older crowd wining and dining was quiet, making it a perfect place for good conversation. A server was quick to take our orders and deliver our drinks, a beer for Ozzie and my go-to Jameson and ginger ale.

"You still do that?" Ozzie laughed and took a swig from the bottle, and I followed his eyes to my left hand.

"Of course." I smiled and looked at the nails on my left hand all painted black.

"Ever considered painting the right hand…?"

"Not really. It's harder to apply nail polish with my left hand as it is, and add in tremors…impossible," I explained. I'd been painting just my left hand black since high school.

"You know there's a place girls go where someone will paint your nails for you," he informed me.

"*There is?* Where?" I gasped like it was a game changer.

"Whatever." He chuckled and shook his head.

"I could go to a nail salon, sure. But I like how I do it myself. Besides, I noticed that Freddie Mercury only painted his left hand black in the early seventies, so now I feel cool."

"You're very cool." Ozzie nodded.

"I know." I took a sip of my whiskey. "Now fill me in."

"Well…" Ozzie sat back against the booth to stretch, thinking through a rundown of my new coworkers. "The four of us have known each other for a long time now, but we've been together, officially, for almost four years. You know I do abstract, and Nick was big into spray-painting when we met but does more prints now. Steven kind of does everything else— painting, matte, oil, watercolor… He's very knowledgeable, so go to him if you're curious. Jax does mostly sculptures and whatever else he feels like.

Jax isn't our boss, but he is the one who got us all together, and it's his place—he owns the building our studio is in. We are all equal, though."

"Jax—with an *X*—short for Jackson? He is your best friend, right? Have I met him?"

"My *other* best friend." He exaggerated a smile. "But yeah, Jackson Caine. He uses his full name only for work—other than that, he always goes by Jax, with an *X*. He hates when people call him Jack. You've never met him. We were neighbors when my family moved here, and he helped me fit in at school—we've been best friends since. He's a good guy. You two should get along. You're pretty similar."

"How so?" I cocked my head and waited for more information, as he took a swig of his pale ale.

"I dunno...same interests. He's very authentic and deep." I smiled at the description and appreciated the comparison. "Steven is pretty quiet and mild but very nice and smart. I met him at Georgetown. He introduced us to Nick. He's loud and obnoxious but fun. Kinda immature...you'll like him," Ozzie teased, and I fake laughed at his immature jab at me. "I'm kidding! Just the fun part, and he's the youngest—well, now second youngest."

"Which is…?"

"Twenty-six. Steven is a year younger than me, and Jax just turned thirty."

"Who was the other guy? The one I'm replacing."

"Yeah, Harrison just moved to the East Coast, which is why I thought you could join us right away. He wasn't with us long and was pretty boring. We're all glad to have you...a woman to mix things up." He shuffled his shoulders around and smirked.

"I'm good at that." I chuckled but wanted to know more. I'd basically accepted the offer and packed my bags without a thought, trusting Ozzie. "Who decides the projects?"

"Jax finds and manages them, but we all have to agree on what we'll take on as a group. We sometimes do solo work on the side if things are slow—which they're not right now. We've been pretty busy. Our reputation just took off."

"What about the business part?"

"Jax takes care of the business side of things—like managing the projects, communicating with clients, and handling the money. But, really, we are *equals*. When we do a group project, Jax divides the money evenly and never takes a larger cut, even though he does more logistical work. It has to be a unanimous decision with everything. Like it was when I suggested you," Ozzie explained, and our food arrived.

"Thank you for that. Really, Ozzie, you have no idea how much this means to me."

"You deserve it, Mia."

"Hm." I nodded. "I didn't realize that you guys were such a big deal until that magazine article. I can't remember the name of it, but Cathy sent us all copies." I chuckled as I remembered his mom sending a box of magazines to my family, rightfully proud of her son.

"*Juxtapose*. Yeah…that was exciting. I guess we are a pretty big deal." He beamed with pride, and I felt immensely happy for them.

"What do you guys call yourselves?" I asked, curious, since I should've known but couldn't think of the name.

"Artists…"

"Yeah, but officially, as a group."

"Oh. Uh…artists." He shrugged. "We've never talked about it… We're pretty well known around here. It started with just Jax and his commissions. He was really successful on his own, then invited us to form a group. His is a bigger name than any of us, but we don't care. We never really needed a name, but now that we've gotten more recognition, it'd be a good idea."

"You guys need a band name."

"*We* need a band name. I know that your drawings are going to step us up."

"Ah, yes." I smiled, feeling special to be a part of their talented group. I was artistic, yes…but I'd never really branched out beyond drawing. I didn't care enough about the other mediums to learn. I had just been enhancing my drawing technique over the years and had created some impressive works. "So, how is the Bishop family?" I dunked a French fry into ketchup, ready for the update. Our connection ran deep, as our two families had been close before I was born. We were all one big, happy group of kids, but Ozzie and I started bonding more than the rest over our fledgling artistic talents. For a while, our two families were in the same economic class—two hardworking businessmen and two dedicated stay-at-home mothers. A lot had happened since then. When his dad became the CFO of a global company, it changed everything. The Bishops moved from Minneapolis to London, then Tokyo, before landing in San Francisco. Even though geography kept us apart, we managed to stay best friends.

"Everyone is great!" Ozzie filled me in on his family. "How's the Bell family?" Ozzie asked curiously before biting into his double cheeseburger.

"Good." I sighed and nodded, thinking of everyone in my family whom I'd just said goodbye to. "Jeff and Carol are…fine." I shrugged, letting him assume that my parents' relationship had been strained ever since I'd disrupted the family dynamic when I moved back home after my bipolar diagnosis. I continued to tell him about my older sister, who'd just had a baby, and my younger sister, who was in college. "Nora and Chris are happy with Ben, who is just adorable. Being an aunt is fun. Stella is doing well in nursing school at the University of Minnesota. And Zeus, my baby, is going to be lost without me," I finished, emphasizing the one positive thing in my life, my dog, Zeus. People said a cane corso was a bad choice for an emotional support animal, but we made it work. I missed him terribly and hoped that someday he'd be able to join me in San Francisco, but first, I had to focus on stability. Ozzie sensed that I didn't want to talk much about my family, and we enjoyed our burgers with more lighthearted conversation.

———

"I'll be the runner, and you just follow with the cart," Ozzie laid out the plan as we entered the grocery store, and started moving before I could agree.

"Ozzie…budget…" I reminded him as I watched him gather prime produce.

"Not for long." He put a few plastic bags in the cart.

"For now." I put the produce back. "I just need Cocoa Puffs, some protein bars, and whiskey."

"Mia, that is not a sustainable diet." He looked at me very seriously. I rolled my eyes because I knew that, but cereal and protein bars were my go-to things to eat when my medications fucked with my appetite and digestion, which was almost always. "Think *whole foods* to make meals."

"Okay, Mom."

"I do not answer to 'Mom.'" Whenever I called him that, Ozzie's scowl was really cute, and I couldn't take him seriously.

"You just answered." I smiled, and he turned and walked away. "Ozzie!"

"Yes?" He spun around and rejoined me at the cart. "Okay, compromise, we get what you want, but I get to add a fruit and a vegetable. And milk."

"Deal." I allowed Ozzie to add apples and carrots to my food haul. With the short grocery list, we were soon checked out and on our way back to my apartment so Ozzie could help me sort through my boxes for the rest of the night.

"So…how are things with you?" he hedged and watched me from a lounging position on his—now *my*—couch.

"Bipolar things?" I glanced at him from where I sat on the floor putting together my new record player, having sensed a change in his tone.

"Yeah. Other things too. I just want to know how you're doing," Ozzie said kindly. I sighed—thankful for his concern but hesitant to answer. I was always reluctant to respond to such questions since I usually had to filter what I said, even with my best friend.

"Bipolar things are fine. I'm stable, so my moods don't swing as much," I answered.

"When was the last time you were depressed? If you don't mind me asking." Ozzie knew that my mood swings swung heavily to the depression side. I had Bipolar II—which meant less severe mania, called "hypomania," and more severe depression.

"Like…twenty-four hours ago." He frowned, even more concerned. "Ozzie, I've been situationally depressed since high school. My life was dark in Minnesota. Honestly, you only know half of it, and you don't want to know the rest."

"You mean there's even *more* to it than what you've told me?"

I took a deep breath before I answered. I didn't want to upset him, but I needed to be honest and own up to my past. "I've told you everything, Ozzie, just not the details." My best friend stared at me with glassy eyes. I never meant for this conversation to be sad. I wanted to focus on the good. "But being here…" I looked around my new apartment, then back to him. "I don't remember the last time I felt truly happy. So… thank you." I blinked back tears and smiled more brightly at Ozzie, who'd made my escape possible. His eyes were still troubled, but he nodded. "I haven't had a major depressive episode in a few months, though," I said. "Those are happening less and less as I maintain stability, but I still feel it, just not as bad."

"Mia." He sighed as he straightened to sit up on the cushion and looked into my eyes, more serious. "You probably won't tell me the gritty details." He watched me for confirmation, and I nodded. "Well, it's horrific, what I do know, and I'll never be able to understand what you have to deal with every day. You're the strongest girl I know. You're awesome and deserve the world." I let his words sink in, but I still found them hard to believe. "How is it being away from your family, though?"

"It's a little scary. Four years after my diagnosis, and they still don't understand me—it's painful, but they supported me even when things got dark or destructive."

"I promise to be here for you, okay?" I nodded. "Seriously, Mia, I will *always* be here for you. You try to hide your moods because you don't want to be a burden, but you're not. Don't ever hesitate to ask for anything—ever, please. I hope you trust me."

"I do. Thanks, Oswald." I smiled, poking fun at his full name, but I meant it, and went to give him a hug. Ozzie spent the rest of the night with me educating me on the art scene of San Francisco.

Once he left, I was alone in the foreign apartment. I walked around, getting used to my new home. I took in deep, cleansing breaths of solitude that I'd craved and started getting ready for bed. It really was an exciting novelty to live on my own. Why was I living with my parents from twenty to twenty-four? Good question—Bipolar II disorder. That bitch of a mental illness had crashed into my life when I hit adulthood. With a history of mental illness in my family, I was diagnosed with depression as a teenager, prescribed Lexapro, and started seeing a therapist once a week. Trauma struck my senior year of high school, which morphed my brain chemicals from a little twisted to intensely fucked up. Everyone minimized what I was going through. I would say, "I had a bad experience in high school." The response: "Oh, high school is hard for everyone." Really? Did everyone's high school experience trigger a mental illness? I didn't think so.

A few dark movements around my room made me flinch as I got into bed. I didn't care, as I felt my nightly medications weigh down my eyelids, and I snuggled under the comforter, a faint smile on my lips as I anticipated the morning and the start of my new job. My eyes flickered open just before I fell asleep, and suddenly, I saw cobwebs. I scanned the room to see a pattern of white streams pulsating around me. I was already aware of the powerful chemicals that rioted inside my brain and never underestimated them, so when I stared into those webs, I wasn't afraid. Rather, I was simply interested. I stretched out my arm and pointed my finger into the streams, curious to see what would happen if I touched the formation. Once I penetrated the unreal embodiment, the white streams all pulled together in a giant figure above me. Now I was scared. The figure grew in size and charged at me as I lay in my bed. Now I was really fucking scared. I screeched, in the line of fire of my own mind, and pulled the comforter over me. I squeezed my eyes shut, counting my inhales and exhales until I fell asleep.

Chapter 2

When my eyes opened in the morning, I felt completely disoriented. It took me several minutes to fight through the grogginess of my medications and more minutes to process what had happened in the past twenty-four hours. I had taken a long plane ride to a new city, moved into a new apartment…and hallucinated a cobwebbed creature attacking me in my bed. I groaned and rubbed my hands over my face, wishing life were just a tad easier. I sighed and looked up to the ceiling, but it was moving, swirling into a hurricane. I squeezed my eyes shut, coming up with a plan to prevent the hallucinations from interfering with my first day of work. Keeping my eyes closed cut off my mind from creating visuals, so I felt my way into the bathroom. As long as I didn't look at anything long and had a distraction, I could ignore whatever my mind tried to throw in my way. I shoved down all the challenges of being bipolar and started getting ready for an exciting day.

Ozzie had given me information overload, and not all of my belongings had arrived yet. I felt scatterbrained and unprepared. I took my time getting ready and decided to try applying makeup. I usually never wore any but wanted a confidence boost for my first day, so I embarked on a journey of putting on makeup with tremor-ridden hands.

I stared into my green-gray eyes in the mirror, trying to look past a hallucination of spiders crawling along the edges so I could focus on my face. My hand shaky, I spent twenty minutes pulling out eyelashes with a lash curler and poking myself in the eye with a mascara wand. Black liquid was dotted and smeared over my lids and freckled cheeks. "Mission abort." I sighed and washed my face for the fifth and final time, giving up. Still, I managed to apply my signature lip stain to enhance my natural color, leaving the rest of my face bare.

I become nervous as I shifted my mind to focus on the new job and all the usual anxieties that everyone experienced. *Are my new coworkers going to like me? What if I don't like them? What if I'm not as good as they thought I was? What if I fail?*

I didn't know how to fit in, especially after the past four cloistered years of my life—if I ever knew how to fit in at all. I wondered what kind of artists the men were. Were they brooding antiestablishment artists? Were they flamboyant look-at-me-and-how-special-I-am artists? Were they self-righteous political artists? Were they gritty and messy artists? I had no idea, so I was self-conscious about how I should present myself on my first day. I settled on my go-to outfit, more like my uniform: high-waisted capri leggings, a baby tee, and chunky sneakers, which complemented my slight figure. My phone lit up with a text from Ozzie, announcing his arrival. I was almost out the door when I remembered the most vital part of my morning routine—meds. I sighed, irritated with myself for almost forgetting and annoyed I had to swallow six pills every morning to survive life—three white, one pink, and two orange. *Bottoms up.*

I stepped outside and into a crisp spring morning and breathed in the novel feeling of hope. I was nervous, but my body buzzed with excitement. The pavement beneath me started to pixelate and shift as shadows crept into the periphery of my vision as I walked down the path to the curb, but I kept my eyes forward. *Mental note—call Dr. Burke.*

I hopped in the passenger seat of Ozzie's Range Rover and buckled myself into the plush leather seat. "Hey, colleague!"

"Hello to you too, colleague. Nervous?"

"Of course I'm nervous." I rolled my eyes, feeling jittery, and he gave me a reassuring smile. I thought about clueing Ozzie in about my little hallucinations, but I didn't want any of my problems seeping into my day. I wanted to enjoy the experience like anyone else.

"They're going to love you. I wouldn't have invited you if I didn't believe in you. Here, take my phone and go to the Starbucks app."

I tapped through the app as Ozzie listed everyone's order—soy latte for me, skim latte for Ozzie, iced caramel macchiato for Steven, and mocha Frappuccino for Nick. Ozzie pulled into the Starbucks parking lot, and I ran in to retrieve our coffees.

"Jax doesn't like coffee?" I asked once I settled back into the SUV and handed Ozzie his skim latte from out of the carrier.

"Oh, yeah. Jax is actually out of town visiting his family, so you won't meet him until next week." After a few more minutes, Ozzie pulled up to the curb in front of a historic industrial brick building. "This is it. Welcome to the office," Ozzie said with a smile that showed his eagerness to be working with me. I hopped down from the SUV and onto the sidewalk and tilted my head back, looking up at the four-story building. It was a lot bigger and older than I'd expected. Ozzie paused with me on the sidewalk once he noticed my surprised expression. "Yeah, it used to be an old factory or orphanage or fire station…I can't remember. Jax renovated the whole thing, so the inside—well, you'll see." Ozzie shrugged and went to the entrance.

I watched him hold a key fob up to the door; then we walked into an elevator. I closed my eyes while the doors were shut, proactively restricting my brain from getting creative with the low lighting while we rode up to the second floor. Ozzie held up his fob again, and the elevator doors opened into a small foyer with double-high ceilings and an open floor plan that included the next level. We ascended the stairway to the third floor. I felt my chest tighten with each step as I felt abnormal anxieties mix in with the normal new-job jitters. *What if I hallucinate something I can't cover? What if they can see through my normal exterior to my inner crazy? What if my mind misfires and they think I'm stupid? What if they see my hands shake and think I'm on drugs?*

"So this is the studio floor," Ozzie said once we got to the top of the stairs, then pointed to the other side of the room, which was still open to the foyer, to a stairway leading up. "Jax lives upstairs. This hallway has the bathroom, supply room, drying room, Jax's room, Nick's room, mini exhibit room, guest bedroom… I'll show you later." Ozzie listed the rooms in order as we walked down the hallway, then lead me to the left, through a big open doorway, and into a massive room with more double-high ceilings. *This is one chopped-up floor plan, but I dig it.* The studio took up the third floor and part of the fourth floor—the other half of the fourth floor was Jax's loft. It was the corner of the building, so two walls were all windows, and skylights let in even more natural light. Four workstations were scattered around the border of the room in the best-lit spots. In the back corner was a modern black leather couch, two matching leather chairs, and a coffee table. The sitting area was surrounded by a big shelf that held records, CDs, books, and a turntable. I then noticed big speakers mounted on the walls. In the other back corner of the room were a table and chairs for meetings.

"Guys! Come meet Mia!" I heard Ozzie call through another doorway before turning back to me. "That's the kitchen." He pointed in the direction he'd yelled. I took a deep breath and felt comforted by Ozzie's presence as I was about to meet my new coworkers. Two men emerged dressed in worn jeans and T-shirts just like Ozzie. One was almost Ozzie's height, with short dark-brown hair and a very slim, even lanky, build. He introduced himself as Steven. The other one, who introduced himself as Nick, was shorter and had shaggy blond hair. He had the most beautiful big blue eyes and long lashes I'd ever seen, and a round face. *He looks like my baby nephew…who looks like the Gerber baby. Nick looks like the Gerber baby.*

"Nice to meet you both." I smiled as I shook their hands. Steven seemed calm and introverted, while Nick was hyper and extroverted.

"So formal. We're not formal," Nick teased and pulled me in for a hug. "You look different than your pictures." He narrowed his eyes to inspect me more closely. I frowned and glanced at Ozzie.

"Is that good or bad…?" I asked nervously. Nick started circling me.

"Nick, reel it in," Ozzie scolded him and gave me a sympathetic shrug.

"Ah!" Nick shouted so close to me, I jumped from the volume and high pitch of his voice. "It's your hair." He nodded and smiled, happy with his detection. Ozzie had probably showed them pictures of me when I was bleaching my hair extra blonde. I admit, my hair looked very different now, since it had returned to my natural sandy blonde. Then Nick actually started pulling on my long hair. *He really is like my baby nephew.* "You're still hot, but I like redheads."

"Good to know." I nodded seriously to match his expression. That's when my focus shifted to Steven, who stood next to Nick with a funny smirk on his face. Steven's dark-brown hair had a red tint to it that I hadn't noticed at first, more burgundy than brown.

"Not you! Ugh," Nick whined and threw his hands up, then took two big steps away from his colleague. I started laughing with Steven and Ozzie. They accepted the coffees Ozzie and I'd brought them, then showed me around the room, identifying their stations and pointing me to the empty one next to Ozzie's near the corner of windows.

"This is your work space, so unpack and get comfortable." Ozzie left me to settle in, which didn't take long. I basically just dropped my purse on the ground next to a bare easel. I picked up my latte and walked around. Nick's and Steven's stations were across the room from me, so I went over to visit. They were drinking their coffees and casually chatting about their weekends. From what I overheard as I approached, Steven had a girlfriend, and I listened harder to make out Nick's voice over the loud slurping of his chocolatey drink and learned that he liked multiple girls.

"Would you mind showing me some of your work?" I asked eagerly, and they happily obliged. What they were currently working on was displayed on their easels and tables—a beautiful landscape by Steven and a vibrant print of the San Francisco skyline by Nick. I knew I was a good artist, too, and tried not to get intimidated, but everything they showed me was impressive. I continued to look around. The walls were white and the floor was concrete with paint splatters throughout and covered in scuffs. The view of the city was gorgeous too, and I was itching to snoop through that media shelf.

"So, what's the daily schedule like?" I asked them and listened to all they had to say. It was an environment of professional artists, and they seemed to work very hard, but I knew I was going to love the group because they didn't take themselves too seriously. That's what I hated about being an adult—everyone took themselves and life way too seriously. Living with bipolar, experiencing the catastrophic highs and suicidal lows, had led me not to take anything less than that too seriously. My new colleagues were dedicated and accomplished artists, but they kept things fun and relaxed.

Ozzie showed me the other rooms around the studio. There was a big functional kitchen that was all mahogany cabinetry and granite countertops, the main studio room where they spent most of the day, then the long open hallway of rooms that ran along the foyer and further down. There was a bathroom; a supply room and drying room; a room full of tools and machines for Jax's sculpting; a small room for Nick's spray-painting that was covered in different blotches and streaks of color on the walls and floor; and a small exhibit room, which had a selection of all of their works. At the very end of the hallway, next to stairs that went up to Jax's loft, was a simple guest bedroom.

I wandered into the exhibit room so I could study the guys' portfolios. I was impressed by everything there but was enchanted by Jax's sculptures. I had never seen anything like them and got excited knowing that I would be able to watch as he made future creations. My eyes tried to focus on one sculpture at a time, to see the fine details, but my mind started to twist them all together. My focus went in and out as the forms stretched across the room and then swirled around me. It was so strange—hallucinating and knowing that I was hallucinating. I could turn it off by closing my eyes, but I didn't want to as I stared, mesmerized by the artwork coming to life.

"You like Jax's work?" Nick's high voice snapped me out of my hallucination, and just like that, the world fell back into place. I looked over my shoulder to see him leaning against the doorway and smiling at me.

"Yeah." I smiled back, thankful that he didn't notice my faraway look. "Very unique." I turned away from the sculptures and met Nick at the door.

"We work right next to him but still don't know how he does it." Nick shrugged and started walking away, and I figured that I was supposed to follow him. We turned into the kitchen, and he opened the fridge door and poked his head inside. "You want a Red Bull or something? We only really have Red Bull…"

"Uh." I considered the energy drink offer, but my eye caught movement next to me, so I reflexively turned that way and came face-to-face with the cobwebbed creature that had attacked me the night before. The white strings were still weaving together and pulsating as I stared into the demonic creation of my mind. "Oh my God." I flinched away with a startled gasp.

"*What?*" Nick's head popped out from behind the fridge door. Thankfully, he hadn't seen my physical reaction, but he'd still heard me. His blue eyes were wide, and I felt bad for startling him.

"Um. Ha. I wasn't expecting…" My eyes frantically searched for anything as an excuse for my outburst. "This fridge is so big! Wow. Impressive appliances." I internally face-palmed but played it somewhat cool. Why did it have to be demonic creatures attacking me? Why couldn't my mind hallucinate cute little cherubs giving me a thumbs-up on my first day?

"Yeah, we're fancy like that!" Nick laughed and closed the door. He handed me a can of Red Bull, then cracked open another.

"You okay?" Ozzie walked through the door with a concerned frown, Steven behind him.

"Yeah, yeah, good." I brushed his question off and cracked open my can.

"This is a good time to get you set up. You'll need our help," Ozzie offered, and Steven and Nick agreed. "We'll bring out your table, and you go explore the supply room."

"Okay." I smiled, setting down the Red Bull, and followed them out of the kitchen. I broke away to explore the supply room while they continued down the hallway.

The space looked like a Blick art store, and I started digging through the pencil cases. I picked out my usual tools, then searched through all of the fancier professional tools I never bought for myself and picked out a few I'd always wanted to try. When I lived in Minnesota, all I used was an HB pencil, an eraser, and a blending stick. Ozzie was always amazed by the artwork I could create with such limited tools and training. As I looked over the supplies I'd picked out, I felt giddy thinking of how much better I could get with professional materials and professional artists around me. I returned to the studio, where Ozzie, Steven, and Nick had set up my station.

"Hey, Mia!" Nick called me over. "Come check it out!" I was happy they were so eager to help me and joined them at my station.

"Your new drawing table." Ozzie waved his hand over the massive drawing table. The legs were adjustable so I could change the height and slant of the tabletop. On one edge, a compartmented shelf was bolted on to hold all my tools. On the other end, a small shelf could be pulled out to be used however I needed.

"Wow. This is awesome!" I did a mini hop of excitement. "Thanks, guys."

All three of them said, "No problem," with a friendly smile. Steven and Nick left to return to their stations, but Ozzie stayed with me.

"An improvement from that uneven little table back home?" Ozzie asked as he watched me transfer my supplies from my arms to the table's compartments. I just smiled and nodded. "It's fun seeing you happy."

"It's fun being happy." I glanced at him, still smiling, as I finished putting my pencils away.

"You're going to thrive here, Mia. I'm so excited for you," he said more seriously and pulled me into a one-armed hug.

"Thanks, Oz." I hugged him back.

"Okay, table is ready to go." Ozzie pointed at my table, then at my easel. "Now, easel. I'm guessing you'll be needing the height adjusted." I tilted my head up to see the easel and spotted the small tray at the top of the mast.

"Was the guy before me a giant?" I joked. I wasn't short, five foot six, but I would've needed a stepstool in order to reach the top screw.

"Harrison, no." Ozzie chuckled as he reached up on his tiptoes to unscrew the tray. "Jax used this a couple times for a project we just finished," he explained as he slid the tray down to my height and then screwed it in again. "Alright. Easel is ready."

"This is awesome." I looked around my station. The easel and drawing table, a view of the city through towering windows, my best friend ten feet to the right, and two new friends to the left. *Pinch me.* For the rest of the day, I continued to organize my supplies, getting more comfortable in my new workplace.

———

Once the workday was over and Ozzie dropped me off at my apartment, I was exhausted. New city, new job, meeting new people, and hallucinating in between was a lot to take in. I sighed as I walked through the door and went straight to the couch, where I plopped down and closed my eyes. I smiled to myself, thankful and happy. The studio was brilliant, and I already loved Nick and Steven as colleagues and knew that we would all be friends. I lived through the day again in my head, and my eyes popped open when I remembered the cobwebbed demon that had scared me and also Nick in a secondhand way. Still lying down, I fished my phone from my purse on the floor and scrolled through my contacts until I found "Nurse Amy." She was the point person for my psychiatrist, Dr. Burke—a psychiatrist who handled medications. I tapped the green icon to dial and raised my phone to my ear.

"If this is a psychiatric emergency, please dial nine-one-one. Press one to be connected to the national suicide prevention hotline…" I nodded along as I listened to the long answering-machine recording until it asked for a detailed message after the beep.

"Hi, Amy. This is Amelia Bell. A-M-E-L-I-A B-E-L-L. I'm a patient of Dr. Burke…" I recited the required introduction for the phone call and finished with my date of birth and phone number. "As Dr. Burke knows, I moved to San Francisco and arrived just yesterday. I've been experiencing strange hallucinations—well, I guess all hallucinations are strange—since last night, soooo…I—I just don't know why it's happening or how to make it stop, so…yeah. Please call me back. Thank you. Bye." I ended the voice mail with a sigh and dropped my phone down on the cushion. I gazed up at the ceiling and saw that, like the night before, it was churning like a hurricane. I kept staring at it because, like the hallucination in the exhibit room with Jax's sculptures, hallucinations could be cool to look at. Like the night before, the hallucinations continued through the evening until I gulped down my medications and fell asleep.

———

I was pulled out of my medication-induced sleep by my phone vibrating, but I was not ready to wake up. I opened my eyes and reached for my phone with the intention of hitting the snooze button but shot upright when I saw who was calling. I cleared my throat to make sure that my voice wasn't laced with sleep and answered the call.

"Hi, Amelia, this is Dr. Burke's nurse speaking."

"Ah! Yes, hi, Amy." I was excited to hear from her and pushed up in bed so my back was against the headboard, ready to listen.

"You said you've been experiencing hallucinations? Can you explain them?"

"Yes." I gave her some examples of how my mind had been messing with me.

"Have you taken any hallucinogenic drugs in the past few days?"

"No. No drugs. Except for medications." I rolled my eyes but understood she had to ask the question.

"And is this the first time you're experiencing this? Your hallucinations are unusual." *No shit, Amy.*

"No, but it's been a long time. The only time I had full hallucinations like this was before I was hospitalized. That's when I was assigned to Dr. Burke in the psych ward. So, four years ago."

"Well, you've made a major life change, moving from your family's home to being alone in a new city. You're stable, yes, but there's still room for inconsistencies, especially if you get behind on sleep." Amy said what I already knew.

"So…it's going to stop?"

"It should. One moment." She put me on hold to consult with my psychiatrist. "Okay. Dr. Burke says to double your Seroquel at night until the hallucinations fully stop. I'll check in with you next week, but call if you need to before that."

"Alright, I'll do that. Thank you so much!" We hung up, and I smiled, comforted to have a plan.

I followed my psychiatrist's directions, and by Thursday, the hallucinations were gone. I was relieved that the cobwebbed demon had stopped stalking me and that objects were no longer moving so I could fully focus on my life, and the first week at my new job was fun and went by quickly.

Chapter 3

In the studio, we didn't do much art because they were waiting for Jax to return to start a new project.

"Do you guys listen to music while you work?" I asked the three boys nearby as I looked at the CDs on the bookshelf.

"Oh, yeah. Those are all Jax's—go ahead and look through them. We approve of everything in there." Ozzie nodded and encouraged me to check it out.

"Oh my God! This is awesome!" I jumped up with excitement when I found Queen and started sifting through the albums.

"I told you! Similar interests." Ozzie chuckled, and I kept looking.

I spotted all my favorites—Queen, obviously, Led Zeppelin, Hendrix, the Doors, the Rolling Stones, Aerosmith, Metallica, and even Nine Inch Nails and Nirvana.

"Y'all like Queen, right?" I called over my shoulder, and the boys all said yes. I found *The Game* CD and put it in the player. I was excited to meet Jax since I believed what Ozzie said about our mutual interests. I especially loved that he had CDs. I had a whole box full in Ozzie's hand-me-down car, as I preferred them over Bluetooth and radio. My love was classic rock, and I always got amped when I found someone to talk to who shared the same enthusiasm. The guys were working on things, so I went to my station and fiddled around as the songs played. I felt comfortable around my new colleagues, so when my favorite song on the album,

"Another One Bites the Dust," started to play, I had to dance as I moved around the room.

"I love this song!" Steven cheered, and they started head-bopping with the beat.

"*Ooh...let's go!*" I sang along and danced like Freddie Mercury. "*Hey, I'm gonna get you too—another one bites the dust.*" I danced around Steven and Nick, who played along, and Ozzie laughed.

I was giggling at myself and walking backward when I ran into the wall. I jumped away and saw that the wall was a man, an incredibly sexy man who I wanted to run into again. I turned to face him fully, but all I saw were broad shoulders and a strong chest. He was well over six feet tall, and I had to tilt my head back to drag my gaze up to meet his dark-blue eyes that glared and intimidated me, so I immediately took a step back. I knew who he was—Jackson Caine. Nothing Ozzie had told me about him prepared me for meeting the man in the flesh.

Jax wordlessly held up a remote and clicked, turning off the music. I couldn't tell much about his body since it was covered in a hoodie and loose jeans, but from the hard exterior I had just run into, I knew it was *good*. I looked away from his fierce gaze, and my eyes dropped to his full and tempting lips that were pressed in a straight line.

"Jax, you're back sooner...?" Ozzie walked over to be next to me but hesitated when he saw how pissed off his other best friend looked. *Why does he look mad?*

"So, you're our new artist," Jackson Caine stated plainly, ignoring his friend as his eyes dragged up and down my body. I nodded—that was the best I could do with that powerful body towering in front of me and those dark-blue eyes now locked to mine. "Working hard?" He lifted his brows with the question and crossed his arm, patiently waiting for my response.

"Um—we were... I just got here, so—um," I stuttered. He nodded along while I tried to formulate a sentence. I took a deep breath and snapped out of it. Squaring my shoulders, I extended my hand toward him. "Yes.

I'm the new artist, Mia," I said with more confidence. He studied me closely, almost suspiciously, before accepting the handshake.

The moment we made contact, I nearly recoiled from static shock, yet I couldn't let go. I felt his fiery energy attack my skin, goose bumps ran up my arm, and that energy burned through my body. The strong reaction felt ominous as I looked up and my eyes connected with his stormy gaze. I felt my cheeks heat and didn't like that asshole smirk on his face as he noticed my blush. I snapped out of the daze just as fast as I was sucked into it and recovered. I wasn't sure of what judgment he was making of me in that moment, but I was very sure that I did not appreciate being judged at first sight. I was embarrassed by my initial timid response to him and irritated by that arrogant smirk on his face. "Nice to meet you, Jackson." I smiled pleasantly, not being able to help myself from making an awkward introduction worse.

"It's Jax." He dropped the arrogant smirk, then my hand, and rolled his eyes.

"Oh. Sorry. Nice to meet you, Jack," I ever-so-sweetly corrected myself. His jaw ticked, and he stared at me like he was deciding whether to put up with me or not.

"Jax…with an *X*."

"But there's no *X* in Jackson?" With a curious tilt of my head, I took the name flop a little further, testing how far I could push him without going overboard—I think I reached the limit.

"No." He smoldered, and once I let a smirk slip, he knew I was messing with him. His jaw shifted, his eyes narrowed, and he scanned my body again before looking past me to acknowledge the other three people in the room. "Hey, guys." He nodded to Ozzie, Nick, and Steven, who had been watching our awkward introduction. "I have news. Stay tuned." He spoke just to them. When he turned back around, his eyes met mine again, but only for a second, before he left, swaggering out of the studio.

I let out a sigh of relief, thankful to be free from that man's intense scrutiny. I stood there, still feeling the aftershocks of his touch but also stung by his rude and dismissive behavior. Blinking several times, I snapped out of the daze and faced my other three colleagues.

"Was that weird...?" I asked nervously as I fidgeted with my necklace, realizing that I'd just made myself look bad by messing with their colleague and friend.

"No," Ozzie assured me just as Nick gave his opinion: "A little."

Nick shrugged. Steven just stared at me, then looked to the doorway Jax disappeared through that led to his loft.

"You could've just called him Jax..." Ozzie hedged, and I felt betrayed but couldn't blame him. *I should've just called him Jax.*

"Ha! No, that was funny." Nick laughed, then came closer to put his arm around me. "You're fine, Mia. Don't worry." I smiled my appreciation for the support but took several steps away from the physical contact.

My confidence started to dwindle, and my mind was overwhelmed by nerves as the boys discussed their "not boss" colleague's rude behavior toward me. "What if he just doesn't like me? What if I'm fired?" I asked with wide eyes, remembering that Ozzie said their decisions had to be unanimous. *What if Jax rescinds his approval?*

"No!" all three boys assured me.

"No one can fire you without a unanimous group vote, so you're not going anywhere. He's *not* the boss," Ozzie comforted me, and I nodded. Luckily, I was already officially hired, and Ozzie was right. Jax couldn't fire me.

Thank God I'd already made a good impression on Nick and Steven before the tragic introduction between me and Jack—I meant Jax. Thank God I had Ozzie for support too—I was going to need it.

"So, did you guys go to art schools?" I asked Nick and Steven curiously. I was sitting on a roller chair and scooted across the concrete in between their stations. They'd met doing an internship together that sounded pretty cool. They asked the same question of me.

"Not really. I went to Florence for an art program, and now I'm here."

"That's so cool!" Steven and Nick seemed very impressed, which made me feel a little more comfortable about fitting in with them. I didn't say that the program had only lasted six weeks, and I had only lasted a couple days before quitting on account of depression. Side note—bipolar followed you everywhere, even to the magical city of Florence.

"Jax studied in Paris. Did you ever go there?" Steven asked me as he rested against his worktable.

"No. I was going to spend a week there after Florence for a drawing workshop, but the Rolling Stones had a concert back home, so I had to leave early."

"You chose a rock concert over Paris?" I heard Jax scoff behind me, and I rolled my eyes before swiveling in my chair to face him.

"I chose the Rolling Stones over Paris," I answered, keeping my reply neutral.

"That doesn't speak well of your priorities as an artist." He arched a judgmental eyebrow. I felt a little flare of passion in my response since he was criticizing my love for the Stones. I had to defend it.

"They're ancient! Mick's heart is unreliable, and how Keith is still alive *and* ripping it on guitar is a rock phenomenon. I'd bet that was my last chance to see them alive, so I took it. Paris isn't going anywhere." I folded my arms and stared him down.

"That's pretty solid reasoning," Ozzie stuck up for me, and Nick and Steven agreed.

"If you say so." Jax sighed and walked away from me, again.

"*Ozzie,*" I whisper-shouted to my friend, then shuffled my feet across the floor, rolling to sit in front of his station. "You never mentioned Jax being an asshole."

"He's really not... I don't know what's gotten into him."

"So he must hate me," I concluded.

"Of course not. He can just be...moody." He shrugged and looked at me with a small smile, as if I would find it relatable. Even though it was true, I didn't appreciate being compared to an asshole. I didn't respond and simply stared back at him, waiting for a better explanation. "Ugh. Mia, I'm sorry. I don't know." He sighed, and I could tell that he was uncomfortable with the situation. I nodded and looked to the door Jax just disappeared through. "I'll talk to him," Ozzie said.

"No. This is between me and him." I shook my head and figured that Ozzie confronting him would just add on more judgment of me. I needed to show that I was confident with my new job and place within this group of talented artists. "I'll try to make it right." I looked at Ozzie to support the decision, and he nodded, then urged me forward.

I stood and walked into the kitchen where Jax was making coffee. He turned around and didn't seem surprised to see me. He leaned against the counter and raised his eyebrows, staring at me.

"Hi." I took a breath and stood in front of him, then leaned against the island counter opposite him. He still didn't say anything, and I was momentarily distracted by his hands. One held the mug and the other rested on the counter. They were veiny and big with long fingers and…

"Yes?" His deep voice snapped me out of my wayward thoughts, and I refocused on him. Now, a little smirk was tugging at his lips. Still in his faded jeans and combat boots, he had taken off his hoodie and was wearing a navy T-shirt that stretched across his broad chest.

"I think we should start over," I said with more confidence, trying hard to keep my eyes on his instead of those hands.

"Who puts nail polish on only one hand?" With a little crease between his brows, Jax cocked his head to the side at his discovery and stared at my left hand. He actually looked cute, as his interest was genuine but also temporary.

"I do. Great attention to detail," I said too sarcastically, and his eyes moved from the black nail polish to mine and narrowed. It didn't seem like he was going to say anything further, so I rerouted to the reason I was awkwardly standing in front of him. "Like I said, I think we should start over."

"Why?" he asked casually, keeping his dark-blue eyes on me as he took a sip.

"Well, we didn't really start off on the right foot," I stated plainly.

"Because I disrupted your dance party?"

"Um…no…."

"What foot should we have started off on, then?" he asked just as plainly.

"The right one…"

"Which means what to you?"

I was not expecting to have to explain to him what starting off on the right foot was. "I—the right one means that…that we should have started…in a good way," I stuttered yet again as I got distracted by his lips when he took another sip of coffee. That asshole smirk was back on his beautiful face. "Our introduction should have been cordial. You should have been welcoming, and I would have been appreciative and happy to get to work with you." I lifted my chin as I responded, again trying to compensate for my flustered reaction to him.

"Okay, Amelia." He shrugged and placed his mug on the counter. He said my full name so casually, it took me by surprise, and I hesitated. *How the hell does he know my full name? Ohh, my résumé.* "Oh, right, it's Mia. Sorry."

"Just whatever. Shake my hand and let's start off on the right foot." I extended my hand toward him and looked into his eyes, but they revealed nothing.

"Fine." He took my hand in his, and my physical reaction was no different than the first time we'd touched. "Welcome. It's so nice to meet you on the right foot." His easy smile was dazzling and overwhelming as he squeezed my hand tightly, causing a jump of excitement and nerves inside me. "Now you be appreciative." I eyed him suspiciously, as I knew he was teasing me, but I had no idea how to handle him.

"Thank you for the welcome. I'm appreciative." I recited my line, trying to keep up.

"Now tell me how happy you are to get to work under me." My eyes widened, then narrowed as his smirk stretched into a cocky grin.

"Okay." I retracted my hand from his. "We are colleagues. You are not my boss."

"Kinda." He shrugged and leaned back against the counter and picked up his mug once again for a sip.

I knew he was just being a dick and that I should walk away, but I couldn't get my legs to take a step away from his body or my eyes to look away from his. "Look, Jax, I want us to get along, but if you insist otherwise, that's on you."

"Mr. Caine." Correcting his name was all of his response, and he looked like he was having way too much fun pissing me off as he smiled.

"Are you enjoying your power trip?"

"I actually am." He chuckled at my scowl, his eyes moving up and down my body, and I wished that I was wearing leggings and not shorts. His presence became too much for me.

"Well, I tried," I said, acknowledging my failed attempt at starting over. "Not nice to meet you, *Mr. Caine*." I glared, then turned and tried to keep my feet from stomping out of the kitchen.

"How'd it go?" Ozzie asked me tentatively when I returned to my station.

"Uh." I sighed, getting my thoughts together. "Maybe better." He was engaging, at least, and had agreed to start over. That was something. Then I remembered his lips and hands, his smile and his dark eyes raking up and down my body. *I cannot let this man fluster me any more than he already has.* "Maybe worse."

"I'm sorry he's in such a bad mood the day you get to meet. It'll get better, I promise," Ozzie assured me, but something told me it was going to get worse. Still, I sighed and nodded. "Let's go for drinks."

"Yeah!" That perked me up a bit, and I immediately grabbed my purse, ready to get out of there.

"We're coming too!" Nick and Steven put down their work and joined us. I smiled in appreciation at my two new friends and Ozzie.

"Bye, Jax! We are bringing Mia to Floyd's!" Nick yelled as we descended the stairs and left the studio, on our way to the bar down the block.

———

"Hey, guys! It's been a while—*what's up?*" The bartender at Floyd's lit up when we walked through the double wooden doors and into his domain. I trailed along behind the guys as they went straight to the counter. I looked down the long bar, then surveyed the half-occupied tables and booths scattered around the open area. The place was quiet, and I wondered if it was part of the San Francisco nightlife or a modest neighborhood hangout bar.

"We had a busy month, but April should be more chill," Ozzie explained as we approached and rested his elbows on the dark wooden bar, then turned to me. "This is Mia. I've known her for forever, but she just moved here and is our new artist."

"Nice to meet you, Mia. I'm Matt." The bartender smiled kindly with an automatically endearing gap-toothed smile, and I said it was nice to meet him. Ozzie informed me that Matt had gone to high school with him and Jax. "Jax still gone?" Matt looked behind us, apparently checking to see if the asshole had come along.

"No, he just got back, but I doubt he'll be joining us." Ozzie shrugged, and Matt started getting them beers and asked me what I wanted. I looked over his shoulder and eyed the counter behind the bar, which carried a vast selection of liquors, until I spotted the green Irish whiskey bottle.

"Jameson and ginger ale, please." I smiled politely, and he responded with an approving head nod.

"So, how do you like working with these guys?" Matt asked as he handed me my drink.

"It's great. I'm excited to be here." I nodded enthusiastically, already feeling comforted with my favorite drink in my hand. We drank and relaxed for a bit, and when we got our second round, I got their attention. "Guys... um—what if Jax really doesn't like me?" I asked, genuinely nervous.

"Impossible. I don't know what his problem is." Ozzie shook his head.

"No way would Jax not like you! I bet that, once you meet him, he'll love you." Matt placed his elbows on the counter and leaned in closer to be part of the group. He smiled confidently at me, and I scrunched my nose.

"I already met him."

"And he doesn't like you?" Matt looked surprised that his friend wouldn't like me. I just shrugged and looked to my colleagues.

"It's weird," Nick confirmed, while Steven nodded.

"What happened when you tried to talk to him in the kitchen?" Ozzie nudged me while the other boys huddled around me.

"He told me to call him Mr. Caine." I thought that was the best way to sum up his behavior in the kitchen. They all started laughing, and I joined in.

"What's so funny?" I froze when I heard Jax's deep voice behind me. I anxiously looked at the guys, trying to communicate that they shouldn't sell me out. "Why do you look so nervous?" He came closer and leaned against the counter, facing me.

"I'm not nervous, *Mr. Caine.*" I looked up at him innocently through my lashes. He narrowed his eyes at me, and the other boys started laughing again.

"Jax, why don't you like Mia?" Matt asked him directly.

"I never said I didn't like her."

"You didn't need to." I rolled my eyes.

"Don't be so sensitive." He turned and took a full glass of beer from Matt.

"Do we all have to call you Mr. Caine now?" Nick poked.

"I was just kidding." Jax rolled his eyes, then looked at me, but I didn't respond, just stared back. "Fine. You can call me Jax." He smiled, but it was still condescending.

"Really? *Thank you*, Mr. Caine." I smiled sweetly back and decided that I'd call him that from then on. He glared at me and leaned in closer.

"I don't trust you." He spoke low, and I thought he was definitely crazy.

"What could I possibly be up to?" I chuckled. He just eyed me and took a long sip of beer. He was standing so close to me, and while he looked me over with distaste, my eyes devoured his striking features—sharp cheekbones and jaw, crooked nose, and full lips. He'd almost be a pretty boy if it weren't for his long sandy-blond hair he kept pushing back, out of his face, and his scruffy facial hair to roughen him up. Our eyes reconnected, and from that asshole smirk on his face, I could tell he knew he was sexy as hell.

He was going to make work very difficult, I just knew it. Unfortunately, he was also so strikingly beautiful that it was hard not to look at him. I bet he'd never heard the word "no." I remembered Ozzie saying that he lived above the studio. I expected many women to walk downstairs, through our studio, and ask how to get to the exit. I already hated him—a quick judgment, but he'd started it.

Chapter 4

"Cheers to Mia! Our team is complete." Nick smiled and held up his drink toward me as we all sat in a booth together. More chairs and barstools had filled since we'd arrived, and the place was starting to buzz. I smiled, my heart warmed by how openly they welcomed me to their team—well, Ozzie, Nick, and Steven. With their glasses in the air, they all shot a glare at Jax, who finally joined in with a sigh. We all clinked glasses.

"I didn't think our team needed a woman's touch, but okay," Jax said, his level of asshole increasing with each word spoken. I sensed the three boys were about to scold him for his rudeness, but I beat them to it.

"You have a problem with that, Mr. Caine?" I quipped, and his brows shot up, then furrowed into a frown. I raised my brows and sipped my drink, proud that I surprised him by firing back and putting him on the spot. I then noticed the other boys staring nervously between the two of us. *So, Jax isn't used to backchat...but he will be soon.* I could see why. Just like I'd bet he'd never heard the word no from a woman, he had probably never been challenged by a man for his formidable presence. I was all too willing to be his adversary but was not at all ready to be his archnemesis once he finally heard the word "no."

"Nope." Jax's scowl turned into a smirk as he apparently thought of a good comeback and shook his head. "I have no problem with a woman's touch."

"Apparently you do, if the team needed it." Jax's face fell back into a scowl, and I turned my attention to the rest of the boys who had been watching us and snickered at my last comeback. "Really, guys." I turned my tone into a more serious one and looked around the faces in the booth. "I am very happy to be working with you."

"And we are very happy to have you." Steven nodded to me, and I smiled back at him and Nick across from me.

"We've been crushing it, but your drawings will step us up for sure," Nick said in his raised, high-pitched voice, and my smile widened with the acceptance I was feeling.

"Yeah, we have so much ahead of us. It's going to be epic. You'll love the projects we get to do," Ozzie said from beside me, and I started to get even more excited for the future. Ozzie then turned to face Jax. "Jax, what's the news?"

"Hm?" Jax straightened in his chair and gave his attention to Ozzie. He had already disengaged from the conversation.

"You said you have news?"

"Oh. Yeah. I'll tell you at work on Monday." He shrugged, then slouched back into his chair.

———

As Friday night progressed, the crowd got larger. As it would turn out, Floyd's was both the bar next door and the fun night out. I went to the bar to order another round for our group, but Matt was busy. I was waiting patiently for him to attend to other patrons and fulfill our order when I felt my skin prickle, and Jax came into view a second later. He leaned on the counter next to me and gave me an up-down with his eyes.

"I'm not so sure about you," he said, stating the obvious.

"That's a vague statement." He shrugged, and I knew he hadn't thought of more to say to back it up. "Kinda seems a little too late for that since I'm already here, sooo…"

"You're pretty bold for your first day."

"Actually, it's my fifth day."

"Fine. You're pretty bold for your fifth day. You should be more concerned with fitting into your new job," he scolded me, then leaned closer, trying to intimidate me with those dark-blue eyes. "*And* impressing your colleagues."

"Thanks for the tip." I rolled my eyes and pushed away from the bar, ready to leave him behind and let him deliver everyone's drinks, but he stopped me, wrapping his hand around my arm. I couldn't ignore that same feeling I got from our handshake, electrifying and ominous, this time more intense as he didn't let go. "So forward, Mr. Caine."

"Shut up." His hand gripped tighter, circling my bicep. "Ozzie may have waved you in, but you still have to prove yourself." I glared at him and tried to jerk my arm away, but he pulled me closer. "Starting now." I yanked my arm away and decided I hated him. I went back to our booth to grab my jacket and purse.

"Bye, guys. See you later." I sighed but tried not to sound defeated.

"Why are you going?" Ozzie's brows furrowed, and he looked past me, wondering about my interaction with Jax as I felt the asshole approach the booth.

"No, we want you to stay!" Nick pulled on my arm.

"Yeah, we are celebrating." Steven smiled kindly, and I no longer wanted to flee from the asshole.

"Okay. If you want me to stay, then I'll stay." I turned to Jax and smirked when the three boys continued to encourage me to stay. I slid into the booth next to Nick.

"Mia, you didn't want another drink?" Ozzie asked, curious, since that's why I'd gone to the bar in the first place. Jax set everyone's drink on the table, except for mine.

"A bit obvious." I rolled my eyes at Jax.

"What? I only have two hands." He shrugged and held up his hands, which were basically baseball mitts—he could've carried another glass. I took an even better look at them, and I tried not to stare. I sighed, about to stand up to fetch my drink.

"I got it." Ozzie stood, glared at Jax, then went to the bar.

"Way to play the victim," Jax scoffed, and I wanted to tell him to fuck off.

"Way to be the villain."

"Not off to a good start."

"Impressing you isn't my main concern right now."

"I would hope not."

"Am I being hazed?" I continued to look around at the group of guys. I actually wasn't kidding.

"Yeah, Jax. Lay off. Seriously." Ozzie sighed as he handed me my drink and returned to his seat next to Steven. Jax raised his hands, backing off, and sat back in the chair he'd pulled up since my addition made their usual booth cramped.

I did my best to ignore him, but once the conversation moved on to something I wasn't interested in, my mind wandered and so did my gaze, which collided with Jax's. He was already looking at me and didn't bother looking away when we made eye contact. I became very self-conscious under his scrutinizing attention. He smirked, knowing he could easily make me flustered, and I looked away and down at my phone and saw that it was nine o'clock. I was getting tired—it had been a long day—but I didn't want to be the first one to go home. I didn't mind staying till close—the boys were fun, and I could keep up with their drinking. They made me laugh, and even better, I made them laugh. It had been so long since I had been able to relax and be myself around others, and it felt so good.

———

"That does not count—you moved your hands!" Nick whined as he called out Steven for cheating. Ozzie and Jax had both gone to the bar, and I sat comfortably in our booth watching Nick and Steven play quarter hockey. As the night went on, so did the rounds. It was that time of the night when we'd gone through so many glasses, a layer of condensation spread across the table, which made Nick and Steven's game difficult but amusing.

"I did not. You just lost." Steven rolled his eyes, then looked to me.

"Referee judges…fair play," I decided.

"Mia, wanna play?" Steven asked. I was having fun watching Nick fumble his thumbs around the coin but was not prepared to participate.

"Um…" I hesitated and looked down at my intertwined fingers in my lap. I held one hand up under the table but quickly pressed both together when I saw it shake. "No, thanks."

"Aw, come on, it's easy," Nick encouraged me and flicked the quarter toward me.

"I'm just not good at it." I shrugged and looked over to the bathrooms as the boys both urged me to participate. "Later. Gotta go to the bathroom." I slid out of the booth and made my escape.

I glanced at the bar and saw Ozzie and Jax talking together at the counter. Ozzie's brows were up, while Jax's were furrowed above a frown. I looked away and continued down a hallway to the bathrooms. When I stepped back into the bar, Ozzie and Jax were still at the counter, so I took an immediate step back into the shadowed hallway. I strained my hearing to pick up on the private conversation—eavesdropping.

"Shit. That's brutal." Ozzie sighed, and I leaned against the wall, getting comfortable.

"Suddenly, he just shattered his phone. Scared the shit out of my mom." There was a pause. "I've never seen him cry, man. Fucking *Britney*."

"Poor Joe."

"Then I fucked up with my mom—"

"Because of Joe's divorce…?"

"No." Heavy sigh from Jax. "Unrelated. I don't want to talk about it, just—God." He sounded really tortured, and I started to feel guilty for eavesdropping. "Too many fucked-up things at once. I just left."

"So all that, then…you drove back here to the studio?"

"Yeah."

I was about to walk away, as the topic seemed too personal for me to listen in on, but then Ozzie said my name. "Where you met Mia."

"This has nothing to do with Mia," Jax said firmly and quickly, trying to shut down the conversation.

"Well, I would be pissed too, if—"

"It's not about Mia," Jax cut him off before Ozzie could call him out on our hostile first meeting.

"Alright, okay." Ozzie backed off, and I heard Jax sigh, like he was going to drop it. "So what *is* about Mia?"

"Oh my God," Jax groaned. "Nothing."

"Why don't you like her? You were on board when we hired her." Ozzie didn't back down, set on getting a reason for Jax's behavior earlier.

"Maybe we hired her too soon."

"What the hell does that mean?" Ozzie's tone got colder, ready to defend me.

"She's really young. Immature. Maybe she won't take the work seriously enough."

"There's no reason for you to think that."

"First time I see her, she's prancing around the studio. Second time I see her, she's admitting to leaving an art school early to see a rock concert. And that's our new artist?" *Ouch.* Jax's reasons for why he didn't like me were hard to hear, and I felt my chest tighten, but I didn't let it shake my confidence. I knew he'd be proven wrong.

"Okay. First, you're going to let that go. Second, you blast Metallica and screw around the studio too. Third, you rescheduled a project to go to a UFC fight with Joe."

"That's different. I'm thirty. She's twenty-four."

"You know that makes you worse, right?"

"Whatever."

"It's as if you don't *want* to like her."

"Maybe I don't."

"Wait, *what?*" I heard a glass slam down onto the counter, clearly Ozzie's punctuation to his question.

"I mean…no. Can we just stop talking about this?"

"Fine. She's not going anywhere, so you'll *have* to like her."

"I'll do my best," Jax professed, but the underlying sarcasm was obvious.

I felt as if I'd been standing in the shadows, listening in on a private conversation for too long, so I sucked in a deep breath, exhaled, and moved past it. I returned to our booth to see Nick throwing multiple quarters at Steven as he tried to dodge them.

"Well, this escalated," I commented dryly as I took my seat next to Steven.

"Okay, put the quarters away before someone loses an eye," Ozzie chastised from behind me as he approached the booth with two beers. He handed them out to Nick and Steven before taking a seat next to Nick. Jax joined us next with beers for Ozzie and himself and a whiskey for me, which he passed out with his large hands.

"Thank you," I said gently as I accepted my glass. I looked up into Jax's eyes as he sat down in the chair he'd pulled up to the booth. Every time I'd looked into those dark-blue eyes, they were stormy and antagonizing. When his met mine now, they were just as stormy but softer and almost vulnerable. He looked away before I could see deeper.

After this next round, the boys got rowdier as Jax got quieter. I didn't know what he and Ozzie had discussed before I'd invaded their personal conversation with my eavesdropping, but it sounded like something had upset him before he'd returned to the studio earlier that day. Again, as the conversation wandered into a subject I didn't care for, so did my gaze. When my eyes drifted to Jax, I expected to already be under his attention. But he was staring at his half-drunk glass of beer as his finger made streaks through the condensation. I enjoyed the small moment to analyze his features without being caught. Vulnerability was obvious in his absent gaze but hooded by heavy lids under furrowed brows—if he really had driven straight to the studio from wherever he was with his family, he was probably operating on very little sleep. Like the moment I met him, his lips were pressed in a straight line, but his mind was clearly somewhere else. Apparently, I had been staring too long as he sensed my gaze, and his eyes rose directly to mine, but only for a second, and he quickly looked away again.

"Mia." Ozzie's voice brought my attention snapping back to his as he rose from the booth and stretched his arms. "Ready to go?"

I had forgotten that I'd gotten a ride with him to work that morning and was dependent on him for a ride home. I'd had Ozzie drive me to and from work all week. The hallucinations vanished by Thursday, but I still was afraid of getting behind the wheel in case they came back. I glanced at my not-quite-empty glass of whiskey and tossed it back before I grabbed my purse from the booth seat. "Yep." I stood, then looked to my colleagues. "Fun night, boys. See ya Monday." I smiled and waved. I heard Steven and Nick call goodbye behind us before we walked out the door.

"You doing okay?" Ozzie asked me when he saw me yawn as he slid into the driver's seat.

"Yeah." I sighed as I pulled the car door closed and buckled myself into the passenger seat.

"It's been a long day..." he hedged as he glanced at me before pulling into the street. "Wanna talk about it?"

"About Jax not liking me?" I clarified, and he nodded. "Actually, yeah, I do." My mind went back to the conversation I'd partially overheard between him and his other best friend.

"Mia, Jax will like you. I'm sorry he was a condescending asshole to you, but he's just having a bad day... He'll get over it."

"Why is it a bad day?"

"It's... He's complicated." Ozzie kept his eyes on the road. I didn't comment and waited for him to explain further. "I told you he was with his family. They're very close. Some shit went down, and he left pissed off and came to the studio. So he wasn't mad at you when you met."

"Okay..." I tried processing what Ozzie had shared but was still confused. "So, what happened with his family?"

"Uh..." Ozzie took a moment to decide how much information he was going to give me. "The Caine family has some fucked-up history that goes back before we moved in next to them, and...Jax doesn't talk about it. He did tell me about his brother, though. Joe's been going through a nasty divorce. They were helping him through some of that when they were together this week. That's when a friend called Joe and told him his wife has been having an affair with his partner at the law firm he works at. Apparently, it has been going on for a few months."

"Oh, God…"

"Yeah. I was at their wedding. I didn't know her well, but I did see them as a happy couple. Everyone did."

"And he had no idea?"

"No idea," Ozzie said with a grave head nod, eyes still forward on the road. "They had been together a long time. Joe feels like an idiot for not knowing the two people closest to him had been fucking him over. Literally."

"That's terrible."

"Britney." Ozzie sighed and shook his head. "Beautiful woman. Narcissist and pathological liar. I hope she hasn't ruined him. Joe is a good man, really." I nodded. "She's been trying to suck him dry this whole divorce. Jax is pretty shaken up about it too."

"Wow… I mean…" I shook my head, not knowing how to respond to such news. "That's why Jax was pissed off when he came to the studio?" Ozzie nodded, still maneuvering through the streets. "And he projected it onto me?"

"I wouldn't say—actually, yeah, I would say that. That's why he was a judgmental asshole when you met him, and I feel like he knows that too. What didn't help a pissed-off Jax was you messing with his name. That's not on you, by the way. He's just…sensitive."

"So I fucked up."

"No, Mia, you really didn't. He'll get over it," Ozzie assured me with confidence, but I wasn't so sure.

"Well, if he thinks I'm not a serious artist…"

"Did he say that to you?"

"No…I may have overheard a few things when you two were at the bar."

"Oh. I'm sorry you heard him say that, but he won't think so for long." Ozzie pulled up to my building and shifted his car into park. "Are you okay?" he asked as he looked kindly into my eyes and placed a comforting hand on my arm.

"Of course I'm okay." I smiled and reached over to give him a hug goodbye. "Thanks for the ride…and information."

"Of course." He smiled back, and I hopped out of his car. "I'll talk to you tomorrow," he called after me before I swung the door closed. I waved before hurrying into the building and up to my apartment.

———-

For the rest of the night, I couldn't stop thinking about Jax. Ozzie had given me a lot of information, but all I could think about was how the man made me feel—other than perplexed and offended. I replayed our first moments together in my mind. The hard body I ran into, his heated stare, his large hand that enveloped mine in a handshake. I ignored everything but the memory of his touch, and I felt my body tingle as I tucked myself into bed. But I could still hear his deep voice telling Ozzie that I was too young and immature, that I wasn't a serious artist.

Thankfully, it was the weekend, giving Jax two days to decompress from all the angst and turmoil that Ozzie said consumed him after spending a dramatic week with his family. I remembered the small admission he'd made while I was eavesdropping that went unaddressed—maybe he didn't *want* to like me. It helped to hear some reasoning for his behavior, but that didn't negate the way he treated me. Either way, I hoped that the asshole I met that day didn't show up on Monday.

Chapter 5

Sunday night, I was nervous. I didn't know what I'd be walking into in the morning. *He was having a bad day... It wasn't me.... It was "Britney" who'd caused him to be an asshole... He was just projecting... Maybe he'll even apologize... We really will start off on the right foot... Jax and I will bond over music... He'll say Led Zeppelin is his favorite band and Queen is second...then I'll say Queen is my favorite and Led Zeppelin is my second... We'll play "Another One Bites the Dust" again and have a laugh—remember when you told me to call you Mr. Caine? Ha ha, good times.*

I sat down at my kitchen table and got more organized, settling into my new life. I had my twice-a-day weekly pill minder out, and all of my medications were spread across the tabletop. I bobbed my head and tapped my feet to the music playing from my new record player.

"Death on two legs, you never had a heart of your own...killjoy, bad guy, big-talking, small fry..." I sang along to the first song on Queen's *A Night at the Opera* album. No, I wasn't playing that song for any particular reason. Yeah, I was thinking about Jackson Caine. It was a good song, though.

I went about being a responsible bipolar-an, sorting my medications into the right boxes in the right dosages. "Lithium, two pills in here... Wellbutrin, three pills in here.... Lamictal, two pills in there... Seroquel, one pill in there... Some other shit for side effects, one pill in here and one pill in there..." I piled the colorful assortment of pills into the Sunday a.m. and p.m. boxes and clicked them closed, then continued down the rest of the days of the week.

Medications. People seemed to make up their own opinions on the subject even when they didn't take any. So many times, I'd heard people saying they wouldn't put anything like that in their body—because they didn't have to! I'd rather not ingest ten pills a day, but I needed them to survive. It took me four years to find the right combination that could keep me stable, that would stop my bipolar brain from spiking to the heights of mania or plummeting to the depths of depression. I never knew when these highs and lows would come, there was no schedule, and I never knew how bad it would get. All I knew was that the chemicals would riot again, so I swallowed ten pills a day to manage it as best as I could. Hopefully, I was past those turbulent years and could manage my mental illness and finally focus on the life ahead of me.

I popped my nighttime handful of pills into my mouth, swallowed with a good slurp of water, and got into bed. My eyes reluctantly closed, and I went to sleep, not wanting Monday to come and not wanting to find out that I'd be working with a beautiful asshole.

———

"Good morning, fellas," I greeted brightly as I joined my fellow artists in the studio on Monday morning. I was relieved when I only heard positive greetings back.

"You're back," Jax said with obvious disappointment.

I spoke too soon, as the aura of positivity was broken by Jackson fucking Caine. His deep voice was somehow rough but melodic at the same time. "Come to put on another show?" Jax asked with crossed arms from where he stood at his sculpting station. I paused and shot him a questioning frown before I realized he was referring to me dancing around the studio.

"No." I rolled my eyes and continued on my path to my station in front of the wall of windows. I dropped my purse on my table, then turned back to face him. He was still watching me, so I placed one hand on my hip. "Disappointed, Mr. Caine?"

"No…" His teasing expression turned into a scowl when I addressed him by his formal name, and he turned away.

I glanced at Ozzie to confirm that he was watching our interaction from his corner station and saw he had his eyes pointed right at me. "*Mr. Caine?*" He spoke in a low voice and gave me a disapproving look.

"What? He told me to call him that," I defended myself quietly.

"He doesn't actually want you to call him that. He was just messing with you."

"Exactly." I shrugged and started sorting through my supplies, ignoring Ozzie's disapproving look.

I knew when Jax corrected me the first time, it was just him being a dick. He didn't actually want me to call him that. But he was still a dick, and I was pleased that something so effortless could irritate him. I did feel a twinge of guilt for prolonging a discord with Ozzie's other best friend, but that twinge faded away when I remembered Jax's sexy scowl when I said his full name. *Oh, well.*

I enjoyed the morning, as Jax left for several hours to take care of some of the business side of things. I spent more time learning all I could about different mediums from Ozzie, Nick, and Steven and their techniques and experiences. I glanced over to Jax's empty station and longed for the same ability with his sculpting that I knew would never come.

———

"Okay! Here comes the news!" Jax's booming voice echoed from the foyer, getting all of our attention. He seemed excited as he basically bounced into the studio, and we all joined him in the middle of the room. "We were selected to be a part of the gallery opening downtown. They asked for three works from each of us to display. Carte blanche and whatever. Obviously, we are all different, but I think it should still be a cohesive collection. We can choose past projects not seen before or something new specifically for the gallery. *Juxtapose* magazine is going to cover it, so we'll have another feature." Jax took a deep breath after his enthusiastic delivery and waited for everyone to freak out. Which they did. I felt a little awkward, since I was so new and jumping in on their success. I told myself that I'd prove my worth and it would be great.

The small celebration was interrupted when my phone started ringing. I had the volume on loud, anticipating a call from my psychiatrist's nurse so I wouldn't miss it, and all heads pointed to the source of the ring, which was my workstation.

"Excuse me…" I murmured and averted my gaze from all of them. I knew it wasn't a big deal, but I was still embarrassed as I rushed across the studio to grab my phone, which displayed "Nurse Amy" on the screen. I then hurried even faster back across the studio to the bathroom, hoping I'd be able to answer in time once I got to a safe place.

I ducked into the bathroom and quickly pushed the door closed, locked the handle, and turned on the sink faucet. "Hello?" My voice was a little breathless from my hustle, but I'd answered in time.

"Amelia, this is Dr. Burke's nurse."

"Yes, hi, Amy." I took a deep breath and leaned against the counter. I pressed the phone closer to my ear so I could hear better over the running water.

"How are the hallucinations? All gone?"

"Yes, it took a few days, but the Seroquel helped. It makes me groggy, but the hallucinations are gone so it's no big deal."

"That's great. How about you do one more night of the increased dose, then reduce the dose to one and a half, then go back to your original dose in a few days?"

"Okay."

"Good. Dr. Burke wanted to check in with you on your other treatment. Are you still seeing a psychologist weekly?"

"Um…it's tricky now that I've moved. Finding a psychologist taking on new patients is rare."

"Talk to yours in Minnesota. I'm sure she'll help make it work remotely. It's important that you keep up that part of your treatment plan."

"Okay, I will." I sighed, agreeing with her but not wanting to have to manage it all. Psychologists spent time with patients for therapy, which supplemented a psychiatrist's prescribed medications. Weekly appointments with my psychologist meant one hour every week that I would have to take out of my workday. Coworkers would notice.

"I think you are due for your lithium levels to be checked."

"Yeah, um, I forgot the lab order form from Dr. Burke back home."

"That's okay. I'll have a scan emailed to you."

"Okay." I sighed a bit more heavily. Lithium had changed my life. It was the mood stabilizer that finally let me breathe again and helped my other medications work better too. Which was why getting my lithium levels checked was important, even though it was a pain in the ass. The drug needed to be within the "therapeutic range" in my bloodstream or else it could cause serious health problems—seizures and even death. The only way to track this was to give blood samples. Every few months, my doctor would give me a piece of paper with his signature, the blood-draw order form, that I then had to hand to the lab tech who took my blood sample so they knew what they were screening for. Based on the results, the nurse would then say it was okay or to reduce or increase the dosage of lithium.

"Don't forget. I'll follow up once we get the results."

"Okay. Thank you, Amy."

"Of course. Watch your email. Take care." We said our goodbyes, and I ran my hand through my hair, very stressed out but grateful for her attention. Everything I had to do started swarming in my mind, overwhelming me.

With bipolar disorder, the extreme mood swings were the hardest, but even being stable was a bitch. There were so many things to keep track of every day to maintain stability. Doctors, blood samples, side effects, medication management, enduring the stigma, and trying to find my way in the world with a mental illness. It was exhausting, and I felt the weight of it all at once. Sometimes I had moments when I let myself feel a little sorry for myself, moments when I wished I was normal. Moments like just now, when I'd just locked myself in the bathroom of my new job and turned on the faucet so my colleagues wouldn't hear me talking to my psychiatrist's nurse about hallucinations. I gave myself only a few seconds to let a couple tears escape my eyes. I gave myself a few more seconds to even out my breathing. I turned off the water, then patted the tears dry on my cheeks to try to minimize the usual signs of crying and fanned away new tears that threatened to escape.

I walked into the studio and looked around the room to see all of the boys focused on their stations. I moved into the kitchen, wanting to be alone. I enjoyed the extra moments of solitude, time for my anxieties to slip away, and pulled Nespresso pods from the cupboard. I had already fixed myself a latte when my body stiffened as I sensed another in the room. From the quick blush of my cheeks and the tingle of my skin, I knew Jax was behind me. I turned and leaned against the counter, held my mug in one hand, and raised my brows as I looked into his eyes. He stood in the doorway and didn't say anything, just looked at me.

"Yes?" I prompted him, then sipped on my coffee.

"How was your phone call?" he asked as he walked further into the room.

"Good."

"Must have been important."

"It was."

"More important than our new project?" Jax inquired with a tilt of his head. He had no idea that I'd cried in the bathroom only minutes before. Now I felt more tears prick my eyes as I felt overwhelmed by his judgment. *Don't cry in front of Jax. Don't cry in front of Jax...*

"Considering the urgency of my response, obviously." I tried to match his hostile yet casual demeanor.

"Mm-hmm. And what do you consider more important than our art?" That tripped me up a bit, but I wasn't in the mood to defend my priorities as an artist to Jackson Caine.

"You'll never know because it's none of your business." I held eye contact. His eyebrows creased, and his head tilted to one side before I walked past him and out of the kitchen. I felt his eyes on me as I returned to my station. That was something that always made me feel bad—no matter how many phone calls I had with Nurse Amy or depressive "sick" days I had to take, I could never reveal my bipolar diagnosis to a boss or coworker, not with the stigma. I looked over my shoulder to confirm that Jax was still watching me from the doorway, but I decided that I didn't care what he thought of me. I admit, huffing and flipping my hair was a bit dramatic as I left him behind in the kitchen, but I meant it—I would never tell him because it was none of his business. I meant it as a promise, one I never planned to break.

Chapter 6

Tuesday, the second day of working with Jax, and it was a battle to get out of bed. The increase in Seroquel handled my hallucinations but also meant an increase in the sedative effects of the drug that helped me sleep. My phone alarm went off at nine a.m., followed by snooze alarms every five minutes, but they weren't powerful enough to penetrate my coma. My cell phone ringing with an incoming call was what finally dragged me back to the surface. I could open my eyes, but my body felt like cement. I lay in bed a little longer, waiting for my limbs to come to life, and my phone started ringing again. I sighed and felt around my bed, searching for the source, and my hand finally found the vibration under my pillow. I saw Ozzie's name on the screen but didn't answer in time, and it ended so I could see my dashboard time—two p.m.

"Shit! Shit, shit, shit." I scrambled out from under the covers and stumbled out of bed. I raced to the bathroom to splash my face with water, brush my teeth, and pull my hair into a sloppy ponytail. I pulled on my Monday outfit, which I'd left on the floor. My phone buzzed again with another call from Ozzie, and I quickly swiped to answer. "Hi, I'm coming. Bye." I basically flew through my apartment until I got to my car, and as I started to drive, I finally let myself breathe.

My eyes were still bleary as I drove through the streets to the studio. *This is so not safe.* I slapped my face awake in the elevator before I had to face my colleagues. Everyone's heads turned to look at me as I walked in.

"Nice of you to join us." Jax's voice was the first I heard, and my eyes met his. He crossed his arms and stared at me. He was questioning my priorities again. I knew it.

"Jax, there's no schedule," Ozzie lightly scolded his other best friend, and Jax put his hands up like he was backing off, then turned back to his sculpting station.

"Hey, Ozzie, Steven, and Nick. How's it going?" I asked pleasantly as I arrived at my station and put down my purse like it wasn't 2:30 p.m. on the workday.

"Hey, where've you been?" Nick asked. The two of them didn't look judgmental, only curious. Still, it made me feel awkward, since I now had to think of an excuse. I couldn't say I'd overslept this late into the day. *Who sleeps until two p.m. on a workday? Someone taking antipsychotic medication, that's who.*

"Oh…" *Think fast, think fast.* "I had to deal with some delayed shipments that finally arrived from Minnesota. I was stuck at my apartment waiting for FedEx." *Damn, that was good.*

"Are you all moved in now?" Steven asked kindly.

"Yep, officially moved in," I said with a sigh, like my fictitious morning of moving into my apartment had been exhausting.

"Well, congratulations!" Nick cheered for me.

"Thanks." I smiled and nodded.

"Does it feel more like home now?" Steven asked even more kindly, and I started to feel bad about lying.

"Yes. It's nice." My smile felt fake, so I ended our conversation by turning back to my station, where Ozzie was already waiting for me.

"What happened?" Ozzie asked me in a hushed tone once the others were back to work. He knew I wasn't waiting for FedEx. "Are you getting depressed?" He also knew that oversleeping was a sign of bipolar depression.

"No, no. It's my medication, Seroquel—it's an antipsychotic. It's like a sedative. I just overslept." I sighed and rubbed my eyes, my mind still feeling foggy.

"I was worried… I was going to check on you."

"Thanks." I smiled at him. "No worries, though. I'm good. I'm lowering my dose soon, so it shouldn't happen again," I assured him, even though I wasn't sure. Ozzie nodded, deciding that he didn't need to be worried about me. He returned to his station, and I went to the kitchen in search of caffeine.

"Who oversleeps until two in the afternoon?" I heard Jax behind me as I stirred a massive spoonful of sugar into my coffee, judgment in his voice.

"I didn't oversleep," I replied as I turned to face him. "I had to wait for FedEx—" I was going to give him my lie but stopped when he rolled his eyes and stepped closer.

"There's pillow markings on your face," he stated as he brought his finger to my cheek and ran it down my face.

"Oh." I raised my hand to cover the marks.

"So, what is it? Hit the town last night? Partied so hard you slept until two in the afternoon?"

"None of the above." I rubbed my hand against my pillow-marked skin and glared in response to his cocky smirk. He thought I was proving his bad opinion of me.

"Then fill in the blanks."

"I don't owe you an explanation."

"So there is a reason." He crossed his arms. He heard me stutter and continued, "And I'll never know because it's none of my business?"

"Yes." I nodded as I dropped my hand from my face and walked away from him…again.

———

The week went by quickly. Five days of working with Jax, and nothing had changed—he hadn't just been having a bad day. My phone call with Nurse Amy and oversleeping didn't help with his opinion of me not being a serious artist. My mind often floated to the words he'd said when I overheard him talking with Ozzie at the bar—maybe he didn't *want* to like me. I had to settle for not knowing his motives and taking it a day at a time.

———

That Wednesday afternoon, the boys were busy discussing past projects in the studio, so I let myself wander into the exhibit room alone. Ozzie had shown me around before and pointed out different styles and phases of their work, but my eyes only sought out the sculptures and fell on one I hadn't seen before. I went to the corner of the room, where the sculpture was almost hidden behind a couple paintings. I nudged them a few inches away so I could see it fully.

While Jax's sculptures leaned heavily on the provocative side of passion, the one I was focused on was more emotionally intense but still soft and beautiful. I guessed the stone he used was marble and the color was a consistent white and gray, so I had to bend down and squint to see the intricate details of the figure. It took everything in me not to touch it, not to run my fingertips along the smooth form of a woman reaching up, her body in an upward spiral, a desperate expression carved so purely on her face. There was no set front, so I moved around the statue, following its twisting direction, and discovered two long, slightly oversized arms starting at the base and holding on to the female figure. The woman's details were soft and smooth, but the masculine arms were as sharp as the hands clawed onto her thigh and calf. My brows scrunched together as my eyes searched the marble for the reason behind the emotional intensity locked inside. What was he thinking as his hands created it? My mind wanted to dissect his, to know what was going on behind those dark-blue eyes.

Even though I was absorbed in the meaning of the sculpture, I felt my skin prickle, and my eyes immediately shot up to where Jax filled the doorway. He held eye contact for a beat before looking away and sauntering into the room to join me.

"What do you think?" Jax asked once he'd woven through the different paintings, prints, and sculptures that littered the room and stopped near the sculpture I was marveling at.

"It's beautiful," I murmured as my eyes continued to search the marble.

"Thank you."

"Is it—" I was about to ask what had inspired this particular work but was cut off.

"Don't ask," he stated quickly before I could reveal my curiosity. His snap reaction didn't surprise me, but it did disappoint me.

"Okay…" I frowned and searched his expression, but he turned his back to me, so I couldn't get a read on him. It wasn't until I moved away from his artwork that he faced me again and rerouted the conversation to me.

"Did you bring your portfolio?"

"Yes, but it's in my apartment," I murmured and felt his eyes follow me as I continued to move around the room.

"You should bring it here—if you want."

"Okay."

"Ozzie showed us your Dante series. That's why I decided to vote you in. Was that a commission?" He followed me around the room, and I shook my head. The Dante series was the project I was the proudest of. I read the *Divine Comedy* in high school, and it had a powerful effect on me as I struggled with depression and bullying. I had spent the past year illustrating *Inferno*, *Purgatory*, and *Paradise* on three poster-size papers, every inch covered in graphite and charcoal, depicting the levels of hell in great detail and my own interpretations of the sins. It was a lot to take in for a viewer, but the emotions I was able to portray throughout the illustrated poem were impactful. "Then what for?"

"Just for fun." I shrugged and glanced at him over my shoulder. His eyebrows shot up, making him almost look surprised, but he recovered and nodded. I understood his reaction, since the hours and days I slaved over that project wouldn't have seemed fun, but I lived for those drawings.

"It's here?" I nodded. "I'd like to see it."

"Sure." I nodded and felt a flutter inside me.

"Maybe you could include it in the exhibit."

"Yeah. That's a good idea."

"Good." I looked over my shoulder again, but he was already out the door.

———

Since my contribution to the exhibit was covered with my Dante series, I found myself bored in the studio on Thursday as the boys worked on their projects. I felt restless and uninspired to absently sketch anything new, and thought back to Dante. I always had the idea of continuing my illustrations on a smaller piece of paper, depicting little scenes or circles from *Inferno* to accent the three large and imposing posters—something more intimate and even more detailed. Many artists had illustrated the *Divine Comedy* before, and I admired the works by Dalí and William Blake, but mostly Botticelli's drawings. Still, I found Dalí's and Blake's works fascinating, since they had different styles from mine. I realized that Ozzie matched Dalí, and Steven matched Blake. I had what I thought was a good idea but was too insecure to mention it to the boys and get shut down—especially by Jax. The next day, I packed a handful of books to bring to the studio.

"Psst. Ozzie." He looked up from his painting, and I waved him over. My three Dante drawings were laid out on my table. "So…how's it going?" I asked and peeked over at his easel.

"Eh. I'm kinda stalling. The painting I'm working on is basically done, but I don't know what to do for the last one."

"How about everyone else?"

"Same." He shrugged. "Lucky you," he mumbled, acknowledging how much work I'd already completed.

"Well…I was thinking about that. There was only so much I could fit on the posters, you know? There's *so* much more content I want to include."

"Mia, it's perfect."

"Well, of course, these are." I smiled, exaggerating my artistic satisfaction over my project. "But there's more to do, and I can't do it alone. It'll also be a little boring if it's all the same."

"Okay…what are you thinking?"

"I've wanted to continue with a smaller dimension and elaborate on the finer details that I wasn't able to include. Like the river Styx! See." I pointed to the fifth circle I had drawn on the *Inferno* poster. "It's there but could be so much cooler featured alone." Ozzie frowned and followed my pointer finger. "Oh! And the flaming tombs." I pointed at the sixth circle. "I did a good job with that, but I only used graphite and charcoal. Using bright, vivid colors would have more impact."

"So, you want to use colored pencils?"

"No." I wasn't doing a great job at explaining my idea to Ozzie, so I pulled out my books and set them on the table. I opened up the pages of Botticelli's illustrations. "That was my inspiration." I then pulled out Salvador Dalí's illustrations, then the book of William Blake's illustrations. "Have you seen these?" He shook his head. "These are Dalí's illustrations. Just look. They're amazing. And, oh my God, William Blake's illustrations. His drawings and watercolors are just beautiful."

"I love this." Ozzie picked the Dalí book up to study it closer.

"I knew you would, because you have a similar style. I bet Steven likes Blake."

"Ha! You comparing me to Dalí. You are too kind." Ozzie laughed like he didn't deserve the compliment, but we both knew he did. "I like this one. I could totally do something like this," he mused as he looked through the pages, then looked up to me. "Ooooh. I know what you're thinking."

"And this." I picked up the third book and opened it to the page with Picasso's illustration for an ancient Greek comedy—it wasn't Dante, but illustrated a different style. "Nick could totally do prints like this."

"And Jax?" Ozzie asked as he continued perusing the books. I shrugged, even though I knew exactly what I wanted from him—a sculpture to depict the second circle of hell, lust.

"He did say our pieces should be connected," I commented and looked around the studio, but Jax had stepped out.

"Guys!" Ozzie yelled to get everyone's attention.

"Oz, I haven't really thought it out yet," I said under my breath, nervous to share my scattered thoughts with the group.

"They'll love it," he assured me and waited for Nick and Steven to gather around us, Jax still absent. "You all need another thing for the exhibit, right?" They nodded. "Mia has an awesome idea." The two boys gave me their attention, and I dove into my idea. My delivery was more coherent and organized than when I'd tried to explain it to Ozzie. They were pleased with my idea, then excited as I had them page through the books.

"How have I never seen this? I love Blake," Steven gushed and took the book with him to sit on the couch.

"Picasso, my man." Nick nodded, and I could tell he was already brainstorming as he walked away holding the book to join Steven and sat in the side chair.

"Success." Ozzie smiled and gave me a one-armed squeeze before taking the Dalí book with him and sitting with the boys.

An hour went by, and the boys were still engrossed in the books that I'd given them and didn't expect to get back. I sat on my knees on the floor, bent over the coffee table with my notebook and sketchbook, scribbling examples of the scenes I wanted to be illustrated and the significant cantos from the poem for the guys to read. I'd ripped the pages out and handed them to one of the boys so they could make their own interpretations.

"Is this an art studio or book club?" I heard Jax say with a hint of amusement in his voice as he entered the room.

"Mia, tell Jax your idea," Ozzie prompted me quickly so he could go back to his studying.

"Are those mine?" Jax frowned as he looked at me, then to his bookshelf.

"No. I brought them."

"So it is book club. Mia, can you do that on your own time?" He rolled his eyes and walked closer.

"Jealous you weren't invited?"

"No…" I saw his eyes start to survey our brainstorming area, then connect back with mine, and he raised an eyebrow. I returned the eyebrow raise, which made one side of his mouth quirk up. "Okay. Tell me your idea." He took a seat on the floor next to me and gave me his full attention. I tried to hide my excitement about his involvement and dove into my idea.

"I've always wanted to go further with my Dante illustrations and elaborate on the smaller details that I couldn't initially fit. I asked if anyone wanted to help…to bring their own style to one of Dante's sins, so, as a collection, it's more interesting and unique. Then all our pieces can be connected."

Jax steepled his fingers and nodded while I anticipated his response. "Okay. Good idea." I smiled brightly. "Does your creativity extend past Dante?" My smile deflated.

"How rude," I huffed and rose to my feet, head held high. "No Dante for you." I felt a twinge of disappointment as I turned my back to him and marched into the kitchen.

The counter and cupboards were abnormally tall, so I had to get on my tiptoes to try to reach a Pop-Tart from the shelf. A large hand beat me to it, and I slowly lowered to flat feet to see Jax standing over me. I expected him to take the Pop-Tart for himself, but he surprised me by handing it over.

"Thanks." I snatched my snack from his hand and turned to put it in the toaster. Then I leaned against the counter to face him.

"I want in." He crossed his arms and leaned against the counter opposite me.

"With Dante being my only area of creativity." I crossed my arms, too, and stared back.

"I haven't seen you do anything else. I still like the idea."

"You've seen one project." He shrugged. "So it's safe for me to assume that your creativity is confined to erotica." He cracked a smile and moved closer.

"That's your interpretation of my work, hm?"

"I wouldn't call it interpretation…you're as subtle as a knife." His smile widened, and he shook his head.

"Let me in on the Dante project."

"What's the magic word?" I teased with a little smirk, liking that I had the upper hand.

"I'm not saying 'please.'"

"Then no." The toaster dinged, but Jax was faster than me and grabbed the pastry. "Hand over the Pop-Tart."

"Let me in."

"No."

"Then no Pop-Tart for you." He smirked, then took a bite off a corner, and I tried not to get distracted by his sensual lips. I rolled my eyes and made a grab for it, but he held it back. Ultimately, I wanted him involved in the project, and I wanted the Pop-Tart.

"Fine. You're in."

"What circle do I get?" He still didn't hand it over.

"The second." I held out my hand.

"What sin is that?"

"Look it up."

"No." He still held my Pop-Tart hostage.

"Lust," I stated plainly and waited for him to hand over my pastry. Those sensual lips curved into an adorable smile, and I had to force myself not to stare.

"Oooh. Why assign that to me, Mia?"

"Naturally, since your creativity is limited to erotica."

"Do you think about my creativity often? I think you're trying to tell me something," he teased, and my eyes widened at his innuendo. I wasn't expecting that and hated his amused look, as he no doubt saw me blush. I abandoned the Pop-Tart and walked away. I went back to sit with the boys and was delighted to see them sharing their ideas and chatting away.

"You guys don't have to do this if you don't want to…" I hedged, still feeling a bit of insecurity and needing to hear their enthusiasm.

"Of course we do!" Nick squeaked from behind his book.

"I love this idea, Mia. I'm so going to use watercolor," Steven assured me with excitement. I smiled at them both with appreciation.

"Brilliant." Ozzie nodded, and I sat back down with them to keep working.

Jax followed me and set my Pop-Tart down next to me on the coffee table before plopping himself in an empty chair to join the group. He picked up the edition of *Inferno* I'd brought and settled in. I watched him page through until he found canto five, when Virgil led Dante past the lustful being punished by an endless wind to get through the second circle.

We spent the rest of the day on the couches and chairs, studying and brainstorming. My excitement grew as my idea started to become real and the boys became even more invested. I looked over the coffee table covered in sketches, pleased with the progress, and happy that I'd decided to share my idea with my talented colleagues.

I felt my nerves amplify with the addition of Jax to our project. His work was masculine and imposing but somehow just as delicate and sensual, as each sculpture defined passion in its own way. I had become increasingly obsessed with his hands and would stealthily watch him work as they flexed and moved, carving, molding, and chiseling blank stone into beautiful artwork. He always looked so intense and completely transfixed on the form in front of him, so absorbed it was like he was somewhere else. I was intimidated by him in every way and very self-conscious whenever he was near. I didn't want the outcome of this project to show my shortcomings in comparison with his and the other boys' work. But worry would get me nowhere, so I shoved it to the back of my mind to focus on what was in my power—dedicating every ounce of energy and creativity to the art in front of me.

Soon, we all had our individual plans decided on, and we dispersed to our stations to get started before the weekend.

Since I finally had something to focus on, I put on my gold wire-rimmed glasses and got to work.

I'd been bending down to reach the lower half of my paper for too long, and my back had started to pinch. I dropped my charcoal and pushed my glasses to sit atop my head and rubbed my hand over my eyes. With a sigh, I sat down on the floor and lay back to rest and analyze my work from a new angle.

"What are you doing?" Jax's rich voice pulled me out of my artistic daze, and I looked up. He stood, staring down at me.

"Resting."

"We have furniture." He motioned to the lounge space in the corner.

"We also have a floor," I countered, still lying down on the concrete in front of my easel.

"How about you act like a professional and lie on the couch instead of the floor, hm?"

"Who says professionals don't lie on the floor, hm?" I smiled as I looked up at him from my comfortable position.

"I do."

"I don't take your views on professionalism as law, so I'll stay here, thank you."

Instead of arguing further, his lips curved in an amused smile, but he tried to hide it. "Of course you don't." He shook his head, then returned to his station.

I tilted my head back to watch him move across the room and felt my body wanting him to stay closer. When he sat back down in his chair, his eyes connected with mine and didn't look away. I diverted my gaze back to my easel when I felt my cheeks heat, hoping he hadn't seen. I remained on the floor for only a few more minutes, then got back to work.

Chapter 7

Later next week, I dipped out of work midmorning to make my blood-draw appointment. Once I'd scheduled it over the phone, it was fairly simple. I remembered the rules, not to eat or take my morning medications until after the appointment for the most accurate results. I pointed out my best vein to the lab tech to save time. I psyched myself up in the elevator before I got to the studio floor, anticipating criticism from Jax because of my absence. As I walked up the stairs, I remembered the bright-pink bandage around my arm and quickly pulled it off and slipped it into my purse. I frowned when I entered the room to see all stations empty. Lunch break. I dropped my purse at my table and went to the kitchen. I stood in the doorway and looked around the room. Steven was sitting on the counter, drinking a SunnyD; Nick was in a kitchen chair with his feet kicked up on the table; Jax sat in the next spot, making his chair look mini compared to his large body; and Ozzie stood at the center island, busy spreading peanut butter on bread.

"Mia, you're back." Ozzie smiled when he saw me, and all the guys looked too. "Want a PB&J?" I noticed then that he had been making everyone the classic lunch.

"Yes, please." I took the offered plate and went to sit at the table, remembering I hadn't eaten leading up to the blood draw.

"Way to skip third period," Jax said as he crossed his arms and stared me down like we were in high school. He sounded more teasing than judgmental and didn't demand I explain myself.

"What's wrong with your arm, Mia?" Nick asked with a mouthful of peanut butter and jelly, nodding to my right arm, which showed the indentation of the medical bandage I'd just discarded.

"Oh…" I hesitated as I looked down at my arm.

"We have a strict no-drug policy here," Jax said gravely, and I rolled my eyes.

"Which only pertains to me, stoner boys?" I looked around to the guys and back to Jax. Yeah, I knew they had their fun. Ozzie, Nick, and Steven all snickered, while Jax just pursed his lips and eyed me.

"Touché." He nodded and joined in with the laughing.

"Blood drive at some church down the street from my apartment. They had that big Red Cross van, so I donated." I gave them another lie to cover up my bipolar issues.

"Good for you, Saint Mia."

"Thank you, Sinner Jax."

"Now, was that necessary?"

"A little." I shrugged and smiled. Fortunately, the interaction fizzled out, and the focus moved away from my needle-pricked arm. Unfortunately, the next topic wasn't much better.

"So, Mia." Nick got my attention from where he still lounged in his chair, feet resting on the table. "Got a boyfriend?"

"Nope," I answered passively and bit into my PB&J, hoping that this topic would also fizzle out.

"Why not?"

"Why don't I have a boyfriend?" He nodded. "I don't know. I just don't." I shrugged and continued to nibble on my sandwich.

"I bet she's high maintenance," I heard Jax say, so I shot him a quick glare. I ignored Jax's jab, and so did the rest of the boys, but Steven jumped in next.

"Don't you want one?" he asked from his seat on the counter. I shrugged.

"Maybe she can't get one." Jax tried again to antagonize me.

"Of course she could!" Nick defended me, then pointed at me. "Just look at her!"

"Not if she's high maintenance," Jax jabbed again, and I rolled my eyes.

"You don't even know me," I defended myself.

"I can just tell."

"How can you—"

"Jax, Mia is not high maintenance," Ozzie interjected before Jax and I could continue our bickering. I flashed Jax a sassy smirk.

"Suuure." Jax eyed me as he sat back in his chair. He had no new jabs so I was fine with ignoring him. Our conversation naturally drifted to our work.

We talked about the Dante project and how we were all progressing at the same pace with our selected circles. Soon, we'd have to start brainstorming how to collaborate together for the ninth and most deranged circle of hell. Eager to get back to our art, we started cleaning up.

"Nick, stick your finger into the Skippy jar one more time, and I'll— *seriously?*" Ozzie actually got mad at the little blondie, and we laughed as he ran away. The rest of the boys followed him into the studio. I took a few more bites of my sandwich before joining them with a grateful smile on my face, happy to be a part of this group of silly boys.

Before long, Nurse Amy followed up and informed me that my lithium levels were within therapeutic range but on the higher end—I had to be hyperaware of any side effects because if they worsened, I could need to be hospitalized. No big deal.

———

To my great disappointment, the boyfriend subject resurfaced at happy hour at Floyd's after work.

"Guys!" Nick perked up with an idea. "Let's get Mia on a dating app!" He scooted in next to me in the booth, delivering a round of drinks.

"Let's not." I shook my head vehemently.

"At least give it a try," Steven said politely, sitting across the table from Nick.

"I'm making you one," Nick announced, then pulled out his phone and held it up to me. "Okay, smile!"

"No." I covered my face and laughed, charmed by his good intentions but still against a dating profile. I parted my fingers to see if he'd put the phone down.

"Come on, Mia. It'll be fun, and we're guys, so we know what to write and stuff," Nick said, trying to convince me.

"Seriously, no." I shook my head with hopefully enough conviction for them to drop it.

"Okay, okay, fine." He sighed and put down the phone. Ozzie, Steven, and Nick went to the bar, leaving me alone with Jax.

"Why not do the app thing?" he asked, his voice more curious than his usual condescending tone.

"I don't want to." I shrugged and swished my straw around in my drink, feeling awkward to be alone with him.

"Don't you want to meet someone?" He thrummed his fingers against the table, which was very distracting. I had never seen hands like that—large with long fingers, obviously strong and veiny but not *too* veiny. I imagined that hand wrapping around my neck and—

"Sorry...what?" I blinked out of my strange imagination and refocused.

"Don't you want to meet someone?" He repeated his question with a small smile tugging at his lips.

"Sure. Not that way, though." I shrugged, and he nodded. His fingers began thrumming again, and I resisted the urge to stare at them. "Do you do that?"

"Apps? No." He leaned back casually, but the way he looked at me excited me.

"No girlfriend?" I put my elbow on the table, chin resting on my hand. He pursed his lips, probably knowing where I was going.

"No."

"A guy like you can't keep a girlfriend? There must be something wrong with you. I bet it's the arrogance thing." I smirked.

"No." He smiled and folded his arms, taking my shot with humor.

"It's your high standards, then. I bet you want big tits, tiny waist, big ass, long legs, and lips like…" I pouted my lips to resemble something close to the popular collagen-pumped look.

"Spot on." He chuckled. "So, if you see any of those women, send them my way."

"I would never condemn a woman to such a fate. How cruel," I said dramatically, bringing a hand to my moral heart.

"Oh, Mia." Jax sighed and leaned closer to me from across the table with a small smirk. "You have no idea what that fate holds." He kept smiling when I didn't have a comeback, just a few blinks as I willed my mind not to imagine that fate.

That's when the boys, thankfully, returned to the booth, halting my imagination and terminating our weird conversation.

"Okay! Check it out!" Nick slid in next to me, holding out his phone. I shot a glance to Jax and saw that he was still looking at me, and with a cheeky smirk, he winked. Feeling my cheeks heat, I looked away. "We made you one!" *Oh, dear God, no.*

"What? How?"

"You're like the only girl with no social media, so Ozzie sent me pictures to use, and we made up the rest." He snickered, and I groaned, dropping my head against the booth back.

"Isn't that identity fraud?"

"We changed your name." Ozzie smiled, and I decided to have a firm talking-to with him later. He was sitting in a chair that he'd pulled up to the end of our booth and looked just as pleased with the profile as the other two boys.

"We did a good job," Steven insisted.

"All right. Let me see." Nick handed me his phone so I could scroll through my fake profile. I shook my head. "You guys named me Mimi? And my bio… I'm a cool girl, new to the city and looking for some fun." I rolled my eyes and scrolled further. "Bikini pictures? Seriously?" I glared at them when I saw pictures from my last vacation with my family in Turks and Caicos. "A bit much, guys. I mean, *really*." I rolled my eyes.

"Hot bod, Mimi." Nick winked. I set down the phone and buried my face in my hands. "The fact you don't have a boyfriend is a tragedy."

"Let me see." Jax's interested voice alerted me, and I lifted my head. He picked up the phone before I could take it back. I watched his expression as he looked at my mostly naked photo. I noticed his jaw tic in a sexy display of intensity, and he raised a brow. I knew it was a very flattering bikini picture—great sunset lighting. He scrolled through. "Damn. Mimi's trying to get some." He let me snatch the phone out of his hand.

"Okay, boys. Get rid of it." I handed the phone back to Nick, and they all protested.

"But you already have matches! Look. This is Gram. He's twenty-five and apparently does a lot of rock climbing. Wait, no, it's just more pictures of the same rock-climbing day." He showed me the picture. I shrugged. "He says he'll take you to dinner and breakfast. Oooh! I see what he did there." Nick laughed, and I shook my head and looked over his shoulder at the screen, curious.

"Okay, this is Drew—"

"No," I denied immediately, on reflex.

"Why?"

"I don't like that name." I sat back, my mind working quickly to stay in the present and not get sucked into the bad memories of being seventeen, pinned below a boy named Drew.

"Picky," Jax pointed out like I just proved his unfounded assumption of me.

"Like I have to say yes to every guy or else I'm a bitch? Typical," I said, voicing my argument to every man I'd encountered who had called me and other women bitches for rejecting them.

"Don't be judgmental."

"I'm not. Not all men are entitled to a chance with me, or any woman, by default. Ahem, male chauvinism. Anyway…say goodbye to Mimi." They all whined, but I was really over it and watched Nick's screen as I made him delete the fake profile. "How about you three single boys? Don't you want to be on apps?"

"I'm already on them." Nick smiled proudly. Ozzie shook his head, and I didn't push him because I was a better best friend than he was at that moment, which left Jax. I aimed my attention at him with raised brows. He shook his head too, but I didn't spare him.

"Let's do it, Casanova. I'll help you." I smirked, and the other boys joined me. "Let's start with your bio. Something simple like, 'Call me *Mr. Caine*...will show you a good time. Disclaimer—won't call you back.'"

"So, you think I'm one of those guys?" He sat back in his chair and crossed his arms.

"I know you are." I was guilty of making snap judgments too.

"You don't know me," he said with sass, mimicking my defensive response to his accusation that I was high maintenance.

"I can just tell."

"I'm a complex, sensitive man, Mia."

"Sure." I sipped my drink. That ended the conversation.

Not long after, a couple girls stopped by our booth. Apparently, they were all acquainted since they did the "oh, hey!" greeting. They made some chitchat while ignoring me completely, and the boys didn't make introductions, which was totally fine with me. I had my head resting against the wall and was starting to zone out when one of the girls started talking to Jax.

"So, Jax." The woman with shiny blonde hair, who they all called Cece, scooted into the next booth over, behind where Jax sat, and leaned over the seat. "You said you'd call."

"Did I?" he answered passively and sipped his beer, but then decided to show compassion and sighed. "I'm sorry. I really didn't mean to blow you off. It's been a busy month." She nodded but continued her glossy pout, her expression confident and seductive as she wore a deep-cut blouse. "I should've called you. We good?"

"Of course. I just missed you." She flirted and purred. "But you won't forget to this time, right?"

"This time?" He glanced over his shoulder at her, and she said something in a whisper that I couldn't hear. Jax paused before responding, and I directed my eyeline anywhere but at him. "That...will work." She smiled and returned to her place next to her friend standing at the end of our table. I stole a glance at him, and we instantly made eye contact. It was intensely awkward, and I immediately looked away, but was grateful to Cece for confirming my judgment of Jax. Finally, after what felt like an hour but was only five minutes, Cece and her friend left.

"They were nice." I spoke out loud even though the words were only for myself—sarcasm definitely evident.

"Oh, shit. We should've introduced you," Ozzie said and looked at me apologetically.

"No, no." I shook my head with a smile, since neither the girls nor I would've wanted that. "It's all good. So, Mr. Complex and Sensitive"—I smirked at Jax across from me—"assumption confirmed."

"Whatever." He rolled his eyes, and I knew he was uncomfortable with me having proof.

"Wham bam, thank you, ma'am," I teased, intending to annoy him.

"Shut up." He glared, and I just smiled.

"Wait, you and Cece?" Steven asked, and I made sure to listen.

"Still?" Ozzie added with a grimace.

"Not really." Jax shrugged, trying to be dismissive.

"Dude, she's such a bitch." Nick laughed, so I put together that it wasn't a terribly sensitive subject. "But hot...I get it." Nick was right. She was beautiful and the exact type I had just been teasing Jax about.

"You showed her a good time and didn't call her back. True to your bio," I teased.

"Jealous?" he accused with a cocky smirk.

"Not even a little." *A little...*

"You remember she's crazy, right?" Nick asked with a smile, but his words were serious.

"Batshit crazy, but so? We don't do any talking." Jax smirked.

"Oh, God. Level of douchebag...too much," I said painfully, covering my eyes and sinking back against the booth cushion, then sliding to rest on Nick's shoulder. Everyone, except Jax, thought I was funny.

"You're so dramatic," he said. I parted my fingers to look at him. He glared at me, but I didn't care and dropped my hands with a smirk. I could tell my opinion of him bothered him. Cece provided proof—he showed her a good time, then never called—but...how he'd spoken to her was kind. He had made plenty of faulty judgments of me that weren't true, so I started to question mine as well.

———

A couple weeks of hard work went by, and everyone was exhausted but mostly excited to see our project come together. Focused at our stations, we were all going over the final touches. I was staring at my depiction of Dante's fourth circle of hell mounted on my easel, head tilted and eyes squinting through my glasses to focus on the small details. I felt my head bob to "Stairway to Heaven" playing in my AirPods. I always picked an album or playlist for each project. I would listen to it on repeat until the project was complete. With my *Inferno* drawings, I was vibing to *Led Zeppelin IV*, the album that had allegedly been influenced by the occult.

My focus was broken when something smacked against the backboard. I blinked a few times and looked down to see an eraser on the floor in front of me. Somehow, I knew who'd thrown it. I looked over my shoulder and saw Jax at his station, so I turned fully around. He was sitting in his chair, swiveling back and forth, while his hand motioned for me to join him. I was intrigued, so I crossed the room until I stood in front of him, his eyes on my legs the whole way.

"Yes, Jax?"

"Want to see my progress?" His eyes lifted to meet mine. I frowned, then looked to his table, and my face lit up. "Yeah, you do." Jax had obviously caught me checking out his work. I didn't hide my smile as I moved closer.

The whole time we had been working, Jax was in his sculpting room, and all I could hear was the sparking and clanking of tools as he worked all day, creating something beautiful. I never dared to interrupt him so I just had to use my imagination and sneak peeks from time to time. Finally, he had carried the sculpture to his station to be seen.

"Show me what you got." I was excited to see his interpretation of the second circle of hell, as I had caught him reading the full text from the *Inferno* book I'd brought to the studio. He kept it at his station so he could revisit canto five while he worked on his sculpture. Ozzie, Nick, and Steven all were working off of my description of their circle.

"Oh, I will." He pushed his feet against the floor to roll his chair to the other side of his table so I could stand next to him and look at his sculpture depicting lust. I was already mesmerized. It was devastatingly erotic and brilliant, pain and temptation twisting together in faceless naked human forms that clung to each other with desire as they tried to get higher, out of hell—but they would never make it, as the sculpture swirled as if it were in the wind and dissipated into nothing at the top.

"Oh my God," I breathed, then smiled as I bent down to take a closer look.

"Did I do good?"

"Fucking hell." I chuckled at the unintentional pun and put a hand to my chest. I was truly overwhelmed. "It's… Can I touch it…?" I looked over to Jax, who was already watching me closely. I didn't know if that was an inappropriate request or not. He just nodded. I bent my knees to be at eye level, then ran my finger along a body that twisted together with others, reaching up and, like a flame, danced higher into nothing. The black metal was harsh but fluid, and intense, but the forms were still so beautiful. How he got metal to look like a windstorm, the circle's punishment, was beyond me.

"So, I succeeded in depicting the second circle of *Inferno*?"

"You succeeded." I smiled.

"Oooh, Sinner Jax can make Saint Mia lustful. Aren't I impressive?" he teased, and I straightened to give him a pointed look, arms crossed. Jax flashed a very-satisfied-with-himself smile as he leaned back in his chair, hands behind his head, and winked. He somehow managed to be arrogant, sexy as hell, and adorable all at the same time. Oh, yeah, Jax could make Mia lustful.

"The *sculpture* is very impressive," I admitted, and he nodded, still smiling. "Is it almost finished?"

"Almost." He switched back into artist mode and sat forward in his chair. "It needs more detail." I could see his eyes home in on those details. I loved seeing him so intense about a project I proposed, and I appreciated the opportunity to see an artist at work up close, not just occasionally peeking into his room.

"Cool." I didn't know what else to say or do, so I just walked back to my station with one final glance over my shoulder to see his focus completely back on his art. His sculpture remained in my mind for the rest of the day.

Chapter 8

"Mia, do not ask me what to wear!" Ozzie laughed into the phone when I called him before the exhibit-reveal party that was later that night. I was nervous on all levels. Our cohesive Dante project, which came from my idea, was finally complete and set to be debuted at the party. I had never shown my work before and did not know what community response to expect. I was nervous to be going to a social function in general, especially a function with my new colleagues that would be my introduction to the San Francisco art world. I was nervous about how I should present myself. I was nervous about the wild card, Jackson fucking Caine.

"But I don't know what to wear!"

"And I do?"

"More than me. I don't know how San Franciscan artists dress."

"However they damn well please. That's the perk of being an artist," he said with encouragement, but I was still wearing my robe and feeling insecure as I stood in my closet. "Want me to come over?" Ozzie sighed, but I knew he had no problem helping me. He'd been witness to wardrobe panic with his sisters.

———

Once he arrived at my apartment, Ozzie dropped onto my couch and made himself comfortable. "Alright. Let's do this." I made him describe the kind of event I was walking into so I could come up with the right outfit. It also helped that I got to see what he was wearing. "Sometimes these things are casual and sometimes not. We almost never wear suits, but tonight is different. It's our exhibit debut but also the gallery's opening night, so think posh and professional." Ozzie then motioned to the posh and professional suit he was wearing. "Still, wear whatever you feel comfortable in. I don't think Nick even owns a suit, so he'll probably be wearing jeans."

With Ozzie's information in mind, I stepped into a simple slip dress and secured the straps on my shoulders before pulling a sheer long-sleeved dress over my head and down my body. It was mini, mesh, and the color was a cute and playful pistachio. With the crew neckline and long sleeves, I was very okay with the short length that showed off my toned legs. Pleased with my pick, I smiled to myself as I strapped on low black stilettos and looked in the mirror before showing Ozzie.

"Oooh la la." He wiggled his eyebrows for fun and nodded.

"San Franciscan art exhibit approved?" I smiled and swayed back and forth, expecting a positive reply.

"Oh, yeah. Mia, you look awesome. Expect a lot of attention tonight."

"Attention? Oh, no. I need to change." I shook my head, honestly wanting to pick a new outfit.

"Don't do that! Own it. Scale of one to ten, how nervous are you?"

"Eleven. So attention is bad."

"I promise, it's really not a big deal. Don't be intimidated. There will be some cameras, you know, pictures for the magazines and blogs, but it's really not stressful. I promise."

"Ugh." I sighed, not comforted.

"There will be an endless supply of champagne."

"I like champagne. Okay. I'm ready." I smiled on a heavy exhale, not ready but ready to act like I was. It took almost an hour with my tremor-ridden hands, but I had managed an easy beauty routine—highlighter on brow bones, inner corner of eyes, cheekbones and cupid's bow; blush on my cheeks, eyelids, and the tip of my nose; Aquaphor dabbed over my brows to keep them in place; mascara; and my favorite pouty lip stain. I let my long blonde hair sway behind my back, allowing my short curtain bangs to fall around my face.

"You look dashing, Oswald," I said in a posh British accent as we left my apartment, making him smile and accept the compliment.

"Why, thank you, Amelia. So, we usually go to these things together, but tonight, we're meeting there." I nodded and hopped into his Range Rover and away we went to the gallery. "Well, that's new." Ozzie chuckled as he looked from my hand to ahead of us, zooming past headlights. I knew what he was talking about.

"I've always done this." I smiled and extended my arm so I could marvel at my nails. "Steven Tyler inspired."

"Who...?"

"Ozzie!" I exaggerated my disappointment in him for not knowing the rock icon. "Lead singer of Aerosmith."

"Ah, of course." He just nodded with a smile.

"It's my fancy nail style. I actually did go to one of those nail salons," I admitted—there was no way I'd be able to paint a small black strip down the middle of my nails.

"Your fancy style." Ozzie laughed at my quirkiness. "You're so goofy."

"I take goofy as a compliment, so thank you."

———

"Mimi, coming in hot!" Nick yelled as a greeting once we found him and Steven at the exhibit. I hated that I felt shy and tried to brush it off. I realized that they hadn't seen me outside of my work clothes. As Ozzie expected, Nick was wearing a pair of jeans and a button-down, while Steven wore the same but added a sport coat. I looked around the posh and professional space and marveled at the big chandelier above us. The high ceilings and the modern design of the gallery were perfect for showcasing the different works of art all around us, and the vastness of the room gave people plenty of room to mill around, viewing the art or chasing after a waiter holding a tray of champagne.

"Hey, boys…what—what are you doing?" I greeted them in the middle of the room with a smile but became off-balance as Nick started to spin me around in place.

"I needed the full picture!" Nick let me go after he was done checking me out. I had become comfortable enough with his personality that I didn't mind his objectification.

"You made me dizzy." The room spun as I stumbled backward a few steps and right into the arms of Jackson fucking Caine.

"Making a scene, already, Mia?" Jax teased as he kept me upright with his hands around my waist. I rolled my eyes and elbowed away from him. He joined our little group and circled me. Once he stood in front of me, his gaze surveyed up and down my body. "Wow. I actually approve." He nodded with a condescending smile to top off his asshole greeting, which really pissed me off. I wanted to say something that would call him out, and I should have. Instead, I arched a brow and did the same, scanning up and down his body, in that posh and professional suit, with critical eyes. I stopped in front of him and pursed my lips with a tilt of my head, judging.

"Adequate." I shrugged, looking bored, and finally brought my gaze to his. His jaw shifted and mouth twisted—he was stifling a smile. To my great satisfaction, Ozzie, Nick, and Steven provided some casual applause for my response. "Thank you." I smiled, proud of myself, but I didn't want to linger.

"Nice claws, by the way." Leaning in with his lips close to my ear, Jax complimented my Steven Tyler nails. I looked up at him, feeling the familiar buzz inside me whenever his large body was so close and his eyes only on me.

"Thank you." I looked away from him and turned back to the rest of the boys. "Who knows where the champagne is?"

"I do!" Nick raised his hand, then grabbed mine and pulled me through the crowd until we arrived at the table with alcohol. "For you."

He handed me a glass, then grabbed one for himself. "For me." I took a greedy sip, and Nick chuckled. "Kinda intimidated?"

"Kinda." I admitted, being honest.

"I was too. Really, there's nothing to worry about. We don't take these things too seriously, just represent our work and have fun."

"Okay." I took another sip.

"Oooh, let's go spy on the people checking out our work," he said with a giggle and took my hand again. We loitered near our collection, people watching and eavesdropping.

We watched the viewers as they shuffled along, starting with our cohesive collaboration on Dante's *Inferno*. They stopped at each circle to take in the different styles of each artist—praising Steven's vivid watercolor, which brought a strange romanticism to his circle, Limbo, which started the journey through hell. More viewers would push through the crowd, urging people to move on to the second circle and see my personal favorite—Jax's portrayal of lust, a metal sculpture of naked figures writhing together, which accomplished the look of being trapped in the endless wind of the sin's punishment with his signature twisting fluidity of the whole form. I was just as captivated as the viewers by his work and couldn't have been any happier that he'd participated in my idea. It was hard for me to look away, but I continued to follow the crowd's progression through our hell. Again, Steven's colorful and weirdly romantic watercolor of gluttons being bombarded with rain, hail, and black snow in the third circle. The fourth circle, punishing greed, allowed me to go into even more pencil-work detail on the muscled figures that exerted themselves in the endless pushing of boulders. Nick killed it with his black-and-white prints of the fifth circle, Wrath, the sinners fighting each other on the river Styx while the sullen gurgled underneath.

"Mia," Nick whispered to me as he overheard the viewers comment on his work at the same time as I did. "I killed it." I gave him a quick squeeze of a hug to acknowledge his success. "Ozzie, though. Damn." He continued to the sixth circle, the sin heresy, where Ozzie used vivid color to create an abstract painting of burning stone coffins—exactly what I wanted from him.

We then followed the crowd's attention to my pencil illustration of circle seven, suicides—naturally, as I was familiar with such feelings and always found the punishment of that sin interesting. I used soft graphite strokes to create detailed trees that sinners would turn into, then charcoal to darken the scene around them.

Ozzie again produced a striking abstract painting of the eighth circle of hell, where frauds were punished and thrown into pits of darkness, forever to be tortured. Ozzie's work was brilliant—the longer you looked into the chaotic and colorful painting, you saw more and more detail all circled together.

Nick and I snickered to each other as we listened to the gasps at the more deranged illustrations of the ninth and final circle of hell, which was by all of us collaborating together. It included sinners trapped in ice, eating each other or being chewed in Lucifer's jaws. Really, the depiction was not disturbing, rather beautiful artwork with a dark side and a tribute to a great poet.

Finally, at the end of the exhibit, my three posters of the entirety of the *Divine Comedy* were displayed. I felt my eyes prickle as I heard viewers marvel over my work and felt Nick's hand land on my shoulder. I looked over to see his boyish smile, and he gave me a proud head nod, acknowledging my hard work.

I wasn't expecting it, but that night was a monumental moment in my life. I felt like I was officially an artist and finally belonged somewhere—and seeing my work hanging on a gallery wall solidified it.

"Guys!" Nick did not use his inside voice when he yelled across the room as we were making our way back to our group. "Mia and I have been spying, and people are going crazy over our work. It's awesome. Go listen."

"It's time for press," Jax informed us, and the boys responded with groans. Apparently, they didn't like press. That was fine with me, since I felt the same. We reported to our section of the exhibit, and Jax said a few words to officially present our work to the crowd.

"This is when we let Jax represent us," Steven whispered to me.

"They only want to listen to him anyway." Ozzie shrugged as he shuffled closer to us, and so did Nick.

"Does that bother you?" I asked the three boys quietly.

"Not at all." Steven shook his head.

"As long as we get credit." Nick nodded.

"Jax is like the front man, but we are all covered in the features and media." Ozzie explained more of their group dynamic, and I was definitely in support of it.

Jax didn't speak for much longer, but I observed that he talked with his hands, waving them around as he talked with no regard for who he might seduce. It was irresponsible. Again, I tried not to stare.

"You definitely noticed our talented new artist, Amelia Bell." I snapped back to attention when I heard Jax say my name. "Our team is even stronger, and her addition has us excited for more diversity in our projects and more cohesive exhibits like the one you see tonight. As artists, passion is the root of our work, and I think you'll feel that tonight. Enjoy."

I stared at him as he talked to the media, surprised and speechless. I felt a nudge on my arm and looked over to see Ozzie beside me with a happy smile. I smiled back, but Jax's words had hit harder than just a supportive colleague's praise. He was always critical, so a public admittance of his acceptance…it meant a lot. I watched him as he pushed his palms together and said goodbye to the media. Jax turned back to us with a goofy grin and shrugged his shoulders, knowing he'd fulfilled his role as front man and that our collection was a success. Once his eyes met mine, his goofy grin fell into a more intimate smile, and he then gave me a head nod. I smiled back but still had to turn away—his eyes on mine were always too intense for me to hold.

The last of our duties was to smile for the cameras. Photographers snapped away as we stood with our collection. To my absolute horror, several members of the media and community wanted to talk to me since I was a new face and obviously stood out by being the only woman in a group of men. *Ozzie did not prepare me for this.* I was polite and represented us well. I didn't know what was expected in an interview, so I just answered questions honestly but minimally. I revealed very little—like nothing—when asked about my background and steered the topic to us as a group.

"Look, it's the most popular girl in school," Ozzie teased once I finally escaped from the media fest. I let out a heavy sigh but smiled, as I was quickly surrounded by Ozzie, Nick, and Steven's goofy round of applause and supportive comments.

"Thanks for the warning, Ozzie. Not." I rolled my eyes, but he just shrugged with a big smile, proud of me. "I need more champagne." I looked around the room and grabbed a golden flute off of a waiter's tray. I stood with Ozzie, Nick, and Steven, but my eyes were searching for the one missing member. I spotted Jax across the room talking to a few women I didn't recognize. One leaned into him and placed a hand on his arm as she laughed at something. I wondered if it was because Jax said something funny or if she just found him attractive. I knew the answer.

My mind went to earlier when I'd circled him and devoured him with my eyes, judging his appearance. I had never seen him outside of his work clothes. He looked sexy in just old jeans and a T-shirt but was straight-up dangerous in a suit. Before, I never wanted to look at him for too long, a defense against his striking features and hot body. I didn't want my head going anywhere I didn't want it to be, even though it skimmed that line daily. Now I couldn't look away....but had to because he was turning my way and I didn't want to get caught creeping. I finished my champagne in two sips and looked around the room like I was marveling at the art. When I glanced back, Jax was walking away from the two women and wandering on his own. I wasn't planning on it, but I just had to get closer, and my feet started moving on their own. I joined him where he'd stopped at a painting in a quiet corner. He looked over his shoulder when he sensed my approach.

"Hey." I forced my voice to be confident instead of awkward. I looked up into his eyes and was immediately intimidated by his intense gaze. *Shit, maybe he wants to be alone.* "Um, never mind." I turned to put distance between us, but he caught my hand and pulled me back next to him.

"What?" He held my hand a moment longer before letting go.

"It's nice and quiet over here."

"That's why I'm here. Avoiding talking to people."

"Oh…sorry." I turned away again, feeling embarrassed. That's what I would've done, too, if I wanted to be alone.

"Not you." Jax chuckled and pulled me back next to him again. "You're an exception."

"Okay." I let myself breathe a little more easily when he smiled and dropped my hand once again.

"So, what do you think?" he asked. I frowned and looked to the painting on the wall in front of us of a bowl of fruit by a different artist.

"Um…it's not my favorite…" I said tentatively, worried there was a right or wrong answer.

"Mia." Jax chuckled and shook his head. "What do you think of your first showing?"

"Ohh." I chuckled, too, because that made more sense. "I really didn't know what to expect, but it's been wonderful."

"Good. I didn't anticipate the press hounding you tonight. I would've given you a heads-up. You handled it well, though."

"Thanks." His compliment perked me up. "And, um, thanks for the introduction."

"You deserve it," he said genuinely, making me smile.

"So…does that mean you consider me a serious artist now?" I asked, wanting him to ease my insecurities by saying it.

"Why do you have to go there?" He scowled, irritated that I'd reminded him of his initial judgment of me.

"Because it's there." He stared at me. I stared back. We were having a staring contest. Jax broke first.

"Yes. I consider you a *serious and talented artist.*" I anticipated a "but" or a jab to offset his compliment, but there wasn't one.

"Thank you." I bowed my head in acceptance, very satisfied.

"So, are we good, Ms. Bell?" He spoke professionally and extended his hand.

"We are good, Mr. Caine," I said just as professionally, and we shook hands. When I connected with his eyes, we seemed to know that it still wasn't over between us. We just stood there, looking at each other with faint smirks but not knowing where to go from there.

"We should…" Jax's eyes left mine and looked past my shoulder.

"Check in with the boys?"

"Yeah."

We were only separated from the group for a few minutes, but when we returned, Ozzie, Steven, and Nick had gotten themselves into a mild argument.

"You're not going to die of thirst." Ozzie rolled his eyes as Nick jittered around, eager to leave the gallery.

"There are drinks here." I frowned and motioned to the tables being replenished with more flutes of champagne.

"Okay, tell me where I can order a vodka Red Bull." Nick crossed his arms and challenged me. I didn't respond, as I didn't have an answer, nor did I think Nick needed any caffeine to spike his already high energy levels.

"Yeah, I could use a Captain Coke," Steven piped in with a hand raised.

Jax looked around the gallery, to our collection and the steady flow of visitors and press. "Actually, we need to do more press."

"Do you want me to die?" Nick asked seriously, and Ozzie and Steven both sighed at the news. I eyed Jax and somehow knew he was teasing them.

"I'm just playing. Let's go." Jax nodded toward the side exit so we could leave without any attention.

"Yeah!" Nick jumped into all of us to get us moving. "Let's go, let's go…to a bar we go!"

Chapter 9

We decided to go to the new restaurant above the gallery since we were all hungry and thirsty and required immediate satisfaction. I sighed when I approached the table and saw that everyone was already seated, meaning I didn't have a choice. The restaurant was the typical high-class steak house—dark hardwood, red leather seating, tablecloths, and dim lighting. I looked around the candle centerpiece at the four boys. After long days in the studio wearing clothes covered in paint and charcoal, it was fun to see us all polished and professional.

"Have a seat, Mia." Jax patted the open chair next to him. "I don't bite."

"Why don't I believe you?" I eyed him with suspicion and remained standing.

"Because you know I'm lying." He winked with a teasing smile, and I sighed as if I were disappointed to have to sit by him as I took my seat. "You're very brave."

"Shut up." I rolled my eyes as if I didn't feel a small flare of excitement to be close to him.

I couldn't explain it, but as I looked around the table to the rest of our group, I knew that if I were seated somewhere else, I'd spend dinner longing to be in the chair next to Jax. Everyone browsed their menus while my mind started to wander. The evening had been a whirlwind for me, and it was hard to process it all, but I was mostly unable to be present with my friends because of the strong body next to me.

"Mia!" Ozzie yelled from across the table, and I snapped out of my thoughts and blinked my eyes into focus.

"What?" I straightened in my seat, trying to reengage, and looked at him with raised brows.

"Ready to order?" he asked, apparently after a couple attempts to get my attention. The server was standing next to me, waiting patiently to take my order with his notepad and pen in hand. I hesitated since I hadn't even looked at the menu, and he decided to give me another minute and stepped away.

"What were you thinking about, Mia?" I heard Jax's low voice in my ear as I read through the menu in front of me. I looked over to meet his teasing gaze; then my eyes dropped down to his tempting lips that curved into a smirk.

I refocused on my dinner choices. "I'm thinking about my dinner." I didn't have to engage with him further since the server returned to my side. "I'll have the half portion of steak, medium rare, and scotch neat. Thank you." I smiled as I handed over my menu.

"You did not just order scotch and a steak." Jax stared at me.

"I did, yeah." I sat back in my chair and folded my arms. I arched a brow at his surprised expression, expecting his criticism.

"I didn't know I was sitting by Ron Burgundy," he commented and smirked like he didn't expect me to understand his *Anchorman* reference. I did.

"Who's that?" I frowned and cocked my head to the side, playing dumb, as he rolled his eyes.

"For you, Miss." The server returned and placed my tumbler of scotch in front of me, and I thanked him.

I knew Jax was watching me as I brought the glass to my lips and took a small sip of whiskey. I savored it as the liquid flowed down my throat and hummed my appreciation for the taste and burn through my chest. I licked my lips as I brought the glass down to the table and looked over to confirm that Jax's full attention was on me. I should've prolonged the tease, but, of course, I couldn't resist a good movie quote. "I love scotch. Scotchy scotch scotch. Here it goes, down, down into my belly. Mm. Mm,"

I recited with my eyes closed and shifted my hips in my chair. I looked over to Jax, who raised his eyebrows in surprise.

"You did not…" He stared at me, and I happily nodded as I took another sip of scotch. I sat back and enjoyed the visual of Jax laughing, the deep rumble from his chest and his genuine smile, knowing I'd caused it.

"What?" Nick bounced in his chair, ready for fun, as the other boys brought their attention to us.

"Mia is just…" Jax mused as he sat back in his chair and glanced over at me, to which I raised an eyebrow. He smiled and answered the question. "Funny."

"Blah. We already knew that." Nick waved us off and returned to his conversation with Steven and Ozzie.

"You think I'm funny?" I asked with a teasing smile as I put my elbow on the table to rest my chin.

"I just said so."

"The Jackson Caine thinks I'm funny."

"You're welcome."

"I'm overwhelmed with flattery."

"Will you ever know when to stop talking?" he asked with a glare.

"Probably not." I shrugged and reached for my tumbler to bring the glass to my lips for a sip.

"Mm-hmm. Until I make you." Jax had leaned in close so only I could hear his low voice. My lips parted, not for a sip of scotch but from a small intake of breath elicited by Jax's threat. My hand froze with the glass to my mouth, and I shot a side glance at Jax. He smirked as he backed away to sit straight in his chair as if he knew that he could make my toes curl with his deep voice.

I blinked away from his deep-blue gaze and focused on tipping my glass back fast enough for a sip of scotch without my hands shaking, then successfully returned the tumbler to the table. "Well"—I cleared my throat and sat up straighter—"your threat is very intimidating, and I'll proceed with much caution."

"Sure you will." We were interrupted by multiple servers arriving at our table to hand out our meals.

All of us dug into our very delicious dinners with jovial conversations between all of us and commentary about the exhibit. All the while, I was hyperaware of every move Jax made. I would periodically glance at his large hands holding the fork and knife as he cut through the full portion of steak.

"Can I help you?" Jax's deep rumble of a voice caught my attention, and my eyes shot to his.

"What?" I blinked into focus, unfortunately knowing that I'd been caught staring.

"See something you like?"

"No…"

"Sure."

"Well, you don't have to clank your silverware against the plate hard enough that it may break."

"That's your reasoning?"

"It's distracting."

"What is? The clanking or my hands?" I stared at him. I didn't have an answer. He chuckled and shook his head. "Eat your meat, Mia."

I nodded and went back to my meal. *Oh, I'll eat my meat.* With an arch to my back, I daintily sliced my steak into a small piece to penetrate with my fork and swirl around my plate to absorb more juices. Just from the tingle of my skin, I knew Jax was watching me. I raised my fork to my mouth and exposed my tongue to taste the steak before my lips closed around the fork and sucked it off. "Mm." I hummed as my eyes rolled back, and I swallowed. I glanced to the side and saw Jax staring at my mouth.

"See something you like?" My question brought his focus back to my eyes, and he narrowed his.

"I didn't know I was sitting by a seductress."

"Are you saying you're seduced?"

"No…I'm just making a comment…based on an objective observation."

"That's your reasoning?"

"It's distracting."

"Sure." I smirked, feeling powerful with the knowledge that I could make him flustered. "Eat your meat, Jax." He dropped his silverware and straightened in his chair to glare at me.

"Careful, Mia," he said very seriously, and I didn't let on that he intimidated me or that my body tingled at his heated warning. I just continued to enjoy my meal.

"Another scotch, Mia?" Jax asked me when the server came around to check on us. I realized that he was only teasing.

"Oh, yes, please." I smiled up at the server, and he scurried away.

"Some champagne at the gallery...some scotch at dinner... Are we taking shots of tequila later?" Jax asked in a teasing way, but, as always, his eyes studied my features, like he was trying to figure me out.

"I prefer añejo tequila, neat." I shrugged and took the final sip of my scotch and placed the glass down on the table.

"Who are you?"

"Maybe someone you misjudged?" I glanced at him with a raised brow as the server appeared and placed the full tumbler on the table, then picked up the empty one. I thanked him as he retreated.

"Apparently." Jax eyed me, and I smiled, surprised that he'd admit it but happy about it nonetheless.

I had been erroneously labeled in my past as a party girl, but the truth was that I just really liked my alcohol—usually by myself. Fun fact, my medications could hold off the effects of alcohol as I drank. I never felt buzzed—unfortunately, because it sounded fun—or drunk and had a shocking tolerance, which meant that I drank for the comfort I felt from the taste. Once I broke through that high tolerance, though...all of that alcohol hit at once, and shit went down—bad, traumatic shit. Which was why I avoided that dark place at all costs.

"So, the exhibit was a success, right?" Ozzie asked eagerly, his question aimed at Jax.

"I'd say so." Jax smiled and sat back in his chair. "The coordinator shared with me that the turnout was greater than expected, media and community, and there are already bids on all of our works." All the boys showed their excitement.

"So, um, all of our work is for sale?" I asked nervously, not ready to part with my Dante series. I felt stupid about my question, as I hadn't thought of it before.

"Potentially." Jax nodded, then keyed into my anxiety. "Do you not want to sell? Mia, I don't know if you're aware of the numbers…"

"I don't really care about a sale, just…if I don't want to sell…would that hurt us?" I asked nervously and looked around the group.

"Not at all. If you don't want to sell, the only negative is you won't get paid."

"Okay." I exhaled and nodded.

"Mia…would you at least like to see the offers? I'm sure it'll be—" Jax said more quietly to me, but I just shook my head. No amount of money could part me from my Dante series. "Alright, the Dante series is not for sale. What about your sketches for the nine circles we did together? I would at least recommend that."

"Yes, I'm good with that." I was just relieved to know that I could hang on to the project I was the proudest of. I relaxed in my chair and smiled with the rest of them. I couldn't remember the last time I'd had so much action in one day, and it left me exhausted. Thankfully, the boys decided to call it a night, though it took some convincing with Nick, who wanted to keep the party going.

———

"So…what did you think?" Ozzie asked me with a big smile, knowing the event was a success as he drove me home.

"Honestly, it's like a dream. I just can't believe this is my life," I marveled aloud, not caring that a major cliché had just come out of my mouth.

"Believe it because you deserve it! I'll keep reminding you. No problem."

"You're a really good friend, you know." I glanced over at him, feeling grateful. Ozzie glanced back in acknowledgment of my appreciation. "Actually, you're a really good *best* friend. Even though I have to share the title."

"Speaking of…"

"Oh, no…I take it back."

"What the hell is going on between you two?"

"Nothing."

"Lie."

"Ozzie, really, nothing is going on. He doesn't like me, we don't get along, the end."

"Looked like you two were getting a little close at dinner."

"So? I had to sit by him."

"And in your own little world. We tried talking to you guys, but you never paid attention, so we gave up."

"Oh…I'm really sorry if I was rude—"

"Not my point. My two best friends whispering across the table, and I have no idea what's going on."

"I don't know what's going on either."

"Yeah, I can see that." He smirked. "It's just…I don't want to insert myself if you're okay, but still…if he ever does something, promise you'll tell me."

"Does something? Like what?" I frowned and tried to understand what direction he was going in.

"You're vulnerable right now and—"

"Ugh." I rolled my eyes and looked out the window, not wanting to be seen as a victim.

"It's true. You know it's true. He has no idea how…" He trailed off, not knowing how to say it without offending me. I turned my head back to look at him, waiting for him to finish the sentence. He was quiet for another block before looking at me. "He has no idea how inexperienced you are."

"Technically, I have experience…just not in the same way."

"Which is still very limited and makes you even more vulnerable. Mia, you know you're naive."

"Yeah, but doesn't knowing that I'm naive make me less naive?" He shook his head.

"Fine. But I'm not as fragile as you think," I said with confidence that I did not have but managed to sound convincing.

"You're the strongest woman I know by a lot." He smiled, and I felt a little comfort in his words, even though I didn't believe it myself. "I just need you to know that you can tell me anything, and I'll *always* be there for you, okay?"

"Okay. Thanks for the ride, best friend."

"My pleasure. You were awesome tonight. See you tomorrow—don't oversleep!" Ozzie reminded me of our brunch date as he dropped me off in front of my apartment, then drove away.

What a weird-ass night. First of many.

———

I lay in bed that night, and despite my nightly medications, which I depended on to knock me out, I tossed and turned. I tangled myself in the sheets as I struggled between thinking about Jax and trying not to think about Jax. As far as my history with men and sexual experiences, it had all been bad. Bad, bad, bad…bad. I'd been in three situations that would qualify as sexual assault—situations I could've taken to the police. The other few interactions I had with men didn't qualify as assault but certainly qualified as traumatic. It was when I still didn't know how to handle my mood disorder, and bipolar mania made me vulnerable and an easy target. I was already naive, and it made me reckless, compromised my decision-making and sense of danger, and I blindly trusted the men I was with and thought they were my friends. I was taken advantage of, and I didn't want any of it.

The shame that followed each scarring and unfortunate circumstance had crippled me. Because of my mental illness and past, I hadn't been able to connect with many people, especially men. It didn't matter their age, status, looks, money, etc. I'd had many opportunities and a few trials, but never did my body respond to any of them. How suffocating it was when a man would get so worked up that they didn't even notice how completely disconnected and scared I was, wanting to get away. Maybe they did notice, and they simply didn't care. It was a miracle, really, that none of those men took my virginity—yes, I was a twenty-four-year-old virgin. Something about my panic attacks when they pushed too far was a turnoff…

No man had ever made me want. I had never felt desire. Then I met Jax. I was afraid to be touched and felt shame when a man looked at me. But when I was with Jax, I wasn't afraid or feeling shame. I even felt myself *wanting* his touch and his eyes on me. My fears were still there, but new feelings had started creeping in. It intimidated the hell out of me, and I didn't know how to handle it…so I kept my eyes closed until I fell asleep and no longer thought of it.

Chapter 10

"Hey," Ozzie said excitedly and hopped into my space as I settled in at my workstation Monday morning.

"Hey…" I eyed him with curiosity since I wasn't aware of anything exciting scheduled for the day.

"Have you seen the *Art of San Francisco* article?"

"Uh…no? What happened?" I frowned as I tried to think of what he would be referring to. He handed me his iPad with an article covering the exhibit opening from last Friday on the screen.

"Oh! Cool. That's us." I smiled and swiped my finger across the glass to scroll as I saw our picture and others.

"Mia, *read* it." Ozzie chuckled and pointed to the text.

"Okay." I read the first couple sentences and rolled my eyes. "*The Jackson Caine and his team of young artists*"—I recited in an aristocratic tone before continuing to read; really, we needed to get a name—"*somehow manage to outdo themselves with each installment and continue to impress and ignite viewers with awe, leaving everyone hungry for more.* You guys are awesome, I mean, really." I giggled, feeling so proud to be a part of the team.

"*We* are awesome," Ozzie corrected, and I realized that the boys had gathered around to listen to the review. "Continue."

"Okay, okay." I squinted and tried to find the line I'd left off on. "*This time, it was their mysterious new artist*—ooh, mysterious—*who…*" I paused as I read on and lost the ability to vocalize the words.

"*Who*"—Jax swooped in and took the iPad from me to finish the report—"*stole the hearts of the crowd*—aw. *The debut of Amelia Bell, a complete unknown, stunned with her work. The group's installment was their most collaborative to date, displaying each artist's trademark style and strengths in one collection. There is no need to be familiar with the poet Dante Alighieri to appreciate and be moved by Bell's illustrations of* Inferno, Purgatory, *and* Paradise, *along with the additions of the rest of the group's artistic interpretations, and this exhibit is a must-see this spring. Consider the collective of Jackson Caine, Oswald Bishop, Nicholas Macdonald, Steven Deacon, and Amelia Bell unstoppable.*"

"Proud best friend," Ozzie announced and wrapped me in a big hug.

"Shout out to Mimi!" Nick yelled and jumped in.

"That's awesome." Steven smiled.

"Congratulations." Jax nodded, and I could tell he really was happy for me.

"Celebrating tonight!" Nick announced, which we all agreed to.

We dispersed to our stations, but it was a lazy day at the studio, as we had finished the exhibit project and were waiting on the next. We went about cleaning our spaces and reorganizing. I started with my easel, having to loosen the top screw to be able to slide the board out. I couldn't reach it from where I stood, so I stepped on the wood base. On my tiptoes, I was able to reach the top, but my body had to twist in order to unscrew it. As my shoulders turned ever so slightly out of line, I felt my entire body leaning that way.

"Uh-oh," I muttered and tried to level my stance, but it was too late. I dropped like a tree. "Ow." I landed to the side and behind my easel, where I was initially reaching.

"Whoa!" I heard Nick's voice and already wanted to die from the embarrassment that was on its way.

"Oh, shit!" Ozzie got to me almost instantly and kneeled by me. "You okay?" He helped me sit up and saw that I was fine.

"Thanks," I mumbled and noticed his eyes crinkling with his suppressed smile. "Go ahead." He started laughing, which had a chain effect— Nick cackled as he ran over, and Steven chuckled as he walked.

"Uh-oh." I heard Jax's sardonic but ruggedly sensual voice, and I looked up to see him entering the studio from the kitchen. "What did you do now?" He joined the circle.

"Let me guess," Ozzie said. "You were adjusting the top screw of your easel."

"Yeah." I sighed, and Ozzie pulled me to my feet. "It's not my fault! I have a spinal fusion," I explained, but they didn't understand what that was, so I explained. "My entire thoracic spine is fused. So it's not my fault."

"What?" Nick tilted his head to the side, then went to stand at my back and poked a finger to my scar.

"Ah." I squirmed from the unpleasant sensation. "Don't do that."

"Were you in a car accident or something?" Steven guessed.

"No, scoliosis. So I have two rods and twenty-four screws keeping my spine straight."

"And that's why you dropped to the floor?" Jax gave me a curious look. With a fused spine, clumsy incidents were normal for me. I decided to have a little bit of fun.

"This easel is dangerous. Unsafe workplace. I could sue you," I said and crossed my arms.

"It's not my fault you don't know how to stand." Jax made a good point and crossed his arms too.

"I demand accommodations."

"What do you have in mind? I cover the concrete with safe padding around your station? Stepstool?"

"Exactly what I had in mind." I nodded seriously. He knew by now that I was messing with him and walked away.

We all went back to focusing on our own stations. Mine was a mess—it took a lot of effort to clean up charcoal crumbled and smeared on every surface, including yourself. I had been in the drying room washing my hands and forearms for a long time when Jax entered. I didn't hear him come in and jumped when he crowded me at the sink.

"You're skittish." He chuckled and leaned against the counter next to me. "You know, you can just ask if you need help with something." I wasn't sure what he meant. "Like handling dangerous easels." I chuckled. "Seriously, though….you didn't get hurt, right?"

"Right."

"Good." He smiled and moved closer to put his hands under the faucet and nudged me away.

"I'm not done, Mr. Caine," I huffed and tried to get my sudsy hands back under the water.

"When are you going to give that up?" He rolled his eyes, and I knew he meant my use of his surname.

"Why?"

"Because it's annoying," he growled and tried to hip check me out of the way, unsuccessfully.

"Then never." I smiled, and he rolled his eyes and flicked water at me. "Oh, no, a drop of water! I'm never going to annoy you again!" I said with intense sarcasm while I reached across him to get a towel from his side of the counter. He just shook his head and smirked.

"Call me Jax. I insist." I shook my head. He sighed and grabbed my wrist in one hand; with the other, he pulled the nozzle off of its stand and pointed it at me. I screeched and tried to get away, but he had a strong hold. After spraying me, he returned the nozzle to the faucet but didn't let go of my wrist. He rested his hip against the sink and looked at me up and down.

"Mia...call me Jax." He was clearly having so much fun terrorizing me.

"No." I tried with all my energy to break free, but I failed, and he sprayed me again.

"So stubborn." He shook his head. "Why do you like to make me mad?"

"What? I don't." I frowned and pulled my arm away, but he didn't let go.

"When you call me Mr. Caine, it makes me mad." *Oh my God, he has a point.* He pulled me closer to his body with a teasing smirk. "And you know what else? I like being mad at you."

"Why?" I asked a bit breathlessly.

"Because I can do this." He smirked as he sprayed me again.

"Oh my God, stop messing with me!" I growled as I felt water dripping down my face and my soaked shirt sticking to my body.

"You're not going anywhere until you call me Jax."

"Fine"—I sighed, and he smiled until I moved in even closer so he could feel my body pressing against his—"Jax." I purred his name in a low voice that actually felt very good, especially when I watched his dark-blue eyes get darker and felt his grip tighten on my arm.

"Now, was that so hard?" he asked in a soft voice with a small smile. I nodded, which made him chuckle and release me, so I took a few steps away.

I wiped the water off my face before glaring at him. "I'll get you back."

"I look forward to seeing you try." He looked so boyish and handsome as his eyes followed me out of the room.

I halted my steps in the hallway when I could see into the studio. Ozzie, Nick, and Steven were all busy with their cleanup, and I really didn't want to give them another round of comic relief today by walking in all wet.

"Come on." I heard Jax behind me, then felt his hand on my arm and my body moving with his as he pulled me into the bathroom. I had no choice but to go with him.

I moved away once we entered into the privacy of the bathroom so I could assess the damage. Looking into the mirror, I could see I was soaked—hair, face, and splashes down my body. I crossed my arms and turned to glare at the perpetrator.

"You look great." Jax smiled with a tilt of his head as he looked me up and down. "You can't be mad at me."

"Oh, I think I can."

"It's your own fault." He shrugged and took a towel out of the cupboard, which I snatched from his hands. I rolled my eyes as I rubbed it over my face, then squeezed through my hair. "You could've just said my name."

"You could've not sprayed me with water."

"Yeah, but I wanted to." Jax continued to smile as he watched me dry off.

I sighed as I looked in the mirror and knew that I'd done my best with the towel. Thankfully, my shirt was a dark color—if it were my usual white Hanes tank, then I would've won the wet T-shirt contest.

"Good for you. Now I have to go home for a change of clothes. Excuse me." I tried to get to the door, but he stayed where he was, blocking the way.

"That's unnecessary… you can borrow one of my shirts. Just take off the wet one and I'll put it in the dryer." He motioned to my shirt like he expected me to pull it off right then.

"Ha. No…" I looked at him as if he were crazy.

"Mia, I've seen a bra before. Get over it."

"I'm not wearing a bra." I rolled my eyes, and his widened. I smirked when his gaze darted to my chest. "Up here." I waved at him, and he didn't like it. He opened the door and left.

I ran my hands through my hair and shook it around, drying it out more so it wouldn't lay flat on my head. I took off my shirt and wrung it out before draping it over the shower rod. That's when the door opened again, and Jax reappeared. I was fast enough to cover myself with my hands.

"Excuse you!" I shrieked as I turned away.

"Sorry." He held out a *dry* navy T-shirt.

"Place the shirt on the counter and leave," I scolded him, much to his amusement.

"I don't appreciate your tone." He chuckled. I rolled my eyes even though he couldn't see. "Just ask nicely and I'll give you my shirt and leave," he explained as if to a child.

"Please hand—"

"Please, Jax." I heard the menacing smile in his voice as he corrected me.

"Oh my God. You already made me wet. Don't keep it going."

"Did I?"

"*Jax.*" I nearly growled and glared over my shoulder, but I couldn't see him with my spinal-fused range of motion.

"I'm having fun." I could hear the goofy smile in his voice and could picture the playful glint in his eyes as he stood just a few feet behind me in the small bathroom. I could have fun too.

"Fine." I sighed like I was going to give in. I turned fully around to face him, and he froze, taken off guard by my boldness as I dropped my hands. His eyes fell to my body, as I was naked from the waist up, and fixated on my breasts. My skin was still chilled and my nipples hard from my wet shirt, and his eyes turned stormy, his jaw ticking with intensity as he stared. I was feeling buzzed at being on the receiving end of that look when his eyes shot up to mine. I grabbed the dry shirt out of his hands and pulled it on. "Thank you." I flashed him a polite and grateful smile before slipping out the door.

I returned to the studio and went back to work. I heard Jax walk in after me, but I didn't look up. Ozzie shot me a questioning look, then straightened when he saw my damp hair and oversized T-shirt.

"What the—"

"I'll tell you later," I promised quickly before he could ask, not wanting his raised voice to call attention to my appearance. His eyes narrowed with suspicion, but he held back.

————

By the time my hair dried, I was out of coffee, so I went to the kitchen. I had just put a pod in the Nespresso machine when I sensed someone near me and knew it was Jax.

"May I help you?" I turned to face him, and he was closer than I realized. I had to tilt my head back to meet his eyes.

"I have seen tits before, you know." His eyes burned into me, and a slight smirk tugged at the side of his mouth.

"Sure." I nodded. "But you haven't seen *my* tits before."

"Aren't you clever." He cornered me against the counter, and I kept my cool.

"I know. So now we are even." I smiled, happy that I was able to get him back for the hose down in the same day.

"Even?" He chuckled, and I frowned, unsure of what I missed. "You just made this a lot more interesting."

"I—um...what do you mean?" I hated myself for letting him fluster me, and he smiled with satisfaction.

"Do you like wearing my shirt?" he mused playfully as he traced my exposed skin along the crew neckline with his finger.

"It's fine..."

"You're blushing." He smirked, which pissed me off.

"I'm not." I glared and tried to duck past him, but he was blocking me.

"You're right. I'm sorry. Your cheeks are just pink."

"Fuck off," I grumbled and turned to the Nespresso machine to put another pod in for a double espresso.

"Cool scar, by the way," he commented behind me. "That straight line that goes from your neck to your hips."

"I know."

"Thanks for taking your shirt off so I could see it."

"You're welcome." He'd gone from teasing to friendly commentary on my scar...with a hint of teasing. I was proud of my scar, and he really made me smile. "I'm going back to work now."

"Not before me." He left the kitchen before I could.

We went back to cleaning our stations but played an awkward game of sneaking glances at each other, then looking away when Ozzie got suspicious.

———

"Alright! I'm done. I'm out. I'm not waiting for you guys," Nick cried out dramatically, as we were staying past his ideal departure time. "Where we going later?" I looked to Ozzie, Jax, and Steven as they started listing places for our fun night out to have a mini celebration for my debut as an artist on their team.

"Bender's. That's where Mia would want to go," Jax threw out, and they all agreed, even though Nick whined about it, not a fan of their choice. I went with the flow, trusting Jax's opinion.

We decided to leave at the same time as Nick. I followed the boys out of the studio, still wearing Jax's T-shirt, but I didn't want to take it off, so I didn't mention it. It felt too good against my skin and too warm covering my body, and I liked the smell too much. I glanced at Jax as we made our way out, and I knew that he'd never ask for it back.

"Mia, I'll pick you up," Ozzie said as we headed to our cars. It wasn't a question.

Chapter 11

"Hey, Oz." I smiled as I slid into the passenger seat once he pulled up to my apartment a little after nine.

He turned into traffic and got to the point. "Hey, I want to talk about this afternoon."

"Can't you just pick up Jax and have him tell you?" I sighed and looked out the window. He hit the brakes harder than necessary at the red light, and I jolted forward.

"So, this is about Jax?" I winced—I clearly gave away too much too fast. "Maybe I should pick him up too." He tilted his head as he stared at me. I didn't know what to say, so I was grateful when the light turned.

"Light's green." I pointed ahead of us, so he had to keep going.

"Just go right into the truth of why your hair was wet and why you were wearing Jax's T-shirt." My mind went through ten different lame excuses I could give, so I really just gave the truth.

"Jax and I were in the drying room. I was annoying him, so he sprayed me with water from the facet. My shirt was wet, so he gave me a dry one." I left it at that, not mentioning that I flashed Jax in the bathroom, and waited. Ozzie looked ahead, watching the road, but I could see he was thinking through what he knew. "I'm not lying. I mean…honestly…what else could have happened to explain my hair wet and wearing Jax's shirt?" Ozzie just smiled and shook his head at my completely honest answer.

"Now I know you're telling the truth." His smile turned into a chuckle, and I sat next to him quietly, not knowing what else to do.

"I don't know what's so funny other than Jax spraying me with water, so…" I frowned and was a little irritated when his chuckle turned into a not-so-contained laugh.

"Ah, innocent Mia. Never change." He sighed and patted my knee.

"I'm considering jumping out of this car."

"No, I'm sorry. I wasn't laughing at you," Ozzie assured me, but I didn't believe him. I knew he was, but I really didn't care. "We're almost there. Wanna go have fun? I think you'll like this bar."

When we arrived, I followed Ozzie through the threshold, and a smile lit up my face—it was a rock bar. Quite obviously, too, as it was sensory overload. I bumped into a few people, not paying attention to where I was going since my eyes were too distracted by the excessive rock 'n' roll decor, ironic and provocative signs and pictures plastered to every inch of the place. Johnny Cash flipped me off several times as I followed Ozzie through the bar and to a booth already claimed by the boys.

"Hey, guys." I noted three empty glasses. "What are we drinking?"

"I'll get this round." Ozzie stood and turned to the bar. "Ah, damn it." He sighed and sat back down. I looked at him and raised my brows, a silent request for him to explain. "Jax beat me." I frowned in confusion and looked at the bar. Jax was talking to a female bartender.

"You like her?" I asked Ozzie, and he nodded. Nick and Steven chuckled, obviously well aware of his crush.

"Bianca." Nick smiled. "Technically, we all like her, but Ozzie likes her the most." I eyed the woman behind the bar as she handed Jax drinks. She was attractive and basically my exact opposite. She was edgy and voluptuous, with black hair and dark makeup. *Of course, she's Playboy Bunny gone goth.* I then quickly averted my eyes as Jax turned to rejoin us.

"Alright, drinks for the people," he announced as he approached the booth with five beverages casually held in his grip. I was momentarily distracted by his large hands as he set down the assortment of glasses and bottles on our table, then pleasantly surprised when I saw that he brought me my go-to cocktail.

"Thanks, Jax." I shot him a quick glance before scooping it up and taking a long sip.

"You're welcome," he said after he pulled over a chair to sit with us at the booth.

I took in a deep breath and sat up straighter in my seat, wanting to harness confidence in my high-waisted jeans and a simple white cotton tank top that exposed an inch of midriff to make it fun. I shrugged my leather jacket off my shoulders and dropped it behind me on the booth.

"Cheers to Mia, up-and-coming artist of San Francisco." I was surprised when Jax lifted his glass, initiating the cheers. The rest of the boys joined in, and we all clanked our glasses together.

"Thanks." I smiled at Jax, then at the rest of the boys. "I'm really thankful to be with you guys." I spoke from the heart, wanting them to know how special they were to me. They all offered supportive comments, saying I deserved it and that they were thankful to have me too.

We were well into our next round, and I was standing next to our booth when a man approached me.

"Hey, babe, join me at the bar and I'll buy you a drink." He smiled, and I looked down at the half-full drink in my hand, then looked back up.

"I already have one, but thank you." I smiled back, and he walked away, looking irritated. The guys all burst out laughing.

"What?" I asked them, feeling insecure.

"He was hitting on you," Ozzie explained to me.

"Well, yeah, but I already have a drink. Was I supposed to double-fist two drinks just so he could talk to me?"

"You could've just put yours down and went with him." Ozzie shook his head.

"I didn't want to." I shrugged and put my glass down on the table.

"Why?" Jax asked casually, sitting back in his seat.

"I wasn't judging him." I rolled my eyes, remembering our conversation about my lack of a boyfriend and my rejection of dating apps.

"I know." He continued to eye me. "So, why didn't you want to?"

"I don't know." I looked around the room, wanting to escape the conversation. It was a simple question I found hard to answer since the truth was too personal to admit—I was afraid of unknown men at bars... or anywhere...and even a simple touch could make me nauseous. "I need a drink," I mumbled and abandoned the booth and my half-full glass on our table to find the bar. I glanced over my shoulder as I walked away and made eye contact with Jax, who was still watching me after I'd dodged his question. I looked away and kept on my path to find a new drink.

I rested my elbows on the counter and felt my eyes going out of focus—my memories from my last night out back home became clearer as I stood alone. Home in Minnesota, my older cousin invited me on a night out with his friends, knowing that I didn't get out much since moving home with my parents. My cousin told everyone to keep a respectful distance. They did, and I felt safe with them when they started calling me Mini-Bell. At the bar, they all said they had my back. I was happy to be with them and even excited to go to the bar, so I put on my favorite summer dress. But after that night, I threw it away and swore to never wear a dress or skirt again.

"Hey, girl. What can I get you?" Bianca appeared in front of me, and I was thankful to be pulled out of my memory by a fellow woman. I made my usual order. "You a girlfriend?" she asked. I gave her a confused look, and she motioned to where the guys were sitting across the room.

"Oh, no. I work with them." She nodded and went to make my drink.

I took a big inhale and exhale, trying to stay in the present. My eyes started to go out of focus again as I watched Bianca fix my drink. Glass of ice, a good pour from the beloved green whiskey bottle, shot of ginger ale from the soda gun, and a lime wedge plopped on top. *Never drink from a glass you didn't see poured. Unless you trust the people around you, right?* Like my cousin and his protective friends. My cousin bought me my second cocktail of the night and asked his friend to deliver it to me. They called him Broder, and I could still see his face in the men that surrounded me, watching me drink the drug-infused Jameson ginger at that bar in my hometown.

"You look bothered, babe." A man next to me nudged my elbow to get my attention.

"I'm fine," I said with my back to him, but he leaned closer.

"You can talk to me." I rolled my eyes and looked over my shoulder to officially tell him to fuck off but froze. I couldn't even tell you what the drunk man looked like since all I saw were Broder's thick black brows and long, dark lashes bordering hazel eyes that had followed my every move throughout the night, waiting for the opportunity to drop something into my drink. I thought Broder was creepy—the way he stared and watched me drink every drop…then it all went blank. I quickly turned away from the drunk man now.

"I'll buy you a drink. How's that?" His offer was slurred, and I was relieved when Bianca placed my cocktail in front of me. I thanked her and quickly handed her my card.

"I'm Mia," I introduced myself to Bianca while she ran my card through the machine.

"And I'm Scott," the man interjected. The creep forcibly shook my hand, but I ignored him. I wiped my hand against my jeans, a reflex after feeling that man's sweaty palm on mine.

"Bianca." She smiled and smoothed out the receipt on the bar and handed me a pen. I slipped my card into my jeans pocket but didn't want to stop talking to her. I liked her. It was true that she was Jax's type, mature and womanly, and I felt like a child in comparison. She smiled and leaned her hip against the bar, but her eyes continued to drift past me to our booth. "So…Ozzie is single." She looked at me for confirmation, and I nodded. "Jax…what's his deal?"

"Uh… he's single." I shrugged, not knowing what she was asking.

"Well, yeah." She rolled her eyes, and I didn't really have anything to say. "Ugh, I'm sorry. It's just…they've been coming around for years, and he's always alone until he leaves with someone. He's such a sweetheart, but I've never seen him with a girlfriend. I just don't get it," she said as she looked past me. "He keeps looking over here." I saw her straighten and swipe her hair over her shoulder, hopeful that she was the focus of his attention. "Has he ever talked about me?"

"Oh, um…" *This is awkward.*

"Shit. I'm sorry. I shouldn't have asked." Bianca winced, then tried to recover with a forced smile and focused back on me. "No strings attached, right?" I slowly nodded, not knowing the answer and not knowing what else to say.

Bianca went to the other end of the bar to help a customer, and I remained where I stood, leaning on the bar counter. I frowned as I eyed my fresh cocktail, but I suddenly couldn't bear to drink it or even look at it, so I pushed it away. I started processing all that Bianca had said. The woman was gorgeous, and I gathered that she'd slept with Jax before, but he apparently hadn't kept girlfriends. He was always alone but sometimes brought home a woman at the end of the night. No strings attached. I started thinking about how she said he was a sweetheart, but my thoughts were interrupted by drunk Scott.

"C'mon, babe, let's get to know each other." His hand reached behind me and found my ass to give it a squeeze. "Where you goin'?" he teased when I jerked away. Then he wrapped his arm around my waist and tried to pull me closer. I felt two of his sweaty fingers slide along the bare skin between my tank top and jeans as his hand grabbed onto my hip. All while his hot breath blew on my neck. I stopped breathing, and nausea started to twist my stomach. It had only been five seconds, but in that time, my vision flickered to black, and I entered the strange state of not being able to see, move, or speak, with only the heightened senses of touch and sound. Five seconds of Scott's breath turning into Broder's and remembering how it felt when he pulled up my dress and pushed his fingers inside me. I thought I was going to faint, but just in time, Scott was ripped away from me.

A large hand grabbed onto Scott's shirt collar and pulled him back, making his barstool fall to the floor with a loud clatter. I whirled around to watch Jax drag the drunk man across the room to the doors like a rag doll and push him out.

"Don't let him back in," Jax ordered the two bouncers at the entrance. Then two of Scott's friends at the bar jumped from their stools, ready for a fight. Jax rolled his eyes when they confronted him, as they were both half his size, and handled them the same way he did Scott. Except, this time, he had two drunk men by the collar of their shirts and kicked them out too. "Those assholes too." I watched the altercation with wide eyes as I stood frozen at the bar. Jax exchanged man handshakes with the two bouncers after he informed them about what had happened.

"Jax…" I stared after him as he stepped back into the bar area, breathing deeply but not from exertion and running his hands through his hair. I watched him approach, but his eyes were far away as he blinked past his intensity and clenched and unclenched his jaw. I knew that look—Scott had pulled him somewhere else too, and he was still in that place as he stood in front of me. "Are you okay?"

"Am *I* okay?" My words snapped him back to reality, and he stared at me. "Are *you* okay?" I nodded, but he still pulled me closer so he could read my expression. "Do you want to go?"

"No. I'm okay. Really," I assured him, and he nodded after taking one more searching look over my features. I offered a small smile. "Thank you for that." He just put a comforting hand on my shoulder, which brought me fully back to the present, and all shame and panic washed away. I finally felt protected. I sucked in as deep of a breath as I could. *Why did no one protect me then? My cousin and his friends were in the same house, but no one came to help me. Why couldn't someone have been there to pull Broder off me?*

"Want your drink?" Jax nodded toward the bar, and my eyes landed on the full glass sitting alone on the counter. I stared at the symbol of my traumatic night with Broder. I blinked and looked up to Jax and shook my head. "Want a different one…?" He frowned as he searched my eyes, and I nodded. "Okay. Go back to the guys, and I'll order you one. What do you want?"

"Um. Jameson ginger ale." His frown deepened when I told him I wanted the same thing. "Thanks." I looked away and went straight to the booth to be with my friends.

"What the hell just happened?" Ozzie asked as he, Nick, and Steven looked at me, then at Jax at the bar, and back.

"Yeah, Jax was watching you talking to Bianca and suddenly got up," Nick explained, and I wondered why Jax had been watching us to begin with.

"Moved so fast, we couldn't even process what happened. Who were the guys that were thrown out?" Steven added.

"Uh." I sighed as I sat down, happy to have a seat to relax against. "Just some asshole being an asshole."

"An asshole who doesn't deserve hands." Jax added his opinion as he approached.

"*What?*" Ozzie and the rest of the boys stared at Jax. I liked the harsh comment, and my lips quirked up as I looked at him. His did, too, as he looked down at me and placed my fresh drink in front of me before taking a seat. We both looked around the table and noted that the boys were still waiting for more information.

"A drunk idiot felt me up at the bar and grabbed me a little." I shrugged and took a sip of my drink.

"Oh, hell no!" Nick squeaked, and Ozzie and Steven joined in with their objections, which warmed my heart.

"We won't let anything happen to you," Ozzie assured me, and they all nodded. They had no idea how much that simple assurance meant to me. After the crowds of men who had proven too late that they couldn't be trusted, or even the crowds of men who just stood by and watched, it felt so comforting, and almost liberating, being around men I truly trusted.

A half hour later, I had forgotten all about Scott and Broder and was enjoying the fun I always had around my colleagues. I headed over to the touch-screen jukebox on the wall, but a man beat me to it. He was older and had the cool-dad look—a worn Metallica T-shirt and Nike sneakers.

"What are you going to play?" he turned to ask me.

"The Doors or Zeppelin…maybe Queen. I haven't decided," I said with a shrug. He smiled and pressed some buttons.

"Alright. I just put ten bucks in there. It's all yours."

"*What?* That's a lot of songs—don't you want to pick?"

"I trust you." He walked away after giving me a wink. *Well, this suddenly got stressful. I can't let Cool Dad down. Deep breath.* "Roadhouse Blues," "Heartbreaker," then "Keep Yourself Alive," "Foxy Lady," "Walk this Way," "Fat Bottomed Girls," "Wild Thing," "Paint It Black," "Big Balls," "Sunshine of Your Love," "Come Together"… I had only one more track to select when I was interrupted.

"What's taking you so long?" Jax said as he came up beside me.

"This guy put in ten dollars and told me to have at it." I smiled and continued scrolling.

"Of course, he did," Jax scoffed, and I shot him a side glance.

"He wasn't hitting on me. Just trusts my taste. Have any ideas?" He looked at what I already had lined up.

"'Big Balls?' Seriously?" I smiled and nodded. That was my favorite AC/DC song.

"Let me guess…that's your favorite song?" I poked him.

"Oh, you think I've got big balls?" He smirked and poked me back. I felt my cheeks flush, and he chuckled. "Let me pick the last song."

"I don't know…" I looked him up and down and pursed my lips. He just rolled his eyes and shooed me away. We returned to the booth and continued to enjoy each other's company, but I mostly enjoyed my music selection. It was halfway through my songs when Cool Dad came up to me.

"Well done, honey." He shook my hand where I sat at the end of my booth with the boys, and we had a little laugh before he left.

"*Wild thing!*" I sang along with the jukebox's next song, and Jax pretended to push me off the bench. "*You make my heart sing!*" I clung to his arm until he pulled me back up, and I started giggling. "*You make everything groovy.*"

"Ozzie, is this Mia drunk?" Steven asked my friend with a laugh.

"Oh, no." Ozzie shook his head seriously, then laughed. I rolled my eyes. I was definitely not drunk.

"Wait a second...how much have you had to drink tonight?" Jax eyed me skeptically.

"However much everyone else has had."

"So, this is your fifth drink?" Jax looked at the almost empty cocktail in my hand. I downed the rest until the ice hit my teeth and set the glass back down on the table.

"Yep."

"Hey, Nick, how does it feel to be outdrunk by Mia?" Jax joked, and the rest of the guys laughed because Nick was the only one drunk.

I went to the bathroom, and on my way back to our booth, I realized my music choices were almost over. The secret last song that Jax selected started to play. The disco beat took over the room, and I started to laugh. *Ooh, let's go!*

Once I was in view of the booth, Jax saw me and smirked. He'd chosen the song I danced to when I first met him and he decided to hate me— good times. I giggled and shook my head, loving that he'd picked "Another One Bites the Dust." Well, I certainly wasn't drunk, but I was in a mood where dancing sounded like a great idea. Ozzie started laughing as I did my Freddie, and the rest of the boys started paying attention. I didn't prolong my performance, and after I did my little dance, I returned to the booth.

"Good choice." I giggled as I plopped down next to Jax.

"That was cute," Jax murmured but tried to play it off as sarcasm.

"You think I'm cute?" I asked loud enough for the whole group to hear.

"I meant the dance was," he clarified.

"Riiiight." I nodded slowly, then started nodding to the beat of the song. As the night carried on, I became more friendly with Bianca and got to see that she really did seem to think Jax and Ozzie were *fine*. She was right: Jax was a sweetheart to her and every woman around him. He was sexy as hell, confident, and effortlessly charming. I noticed he never approached anyone. He just sat back and let his alpha-male energy draw them in. He was always polite but was the most engaged with the women who fit his type—gorgeous, mature women with *Playboy* figures. I hated that insidious jealousy that snuck up on me every time I had to watch him leave the bar with a different woman. He'd say, "Ready to go, darlin'?" Then put a hand on her lower back and hold the door open for her to walk out first. Then they were gone. Bianca was right. Other than the end-of-the-night exit, he was always alone.

Then it was that bar time when we—ahem, Nick—started to get sloppy, so we called it a night.

"I can drive Mia home," Jax offered to Ozzie, who looked at me.

"Is that cool with Mia?" my protective best friend asked, and I shrugged. He still didn't seem convinced, so I double shrugged. "Verbal response, please," he said.

"That's cool with Mia." I rolled my eyes and smiled at Ozzie. Then it fully hit me that Jax would be driving me home. *Why does he want to drive me home? Is he interested in me? He doesn't like me...right? Of course, he doesn't like me... Oh, fuck it. Don't overthink it.*

"Ready?" Jax looked at me, and I nodded as we all exited the bar. *He didn't call me "darlin'" and he didn't put his hand on my lower back...and that's okay.* Ozzie and Jax were both at a legal alcohol limit to drive, so Ozzie, Nick, and Steven went one way to his SUV, while I followed Jax the other way. He clicked his keys, and I saw his car light up. *Is that...?*

"You drive a *Camaro*?" I hopped with excitement, then tried to play it cool. "Bitchin'." *Fail.* "1969?" I guessed, and Jax was surprised that I'd guessed correctly.

"Yep. Get in." He chuckled at my excitement and stood next to his Camaro, waiting for me to get in. I didn't and instead took a lap around the vehicle to check out the whole badass black car and then stopped at the passenger side.

"I did not expect this very enthusiastic approval of the car I drive."
Jax laughed as he bent his large body to fit into the car, and I got in. As
he started the engine, I started looking around and checking out the dash.
"Did you smoke something earlier?" he asked. There was warmth in his
eyes that I hadn't seen before.

"No. This is…"

"Bitchin'?" He finished my sentence with a smirk, and I nodded.
"Buckle up." I sat back in place and tried to reel it in. Jax drove through
the streets, already knowing my address, as it was Ozzie's old one. It started
raining, and it was hard to see where we were going, so I just got comfortable and felt cool riding in my dream car. We fell into a comfortable
silence, and I started to zone out. I was staring at the rain dripping down
the windows, lost in my head, until I felt a gentle nudge. I straightened
in my seat and looked to Jax.

"Hm?" I frowned, not knowing if I had imagined the nudge.

"You okay?" He placed his hand on my leg but immediately with-
drew it.

"Um. Yeah. Why?"

"Because we are at your apartment but you haven't moved."

"Oh." I felt awkward as I saw that the car was in park outside of my
apartment. "Ha ha. Yeah." I un-clicked my seat belt and reached for the
handle, but Jax put his hand over mine.

"Mia." I remained seated and faced him, liking the warmth of his
large hand covering mine. "What were you thinking about?"

"Um…the drunk guy at the bar. Thank you for noticing and, um,
thank you for stopping him."

"I won't let anyone hurt you or even bother you," he said seriously,
and I felt his fingers curl under my palm to hold it, like the touch was
backing up his words. My small smile was the only way I could respond
to his gesture.

"Why did you want to drive me home?"

"To make sure you're okay."

"Why do you think I'm not okay?" I questioned. He poked the spot between my furrowed brows so I'd relax. "Well, then, are you okay?"

"Why wouldn't I be…" I poked the spot between his furrowed brows. "Okay." He chuckled and relaxed more in his seat, making no move to urge me out of his car or put it in drive. I didn't know what to say, so I just looked back into his eyes for a few mesmerizing seconds.

"Jax, why don't you like me?" I asked quietly, thinking back over all of our interactions up to this point and taking the chance to ask a question he'd hopefully take seriously in the insolation of his car. The windows were blurred by the heavy rain, the only sound rain pattering on the roof of the car. He was still holding my hand, and I hoped he wouldn't pull away.

"Why don't you like *me*?" he shot back, and I raised my brows and stared at him, letting the obvious answer remain unspoken. "Don't answer that." I smiled and waited for him to answer me. He sighed and looked away, gathering his thoughts. "I don't not like you."

"Okay…"

"You're just…different."

"In a bad way?"

"No."

"That doesn't make sense." I frowned, already knowing I was going to overanalyze this conversation all night.

"I know." He was still holding my hand but let go and sat up straighter. Now I could tell he wanted to urge me out of his car and put it in drive.

"Okay, then." I pushed the door open. "Thanks for the ride." I shot one more glance at his now-impassive face before I shut the door and hurried through the rain to my apartment.

Chapter 12

I went straight to my room, peeling off my wet tank top on the way, and dropped it on the floor. I wrestled off my damp jeans and continued to undress until there was nothing left to take off. I was tired and chilled by the rain, so I skipped my nightly routine and went straight to my bed and slid under the covers.

As I tried to fall into sleep, my eyes popped open. "Ughh," I groaned in frustration as I remembered that I hadn't taken my nighttime medications but really didn't want to leave the warmth of my bed. *I could just skip it... No big deal...* But it was a big deal, and I knew it. My stability was fragile, and I had to be responsible and keep it that way. With a heavy sigh, I pushed the covers away so I could swing my legs over and off the bed. I felt my way through the darkness until I found my medications atop my dresser. I could identify each medication by the sound of the pills rattling in their orange bottles. I slid four pills into my hand and tossed them back, skipping a sip of water. I hurried back to bed and crawled under the covers, eager for the warmth and comfort.

I willed my mind not to let me fall asleep with Broder's face in my head or the memory of his fingers. I could have died that night. With the amount of medications in my system, I was surprised the drug-infused cocktail didn't kill me. For a small time after that incident, I wished it would have. But those dark thoughts were behind me, and

I hoped they'd forever stay there. I pulled the duvet tighter around me and closed my eyes.

———

I didn't set my alarm so that I could sleep well into the afternoon but was still woken up too early by my phone vibrating with a call from Ozzie. He simply said he was coming over. I wasn't happy to have to get out of bed but did anyway to see my friend. I met him outside my apartment, and we walked to a nearby café. I tilted my face to the sun and savored the warmth on my skin.

"Everyone said that it rains a lot in San Francisco." I looked at the native for his opinion. So far, it had been consistently gorgeous.

"It's usually more chilly this time of year. Maybe climate change? I dunno. We have some things to talk about."

"Okay, fine." I sighed, knowing he was going to bring up Jax and my ride home. "Bianca is cute." I nudged him as we walked down the sidewalk.

"I wouldn't call her cute." He chuckled and kicked around a rock as we went. I had to agree that 'cute' didn't cover it.

"Bianca is smoking hot, man," I tried again and nudged him harder.

"Yes." He nodded, and I waited for more information. "I haven't made a move or anything."

"Why not?"

"She's intimidating." He glanced at me. "And she's been with Jax. I'm not too eager to follow up."

"Oz." I was sad that he felt inferior. "You're hot. Objective opinion," I added, which made him smile. "Jax isn't better than you."

"You don't know him." He sighed as we approached the café and held the door open for me.

"What's that mean?"

"She'll just be hung up on him, and I don't want to deal with that."

"That's fair." I nodded as I sat across from him in a booth.

"Speaking of Jax." Ozzie leaned forward and rested his elbows on the table, eager to get to the topic.

"Who?" I asked innocently, but he looked bored by my evasion. "What about him?" I felt even more awkward talking to Ozzie about Jax, as I continued to feel more drawn to him. Especially when I thought that there was no way my feelings could be returned.

"What is going on with you two?" He became more serious, and I sighed.

"Nothing. Honestly." I looked him in the eye so he knew I really was being honest, because it was true.

"Why'd he want to drive you home?" he asked with a raised eyebrow, suspicious.

"Just to make sure I was okay. You know, after the drunk guy felt me up." I shrugged like it was no big deal.

"Oh, that's right. I'm sorry, Mia." Ozzie looked sad for me, but again, I shrugged it off. "So, Jax came to the rescue? I told you he's a good guy."

"Yes, I know." I nodded, happy to have seen that part of him for myself.

"Still…" Ozzie cringed over what he was about to bring up. "I feel like I have to warn you…"

"You don't even need to warn me. I'm guessing I'm not his type," I said casually as I opened up the diner menu even though I knew I was going to order waffles.

"So? You're still a beautiful woman. Objective opinion. I'm still on the outside of your weirdo dynamic. Warning stands." He bumped his fist on the tabletop like a judge, wanting me to take him seriously. I really didn't.

"Why aren't you warning Jax about me?" I rolled my eyes, knowing the answer.

"Mia, we've talked about this. Jax is, like, a million times more experienced than you, and he's…I don't know. He's a lot."

"And little me can't handle the big bad wolf?"

"Yes. Sorry, but it's true. You're vulnerable right now, and Jax doesn't know how inexperienced you are."

"Oswald Bishop, you promise me right now that you will never tell him or anyone that I'm a virgin." My intensity escalating, I pointed at Ozzie to make sure he knew that I was deathly serious and bumped my fist on the tabletop as well.

"Yeah, okay! I promise. Just be careful."

"Sure. Let's order."

———

On Monday morning, my week was off to a good start. Once I arrived at the studio and exchanged greetings with the boys, I made my way to my station and found a surprise.

"No way." I stared at the stepstool in front of my easel and burst out laughing. Jax had actually gone out and bought the accommodation for me. It was plastic and royal blue, definitely from the kids' section of the store. I dropped my purse and stepped on and off it, trying it out. I looked over to Jax's station and saw him swiveling in his chair, watching me with a little smirk. Even though he was teasing me, the gesture made me very happy. I didn't say thank you, but we did share a smiley moment when our eyes met across the studio.

———

"Who's down for a road trip?" Jax asked with a clap on Thursday morning. He stood in the middle of the studio and waited for all of us to gather around. I hopped down from my stool, and we huddled together. "Friday to Monday...maybe later...probably later...definitely later." He didn't give any more details, but Ozzie, Nick, and Steven agreed immediately. I hadn't said anything yet, as I was just trying to process the sudden project ahead of us that I didn't know about. "Miaaa, road trip?" Jax asked, singling me out. "Unless you have something else planned," he teased, knowing that my social life began and ended with our group.

"Nope. I'm down."

"Perfect. Details. Someone referred us to an older gentleman to update his family mansion three hours east. He wants it done ASAP, and since we have the gallery sorted, we have time to fit it in. He's offering a *lot* of money…so, why not? Questions?"

"Update family mansion? Is he expecting restoration work..?" I asked, still not clear on the task or how they usually handled off-site projects.

"Right, I wondered that too, and the answer is no. It has been neglected for a while, and he wants the artwork updated. It'll make sense once we get there. We leave tomorrow morning at ten. Mia, be on time."

"I was late one time," I grumbled.

Well, this is going to be fun and then probably a disaster. That would continue to be Jax and my theme. By the end of the day, we had all of our supplies packed and ready to go.

———

Friday morning, I had no idea what to expect. Jax said we'd go for the weekend but maybe for a week—better to overpack than under-pack. I put together a duffel with what I thought would be appropriate for an old mansion in the middle of nowhere. Art scrubs, my signature Mia uniform, toiletries, art supplies already packed—that should be it. *I'm definitely forgetting something. Ah! Medications.* That would've been so bad. I had plenty of time before I had to meet everyone at the studio and decided to stop by the deli on my street to pick up breakfast. I knew the boys might have already eaten, but as I'd gotten to know them, I'd realized that their stomachs were bottomless pits and any free meal was rejoiced over.

"Hello," I greeted the man behind the counter once I arrived at the deli. I had been reciting all the boys' bagel orders in my head before I got there so I wouldn't forget. *Ozzie likes smoked-salmon bagels because he's fancy like that… Steven likes egg and cheese… Nick has the same order as my younger sister, cinnamon bagel with strawberry cream cheese... Jax, the simple everything bagel and plain cream cheese.*

I had a little pep in my step as I walked out the door and drove to the studio, excited to do something nice and for the new little adventure.

"Good morning, boys," I said brightly when I saw them all gathered around the couch and chairs. "I come with bagels." I held up the paper bag, and they all cheered. I dug my hand into the bag to fish out their orders and tossed them out. "Steven...Ozzie...Princess Nick..."

"Thanks, Mimi!" Nick said, already taking a monster bite of his sugary breakfast along with Ozzie and Steven. I looked around and didn't see Jax, but he soon appeared in the doorway of the kitchen.

"What'd you do?" He frowned but got his answer when he looked around to everyone eating breakfast, then spotted the bag I was holding. "Do I get one?" He looked adorable when his eyes met mine and asked with such hope.

I walked up to him to make the delivery. "Everything bagel with plain cream cheese." I handed him his bagel.

"Well, that was sweet of you. Thanks."

"Mm-hmm." I offered a sweet smile in response and went to sit with the boys and enjoy my breakfast.

"Okay, let's go." Jax stood up once he'd finished his food and started to move.

"I'm not done." I looked up at him towering over me as I remained seated on the floor. I still had half of my bagel left, while everyone else had finished.

"We have a timeline. And you eat like a chipmunk."

"Should I eat like a caveman, like you?" I teased, maintaining eye contact as I took a monstrous caveman bite from my bagel.

"Cute." Jax was aiming for sarcasm, but his mouth twisted as he hid a smile. "Now chop-chop, chipmunk, we gotta go." He patted my head as he walked past me to start getting our supplies ready to go.

I regretted my caveman bite as I felt a twist of nausea in my stomach once I swallowed. Nausea was one of the side effects of lithium that I often dealt with and needed to monitor closely. I sighed and looked down at the half of the bagel I still had left. I wanted to finish my breakfast but didn't want to put anything else in my stomach before our road trip. I picked up my bagel and the mess the boys had left behind and threw it all away. I jumped into helping everyone with our supplies, and we were soon ready to go.

Chapter 13

We waited on the curb for Jax to bring around his car. I was surprised to see him pull up in a big pickup truck. *So he has an old Camaro and a new pickup...okay.*

"You drive a Ford Raptor?" I asked and didn't mask my surprise. "How overtly masculine."

"Shut up." Jax sighed and pushed me aside to pick up a crate. We all helped load our supplies and luggage.

"Shotgun!" I yelled once everything was secure in the bed of the truck. I made a run for the front seat, and to my surprise, Jax didn't stop me.

"Need help?" He chuckled when he saw me trying to get into the lifted truck.

"Nope." I rejected his offer but really shouldn't have. I slipped from the footstep on my first try, then fumbled to pull myself into the high seat. Eventually, with the help of the handle and some encouraging statements from the boys, I made it into the front seat. I was breathing heavily, just a little, as I buckled in and pushed my hair out of my face.

"That was a treat to watch." Jax continued to chuckle, and since I was the last one into the truck, he put the truck in drive and pulled away from the curb.

"Well, then, you're welcome." I nodded seriously and looked in front of me out the massive dash of the truck. I didn't think he'd actually let me sit in the front.

"Okay, front-seat attendant, are you prepared to take on the responsibilities?"

"Like what?"

"Directions…radio…entertaining the driver…"

"I'm up for the task." I sat up straight and nodded. Jax told me the address so I could program into my Maps app. We started our three-hour journey, and the boys in the back seat put in their AirPods to sit back and zone out. Ten minutes went by, and I forgot to direct Jax on two turns.

"Alright, you're fired." Jax sighed and propped his iPhone up on the dashboard and clicked on our destination in his maps.

"I can still be helpful. DJ Mia." I reached for the USB cord, but he wrapped his hand around my wrist and held it away. "Hey."

"No. You already failed as front-seat attendant."

"Aw. Give me another chance." I leaned toward the console and pouted my lips to look extra cute. I didn't try to pull my arm away from his grasp, as I didn't mind the feeling of his hand wrapped around my wrist. His eyes glanced to mine, then dropped to my lips for a second before refocusing on the road.

"Convincing argument. You have another chance." Jax released my arm so I could grab the cord and plug in my phone. "Lot of pressure here, Mia. Don't disappoint the driver."

"Uh-oh…what happens if I disappoint the driver?" I asked with big eyes, staring at him like I was scared.

"You'll find out," he responded casually, and I watched him make a turn, using one hand to circle the wheel. I glanced back to his face to make sure he hadn't caught me staring before refocusing on my task. I found scrolling through my iTunes library to find the right song to play very stressful.

"Oooh, surround sound." The first guitar riff of the song played, then repeated itself through every speaker. I pointed my smile at Jax when the lyrics came on.

"Of course." Jax chuckled when he heard "Big Balls" by AC/DC.

"Your favorite song, right?" I giggled when it came to the chorus and sang along. *"I've got big balls…I've got big balls…And they're such big balls…"*

"Alright, front-seat attendant, well done." He nodded and urged me to continue. "Keep it coming."

"Okay, okay. Let's play a game." Jax glanced over to me with a raised brow as if he were up to no good. "I bet I can find a classic rock song that you can't identify."

"Bring it on." I happily searched my music to play deep tracks of my favorite bands to try and stump him. I went through five songs, and he guessed correctly each time. It was an easy game. "Ha. I win," he said.

"One more." I refused to lose a random car game I made up and went deeper. "Ha." I smirked and tapped play on what I knew would be a winner.

"What is this?" Jax frowned as he listened. "This isn't classic rock."

"But it is. Ha! You lose. 'Misfire' by Queen from their third studio album, *Sheer Heart Attack*, 1974."

"Thank you, Classic Rock Encyclopedia." Jax chuckled and shook his head.

"There's more. Written by the bassist, and it's rumored to be about premature ejaculation." Jax's eyebrows shot up, and he stared at me for a beat before laughing.

"Mia! So inappropriate."

"It's fact."

"Just was not expecting to hear you say 'ejaculation.'"

"Why is that so unexpected?"

"Because look how cute," he teased and squeezed my cheeks, but I swatted his hand away. *I don't want to be cute. Damn it.*

"Whatever. Ejaculation." I leaned back and looked forward to the road ahead as well. My legs suddenly felt cramped, so I raised them to try and stretch.

"Don't do it." Jax's deep voice brought my attention back to him, and I paused my movement, feet in midair.

"What?"

"Keep your feet away from the dashboard."

"Why?"

"Because I said so."

"Okay." I actually laughed at his warning and laid my toe against the dash. "Uh-oh. Your order wasn't obeyed."

"If I weren't driving…" He let the threat trail off.

"You'd what?" I teased and then officially rested my feet on the dashboard of his Ford Raptor.

"Make things interesting." He glanced over at me with a smirk.

"And how would you do that?" I taunted him from the safety of the passenger seat, but even from behind the wheel and wearing a seat belt, Jax still looked dangerous. Focusing on the road, he pursed his lips and tilted his head like he was thinking about it, but once his eyes went to my legs, he didn't look away. I could feel his gaze run from my feet, up my legs, and to my thighs.

"You're not ready for it, darlin'," he said once he gazed into my innocent eyes with a wicked look in his. I felt a spark of something when he called me "darlin'." He focused back on the road, but I wasn't done with the topic.

"Ready for what?" I taunted further and rubbed my socked feet back and forth against the leather. Jax smiled at my curiosity and shook his head. He didn't answer me—instead, he extended his arm across the console so his hand could squeeze the funny spot above my knee. My leg pulled away on reflex, but I laughed as I pushed his hand off.

"Stop annoying the driver."

"Fine." I sighed but extended my legs further so my toes hit the windshield.

"Front-seat attendant, play more music," Jax ordered, which I was fine obeying.

The rest of our road trip went by with Ozzie, Steven, and Nick listening to their own music on their AirPods and playing mindless games on their phones, while Jax and I talked in the front seat, with a brief break when I handed out snacks at the halfway mark.

"Mia," Jax whispered after a period of silence, so I brought my attention from looking out the window to him. "Look back." I frowned and turned around to see that the three boys had fallen asleep. Ozzie was slumped against the window with Steven's head resting on his shoulder, and Nick was cuddling Steven.

"Oh my God." I started to laugh, but Jax shushed me so I didn't wake them. "That is the cutest thing ever."

"Let's document it." He nudged my iPhone on the console toward me. I picked it up and took a picture of the three of them, then sat forward and put the camera in selfie mode. "No." Jax shook his head, not wanting to be in a picture.

"You have to. Don't ruin the moment," I said sternly, then held up the camera to get a picture of the three boys in the back with the addition of Jax's and my heads popping up from the bottom. "Ha ha! Look how great this is." I showed him the two pictures, and we both must have laughed a little too hard, since we woke up the backseat passengers.

"What'd I miss?" Nick sat up straight with a bolt of energy, followed by Steven and Ozzie.

"Ugh. My neck hurts," Ozzie grumbled and rubbed his hand over the back of his neck as Steven yawned and stretched his lanky limbs.

"Nothin'." Jax shook his head and looked forward.

"Yeah, we've just been playing music. Boring." I glanced back at them and could tell they were still sleepy. Jax and I exchanged a sly smirk, knowing we'd keep the picture between us until the opportune moment. I opened a new message to send the two pictures to Jax, excited to start a thread with him, since we'd never contacted each other on the phone before.

"Almost there," Jax announced, and we all got ready to shed the road-trip energy and start working on the job we were approaching. We were all in our professional-artist mode by the time Jax pulled onto the property.

"Front-seat attendant, dismount," I announced as I hopped down from the lifted truck. "How did I do?" I asked Jax with a big grin when he stood in front of me.

"Directions, fail. Music, pass. Entertaining the driver, pass."

"Two out of three." I nodded with self-satisfaction and held up my hand. At first, Jax stared and didn't get it, but he soon understood my gesture. He shook his head and high fived me back. I slipped around him to start unloading. We all gathered our duffel bags and decided to bring in the other supplies later. Ozzie, Nick, and Steven offered to carry my bag, but I declined. I didn't know that it was a long walk across the grounds to the mansion. I was definitely not going to help bring in the supplies. Not long after our journey down the uneven, rocky path through tall, flowery bushes, my back started to pinch, so I transferred the bag to my other shoulder, but that just spread the pain. I ended up adjusting my grip and carrying it awkwardly with both hands. Jax walked by me and took my duffel with him.

"Jax." I hurried my steps to catch up to him. "I said I can carry it."

"I know." He nodded but kept walking. I grabbed for it, but he easily held it out of my reach. "Does your back hurt?"

I wasn't expecting his concern and knew my back needed relief. I admitted to needing help. "A little."

"So let me do it." Jax looked down at me as I tried to match his long-legged pace. I simply nodded, and we continued our journey to the house.

I was distracted by the cramp in my spine as I tried to realign my back by wiggling my shoulder blades, so I didn't notice that Jax was staring at me at first.

"What?" I shot him a sidelong glance, still stretching.

"Nothing." He chuckled and looked ahead. I looked ahead, too, but stopped in my tracks. We'd arrived, and all of us were blown away by the estate—a monster-size Tudor-style home surrounded by gardens and acres of groomed land in the middle of a forest. I tilted my head back to look up at the four stories of brick covered in vines and expansive windows and balconies.

"Hello!" we heard a chipper voice welcome us at the door, and a small old man scurried outside to greet us. "I'm Lawrence, the groundskeeper. Please come in."

We followed the man as he moved through an elaborate entryway. The place was beautiful but very muted from years of neglect. Humble relative to the usual mansion worth that much money. "Okay, artists." Lawrence clapped with excitement. "Go up this staircase, and you'll find that you all get your own room, so just follow down the hallway. Mr. Sinclair won't be here until later, so whenever you're ready, I'll show you around." He motioned for us to go upstairs. I ran up the stairs ahead of all of the boys, hunting for an en suite bathroom. I poked my head into each room until I found one at the end of the hallway. I jumped on the bed to claim my spot. Once the boys got to the second level, they realized why I'd been in such a hurry.

"Mia! You took the only room with a bathroom," I heard Nick complain from down the hall. As the only woman, I didn't feel bad. Jax then appeared in my doorway and walked in.

"Your bag, Ms. Bell," he announced as he dropped my duffel next to where I was lying on my bed. "How's your back?" he asked, standing next to my bed.

I took a second to stretch, trying to detect any pain, but the pinch and cramps were gone. "It's good." I smiled up at him and saw that his demeanor had changed within the few seconds he'd been inside my room. His eyes darkened as he watched me stretch my body across the bed, lying down and looking up at him with a genuinely innocent smile. When I noticed the sexy tic of his jaw, I knew it was time to change positions. I not so sexily rolled to my side and used my arm to push myself upright into a sitting position—spinal fusion style. "What?" I asked.

"Hm?" Jax's eyes shot to mine, and I could see the smolder fade away as he looked at my face. "Uh—your back is good. So that's good." It was fun to see him flustered, even for just one second, because a second later, his playboy effect was back. "So…I helped you with your bag. Aren't I nice?"

"Yeah…"

"I don't get a 'thank you?'"

I eyed him and his up-to-no-good smirk. "Thank you."

"Hm." Jax held his chin between his fingers and nodded as if he were thinking through a serious decision. "I think you can do better than that."

"Are you giving me another try?" He nodded. "Okay." I cleared my throat and composed myself. "Jax, I am *so* grateful for your big, strong arms carrying my duffel all the way from the truck up to my room. You're my hero. How can I ever repay you?"

"Well, since you asked…"

"Okay." I stood and tried pushing him toward the door, but he didn't move. He just looked down at me and smirked, then gave me the lightest push, which caused me to drop back onto the bed.

"We can circle back later," Jax said like we were talking business, then winked before swaggering out the door.

———

A little while later, Lawrence showed us around the house and grounds. The place was fragmented with twists and turns and many levels and steps—I got lost within the first ten minutes of the tour. The groundskeeper showed us around the kitchen and wrote down directions to get to town.

All we were shown beyond our lodging floor was the first level, where we would do all of our work, and outside, just for fun. The grounds were just starting to be worked on by gardeners, and I could tell it'd be an impressive display when the plants bloomed. I gazed at the exterior of the house from the backyard and was blown away by the architecture. There were two more floors that remained a mystery. On the top floor was a massive circle balcony that I promised myself I'd get to. The tour took a long time since Lawrence shuffled instead of walked and provided an excessive amount of information on the details of the estate and the history of the family.

"Okay, artists. Mr. Sinclair has arrived. Let's go welcome him," Lawrence said cheerfully and led us to the entryway.

Mr. Sinclair was a tall, very polished man in his late sixties. He had a deep, rich voice, and I loved his skinny mustache. He'd just taken off one of those flat caps when he shook all of our hands.

"Welcome! Thank you for coming at such short notice. We are hosting a big—too big—family and friends reunion party at the end of May, and everyone expects to be wowed." He smiled warmly and started telling us, mostly Jax, about what he expected from us. He basically wanted us to make the foyer, parlor, family room, dining room, and study works of art to rival the traditional splendor with a modern influence. So…we'd be there for a week, at least. He showed us around the house and pointed out dated art pieces.

"I want this place to still feel like home, so I want you all to replicate these pieces in a refreshed and updated way in the rooms I showed you."

"Look here." He handed Jax a binder and kept walking. "Now you, my dear." He turned and focused on me. "Mia? Is that short for Amelia?"

"It is, yes." I nodded and smiled softly.

"Then, Amelia"—he put his hand to my back and steered me forward to the parlor—"this was my mother's and my grandmother's *favorite* room."

"I can see why." I admired the tall, concave windows that flooded the room with light.

"Yes. They were lovely women. So beautiful and delicate. Classic women." He seemed to be lost in a memory, so I waited for him to continue. "Well." He sighed and then refocused his eyes on me. "You remind me of them. Which is why I want you in charge of this room."

"No pressure." I giggled softly and he looked at me with affection. *Does he have a mom thing? Like an Oedipus complex…*

"I have faith in you, Amelia." He winked. *Oh, Lord.* He carried on with Jax for a while, and I exchanged weird looks with the other boys, who had kept their distance while our employer focused only on me.

"Mr. Caine, I think I've rambled on long enough. I best be going," Mr. Sinclair announced and shook Jax's hand, then turned to us. "I'll leave you all to what you do best." He looked at me and smiled, gave me a little head nod, and left.

"So…what to do for the rest of the night at an old, secluded mansion?" I mused and waited for the suggestions.

"Liquor run!" Nick cheered, and all the guys were in favor.

Chapter 14

Since Jax was the one with a means of transportation, he was automatically assigned to do the liquor run.

"I'm not going alone, guys," he announced as he leaned against the kitchen counter, arms crossed. I felt my arm instantly want to lift to participate, but I kept it down. "So, who's it gonna be?" Jax's gaze moved to each member, starting with the boys sitting at the kitchen table. "Steven? Nick? Oz?" They all shook their heads even though his eyes moved past them before they could even reject his offer. Then his gaze landed on me. "Mia." I shook my head like the others, but he ignored me. "You're the winner. Let's go."

"Oh, gee, I won a trip to the liquor store?" I forced my words to be sarcastic to match an eye roll, but my smile was genuine as I followed him out of the kitchen.

"Lucky you." He smirked and opened the main door and let me pass through first.

"Back to front-seat attendant again." I sighed and hopped into the truck.

"You get a chance at redemption." Jax reminded me of my poor job during our road trip. "Directions. Enter the town Lawrence told us into your Maps."

"Fine. Give me your phone." I held out my hand, which he just glanced at, then looked ahead again.

"I'm not giving you my phone." He shook his head as he eased his way through the winding driveway.

"Oooh, why not?"

"Would you give me yours?"

"Of course. I have nothing to hide," I said as my brain searched through my phone.

"Ms. Perfect?" Jax arched a brow and glanced over at me.

"Not even close." I chuckled to myself but really hadn't meant to say that out loud.

"Why?" Jax asked with a frown, but I ignored him.

"So I don't have my phone, just Lawrence's scribbles." I held up the paper. "Just put liquor stores nearby into your phone." I motioned to the little stand on the dash that could hold his phone for directions.

"Hm." He looked at the paper I held up and squinted, realizing that the scribbles were almost illegible. He glanced over at me. "I think we should trust the directions of a local, don't you?"

"Oh, definitely." I nodded in agreement. I knew I wouldn't be able to read the old man's handwriting and could potentially get us lost. I was okay with that. "Oh, God, it's written in cursive." I started to laugh since I couldn't read cursive even with perfect penmanship.

"Front-seat attendant, remember this is your chance at redemption," Jax said very seriously, and I couldn't stifle an excited smile.

"Let's go." I sat up straight in my seat with Lawrence's directions in my lap. "Right." I pointed, and Jax pulled out of the driveway, and our journey began. It didn't take long for us to get lost.

"We've passed this little chapel three times." Jax groaned as he made another turn with the palm of his hand circling the wheel, which temporarily caught my eye.

"I'm telling you the directions." I looked through the paper again. I was reciting each word, but because of the scribbled cursive, I sometimes misinterpreted it. "Okay, just choose a street and we'll go down it. Like this one."

"Mia, that's a state highway."

"Oh." I looked at the street sign and laughed.

"You have until sundown to get us to alcohol or else you missed your chance at redemption."

"It's already sundown." I frowned as I peered out the window to the sky. When I looked back at Jax, his eyebrows were up and waiting for me to get it. "No!"

"Sorry." He shrugged and made a U-turn.

"A third chance!"

"You're getting an awful lot of chances, Mia." He tsked and maneuvered through the small-town roads. I nodded. "Alright. Get us to alcohol before the end of the world and you are redeemed." Five minutes later, we found the liquor store. I honestly hadn't been trying to get us lost. I also hadn't given the task much effort. We missed the store by one block four times.

"I did it." I strutted through the parking lot like I'd won a gold medal. I looked at Jax over my shoulder and pointed to the sign that stated "LIQUOR," then went into the store, Jax behind me.

"You're right. We found alcohol before the end of the world." Jax nodded as he picked up a basket and followed me further into the store. I stopped in the whiskey aisle and put a bottle of Jameson in the basket Jax held. I continued to locate everyone's go-to drinks. Once we had everything we needed, I followed him to checkout.

The cashier scanned through our bottles and cases of beer. The boys could drink—well, I could too. We waited for him to organize our purchase into two boxes on the counter.

"Don't even try." Jax chuckled when I put my hands on one of the boxes.

"I can carry it." I rolled my eyes.

"How are you gonna do that with little arms and a fused spine?"

"I could grip it by the husk." The Monty Python quote just came out of me, accent and all, and I hoped he understood the reference so an embarrassing moment wouldn't get even more embarrassing—movie quotes were always a gamble. Jax stared at me for several seconds, then burst out laughing. Even the man at the register was laughing. *Thank God.*

"I can't believe you just said that."

"Mm-hmm." I smirked as I tried to pick up the box. I couldn't get it off the counter—I really couldn't handle any weight with my back and no arm muscle. I abandoned the box but didn't want to give up, so I picked up the bottle of Jameson and stepped back.

"Nice." Jax chuckled and gathered our haul. He carried the two boxes, and I followed, carrying one bottle, through the parking lot.

"Good for you, muscle man." I rolled my eyes and climbed into my seat.

"Thank you, European swallow." He smiled as he made another *Holy Grail* reference as he got into the truck.

"Ha ha. Hilarious."

"You are." He nodded, and I didn't let on just how delighted I was by his compliment.

"So it may be harder for me to interpret directions backward." I picked up the sheet of paper and twisted it around a few times until it was the right side up. I started reading the bottom line when Jax's hand came into view and pulled it from my grasp.

"I got this one." He chuckled and tossed the sheet onto the dashboard and proceeded to drive us back to the mansion by memory.

"So." I relaxed against the seat, relieved of my duty, and propped my feet up on the dash. "What do you think about the project?"

"It's interesting. We haven't done anything like this before. You know like commissions, art shows, a community project here and there, our new place in the gallery…never anything close to restoring the lost art of an old family mansion."

"Is this usual? What Sinclair is asking for?"

"No. I'm a little wary about his expectations. I understand what he wants, but we need to be careful about how far we take our creativity."

"Yeah, I feel that. How much work do you have to do?"

"Two pieces to be mounted on the wall in his study," he answered, then glanced at me. "You, though…you have a whole damn room."

"Yeah, for the man's maternal lineage. No pressure." I chuckled, but stress was evident in my voice.

"That level of sentimental…it's a lot of pressure," he agreed but then added supportive words I needed to hear. "The guy lucked out. You're the perfect artist for the job."

"You think so?"

"You felt how much emotion is in that room. I don't know how, but you understand those levels and it comes through in your work." Jax spoke casually, but I could tell his words were heartfelt.

"I'll do my best." I nodded and looked out the window, loving what he'd said but feeling vulnerable by how deeply he seemed to understand me.

"Ten minutes," Jax announced as we neared the driveway to the mansion. "Twenty-five minutes there and ten minutes back."

"Huh, you must have taken a shortcut." I shrugged and slid down from my seat and onto the gravel once the truck was parked.

Jax picked up both boxes of booze from the back seat, and I skipped along next to him with my Jameson bottle.

Once we got back, I poured myself some whiskey and spent the rest of the night in the parlor. Looking through the photos Mr. Sinclair left me, I glanced back and forth between a picture of a young grandma and a young mom, and they looked virtually the same, just from different time periods. They were stunning and feminine, but both had the same cheeky smirk. I continued to inspect the furniture, decorations, colors, and themes. Jade, the stone and the color, was everywhere, along with touches of powder pink and ivory. I started forming a plan.

"Band meeting!" I heard Ozzie call, and I followed his voice to the great room. We all gathered and talked about ideas and plans. It was settled that we'd probably be there for a week. Steven groaned and went to his room to call his girlfriend, Lizzie, but the rest of us were excited.

We retired to our rooms after dinner to chill and get a good night's sleep since we knew we had a big job ahead of us and anticipated plenty of late nights. I was lying on my bed, looking up at my iPhone in my hands above me as I searched through my music to put together a playlist for my project. "Elvis…Roy Orbison…Otis Redding…" I mumbled to myself as I added them to a playlist.

"Do you always talk to yourself when you're alone?" Jax's deep voice startled me since I hadn't heard him open the door.

"Jesus." My phone slipped from my hands and onto my face. "*Ow.*" I groaned and rubbed my nose, then looked up when I heard Jax's chuckle. I rolled my eyes and pushed myself into a sitting position in the middle of my bed. "Do you always creep into people's rooms without warning?" He just shrugged and remained leaning against the doorframe. "What do you want?"

"I have some bad news." I watched him carefully as he walked into my room. "There's something wrong with my room, and this is the biggest one. Looks like we are bunking together."

"No," I objected, and he jumped onto the bed with me, so I rose to my knees, ready to run if needed.

"This bed is big enough for the two of us. Don't be selfish." I stared at him, hoping he was kidding. "You seem like a kicker." I pushed him off the bed. "*Ow.*" I laughed, impressed with myself that I was able to pull it off, and crawled to the edge of the bed to make fun of him. He quickly grabbed my wrist and pulled me off the bed so I fell on top of him. "Uh-oh…am I going to need to build a pillow wall?" he teased with a playful smile and hands around my waist.

I lifted myself onto my hands and knees and pushed a lock of hair behind my ear. "I'm sure there's a couch open somewhere in the house for you to sleep…or a chair…or rug…or shed. You're not staying here."

"Relax, I'm kidding." He chuckled, and I tried to stand but he didn't let go. "What are you so afraid of?"

"N-nothing…" I said breathlessly. "What are you doing?"

"N-nothing." He mimicked me and smiled, knowing that he was affecting me.

"Let me go," I ordered.

"Why?" He was still gripping my waist, and I glared at him. Bastard knew he was getting me flustered, but I could turn the tables just as easily. I pushed my hair to one side and smirked.

"You know what?" I sighed and lowered my voice to a more seductive level. "I'm comfortable right here, *Jax*." I shifted my weight and extended my hand across the floor to lower my body closer to him but was sure to not touch him. His eyes widened, and he basically threw me off him. "Why'd you do that?" I acted surprised but started laughing as he stood up.

"Time for bed. Good night," Jax said, already walking away and out my door.

"All right, sleep well!" I called after him. My laughter faded, and I picked myself up from the floor. I wasn't prepared for the longing I had for him to come back once he was gone, and I hated it. I felt instantly nervous.

I can't have feelings for him. He's hot—in an obvious and dominating way. But he doesn't affect me. Not at all. Never will.

"Mia." Ozzie walked into my room and closed the door.

"What's up?" I bounced back onto my queen-size bed.

"What's going on with you and Jax? *Seriously* just tell me."

"Ugh, I've told you. *Seriously*, nothing."

"Then why were you two on the floor?" He stared me down, and I hesitated. I didn't know he'd seen that.

"He was being stupid, and I matched his stupid." I shrugged, not realizing just how accurate of a description that was for our interactions.

"Just be careful." Ozzie sighed.

"*Why?*"

"I've told you. Just be careful, okay?"

"Thanks for the advice, but I'll be fine." I smiled to assure him, even though his warning freaked me out. I wanted to question his reasoning further but didn't want to prolong our conversation.

"All right." He looked around my space. "You got the best room."

"I know." I smiled, glad I'd made the run for it. "Good night."

"Sleep well." Ozzie smirked, then left my room and closed my door. I went to dig around in my duffel, starting the process of getting ready for bed, not knowing that it was going to be a long night.

Chapter 15

Soon, the house was quiet, and I could tell everyone was sleeping—except me. My mind was buzzing, and I couldn't sleep, not even with my nightly pills, which should've knocked me out. I was on the border of hypomania—bipolar mania but less severe. I could feel it coming with my inability to shut my eyes and the light buzz that hummed through my body.

I glanced around my room, making sure my mind wouldn't conjure up any hallucinations. I chose an item to fix my gaze on, an empty vase in the corner, since sometimes it took a second for an item to contort. I relaxed, as my vision was steady. I didn't know if my inner feelings around Jax were heating up or the chemicals in my brain were dancing over my hypomanic mood that made me feel just a bit of sexiness. I stretched across the comforter to lay on my front, wearing only my Calvin Klein underwear, and swayed my feet back and forth while I sketched. Even the itchy old comforter felt good rubbing against my skin as I spent hours listening to my new playlist and sketching random ideas I had for my project.

"Sigh." I vocalized the deep breath I let out as I turned to my back. I stared at the beams of the high ceiling and felt my mind start to count all of them. *One…two…three…ugh, I messed up. One, two, three, four…five… this is so boring.* The longer I lay still, the more restless I felt. I dropped my head to the side and spied my empty whiskey glass. "Aha." I smiled and bounced off the mattress to find my robe. I pulled out my long-sleeved, knee-length flannel robe from my duffel and wrapped it around my body, tying a secure knot at the side. I grabbed my empty glass and slipped out of my room on a quest for a refill. I walked down the hall, my destination the kitchen, where a bottle of Jameson waited for me. *Scotchy scotch scotch. I love—balcony!* I suddenly remembered my promise to find the top-floor balcony and rerouted.

I found a staircase at the other end of the hall. I followed so many twists and turns, I didn't expect to be able to make my way back, but I didn't care. Dark shadows surrounded me, so my eyes depended on the soft streaks of moonlight that came through the windows to light up my path. *A ghost is going to pop out in front of me…or a psycho killer will come up behind me…any second.* I kept climbing any staircase I found until I arrived at the top level and the balcony was right in front of me.

I walked outside and looked up into the glorious sky—no clouds, revealing a crescent moon with constellations and stars splattered across the night. It reminded me of the night sky back home and how I'd lie down on the dock at the lake and just gaze above me. "This is beautiful," I murmured to myself as I tilted my head back to see more.

"Hey." I heard a strong voice come from beside me, the figure shadowed by the night. I jumped with a screech away from Jax.

"Oh my God!" I put a hand against my pounding chest and waited for my heartbeat to return to normal.

"Did I scare you?" He chuckled and walked into the soft moonlight.

"Psh. No." I pushed a lock of my hair behind my ear and steadied my breathing.

"So you do talk to yourself when you're alone."

"I'm good company."

"That's a good point," Jax agreed, which made me smile.

"What are you doing here?" I asked as I took in my surroundings again. Standing on the stone balcony, we could gaze up at the sky or look down at the vast grounds of the mansion below.

"Probably what you're doing." He shrugged.

"Couldn't sleep?" I guessed. He moved closer to me and nodded.

"How about we can't sleep together?"

"Okay." I took a sip of my drink, the last drop, and sat on the balcony ledge. *Damn, I forgot about the refill.*

I quickly glanced from him to the doors and around the small area we shared, alone. My restless energy still buzzed just beneath my skin. I felt nervous being around him, nervous I would act like a hypomaniac—rapid and frenetic talking, oversharing, strange ideas, or agitated behavior—which would make him uncomfortable. I looked back to his face, and I felt my restless energy start to ease, his dark-blue eyes having a calming effect on me.

"Why do you drink Jameson?" Jax asked as he sat next to me on the ledge, which was wide enough for me to pull my legs up and cross them, careful to keep my robe covering me.

"I want to," I said simply. He nudged my knee, and I noticed that he had a tumbler of dark liquid as well. "My dad. I watched him make a Manhattan a million times, so one night, I wanted to impress him and made one for him myself. So I always did after that and would make one for myself without him noticing."

"How old were you?"

"Sixteen." I furrowed my brow, making sure I guessed my age accurately, then nodded. It wasn't often that my dad would drink, so I wasn't a boozing teenager, just the weird teenager, staying at home with a Manhattan on a Friday night. "And you?"

"My dad, as well. Although I never fixed him a cocktail. Kiss-ass," he teased, and I rolled my eyes. I guess that was true. "So you must be your dad's favorite."

"Ha. You'd think so." I chuckled to myself and lifted my glass to my lips, forgetting it was empty, and put it down.

"What do you mean?" Jax asked with a tilt of his head, and all I could do was blink. *I've been supporting you for four years, and you're still bipolar? I raised you the same as your sisters—they're successful, so why aren't you? Nora was already married at your age. Stella is closer to a degree than you. What do I tell my family and friends when they ask about my failure daughter still living at home?* My dad's voice rang in my ears. Living at home was hard. I didn't want to talk about family.

"I don't know." I shrugged it off and picked up my glass, forgetting that it was empty, and put it down. *No. I don't have daddy issues. No. But... kinda...yeah.*

"Did you get your taste in music from him too?" Jax asked, and I chuckled and shook my head, thankful that the topic had turned to music.

"Not at all. He's into John Denver and Neil Diamond. Which is a major disappointment because he should have awesome concert stories to tell me, but alas, all those bands went through his town, but he never went." We sat on the stone ledge of the balcony and talked about music for an hour. We tried coming up with an alternate universe where Bonham didn't drink so much and Freddie didn't get AIDS, where Jimi and Jim didn't die and Kurt never killed himself.

"What was your favorite thing about Paris?" I asked him with keen curiosity. He smiled and started telling me about the amazing art and culture, and I loved listening to him talk.

"Did you really skip France for a Stones concert?" He looked at me with a judgmental arch of his brow.

"Yes." I sighed, and he exaggerated his disapproval. "Okay! Jax, you know they could drop any minute! Paris will always be there!" He shook his head. "You would do the same thing!"

"I would not."

"Yes, you would. I know you would."

"Really?" I nodded. "How would you know?"

"Because I did." I smiled proudly at my argument and watched him stare at me and purse his lips, trying to decide if he'd admit it or not. "So, you would. Admit it."

"I can't do it." He sighed and shook his head, but I still waited for him to give in. "You can't make me."

"I think you just did."

"Nope." He shook his head again before redirecting. "I actually wanted to study in Italy."

"Michelangelo?" I asked, and he nodded. "Why didn't you?"

"My godfather had certain connections in Paris that I wouldn't have made in Italy. It worked out."

"Have you been?"

"Once, when I was a kid… I can't believe I haven't gone back yet."

"Is that when you became interested in sculpting?"

"In Florence." I could see in his eyes that he was in a memory. "I just became obsessed with it even though we were only there for three days. I don't remember much…but seeing the statue of David, I'll never forget that. And there was this kinda outdoor gallery with rows of incredible statues."

"I know what you're talking about. Piazza della Signoria…it was my favorite place. I spent a lot of time there. Do you remember any of the statues?"

"Yeah. The one of Medusa decapitated."

"Naturally."

"The other one that I remember"—I saw his eyes light up, and he brought his hands together—"was of a woman and two men, and they were twisted together in this struggle…a very intense, upward spiral, and you could just, like…feel it, you know?" He twisted his hands around each other like the statue. A small smile curved my lips. "Sounds dramatic for a ten-year-old, but whatever. It's always been special to me." He shrugged it off, but I could still see the passion in his eyes. I knew exactly the statue he was talking about, and it happened to be my absolute favorite. I had spent many hours in that square sketching it from every possible angle.

"*The Rape of the Sabine Woman*," I said.

"That's what it's called?" I nodded. "What do you think of it?"

"After seeing all of the art there was to see, that is my forever favorite." Something then sparked in my brain, and I hoped that my connection was accurate. "Has"—I hesitated and looked at him more closely, not wanting to be wrong—"has that been the heart of your work?" I asked softly. I didn't want to get too personal, but I was so fascinated with his art that I had to know. He looked closely at me, too, and I was ready to revoke the question.

"Oh, Mia." Jax sighed and looked away for several moments, then looked back at me. "How are you the only one who knows this?"

"What do you mean?"

"Tell me about your time there." He tried rerouting, but I wasn't done yet.

"Your sculpture in the exhibit room." I sat up a little straighter as I remembered it. "Was that inspired by the Sabine woman? I knew that's why I loved it so much! Oh my God, how you made it so powerful but soft, and the emotion—"

"It's not," Jax interjected forcefully to get me to end my praise of an apparently very sensitive artwork. I shut up and nodded. "Now tell me about your time there."

"My time in Florence?" I asked. He smiled with an adorable grin and clasped his hands together to be a good listener. "The first week was just me getting lost."

"Not surprising."

"Yeah, yeah." I looked into his enchanting dark-blue eyes. "It was amazing. Honestly, it really was—like, what you said about Paris. I lived down the street from the Duomo and from Santa Croce. I would casually walk across the very bridge where Dante met Beatrice again. It was just…" I sighed, not having the words to describe it and trying to calm my excitement as I got deeper into the memories. I could tell he understood.

"Is that when you decided to illustrate the *Divine Comedy*?"

"No, I wanted to ever since I read it the first time in high school, but it was intimidating. It was seeing the first portrait of Dante in the Bargello that got me going. I did all the rough sketches there, then did the final series when I came home."

"That's a beautiful background. I think your work is brilliant, so it's nice knowing the inspiration behind it." I never felt such happiness from a compliment in my life. "Was art history part of your degree?" I shook my head, hoping he wouldn't ask anything else about education.

"I admit, the project you brought us in on was fun. Especially since I had such good material to work from." He actually winked as he reminded me that I'd assigned him the second-circle sin, lust. "Tell me why."

"All the other circles were taken." I shrugged, and he shook his head with a teasing smile. "Fine. Your sculptures are very—um, passionate. I wanted to see what you would do with incorporating the perspective of lust as a mortal sin. Pleasure, meet pain," I admitted but stopped myself there before I started rambling and admitting to anything more.

"Honestly, I didn't know anything about *Inferno* or Dante, but after reading it, I can see why it's been a big part of your art."

"Wait, you read the whole thing?"

"Of course I did. So, what did you think?" he asked. I looked at him. "I mean, about my sculpture of the second circle…how did it make you feel?"

"Um." I wasn't expecting that question. I blinked a few times, trying to decide if I were going to give an honest answer or not. "It's a reminder. Your sculpture shows the lustful sinners trapped in an eternal wind, but it's not really a deterrent…" He arched a brow, and I smiled. I knew he was interested in my opinion, so I continued, "It's dark but beautiful, erotic, passionate… It's a reminder of darker desires…which everyone has. They're either accepted or suppressed."

"And you? Are your dark desires accepted or suppressed?"

"It's a secret." I looked him in the eyes and smirked, planning on giving nothing else away.

"Of course." He sighed but had a little glint in his eye. "But can I coax it out of you?"

"Nope. Oooh. Mr. Sculpture Artist evoking dark desire…what did you feel?"

"Good question." He chuckled. "It's a secret."

"Of course." I wasn't over the subject. "Has it sold?"

"Yes."

"Aw. I wanted to see it again."

"Maybe you will." I cocked my head to the side, wondering what he meant and hoping I would. He didn't explain but still looked very pleased with my response. "Impressive analysis, though. I expected your answer to be lust." He smirked, and I couldn't tell if he was being serious or not.

"I'm that shallow?" I glared at him, mildly offended, and he just chuckled and shook his head.

"No. You're definitely not. How did you learn so much about the *Divine Comedy* and all those illustrations?"

"I dunno. Just…reading stuff."

"Reading stuff? I don't buy it." I shrugged. "You're just that passionate about a weird Italian guy's poem about heaven and hell?"

"And purgatory."

"Oh, you are." Jax's eyebrows rose, and then he smirked and rubbed his hands together, like he was analyzing me and on to something good. "So, what made you fall in love with it?"

"Um…" I held up my empty tumbler. "Oh, no…time for a refill." I shrugged, but Jax just chuckled and picked up the Jameson bottle from the stone floor that I didn't know he'd brought and poured some into my glass. "Thank you…"

"Follow-up question. What makes you evade a question about Italian literature?" I didn't say anything and took another sip from my newly filled glass. "Fine, Miss Mysterious. What else can I get out of you… oh." I didn't like the playful, menacing look in his eyes. "You were never formally interviewed."

"Yes, I was."

"Not really. Ozzie waved you in."

"Well, I'm here, so no need to dig up the past."

"What was your major if it wasn't art history? I do remember a long list of universities on your résumé. What degrees do you have?"

"I never finished." I sighed, regretting the entire conversation. Jax looked surprised, while I tried to act casual, as if the subject weren't a painful one and didn't make me incredibly insecure. A long list of colleges and universities either meant a long list of degrees or a long list of failures.

"Uh-oh. Did someone lie on their résumé?" he teased, but I could tell he was studying my facial expressions and body language, no doubt picking up on my awkward reticence about answering his very simple questions.

"Of course not," I huffed with mock offense at my integrity being questioned. "Read the fine print. Nowhere does it state a graduation date or degree."

"I believe you. Now, Ms. Bell, as for the interview, I would like to continue with your educational history. Here you are, a talented and brilliant artist, yet there is no degree. Instead, a list of colleges with no listed majors. What is your secret?" His tone went from professional to suspicious as he studied me, having his fun. I rolled my eyes as he spoke but froze when he asked about my secret. Jax had a playful smirk on his face but dropped it when he saw my expression. If he was reading me right, he would see sadness in my eyes and vulnerability in the twist of my brow and the way I wrapped my robe tighter around me.

"It's getting late." I looked away from him and turned to hop down from the balcony. Jax reached his hand toward me and placed it on my knee before I could unfold my legs.

"Mia…I was just playing. I didn't mean to upset you." His deep, soft voice seemed to soothe my anxious body. I looked into his eyes, and, again, my breathing seemed to calm as I stared. "Will you stay here with me?" For a moment, my brows furrowed further, and my eyes blurred out of focus from the gentle way he was treating me. He didn't just sit back and let me run away. I took a deep breath and nodded.

"I'm sorry. I…" I murmured as I straightened back into place, sitting on the balcony ledge.

"Don't be sorry," Jax said quietly as his head dipped a bit lower to study my features. "I really didn't mean to, um…" He couldn't finish his sentence since he didn't really know what he'd done.

"No." I shook my head as I regained my confident voice. "I just…" I rolled my eyes at myself and flitted my hand into the air, dismissing the whole reaction.

"Okay." He nodded but continued to watch me. I was finally relaxed but didn't know what to say. "I just want to get to know you more," he said. "I don't think you have secrets."

"Yeah, you do," I said, and my lips curved, my reaction proof that I had secrets.

"A few," Jax confessed with a smile and shrugged. I nodded and took a sip of whiskey, then looked out into the sky. "I went to UCLA," he said. I faced him again with my brows up. "Mm-hmm. I went to Paris for an internship, then to UCLA. I majored in business." My mouth twisted, finding it funny to picture him in business. "Yep. I was in business for a couple years with my dad before quitting to pursue my art full-time."

"Which paid off quite well," I commented, happy for him but also for our group. It was so nice getting to know him better. Shit…that was what he was trying to do, get to know me.

"It did. We have a pretty special thing going on," he said and lifted his own glass of whiskey for a sip. He eyed me for a few seconds before continuing. "Can't I get to know you a little better?" I slowly nodded. "I just want to know where you went to college. That's safe enough, right?"

"It is." I nodded, even though it wasn't. The way he leaned in with his hands together, wanting to listen to me, how he actually wanted to know more about me… I felt honesty bubble up in my response. It took me a few seconds to gather the courage to speak while Jax sat patiently. "I went to the University of Washington after high school but only stayed one semester."

"Why'd you leave?"

"Just wasn't my vibe." I shrugged. "I only went there to get far away from home."

"Why's that?" Jax cocked his head to the side, and there it was— another question I couldn't answer.

"Um…" *Because at a sleepover, my senior year of high school, my two best friends purposefully got me drunk, my first time. I remember passing an Ice Mountain water bottle filled with Grey Goose back and forth with the two girls—sip, pass, having fun, sip, pass—but I didn't know they were only touching the bottle to their lips and I was the only one drinking. I haven't tasted vodka since that night seven years ago. When I became wobbly and unable to see straight, they guided me into my car to sneak over to another sleepover. They drove me to a boy's house, and I was so wasted, I couldn't stand, so other friends from the house came to help carry me inside, right to a bedroom in the basement where that boy named Drew lay waiting for me in a bed. The other boys watched him do things to my limp body. I can still remember how he smelled and the feel of him under my palms when he used my hands like a puppet. I can still remember his sausage fingers. My two best friends were pissed because after Drew was done with me, the boys kicked us out, saying that if I died of alcohol poisoning, they didn't want it to be in their basement—they were my friends too. I was carried back to my car, and I got sick in the backseat. The girl driving purposefully swerved around the road, and I tumbled around with no seat belt. The next day at school, everyone was waiting for me before the first bell. The boys demanded an apology for being a bad hookup and not getting Drew off. You know what I did? I actually apologized. My God, I felt shame just from that. After, no one spoke to me besides the teachers. Those kids had been my friends for five years. That's why I loved* Inferno *as a high school senior—Dante was in exile when he wrote it, and he made the ninth circle of hell for betrayers. After graduation, I wanted to get far away…so I went to the University of Washington.* "To see a different part of the country…?" I squinted and trailed off, coming up with my answer as I spoke.

"Are you asking me?" Jax asked with a chuckle, and that got me to smile and shrug. "What was next?"

"Well…it's an all-girls college."

"What?" He laughed again, and I shrugged again, laughing as well. "Why?"

"I had a scholarship, and it was chill. I didn't like college life."

"Why not?"

"Lots of college students…sloppy parties…frats and sororities… campus living…"

"Excuse me, but did you just say you didn't like college students when you were a college student?" he asked, and I nodded. "And you didn't like parties?" I nodded again. "What college student doesn't like parties?" I raised my hand, and he chuckled and shook his head.

"They're so lame!" The truth was I never really had the chance to have a normal college experience, and it made me sad that I could never relate or connect to any of it. I knew I'd missed out on a lot.

"How many college parties have you been to, though?" Jax eyed me with suspicion, implying I was judging something I never experienced.

"Mmmm. Five. Well, one party doesn't count because I sat on the front porch reading my Kindle and drinking shooters of Jameson that I'd brought in my purse. The cops showed up and thought I was hilarious. I was spared before they busted in. Everyone got misdemeanors."

"Wow." Jax was laughing hard at my lame college story, and I joined in. "If I were there, though, and saw you on the porch, I would've joined you."

"No way." I shook my head.

"Of course I would. Look how cute," he teased and nudged my foot.

"Ha. I wasn't cute back then." I chuckled, knowing that he would never have even noticed me. High school harassment wasn't far behind in college. Depression diet and stress skin care meant I gained twenty pounds and had extreme acne—shout-out to Accutane. I shivered just thinking of seeing Jax when I had such low self-esteem. I wasn't doing much better in front of him now.

"I don't see how that's possible, but okay." We both let the topic fade away. "So, what was after the all-girls college?"

The University of Minnesota. "That's all of them." I shrugged and felt my honest answers closing off. I stared down at the stone ledge, my eyes already fading out of focus, the traumatizing memory too close.

"Only two?" he asked. I nodded. "Are you lying?" I nodded. "Why?" I didn't respond—suddenly, all words were hard to form. "Okay, I'll guess."

I looked away, not wanting him to be able to read my emotions again. "Because you're legally bound to secrecy—spy school." My eyes finally met his. The dark blue was soft and kind but still contained a spark of intensity as he looked at me. My shoulders relaxed, and I let go of the anxious breath that had been twisted in my lungs. He made me laugh.

"Well, my cover is blown. I have to kill you now," I said very seriously.

"I'd like to see you try," Jax teased and smiled at the idea.

"I was the crafty one. When you least expect it."

"Then I'll be keeping an eye on you," he warned, eying me up and down.

"You do that." I slowly nodded, and his wide grin was so dazzling. I welcomed the distraction.

"I think the sun is rising," Jax noted as he looked to the brightening sky. Most of the stars had disappeared, and the night was now illuminated by the sun just below the horizon.

"We've been out here that long?" I frowned and looked up as well. Jax had stood from the railing and offered me his hand to help me hop down.

"Past five a.m.," he announced as he looked at his phone, then back to me. "Aren't I good company?" He pinched the spot at my neck to make my shoulders squirm. I pushed him away and followed him to the door. Once he opened it, he shot a look over his shoulder at me, then stood aside and made me go first. "I'll be keeping an eye on you."

"Sure." I went through the doorway but had no idea how to get back to our hallway of rooms.

"Straight across the hallway to the side staircase." Jax chuckled from behind me, knowing I didn't know where to go. He gave directions until both of us were in our rooms.

I sighed as I collapsed onto my bed and looked up to the ceiling. I knew that I wasn't going to be able to sleep much, so I crawled under the covers and tucked myself in, getting comfortable for the overthinking I had to do.

How could I sleep after that? It was like I'd been in an alternate universe where Jax and I were…friends? I liked it. Okay—loved it. But…it couldn't have been real. It must have been an isolated incident. I never let myself get too optimistic. I knew that sounded so…pessimistic. I had no expectations of my future because I didn't want to be let down. Nothing was promised to anyone, and I had to appreciate the moment. I really appreciated that moment.

I hadn't meant to show Jax the vulnerable side of me. I knew he hadn't intended to either. How could he? Simple questions about one's past college years should have been easy to answer. The explanation was plain and simple yet still complex and heartbreaking, something too painful to admit. I wished I could converse with him like normal—not have my lungs contract, my heart tighten, my eyes fog when he asked me simple questions. He could read my emotions, to some degree, and continued to want to know more. Which was why I let the conversation about college go on too long. Once he'd asked about what came after the all-girl schools… there I went, back in that dark place.

College number three. I didn't think I had ever spoken of it out loud outside of my psychologist's office. I didn't want it in my head. Ever.

The University of Minnesota. I was enrolled there until November 13. Just half of a semester of my junior year. That was when my moods started to swing. And they swung. Depression to mania, depression to mania…it was a spiral downward and upward at the same time. Depression hit hardest, and my roommate found me in the corner of my bedroom crying. *I can't live another day like this. I can't live another hour, another second. Make it stop.* I had wrapped my arms around my legs and buried my face in my knees. Tears poured from my eyes as I squeezed them shut, and my lungs shook as they tried to keep up with the pain inside me. Every molecule of my being hurt, and there was nothing in front of me. That was how bad it could get, where nothing mattered anymore other than the desperate need to make the pain go away.

"Mia…. what's wrong?" my roommate, Emily, asked gently and put a hand on my arm.

"I don't want to live anymore," I said in a whisper, eyes blurred by tears and voice weak and shaky. I knew the weight of those words, and I meant it. Concerned and not knowing what else to do, Emily left my side.

I didn't know how much time had passed as I was alone in the corner of my college room. "Mia?" a foreign voice said, and I slowly lifted my face from hiding behind my knees and frowned when I saw paramedics in my room. A young man in a blue uniform approached me slowly with his hands up. I dropped my arms from my legs, and the man backed up several steps. "It's okay. We are here to help."

"What?" I squinted and looked around my room, feeling my heart drop as I realized it looked like a true maniac lived there. I watched the paramedics stepping over art supplies that were scattered across the carpet—charcoal, pencils, and paints with scribblings and splatters over canvases and sketchbooks and spills on the carpet. I had four lamps without the shades on top placed around where I worked and an empty bottle of Jameson and empty package of Oreos on the floor. Worst of all, charcoal smudges on the wall—my manic mind had hallucinated skulls dancing across my bedroom walls, so what did I do? I used all of my charcoal to trace them—it really wasn't creepy. It looked cool and artistic, in my opinion. Manic, I had spent the previous week with no sleep and alone in my room, getting drunk and making art while dancing around to Metallica. Only a day before, I'd felt like I could fly, but suddenly, I wanted to die, and found myself cowering in the corner of my bedroom with paramedics around me. Another man was behind the first, and my roommate was watching from the doorway. "Emily, what's going on?" I asked.

"I called for help," she explained.

"I don't need help!" I stood, and the paramedic made a grab at me. "Get off!" Scared, I pushed him away.

"It's okay, Mia. Don't fight," the paramedic said slowly to me with his hands up.

"I'm not fighting!" I remained in the corner of my room, trapped. "What did I do?" I frantically looked over all faces in the room, confused and scared.

"You are not in trouble. Just come over here, and we will help you."
He spoke softly to me, like I was a danger to him. He was several feet
away from me, but his knees were bent and his hands out like he was in
a ready position, his energy aggressive and triggering. He scared me, and
I wrapped my arms around myself, not wanting him near me.

"No. Go away." I frowned and shook my head, trying to back further
into the corner and disappear. "I did nothing wrong."

"Your roommate here said that you are a danger to yourself, so we
have to bring you to a safe place."

"Emily?" My wide eyes shot to where my roommate stood back and
watched the drama.

"I thought it was an emergency."

"It's not, so you guys go away," I demanded, and I saw them look
around my room, then back to me like *they* were scared. They appeared
young enough to be college students.

"We are here to help. Just come with us willingly, okay, Mia?" I glared
at the paramedic and hated him for using my name like he cared. It became
harder to breathe, and I tried holding back any hysteria that would cause
them to restrain me. They restrained me anyway.

I had never felt so defeated in my life. I was taken to the university
hospital across the river from main campus and forced to wait in a small
room alone for six hours until someone came to bring me to the psych ward.
They made me take off my clothes so they could remove the drawstring
of my sweatpants and searched for anything sharp. I was escorted to my
room and sat on my wooden bed. There were stains on the dull yellow
walls that made my stomach churn, and I looked out my barred window
to see the campus of the college I was dropping out of below me. I was
there for two weeks, and my time inside the psych ward… I didn't want to
relive it. I was diagnosed with bipolar, assigned a psychiatrist, prescribed
medication, and finally discharged.

University of Minnesota—bad memories.

Chapter 16

That morning, I was lying awake in bed by seven o'clock, unable to sleep any longer but too drugged from my nightly medications to do anything about it. The beginning of mania was the best phase of bipolar, in my opinion, and I hated having to squash it, but I had to. The consequences were too great if it got out of hand or if the depressive downfall was bigger than expected. So, like the responsible bipolar-an I was, I squashed it. I would adjust my medications for the next few days to smooth out the blip so I could continue into the sunset of stability.

I felt around the bed for my phone and slid it out from under my pillow. I canceled my morning alarm and waited until I could drag myself out of bed. I was showered, dressed, and pepped by eight o'clock and beat everyone to the kitchen.

"Oh, no." I heard my best friend sigh behind me as I stood at the counter, almost done making coffee that I'd found in the cupboard.

"Good morning, Oswald." I smiled once I turned to face him and handed him a mug.

"You're never the first person up." He eyed me and accepted the coffee. "Please tell me you slept." He grimaced, nervous to hear my response, since he somewhat understood my irregular sleeping patterns.

"Yeah. I slept." I nodded and leaned against the counter.

"How long?" He eyed me over the brim of his mug as he took a sip.

"I dunno. Like, four hours," I lied with a shrug.

"Does this mean you're, like, on the up?" he asked, unsure how to phrase it.

"No. Well, yeah. But no." I frowned, still finding it hard to explain. Ozzie frowned, too, so I tried my best. "You know I'm stable, right?" He nodded. "So stable means that my mood swings are contained within the range as close as I can get to a normal brain and still be able to feel emotions." I paralleled my hands to show a range, then narrowed them. He nodded. "So, within that range, there's still room for mood swings, but the swings are contained and minimized. I'd typically be rising into a hypomanic episode right now, but because I'm stable, those symptoms are contained, and my mood doesn't spike to higher levels. The best way to track this is my sleep. Does this make sense?" Ozzie stared at me, and I could see in his eyes that he was trying to piece it all together so he could understand. "I can draw a diagram if you like," I teased but wouldn't mind going that far.

"Okay. I understand." He nodded. "As much as my neurotypical brain can understand."

"Thank you." I nodded, happy I was able to explain myself.

"Eight o'clock, and I've already learned so much." Ozzie smiled. "Thank you for explaining this stuff to me. You probably have to repeat yourself sometimes, but I'm always listening."

"And thanks for that."

"This coffee sucks by the way."

"I was the first one down! There was no one to help me." I laughed at myself and stood back as Ozzie made a new pot.

By nine o'clock, everyone was present in the kitchen, and I made sure that the boys were all thoroughly caffeinated. Jax yawned, and Steven asked how he'd slept. According to Steven and Nick, the beds were like wooden boards. I didn't mention that my bed was soft and luxurious.

"Oh, fine. Just didn't get enough of it." Jax took a long sip of caffeine and sat by Steven at the kitchen table. Ozzie shot me a nervous glance.

"I told you to be careful," he murmured so only I could hear.

"I am. We both couldn't sleep…nothing happened," I whispered back, and he kept frowning.

"Wait…shit." Jax rose to his feet and brought his mug to the counter where I stood. "We have no food, and I'm hungry," he grumbled and continued to the door. "Designated front-seat attendant. Grocery store," Jax called from the other room, on his way to the truck.

"I guess that's me." I sighed with a heavy eye roll as I left the boys in the kitchen. I caught up to Jax.

"How are you this chipper?" Jax asked, eying my appearance, and I smiled. "You're not a morning person."

"I am today." I shrugged as we approached the truck. "Oh, shoot." I climbed into the front seat and sighed. "I forgot my phone again."

"*Oh, shoot,*" Jax mimicked me. "I did too." My eyes lit up at the idea of another adventure into town.

"Since I redeemed myself last time," I said, "I think it fair to say directions are the front-seat attendant's responsibility."

"It's only fair." Jax eased down the driveway to the street, then looked at me for the first direction.

"Left turn," I said with confidence.

"Last time, you said right."

"For the liquor store. Now we are going to the grocery store."

"This is definitely a mistake, but let's see how you do." Jax turned left. We got even more lost than we had the last time.

"Where even are we?" I laughed and looked out the window at the random fields.

"As if I'd know." Jax shook his head, and we continued to bounce down an uneven gravel road. "This is even worse than last time. What did you do?"

"I used my directional intuition."

"I made a terrible mistake."

"Take it back!"

"Take me to a grocery store!"

"Fine." I closed my eyes and put my hands together. "Turn…right." Suddenly, the truck stopped, and I opened my eyes. I looked at Jax, and he just sat there with his arms crossed, staring at me. Apparently, he was cranky when he was hungry. He nodded his head out my window, to the right. It was a farm pasture, and I started to laugh.

"You're annoying," he grumbled and made a U-turn at the dead-end country road. His surly demeanor remained until we found the grocery store.

———

"Let's just get cereal and milk and call it a day," Jax suggested as he pushed the cart through the produce section and I dropped in bananas.

"Cereal for breakfast, lunch, and dinner?" I chuckled.

"Yeah. We can order pizza," he suggested casually, and I brushed him off.

"For a week? No." I ran around the store, getting together plenty of food for snacks, meals, and s'mores. "Steak!" I beelined for the meat counter. I had to keep reminding myself that I was shopping for four men. I grew up with sisters, and our portions were nothing compared to guys'. I looked into the cart and judged how I did. "Good. Let's go." I smiled at Jax, and we went to check out. I looked over the usual racks in the line displaying magazines, gum, and candy. I picked out a Snickers bar and dropped it in the cart with the rest of our things.

"I can manage a paper bag, Muscle Man." I rolled my eyes when Jax arched a brow at me when we started grabbing our bags at the end of the counter.

"Well, then, after you, European swallow." He motioned his arm toward the doors so I'd go first. Jax carried two bags, and I carried one across the parking lot, and we loaded them into the back of his truck.

"Okay, let's goooo. I'm hungry." He brought his hand up to the gear stick to put the truck in reverse, but I interjected and pushed the Snickers bar into his palm. He paused for a moment and frowned but, a second later, understood and started laughing. I loved his laugh. "Thank you." I sat back in my seat and smiled, happy that he'd actually peeled the wrapper back and started eating the candy bar. After a few bites, he offered me one.

"Oh, no, you need the whole thing."

"Stop being cute." He chuckled and ate the rest of the Snickers. Jax glanced over his shoulder to take a left turn as I looked out my side window. *I don't want to be cute.* Like the ride back from the liquor store, Jax knew the return route and brought us back to the house in half the time.

———

After breakfast, we all got busy setting up our supplies, then dispersed. We got to work quickly, and I spent all of my time in the parlor, alone. I sorted through the many, many sketches I'd done the sleepless night before and selected the ones that fit in the best with the room. Still coming up with ideas, I picked out pieces to keep as focal points and to gain inspiration from. I did a lot of prep work, which was always exhausting.

"Mia." Ozzie opened the door, interrupting Roy Orbison's dramatic crooning. I shook myself out of my creative zone and paused the music.

"Hm?"

"It's seven p.m. Aren't you hungry?"

"Or are *you* guys hungry?" I chuckled, knowing that he probably wanted me to cook. At the thought of it, I suddenly became aware of just how famished I was. I held up my hands and noticed them shaking. "Yep. I'm hungry." Ozzie shot me a comforting smile since he knew about my tremors and how they got worse if I didn't eat enough.

"Alright. What are we having for dinner?" I questioned the kitchen full of boys drinking beer and waiting for me. They all looked up at me, surprised expressions on their faces.

"Oh...we thought..." Nick looked around, then back at me, and I shook my head.

"I'll make steak." I chuckled and fully entered the kitchen. I was craving the tenderloin I'd gotten from the meat counter at the grocery store. "Actually...who's good with a grill?" Jax then took charge of grilling, and I started cooking the rest of our meal. The three other boys headed off to show each other their ideas. I made mashed potatoes, put bread rolls in the oven, and joined Jax on the patio to grill Parmesan-sprinkled broccoli. Back in the kitchen, I stretched to the top of the fridge, where the taller-than-me boys stashed the booze, and brought down the bottle of Jameson.

"Pour me one too, please." Jax smiled as he joined me in the kitchen, so I grabbed two glasses from the cupboard.

"How many fingers?" I asked and looked up to meet his eyes.

"Two." He smirked and leaned in closer. We were the only two in the kitchen, and I became very aware of his large body so close to mine. "Although that's probably three to you." I furrowed my brow, unsure of what he meant, which made him chuckle. He picked up my hand and held our fingers next to each other. *Oooh. His are bigger. Duh.* I felt a flush creep up my cheeks as I stared at his hand, then quickly pulled away from him. I picked up the bottle but immediately put it down—my tremors were bad, and holding the heavy bottle would only exaggerate them. I couldn't lift it in front of him, so I slid the bottle and glasses on the counter toward him. He poured one for himself, then looked back at me.

"How many of my fingers do you want?" He smirked, and I almost dropped dead from the blatant innuendo. I felt myself blush, and I instinctively swallowed and licked my lips, completely taken aback by the novel feeling rising inside me. Jax's gaze darkened as he watched my mouth, and his eyes narrowed once they'd met mine. I took action and grabbed his glass for myself, then took two big steps away and took a long sip of whiskey.

"Easy there, Mia." Jax's voice was low, and his gaze raked up and down my body.

"*Easy there, Jax,*" I mimicked, and he chuckled.

"Come back here."

"Why?"

"Because I said so."

"You know you just confirmed that I won't be cooperative with that response." I crossed my arms, and he shook his head with amusement and went back to the grill. I let out a big sigh. That was horrifying but also the most exciting exchange I'd ever experienced. I was twenty-four, and this was the first time I'd ever been aroused. With my past traumas and mental illness, it made sense to me that no man had ever made me feel…just feel. I was used to it. All of a sudden, one man could make me feel everything. And he was right outside grilling steak. It freaked me out.

I heard the back door open, then swing closed, alerting me that Jax had returned from his post at the grill. "Steaks are done," he announced behind me, and I slowly turned around to face him as he placed the main dish on the counter.

"Ah, perfect. I'm hungry." I eyed the perfectly grilled medium-rare meat with desire. I loved steak and even salivated, but I wasn't about to announce that.

"Me too," Jax said, but he was looking at me. *Oh, hell.* He took a few steps and maneuvered me so I was trapped between him and the counter.

"Jax…" I said in a warning tone. "Why do you look like you're up to no good?" I asked with a narrowed, suspicious stare.

"Because I am." Jax smirked, his eyes dark and alluring. My body betrayed me as my pulse quickened and my cheeks heated once again. He knew it, and both of his arms caged me in as he held on to the counter on either side of me. "But I promise it'll be very good." His body was so close to mine, and the seductive curve of his lips was overwhelming. I couldn't look him in the eye. He then brought one finger up to trace my jaw to my chin, lifting it slightly so I would look at him. I let out a little breath of surprise, which made him smile, and he bent down to kiss me. I couldn't let him and turned my face away.

"Jax, let's not do this…" I spoke softly, unable to get a handle on my nerves. Jax didn't say anything, just used his finger to turn my chin toward him again so I'd face him.

"What?" He frowned and stared at me, surprised or confused or both. "This…"

"Which is *what*?" He sounded a little irritated. He dropped his hand from my face to the countertop so his arms caged me in again.

"Is this…" I said meekly, leaning farther back into the counter, and quickly used my hand to motion between the two of us, then dropped it.

"Can you form declarative sentences, please?" Jax raised his brows, calling me out for being timid. I felt so embarrassed. Seconds ago, I was flustered from the heated way he was looking at me and scared of the new feelings inside me, and a second later, I was having to back up why I'd stopped him as he stared down at me.

"I don't think we should kiss," I said with forced confidence in my voice as I straightened to look him in the eye. I knew he wasn't going to drop it.

"When did you make this decision? Five seconds ago?"

"When faced with the situation of you trying to kiss me…"

"This whole time—" Jax straightened to look down at me, and I heard his voice deepen, ready to be defensive.

"This whole time what?" I narrowed my eyes and crossed my arms.

"I would've already told you if you didn't interrupt me. *This whole goddamn time* you've been teasing me." Jax dropped his hands to his sides so he wasn't caging me in anymore.

"I have not!" My eyes widened at his accusation, as I didn't feel like I'd been teasing him.

"Oh, please. You're always running around being all sexy, trying to piss me off and turn me on."

"*What?*" Jax stood tall, arms folded with an arched brow as he stared down at me, daring me to prove him wrong. *Running around being all sexy? More like floundering around being all awkward.* I thought his accusation was ridiculous. "That's all in your head."

"You flashing me is definitely in my head." I stared back at him as one side of his lip curled into a not-so-amused smirk. That was a hard point to argue. I shook my head, but he nodded as his eyes dropped down to my chest. "Mm-hmm. It's in my head right now."

"So what?" I crossed my arms to feel more secure, wanting him to get to his next point.

"So now here we are, and you are all like, *Jax, let's not do this…*" He tried to mimic my delivery, and I started to get angry.

"Did you forget we don't like each other?" I glared at him, making a dumbass point. I felt so bad and out of my depth with all of the weak explanations I was giving.

"What a dumbass thing to say." He stared down at me. "What have we been doing this whole damn time we've been here? Not liking each other?"

"Ugh. Whatever." I sighed and brought my hands to my head, trying to think of something to say. I dropped my arms to my sides, close to giving up.

"You still think I'm the asshole you first met?" I didn't say anything. I wasn't expecting him to get so real. He took my silence as an affirmative, hurt hidden in his dark eyes that swirled with more anger, and slowly nodded.

"Jax, I…" I didn't know what to say, but I knew I didn't want him to believe I still thought of him only as an asshole.

"If that's how you feel, why are you still here?" he asked simply.

"Why am I here? Seriously?"

"I'd like to know."

"Because I'm an artist with three other colleagues who respect me despite the one asshole making it a hostile work environment."

"If you have a colleague who's such an asshole, making it a hostile work environment"—he leaned closer—"*leave.*"

"*Make me.*" I glared and gave him a shove, but he caught me and didn't let go. I felt a surge of excitement as his hands circled my biceps and squeezed. His fiery eyes were locked on mine, and I felt him start to pull me closer, but we were interrupted.

"Okay!" Ozzie broke through the doorway, and Nick and Steven followed him into the kitchen. Ozzie stepped between us. He pushed Jax away from me while Nick pulled me away from Jax. "What the hell is going on?" Ozzie demanded, but Jax and I hadn't stopped glaring at each other over the shoulders of our friends, eyes filled with heat, not hate. There were too many people in the room, and I felt claustrophobic. I pushed past Nick and dodged the rest of the boys to get out of the kitchen. I ignored Ozzie when he called my name, hurrying to be somewhere alone. I neared the stairs, heading for my room, but decided that it wasn't far enough away. I walked out the front door.

Chapter 17

I paced back and forth outside, not knowing what the hell to do. The only way out was in Jax's pickup truck, so I felt stranded.

My mind couldn't get Jax's face out of my head when he looked like I hurt him. His brows, knotted together as he called me out, loosened. His eyes, piercing and intense as he challenged me, blinked temporarily out of focus. His jaw, clenched and intimidating, relaxed, but only for a moment. It was only a second that I could see true emotion cross over his features. And then his face was stone, and our fight continued. *How did I fuck this up so much?*

I felt tears prick my eyes, but I blinked them away as I focused on even breathing. I wanted him to kiss me. I knew that even though my body wanted it, my mind wasn't ready for it. I knew I'd done the right thing by stopping it, but I had no idea what would happen going forward.

"Mia!" I was startled when the front door swung open, and Nick's siren voice called my name. "Oh. Ha ha. You're right here." He hopped down from the entryway steps to stand by me on the path. "Wanna talk?" I sighed and let him pull me toward a nearby bench. "What happened?" he asked. I glanced into his baby-blue eyes—he looked so eager to help, but I didn't want to tell him what happened.

"Just…" I sighed again, looking off into the distance and running a hand through my hair. "I don't want to talk about it." I dropped my arm onto the armrest and reclined more in the bench seat.

"That's okay. We all called Jax out for being an asshole, so don't worry about that," he assured me like it was going to make me feel better, but guilt twisted my stomach instead.

"What's happening inside?" I looked over at him, nervous that Jax was getting an unfair amount of censure.

"Ozzie is talking to him." I nodded. "Just relax, Mia." Nick patted my back. "You know we all love you being here. We don't want you to leave like Jax said."

"Oh."

"Honestly. You complete our group. Now that we have you, you can't leave us."

"I don't want to leave you guys." I offered a very honest statement, as I didn't know how else to respond.

"I knew I could convince you to stay!" Nick bounced to his feet and smiled proudly. I didn't think it necessary to tell him I was never leaving. "Okay. Let's go! I'm hungry." He grabbed my handed and pulled me to my feet, then into the house.

It was almost nine o'clock by then, and I knew all the boys were hungry. We neared the kitchen, and Nick put his hand on my shoulder to stop me from going further. We could hear the boys talking, and Nick looked at me, nervous about what I might overhear.

"I've told you to back off from Mia." It was Ozzie's authoritative tone, and I obviously knew who he was talking to. I cringed, imagining Ozzie giving Jax the same warnings he'd given me…just from the opposite angle.

"Well, I'm not…*on her*…so…" Jax responded, sounding bored of having to listen to Ozzie's scolding, which I assumed he'd been getting the whole time I was outside.

"Jax, I'm serious," Ozzie replied even more sternly to Jax's flippant response. "Go apologize so we can have dinner."

"I'm not apologizing," Jax stated simply.

Ozzie raised his voice. "You told her to leave!"

"I didn't mean it!" Jax matched his volume.

"Then why the hell say it?"

"Because she was… I—I don't know why. I just don't think straight when I'm around her," Jax defended himself.

Ha, no shit he doesn't think straight. Wait…what the hell does that even mean?

"Apparently." Ozzie scoffed at Jax's weak reasoning.

"You don't know what happened."

"I know Mia is upset. That's all I need to know."

"Well, I'm upset too."

"Why would *you* be upset?" *Because I rejected him.* I didn't know what part of the rejection upset him—was it the first time playboy Jax heard the word "no," or could there be something more?

"Because! Because she… I just thought… But then she…" I held my breath, nervous to hear what Jax had to say about me. "She's not so innocent."

"Jax, Mia is very innocent." I rolled my eyes.

"Well, you wouldn't know! She's like a seductress, I swear," Jax professed rather dramatically, which made me smile. *Me, a seductress. Ha.*

"Oh, God." Ozzie sighed, and I could almost hear his facepalm as I pictured him shaking his head at the absurdity. "You are so wrong."

"Mia," Nick whispered and started tugging on my arm. "Let's go." He pulled me out of hearing range, so I didn't hear what came next in the conversation. I waved Nick off and walked back toward the kitchen.

"I don't believe you," Jax responded to what I'd missed.

"Don't repeat that. Now officially back off." Ozzie gave the order while I held Nick off from dragging me away again. *What's not to be repeated?*

I was getting irritated knowing the topic of their conversation was about me while Nick kept trying to get me away from it. I decided to stop it with my presence.

"But—" Jax was clearly going to keep arguing about backing off but shut up when he saw me.

Ozzie stood at one end of the kitchen, Jax at the other. Steven sat at the table with his headphones in, playing with his phone.

"Hey, guys," I greeted them casually and walked to the stove to get dinner ready. "I'm hungry." I nodded to myself and quickly assembled the food to be reheated.

"Mia..." Ozzie said softly. He studied me to try to gauge my mood. "You okay?"

I realized then that he probably had no idea what had transpired between Jax and me earlier. I glanced to the other end of the kitchen and saw Jax standing against a wall of cupboards and staring at me. Once our eyes met, my mind went to standing against the counter, Jax in front of me with one finger tilting my face up, his lips only inches from mine... then me rejecting his kiss. I quickly looked away from him.

"Yeah. Come help me." I gave my best friend a reassuring smile and told him to find the plates and silverware. Jax approached the counter first, and I took a step back.

"Ladies first," Jax said in a low rumble and put a hand on my lower back to urge me forward. I stopped breathing. I had never felt his hands on me before, and the warmth that came from his simple gesture surprised me. I looked up at him when he didn't back off and saw that the up-to-no-good glimmer in his eyes was back. Before he could see me blush, I pushed his arm away and grabbed a plate. I dished up some steak and the sides I'd prepared. I'd set my plate on the long wooden table and was lowering into my chair when I froze as Jax come up beside me and put his plate next to mine.

"Seriously?" I rolled my eyes and settled into my seat.

"What? You don't want to sit by me?" Jax innocently asked me. I didn't respond. "Oh, that's right. We don't like each other." He stared me down, looking for some kind of reaction. My eyes narrowed as I tried to figure out which Jax I was dealing with—teasing, surly, serious, or asshole. Maybe all of the above.

"Nope," Ozzie said once he'd brought his plate to the table and gestured at me and Jax. "Jax, sit over there." He pointed to the opposite end of the table. Jax stared at me and shifted his jaw, trying to decide if he was going to argue or not. He didn't argue, just wordlessly picked up his plate and carried it to the other end. Even though a long table separated us, we were still face-to-face.

"Thanks for dinner, Mimi!" Nick bounced his way to a seat at the table, followed by Steven. Steven and Ozzie thanked me for dinner too. The three boys' heads swiveled to Jax when he stayed silent.

"Thanks for the broccoli and potatoes, Mia," he said politely but with sarcasm since he was the one to cook the main dish.

"You're welcome," I answered and dug into my meal, starting with the perfectly grilled tenderloin.

Ozzie, Steven, and Nick tried to keep a conversation going, while Jax and I remained silent, shooting looks at each other from across the table. The boys kept looking between us, nervous we were going to break into a fight at any second. Soon, only the scraping and clanking of forks and knives against plates could be heard.

"Okay." Nick spoke up as he sat back in his chair and dropped his utensils. "This awkward tension is killing the vibe."

"We're not being awkward." I defended the both of us, while Jax did the opposite.

"We're being awkward," he admitted.

"So go be awkward somewhere else," Steven said, uncharacteristically getting involved.

"That's not fair," I objected.

"That's fair," Jax admitted, and I shot him an evil glare. As much as I longed to be alone with him again, I really did not want to be alone with him again. Jax responded to my glare with a devious smirk as he stood from the table. He looked way too eager to get me alone. "Let's go be awkward somewhere else, Mia."

"I'm not going anywhere," I objected and remained seated. I looked around to the boys, not wanting to be kicked out. Ozzie, Nick, and Steven all looked torn between kicking me out or letting me stay for dinner. I looked back to Jax, as he was waiting for me. "*You* go be awkward somewhere else."

"Mia, *let's not do this*," Jax said with a sigh like I was being so difficult, his words also mimicking mine from our earlier fight.

"You don't have to be an asshole about it," I bit out, but my death glare had no effect on him.

"What? Isn't that what you expect?" Jax asked with raised brows.

"Alright. Both of you. Out," Ozzie declared as he stood from to table and walked to the back door and opened it.

"Okay," Jax said with a shrug and came over to where I was seated. I made no move to stand, so he grabbed my hand and pulled me to my feet, then to the exit, where Ozzie held the door open.

"Figure it out," Ozzie demanded and gave us both a push outside, then pulled the door closed with a bang, leaving us alone in the gardens.

We were standing outside like two kids on a time-out for fighting. *Whoa…that's exactly what it is.* I looked up at Jax, who looked at me and offered a small smile. I just rolled my eyes as I pulled my hand from his and started walking.

"Mia." Jax sighed and followed me.

"Are you chasing after me?" I taunted and kept walking.

"Oh my God. Shut up." He caught up to me quickly, and I changed course. He groaned with irritation but kept up. "Where are you going?"

"I don't know.'" I sat on one of the many stone benches around the garden. He sat down next to me, so I scooted to the other end. He chuckled and scooted with me so I was sandwiched between him and the armrest. "Just leave me alone, Jax." I sighed and tilted my head back to see the stars.

"I can't." He spoke softly, and I felt his intense gaze on my profile, but I didn't look away from the sky.

"You're the one who told me to leave," I reminded him, waiting for a potential apology.

"Then you said to make you leave… Should I make you?" He smiled, his voice rich and smooth, already up to no good.

"Do you want to?" I arched a brow and looked at his teasing face, which softened a little. He shook his head. "So, you want me to stay?" I asked, clearly wanting to hear him say it.

He rolled his eyes. "Yes, Mia. I want you to stay."

"I'll think about it."

"I can make you stay too." That up-to-no-good look was back.

"You sure you want to work with a seductress?" I smirked, remembering what I'd overheard him say to Ozzie.

"You'll definitely drive me crazy, but I'll try not to take it out on you. You don't know any better." He sighed, goading me.

"What's that supposed to mean?"

"Well, Mia, *usually*, a seductress has plenty of experience with the pleasures of sex. Clearly, not in every case," he explained casually, but his eyes were intense, and I froze. I hesitated in my response, and he raised an eyebrow, waiting. *Oh, no.*

"Um…w-what?" I stuttered, horrified about what he would say next.

"Oh my God. It's true," he said mostly to himself and looked surprised, but then his expression fell into a satisfied smile. I didn't say anything, just shook my head. "Did you not understand me, darlin'? I'll be more clear. I don't think that you've ever known *pleasure*." He saw my cheeks go up in flames and grinned. He leaned in, and I got goose bumps when he spoke softly in my ear. "Tell me I'm right, Mia." He pulled back to further watch my reaction. Bastard. All I could do was barely shake my head, but he nodded. "Tell me." He spoke softly but roughly.

I couldn't just sit there, so I shot up to my feet and ran away like the mature adult that I was.

"*Oswald!*" I yelled as I got close to the house and ran inside. I was breathing heavily from the short burst of exertion, which alarmed Ozzie, who stood from his seat at the kitchen table and ran to me.

"What happened?" He looked me up and down with concern, making sure I was okay. How nice.

"Judas." I glared at him and headed for the other door. *It's time to be alone.* But alas, I didn't get what I wanted, and Ozzie pulled me back into the room. Nick and Steven were staring at me too.

"Mia! What's wrong?" Ozzie looked into my eyes, seeming nervous. I usually never got mad at him, so my outburst was cause for alarm. Then Jax followed me inside.

"Jax…" Ozzie looked at him, still unaware of what had happened other than the fact that Jax had clearly upset me.

"Calm down, Oz," Jax settled him. "I'm just getting to know Mia better." He looked over at me and winked. Ozzie's eyes widened and shot to mine. I realized then that Ozzie sharing my virgin status with Jax was the part I'd missed when eavesdropping. Jax's comment and the scowl on my face alerted Ozzie that Jax had repeated what he'd heard.

"Oh, shit." Ozzie face-palmed, then glared at Jax. "I told you not to repeat that."

"I didn't believe you." Jax shrugged.

"Mia, I'm so sorry," Ozzie apologized, but I didn't feel like forgiving him. I wanted to be alone and turned my back to him. "Where are you going?" he asked as I walked away.

"Don't follow me," I shot over my shoulder as I left them behind. There was one place I wanted to be to be alone, and I started climbing the multiple staircases.

Once I stepped out onto the balcony, I finally felt like I could breathe. I sucked in a deep breath, then sighed heavily, savoring the feeling of being alone. I walked out further and took a seat on the balcony ledge. I tilted my head back so I could gaze up at the night sky and clear my mind. I enjoyed maybe thirty minutes until someone interrupted my solitude.

"I knew I'd find you up here." I heard Jax's deep voice coming from inside, but I didn't turn to face him. "May I join you?"

"No," I denied him, not wanting my alone time to end quite yet.

"I brought whiskey." Jax said the magic word, and I turned around to see if he was telling the truth. He stood at the threshold holding two glasses and a Jameson bottle. "Peace offering."

"You may join me," I said reluctantly. Jax smiled as he approached and sat on the ledge, our positions the same as the night before. "Only because I abandoned my drink downstairs."

"Oh? The glass of two of my fingers of whiskey?" he asked with a smirk as he poured Jameson into my glass. "Here's two more." He held it out to me, but I just crossed my arms and stared at him so he knew to try again. "I may have taken the wrong approach." I nodded, and he started over, but that little smile on his face meant that he found himself quite amusing. "A peace offering, Mia?"

"Offer accepted." I accepted the glass from his hand and took a sip, solidifying the peace. Jax poured a glass for himself. I didn't know what to say, so I kept quiet.

"I don't know where to start." He looked at me for a prompt, but I didn't give him one. He nodded and fiddled with his drink for a few more moments before reconnecting his eyes with mine. "It's not bad to be a virgin," Jax said a little awkwardly. "Don't be embarrassed."

"I'm not embarrassed." I was a little embarrassed.

"Then why are you so upset Ozzie told me?"

"Because it's personal information."

"Why are you secretive?"

"You're asking someone secretive why they're secretive?" I asked. Jax's lip quirked up, and he nodded. "It's a secret."

"Naturally." He chuckled and shook his head. "How about why are you so mysterious?"

"It's a mystery."

"Forget it." He sighed, and I let myself smile. "Mia…" I raised my brows to show that I was listening. "I…I'm sorry about earlier."

"You got mad at me."

"Yeah." He sighed and scrubbed his hand over his face.

"Why?" Jax blinked and stared at me. I didn't know if it was because he thought it was an obvious answer or if it was just annoying to replay our fight. "Ooooh, was this the first time you've ever heard 'no?'" He scowled, and I smiled. "I knew it."

"Judging much?"

"Am I wrong?" I teased, wanting him to admit it.

"Fine." Jax sighed with an eye roll. "You're the only woman who's shot me down." I nodded. "So, why did you?"

"What?"

"Why'd you shoot me down?" Jax asked. I wasn't expecting the question.

"Oh. I just wasn't feeling it," I lied with a shrug.

"I was sure that you were feeling it," Jax shared honestly and looked into my eyes.

"Well, then, I changed my mind," I said as I looked away, not wanting him to see more than I wanted him to as he studied my face.

"Why?"

"Because…we are colleagues. It would be inappropriate," I lied again.

"I don't think that's it, but still a good point." I nodded. "Well, here's to being colleagues," Jax toasted, and I smiled as we clinked glasses together. As exciting and heart-pounding as it was to be around him, it felt so calming and right when we agreed on something.

"Jax…" I quickly changed the subject before he could ask any more questions I'd have to lie about. "I don't think you're the asshole I first met." Jax perked up with my admission.

"Thank you." He smiled, and I felt good about making him look so happy. That's when my stomach growled, making us both crack up—I still hadn't finished my dinner. "Let's go." Jax stood and offered his hand to help me hop down from the ledge, and I followed him inside.

We returned to the kitchen and rejoined the rest of the group. Ozzie pulled out my plate from the microwave and handed it to me. No one mentioned any of the drama of the night, and the boys kept me company while I ate my dinner at the kitchen table. It had been an emotional night, and I felt exhausted, so I managed to eat my serving of steak and a bite of mashed potatoes before I said good night and went to my room.

"Mia." I heard Ozzie's voice behind me as I walked into my room, but I pushed the door closed, leaving him on the other side. I bounced onto my bed and lay on my back, staring at the ceiling. "Permission to enter?"

"Enter at your own risk." I heard my door click open, then closed, and felt the mattress dipping in weight next to me.

"I'm sorry," Ozzie offered, but I didn't say anything, so he lay on his back next to me and waited. I knew he wouldn't leave until I acknowledged him.

"You promised not to tell anyone, and you told Jax," I said.

"I'm sorry. It's not a bad thing, Mia," he said and sat up, pulling me with him so we both were sitting on my bed.

"I know. Still, you said you wouldn't tell anyone." I gave his shoulder a good smack with the back of my hand.

"I'm just looking out for you," he said. I gave him a sidelong glare. "Mia, I'm sorry I told him, but he needed to know."

"Why the hell would he need to know?"

"Be real with me, Mia. You two have been getting…close. Like he-made-a-move-on-you close."

"He told you about that?"

"No, but you just did."

"Clever." I ran my hand through my hair, feeling awkward. "You shouldn't have told him, but you're forgiven."

"Mia." Ozzie dropped his head with a sigh before straightening. "You weren't being honest with me. He wasn't either." He stopped me when he saw that I was about to object. "We both know you two were getting closer. Jax is a lot and didn't know how innocent—I mean, inexperienced—you are. Maybe he would've come on stronger, and it would've freaked you out." I was quiet as I thought through his reasoning. "You know I'm right."

"Ugh. Whatever." I dropped to my back again.

"Mia…he thought you were a seductress." I glanced over to where Ozzie was looking down at me with a small smile. I couldn't help the chuckle that rose from my throat, and I brought my arm up to cover my eyes as I started to laugh. Ozzie joined in with me.

I finally came up for air to defend myself. "I never tried to be!"

"Oh, I know that." Ozzie twisted to lay on his front next to me.

"*The* Jackson Caine thinking that *I* am a seductress." I shook my head.

"I should've caught on to it sooner." Ozzie sighed. "You're a beautiful woman, and he's…Jax."

"Yeah," I acknowledged, understanding his view.

"But…if you like him…"

"I don't like him," I lied.

"Okay. That's probably best. Don't need you two weirdos stirring up more drama." He chuckled and shook his head, like that would never happen. It would happen.

"I'm not a weirdo," I huffed, but Ozzie shot me a look to challenge that, and I laughed.

"So…I'm off the hook?" Ozzie asked hopefully, and I glanced over at him and his sweet best-friend smile.

"Yeah." I looked up to the ceiling.

"Maybe best friend bonus points for looking out for you…?" I glanced over to him again with an even wider grin.

"You're pushing it, Oswald Bishop, but…fine."

"I love you, you know."

"I love you too." We had a best friend hug, and he drifted off down the hall and to his room. "Weird-ass night," I muttered to myself as I readied for bed.

Chapter 18

We all had a long, tiring day, as the beginning of a project was always the hardest—expanding creativity, making decisions, and starting with a blank canvas could be maddening. The five of us were so engrossed that we hardly even talked to each other until the sun went down and we all got hungry. The boys decided to order pizza while Ozzie made margaritas.

We gathered on the patio with our pizza boxes, and I picked up a slice of pepperoni. Nick and Ozzie complained about difficulties with their parts of the project. Jax and Steven had their own conversation going as we all sat around a steel fire pit. I didn't have much input since I was having a fine time myself—I was making good progress in the parlor. Stress-free, I zoned out and enjoyed my food.

"So, Mia." Nick got my attention from across the fire pit. "Do you miss Minnesota?"

"Not even a little." I chuckled at the thought, then realized that my reaction might seem odd. "I mean… I miss some things."

"How are you liking SF?" Steven asked.

"I love it, really." I felt my face light up as I answered.

"You haven't dated since being here, have you?" Nick asked me with a tilt of his head.

"Well, we know she's not on any apps," Jax reminded everyone.

"No." I shook my head. "My life here pretty much begins and ends with you guys."

"How was the dating scene in Minnesota?" Steven asked.

"Um, it was okay." *I wouldn't know*. I shrugged and sipped my margarita.

"Ooh! Worst date. Nick goes first," Jax suggested and sat up straighter, apparently already aware of Nick's worst date.

"This is such a boring story." Nick groaned and dropped his head back, but the guys heckled him, urging him to tell it again. "Fine. I matched with this girl on Tinder, and we met up at a bar. She showed up and kept calling me Mark. I was like, no, I'm Nick. We were both pretty hammered, and she kept calling me Mark, so I just went along with it."

"Why would you go along with it?" I laughed, already loving his anecdote.

"She was hot." He shrugged. "So we had a fun time, fooled around in the bathroom, and she invited me back to her place, but before we got into our Uber, the *real* Mark called her. She freaked out, said I was twenty-first-century Ted Bundy, and jumped into the car without me. There was a cop like right fucking there, and he questioned me on the sidewalk."

"Oh, no." I laughed despite his sour expression. "Did you get any jail time, twenty-first-century Ted Bundy?"

"No." Nick pouted.

"My worst date…I got stood up once," Steven shared with us.

"Awww, no." I frowned, not liking that Steven, the sweetest man ever, had been stood up.

"Yeah. But then I realized I'd told her the wrong restaurant. So I just went home." He shrugged, and we all laughed because *that was so Steven*. "Jax," he prompted.

"My worst date. Uhh…" Jax sat back and squinted, searching his memory. "I haven't been on a date in years." Nick started to slow clap for him, and the others joined in. I was having fun. "Okay! I went on a date with this girl, Ellen—she was beautiful but was sooo boring."

"That's it?"

"Yeah."

"How did it end?" I asked with a small smile, predicting a happy ending.

"I called her an Uber and said take care." Jax shrugged, and my smile widened. Jax turned to the next man in the rotation. "Ozzie?"

"I don't know. I'm boring. Oh! This girl in college heard that I had lived in England, so she messaged me on Insta...no, that wasn't around, Facebook. She asked me out, so I met her at the usual college bar, and she was *so* disappointed that I didn't have a British accent that she ditched me." We had a good laugh at that one, and Ozzie didn't call me out to go next.

"Mia's turn!" Nick announced.

I wished I had already come up with a story of my own to share, but I'd been too distracted learning more about my colleagues. I honestly hadn't been on a date, a real date, and jumped into a story I wasn't prepared to follow through with. "Uh...I once went on a date not knowing it was a date. Like, this guy invited me to a party, but the party left once I got there."

"Ooooh, that's kinda smooth!" Nick laughed, and I nodded. *And then he wouldn't let me leave.*

"So, how'd the date go?" Steven asked, and with everyone engaged in the conversation, I felt pressured to answer.

"It was—um. He—uh... I didn't—um." I swallowed and felt the forced jovial expression on my face stiffen as my eyes moved out of focus and my mind jumped back a few years. I remember being so excited to be invited to a party. I was newly diagnosed with bipolar, and I wanted to try to be a normal twenty-one-year-old, having fun. When I'd arrived, it was just the man who'd invited me and a few of his friends. After ten minutes, all of his friends left. I wanted to leave, too, but he wouldn't let me. People talked about fight or flight. They never talked about freeze. "It was okay." I shrugged and sipped my margarita, hoping someone else would move the conversation along.

"Well, props to him for pulling that off." Nick laughed but I didn't move. I was able to feel the tears I'd shed that night run down my face, and I was worried real tears weren't far behind. He had gotten rough with me, and I'd frozen. He'd pushed me around and pinned me down. I had just cried and waited for it to end. Considering the force he used, it was a good thing that I didn't fight back. Sitting at the fire with my friends around me now, I felt my lungs contract and my brows furrow together, remembering the feeling of his hands in my hair, pulling my head down to his lap. I felt my mind falling down into those memories, the ones I'd buried and struggled daily to keep there. I knew it was too late. Once my mind fell, those memories took over.

"Yeah." I stared at nothing in front of me, then rose to my feet. "I'll be back." I forced my voice to sound casual and moved my eyes around the circle but avoided looking at any of their faces. I hurried to get inside.

I went into the quiet kitchen and leaned against the cabinets, my whole body trembling, and I sucked in deep breaths to calm myself and to hold back the tears. I cursed the world and how a fun conversation with colleagues could end up with me isolating in the kitchen. I was so happy to be a part of the group, so why did my past have to drag me down into the darkness of those memories? Sharing stories around the fire, I truly didn't expect a panic attack, but here I was, having a panic attack. I felt my heart rate speed up as I squeezed my eyes shut, trying to force out the vivid memories. It wasn't just the visions in my head. I could still feel him and knew that I always would. That touch would never go away. I could still feel the sting on my scalp from when he'd fisted his hand in my hair and shoved my head down on his lap. I could still feel him in my mouth and throat. I could still feel the panic I'd felt when I couldn't breathe and the fear that jolted through my body when I blacked out. *Note to self: stop closing your eyes when having a panic attack.* As the sensations of the memories came back, I started to feel like I was choking and my jaw locked as nausea built up. I couldn't breathe; I was suffocating all over again.

"Mia?" Jax's soft voice sounded from behind me, and his hand gently touched my arm. But I wasn't in that kitchen anymore—I was in the darkness of my own mind. I recoiled from his touch in terror, trying to get away. I stumbled into the corner counter and sank to the floor, cowering against the cupboards. I covered my face with my hands, still scared and in my head. I heard Jax curse under his breath, and he knelt next to me.

"Hey, Mia. You're safe. Okay?" He stayed next to me on the floor while I sat, petrified with fear. "You're safe."

I still trembled, and tears kept pouring down my cheeks, but my breathing was slowly getting under control.

"Can you lower your hands?" he urged me gently, and I did but didn't open my eyes. "Look at me." I shook my head. "Please."

With another deep breath, I let my eyes blink open. Jax was kneeling in front of me, close but not touching me. He studied my features, searching for an answer. I looked away, not fully in the present. I covered my mouth with my shaking hand and waited for the bile to subside. *Swallow. Swallow. It's not real. Breathe. You're not suffocating. Breathe.*

"What just happened?" he asked gently after waiting for my body to relax. I removed my hand from my mouth and dropped my head against the cupboard, then gave him a look to say, *As if I'd tell you.*

"I'm okay," I murmured, still avoiding his eyes. He brought a hand to my forehead and felt cold sweat.

"I should get Ozzie."

"No. I'm okay. Really." I looked into his eyes, to hopefully show him that I was okay even though I wasn't. "Um, bad pizza."

"Don't," Jax gently chided me for lying, and I knew he was right. I took his offered hand in mine. He helped me slowly stand.

"Thanks." My gratitude came out in a whisper as I felt the intense vulnerability from Jax witnessing the dark part of me that I so desperately kept hidden. He nodded, still studying me.

"Want to go back or…?"

"I don't know." I tried weighing the option of returning to the group versus going to my room, alone. I had regained my bearings, but those dark memories weren't far off and would too easily come back if I were alone with my thoughts. "I should go back." I sucked in a breath, still feeling the effects of the panic attack, which were subsiding but still too close. Jax stepped toward the door but paused when I didn't follow. I didn't say anything as I walked further into the kitchen. I grabbed a fresh glass from the cupboard, then the bottle of Jameson, and brought them both to the kitchen table, ready to sip on some whiskey, alone and dejected. I heard a couple clings and a light thud. When I looked up, Jax was settling into a chair a couple spots away.

"Jax, you don't have to…" I felt extremely awkward as he sat with me. Back home, no one wanted to be around my problems. Something about intense emotional breakdowns made people uncomfortable…I understood. If I wanted comfort, I'd have to insist, and even then, they'd withdraw. No one wanted to have to beg for attention, so I got used to being alone.

"Have to what?" he asked simply as he took the Jameson bottle, poured some into my glass with his long arm, then poured some for himself.

"You don't have to stay with me," I said softly and picked up my glass to sit back in my chair, pulling my legs up onto the seat. "I'm okay. You can go back to the party."

"Do you want to be alone?" he asked with a concerned frown, and I could tell that he was genuinely asking me—not just hoping for me to confirm that he could leave with no guilt. I just stared at him, surprised, not knowing what to say. "Okay, uh, Mia, I'm sorry. I just thought… I'm sorry. I'll go," he said awkwardly and stood.

I put out my leg to get in the way of him leaving. "Do you want to stay?"

"That's why I sat down…" He frowned, and I smiled.

"Then take a seat, Mr. Caine." He was going to smile back, but his face turned into an adorable scowl.

"Not if you call me that."

"Jax." I was still smiling. I would've been happy if any of the boys reacted like he did. That it was Jax…it was even more meaningful.

"Was it talking about the date?" His voice was gentle as he sat back down. My mind was sucked back into why we were in the kitchen to begin with. I froze, and he sensed my answer. "Do you want to talk about it?" Again, he asked so gently and genuinely. I shook my head. "Okay." He nodded and took a sip of whiskey, still watching me over the rim of the glass. I could tell that he was seeing more than I wanted to give away. I didn't know if it was because he actually looked when most people looked away, or if there was something in him that could see deeper inside me than anyone else ever could—probably both. He could tell I was feeling very vulnerable and that my head was still in a bad place. "My older brother, Joe—don't get any ideas because he's not sugar-daddy old—he lost his virginity…guess where."

"Ha. Motel. Prom night." I leaned my head against the chair back and looked at him, appreciative of the conversation change.

"Psh. How basic. Use your imagination."

"Okay." I laughed and thought through options. "Golden Gate Bridge."

"That's not even believable. Come on, you have to guess."

"Alcatraz?" My guess made him lift his brows and look weirded out. "What?" I said. "That's believable. There's plenty of places to get it on."

Jax couldn't hold in his hearty laugh. "No, freak."

"Playground?"

"Mia! Think of the children!"

"Under the bleachers of a high school football field!"

"Closer."

"Concession stand? Behind the popcorn maker?" He shook his head, and I kept guessing.

"Forget it. You'll never guess."

"Then tell me!"

"His bedroom." He smirked. I laughed but didn't want to accept it being so simple.

"Under the bed?"

"How would that even work?" He shook his head. "No. In his bed." He smiled as he finished off his whiskey.

"Wow. All this time, I thought there was going to be a good story. Basic."

"I never said it was a good story." Jax snickered, knowing he had led me on. "He did have sex on a playground, though. Guess when."

"Last week." That got him laughing again, and I smiled, savoring the sound.

"High school."

"Ugh. This Joe has boring stories." I sighed, then glanced at him with a smirk. "But I bet you don't."

"Naturally."

"Tell me!"

"Mmm, no. Maybe when you're older." He patted my head with a condescending but somehow sweet smile and stood, picking up both of our empty glasses. "Return to the party?" He could tell that I really didn't want to. "Don't you want s'mores?" I instantly stood and went to the cupboard.

"Yes," I said as I pulled out all of the ingredients, my past traumas forgotten for the moment. He refilled our glasses with two of his fingers of Jameson and followed me back to the patio.

"S'mores for the lads," I announced and put down the marshmallows, chocolate, and graham crackers before taking my seat. I looked over to Ozzie and saw that he was clearly concerned and suspicious about my disappearance with Jax. I gave him a reassuring smile, then a bigger one, but he kept giving me that look, so I made some funny faces. Surprisingly, none of the boys questioned our absence. Probably because of the empty pitcher of margaritas and the empty beer bottles I spotted littered around each of them.

The night went on with fun and games, but I went to my room to go to bed first. I was looking through my duffel on the bed as I brushed my teeth when Jax opened the door. I startled a little but then rolled my eyes when I saw him and went to spit in the sink.

"I could've been changing." I glared at him when I reentered my room.

"I know." He smiled and sat on my bed. His eyes then traveled up and down my body, and I refrained from shifting around awkwardly. "Is that Kurt Cobain?" He reached out, grabbed my shirt, and pulled me closer to him. I was wearing a comfy oversized T-shirt with an image of Kurt underwater from the *Nevermind* photo shoot, which I often wore to bed. Oh, and nothing else but Calvin Klein cotton underwear.

"Yes." I swatted his hands away, as he'd clearly just realized that there wasn't much else underneath.

"You have long legs for being short."

"I'm not short. You're tall." I crossed my arms and stared at him, about to ask him why he was in my room, but he asked me something before I could.

"What happened in the kitchen?" he asked softly and stared into my eyes.

"I'm not going to talk about that," I said firmly, and he studied me. "Why not?"

"Because I don't want to." He was about to ask me again, so I covered my ears. "Stop. I want to forget it."

"Are you okay now?" He was being genuine, like how perfect he was earlier, and I wished I could answer his question honestly. Of course I wasn't okay, but…he made it okay.

"Yes. Thanks." I nodded, and Jax sat there longer, watching me. I shifted awkwardly, not wanting him to ask any more questions. "I'm going to go to sleep now, so…"

"Thanks for asking, but I'd rather sleep in my own bed." He smirked and stood up, knowing that's not what I meant.

"I doubt that." I smirked back at him, and he arched a brow in warning. "Good night." I smiled and pushed him out into the hallway and closed my door.

With a deep sigh, I took my evening meds and crawled into bed. I let my mind unwind. Jax had witnessed my panic attack. I hated that he'd seen that. He'd witnessed a snippet of who I really was—which was something I hid from the world at all costs. I hated feeling exposed. The level of vulnerability and rejection I'd faced throughout my life was relentless and had left me with a constantly breaking heart. I despaired over that for a while as I stared up at the ceiling until a new thought sparked in my head. Jax *helped* me. Every panic attack I'd had before, the presence of anyone else heightened my fear. Jax should've frightened me and made me sob uncontrollably. I would've kicked him away. I would've remained on the kitchen floor for another hour. His touch had startled me when I didn't know it was him, but then I'd heard his voice, and he'd *helped* me.

I was a second away from puking my guts out, but I didn't. He came near me, and I didn't run, hide, or kick—I even wanted him to be close. The intensity of my panic attack symptoms was quickly washed away as he stayed on the floor with me. *Huh. Weird.* I knew that there was something unique to him that made me feel safe. His actions weren't actions those of someone who was foreign to that level of emotion. How did he know not to touch me? How did he know what to say? There was something there, and I knew it.

Jax helped me come down from that intense, painful place in my head that had me trapped. I knew it was because he truly wanted to…not out of obligation as a human, like when someone helps you because they want to be a good person. So many people approached me like that, and it was so damn obvious. That Jax genuinely wanted to be there… That blew my mind. I pushed all of that angst aside so I could relax, and I hoped the effects of my medications would quickly drag me into an unbothered sleep.

But the darkness of my past was still there. While it had briefly been held off by friends and s'mores, it crept its way from the corners to the front of my mind as I struggled to sleep. Trauma took over every sensation of my body. I closed my eyes and allowed myself to cry. I missed Jax and wanted him with me. I lay there, lonelier than ever. I hardly slept at all.

Why can't it be good memories that possess my conscience and self-esteem? Why is it that the most painful traumas of my life follow me wherever I go? I'd actually really like to know! What cruelty plays these experiences in my head on repeat? Why, when I'm recovering and trying to find happiness, do those images and feelings invade and tear me apart all over again?

Why, when I'm sitting around a fire with my new friends and colleagues, do I feel hands all over me?

Why, when I'm just having a cup of coffee, do I remember how it felt when that man forced his fingers inside me?

Why, when I'm walking my dog, do I see that man on top of me?

Why, when I'm trying to sleep at night, do I see his face and hear him panting in my ear and feel his hot breath on my neck?

Why, when I'm driving in my car, do I feel those tears and sobs on my face after I said no?

Why, when drawing at the studio, do I see that popcorn ceiling I stared at, hoping for it to be over?

Why, when I'm laughing with my family, do I want to throw up, remembering that man forcing me to choke?

Why, when I'm existing, do I feel crippling shame?

I already experienced it! Isn't that enough?

Universe, you sick, sick bastard.

Chapter 19

It had been a rocky first few days at the mansion, to say the least, but the rest of the week went by smoothly as we all got more intense with our projects. I slaved away in the parlor, demanding perfection from myself to honor our employer's maternal lineage. We were all exhausted and did a hundredth walk-through to critique ourselves. Finally, we were satisfied and brought our stay at the mansion to an end.

———

For the road trip back, I beat everyone to the truck and sat in the front seat again. We were halfway home from the mansion when my body reminded me that I was a disaster—as if I could ever forget. The lack of sleep during the week had built up and exaggerated my nausea, a side effect of my medication, tenfold. I'd managed to operate effectively as we finished our work and packed our gear, even though nausea had a crippling effect on my body. The car ride made it worse.

"Um, Jax..." I said quietly as the truck cruised down the road, "can you please pull over?"

"Why?" He looked at me like my request was bizarre, and I guess it was. We were on a country highway in the middle of nowhere.

"Can you?"

"No, we can't pull over here." He didn't look at me and kept driving. Panic started swelling up as physical sickness signs warned my body. *Here come the mouth sweats.*

"Jax, *please*, pull over." He stared at me, studying my features to gauge what was wrong, but I just stared back with raised brows. He slowed to a stop on the side of the road.

"Mia, what's—" I stumbled out of the truck and ran to the back so no one could hear or see me. I heard Ozzie, sitting in the middle back seat, tell Jax to help me, and I hoped to God he didn't as I dropped to my knees in the dirt and puked over the side rail. *Fuck, that's gross.* I stumbled away from the rail and dropped back, falling on my ass to rest. "Mia?" I tensed when I heard Jax squat next to me. I bent my legs and rested my elbows on my knees as I took calming breaths with my hands covering my face. He gently took my wrist and pulled away a shaky hand to see my face, but I looked away. "Hey. What's wrong?"

"Just um...sick." He went to the truck and returned with a bottle of water. "Thanks." I took it and tried to rehydrate. It was awkward, him seeing me like that—especially when I saw him notice my shaking hand as I tried to hold the bottle to my lips. Jax just sat with me and held up the end of the bottle to steady it so I could drink. I finished half the bottle, stopping when it made my stomach queasy. After he set down the bottle, he brought his sweatshirt sleeve to my mouth and wiped away the water droplets that clung to my lips. I looked at him and saw that his eyes were so tender and kind, which warmed my heart. My mouth curved at the side when he held up a piece of gum, and I took it. "How much longer is the drive?"

"Hour and a half," he answered gently, and dread filled my whole body.

"Oh, *fuck*," I groaned and tipped over to my side on the ground.

"What's wrong?"

"Nothing," I said as a reflex.

"Don't. Mia, *what's wrong?*" Jax wouldn't accept a lie, which I respected, but I still couldn't answer truthfully.

"Um. Car sickness." Just knowing there was an hour and a half of torture made me even more nauseous, worrying we'd have to pull over again.

"Why don't I believe you?" Jax stared at me, and I wanted to disappear.

"Because I'm lying," I mumbled, giving him some truth.

"Mia." Jax sighed. "What can I do for you?"

"Literally nothing at all." I took a deep breath as I closed my eyes. "Just leave me here. That would be best."

"I'm not doing that."

"You sure?"

"Yes, I'm sure. Come on," he said more forcefully, and I knew I had to get up, but I didn't want to.

"Don't get mad at me if I tell you to pull over in an hour."

"I won't. Let's go before we get hit by a car," he said quietly. "Ready?" He waited for my head nod and offered his hand to pull me to my feet.

"You okay, Mia?" Ozzie asked me with underlying anxiety once I climbed back into the truck. He hadn't gotten out of the truck himself because he was stuck in the middle seat. If he'd gotten out, he would've brought the boys with him to see me puking, and I would've had a very grossed-out audience. I was thankful that he hadn't.

"Yeah...um, car sickness," I said as I got situated back in the truck and clicked together my seat belt.

I was sitting sideways in the chair, leaning against the seat and hugging my legs. It was the best position possible in a car to avoid aggravating the nausea. I felt Jax's eyes continue to glance my way with curiosity.

We had only one hour left when my nausea threatened to be too much. *Please don't puke. Please don't puke.* My mouth started to water. *Fuck—I'm going to puke.*

"Jax..." I whispered with my face pressed against the seat cushion. He looked over at me, already knowing what I needed, and pulled over. The scene unfolded as it had before—I stumbled out of the truck, puked over the metal barricade, then Jax comforted me. He didn't ask any further questions, but his constant concern and curious glances didn't go unnoticed—but did go unanswered. We got back into the truck, and I curled back against the seat.

The boys in the back started complaining about hunger. Steven wanted Subway, Nick wanted Taco Bell, and Ozzie wanted McDonald's. Jax was the tiebreaker, and we stopped at McDonald's.

"Happy Meal for Mia?" Jax teased, and the boys laughed.

"Ha ha." I rolled my eyes but hesitated. "Yeah." The boys all thought that it was the funniest thing, but a cheeseburger Happy Meal sounded awesome on my empty stomach. "Whatever. You don't get to play with my toy," I said, all haughty, and picked up the cheap plastic figurine of Batman from the box.

"Sharing is caring," Jax teasingly scolded me.

"I'm Batman." I held up the toy to my face and tried to mimic his iconic deep voice.

"That was the worst Batman I've ever heard." Jax shook his head. I pouted, which prompted him to reconsider. "Actually, you're the second. Nick is the worst."

"Hey!" came Nick's high-pitched voice from behind us, proving Jax's point.

Relief washed over me as we pulled up in front of the studio. Once Jax put the truck into park, I jumped out and ran inside. I had been holding in the contents of my stomach for as long as I could and was grateful when I made it to the studio bathroom. I puked my guts out, then washed my hands and mouth in the sink. After a deep breath, I opened the door. Of course, Jax was right there staring at me with that constant worried and confused frown. He didn't say anything, so I didn't say anything and just left. I drove straight home and slept for fourteen hours. When I woke up, the nausea was gone and I could function again.

Chapter 20

During the middle of the next busy week, the boys were planning to have a party in the studio, which I figured was a bad idea. With every room full of our artwork and supplies, I wanted to say, "Don't let a drunk crowd in," but that's just my opinion.

I was in the kitchen making coffee when I heard them talking about it, and my heart dropped. I hated parties. I knew that seemed antisocial and lame, but it was true. Especially when I was the only stranger in a crowd of friends.

"Did I hear 'party?'" I asked casually as I breezed back into the studio.

"Party? Where?" Jax asked as he looked around the room, then back at me, a sly little smile on his lips when he shrugged and leaned against the couch. I rolled my eyes, like I didn't think he was adorable, and looked to the rest of the boys in the room for an answer.

"Yes, you did," Steven said as he jumped up to bring his used brushes into the drying room.

"That's cool. Have fun." I acknowledged them politely and then settled into one of the leather chairs with my coffee. I sat sideways on my knees so I could face the boys at their stations and act like I was ignoring Jax on the couch.

"Mia, of course, you're invited." Ozzie chuckled as he turned away from his easel, already knowing that I wouldn't want to go.

"Yeah, Mimi! You can meet all of our friends," Nick said enthusiastically and rolled, kneeling on his chair, over to where I sat. Jax then groaned as he dropped his head against the back of the couch. "Ignore him." Nick rolled his eyes.

"Obviously." I smirked, not looking at Jax and sharing a chummy moment with Nick. I asked them when it was.

"Friday."

"Ohh. Shoot. I'm busy Friday. Ah, well, you'll have to tell me all about it on Monday." I shrugged, hoping they wouldn't press too hard for my attendance.

"You have plans?" Jax asked like it was a shock.

"Do you guys hear that?" I asked Nick and Ozzie. "That really annoying sound coming from that direction?" I waved my hand around in the direction of the couch, still not acknowledging him.

"Oh, come on, that was a fair shot." Jax stuck up for himself.

"Seriously, do you guys not hear that?" I leaned toward the two friendly boys and asked them again while looking around the room as if searching for the source. Ozzie, Nick, and Steven were there to validate my humor with their laughter. I soon returned to the kitchen to refill my coffee.

———

We weren't far into our workday on Friday when the boys huddled around the couch and chairs and began planning how to organize the studio for the party.

"So…how do you expect to have a crowd of party people in here and not get anything ruined?" I asked with crossed arms, skeptical of their plan.

"We lock the doors to the hallway rooms—" Ozzie began.

"Except the bedroom." Nick snickered, but we ignored him.

"And we push all of our stuff to the side and cover it. Easy," Ozzie finished, then eyed me as I looked around the room. "Mia…you're coming to the party, right?"

"No, but I look forward to some good anecdotes on Monday."

"Seriously, we want you to come." Ozzie got more serious, as he knew I really had no intention of attending.

"Of course you're coming!" Nick whined, and Steven joined in.

"She said she's not coming. We should respect that," Jax backed me up, which I appreciated, even though he was still being an asshole.

"No way. Mia, we are having a party. You are a part of the 'we,' and *we* all need to be here," Ozzie reasoned. It was a nice thing to say, but I wasn't convinced.

"Yeah, and you can meet our friends," Steven piped in, but I still wasn't warming up to the idea.

"You're all a big friend group from school. Everything is going to be based on insider information. Like, 'Hey, guys, remember that one time in college when Chad did something douchey at Chi-O-Delta-Mega-Pizza-Pie?'" I did a poor imitation of a frat boy, which earned me laughs.

"That's very true. Good point." Jax nodded as he further encouraged my absenteeism.

"Or, like, 'And remember when Jax was a jackass like always? Memories, bro!'" I ignored Jax and got the guys cracking up again. He just scowled.

"Don't worry. They'll love you. Everyone loves you!" Nick tugged at my arm like a little boy, and I laughed, feeling the warmth of their encouragement.

"Seriously, Mia doesn't want to come, so she's not coming." Jax smirked at me, and I couldn't stand that he was agreeing with me. I couldn't give him the satisfaction.

"You know what." I sighed, and they all looked at me. "I'm a part of the team, and I should come, so I will." Ozzie, Nick, and Steven all showed their excitement and kept reassuring me that it would be fun. I glanced at Jax, and he still had that scheming smirk on his face. *Did I just fall for reverse psychology?*

"Settled. Mia, you're assigned to the liquor run," Jax ordered, and I rolled my eyes, not about to buy all their liquor.

"Oh. Shoot. I don't have my ID." I shrugged, and Jax walked away, heading to my purse. "Excuse you!" I hurried over to retrieve it.

"Aha." He smiled when he took out my ID and handed my purse back to me. "Nice fake, Mia. Looks just like you," Jax said as he held on to my driver's license. His little smirk made it obvious he was trying to provoke me.

"Think the liquor store will buy it?" I asked hopefully, playing along instead of fighting back.

"Let's go find out." He pushed me out of the studio to go to the liquor store with him.

"You can stay in the car. I'll crack the window," Jax tried to tell me when we got there. I just laughed at him and walked ahead into the store. He grabbed a whole cart to stock up, and I followed him through the aisles putting random bottles in the cart, which he would immediately put back, just to annoy him.

"The fuck is this?" he scolded me, and I smiled when I saw the bottle he was holding up. "We aren't getting this."

"Sorry, I thought that was your drink." I shrugged. It was the big pink bottle of Kinky vodka. After he put it back, I hunted down my favorite añejo tequila and went to join Jax at checkout.

"What did you get? Is it expensive?" he asked, but I'd already put it on the counter.

"Very." He rolled his eyes but still bought it for me. The booze was crammed into two boxes, and I went to grab one.

"Don't even try. I got it." Jax chuckled, but I held on to the box. "Are you going to grip it by the husk?" he teased, as I'd said that to him before. I backed off and let him carry it.

"You're going to change before the party, right?" He glanced at my body on our ride back.

"Why?"

"Well, are you?"

"Why?"

"You should."

"Why?"

"Stop saying why. You sound like my three-year-old nephew."

"I bet he's adorable."

"He is. Wait—shut up."

"What should I wear, then?"

"I don't know. Your wardrobe is like a ten-year-old going to arts-and-crafts camp." He was trying to insult me, but I burst out laughing. That was the greatest insult I'd ever gotten. "It's true!"

"Jax, I have way more to my wardrobe than what you've seen." I let my laughter die down.

"Then let me see."

"Ha ha. No."

"Too bad." He smiled and he pulled up to my apartment, and we got out of the car.

"Okay." I stopped him before I opened my apartment door. "You're not picking out what I wear, just to be clear." He nodded, and I let him in.

"Weird. It's still Ozzie's apartment," Jax mused as he looked around the living area.

"He left me most of the furniture." I shrugged. The space hadn't changed much since I'd moved in. All I'd added was an oriental rug for the love seat and couch. Even though I was an artist, I didn't care about decorating, which left my place sparse and awkward. Still, I thought the natural light that flooded through the tall windows and lit the hardwood floor made it warm and comfortable.

"All you brought was a record player."

"And records."

"Ooh." He started perusing my collection, which I had stacked on the floor in the corner. I hurried to my bedroom, then locked the door so I could clear out the bipolar paraphernalia from my room by shoving the pharmacy of medications into my top dresser drawer.

"Uh, knock-knock." I heard Jax from the other side of my door. "Miss Mysterious, may I enter your domain?" I went to the door to unlock it but didn't wait for him and went to my closet. I was alone with him in my private space, but he wasn't making me nervous, only excited.

I rested my hip against the closet doorway and watched him enter my room, his subtle swagger still there in the few steps he took to meet me at my closet. "So, this is Mia's room."

His eyes scanned the room, then he looked at me and smiled.

"Yep." I grabbed his arm and pulled him into my closet before he could look around more. It was a walk-in, which I was thankful for, considering the storage space required to fit my clothing and Jax, the giant.

"Ooh, you're either very excited to get me into the closet with you or you are distracting me from looking around your room," Jax teased, and I didn't expect him to catch on to that.

"I'm just ready to get this process of picking out my outfit going," I lied.

"So, both." Jax smiled and winked at me, then turned to face the long racks of clothing. "Damn, shopaholic." He chuckled. Over the last four years, when I was lonely and depressed, my comfort was online shopping—and my weakness when manic. I was left with a kickass selection of clothes, though. Jax skimmed through the dresses hanging from the racks, all colors and textures represented. I watched his hand run along the fabrics, sometimes pulling one out to see it better. A yellow linen summer dress, a blue tulle, a pink collared knit, two of the same silk dress but one in black and the other in a turquoise tiger print, and thirty more. The majority of them still had the tags attached. Back home, I'd be staring at my laptop screen with bloodshot eyes, scrolling through designer websites, and clicking "add to cart" at four in the morning— everything in excess and out of my budget. When I was hypomanic, erratically spending lots of money was a usual symptom. I would spend thousands of dollars at a time until I went broke. "Mia, you have a Dior gown?" Jax glanced at me over his shoulder with raised brows. "Where were you going? The Oscars?"

"Oh, ha, yeah. Um, that was a hand-me-down from a friend. She's loaded," I lied, and he went back to looking through my closet. That was the worst offender—a $2000 online purchase at four a.m. By the time the package arrived, I had returned to a level mood and felt so embarrassed. I cried when I realized it couldn't be returned. I still shuddered remembering that as I stood in my closet with Jax, years later.

"I'm overwhelmed." Jax sighed as he stood back and stared at the unorganized and very cramped wardrobe. "How do you do this every morning?"

"I don't. I just use my arts-and-crafts camp drawer," I said very seriously, and his mouth twisted until he started laughing at his own dig.

"I'm not taking it back."

"You don't have to. Now, focus. What do the women in your friend group wear?"

"Leather. Lots of leather," he informed me very seriously, so I decided to play along.

"Oh, perfect! I have lots of leather."

"Wait...you do?" He frowned and looked around my closet to find it. "So that's your secret."

"Mm-hmm. I'm a dominatrix."

"Now I know you're lying."

"Appearances can be deceiving."

"Mia the dominatrix." Jax made the sound a whip would make as he motioned with his arm. I smiled and nodded. "Where's your whip? Show me."

"It's not here. It's in my locker at the sex club. I'm a regular."

"You're a regular?" He eyed me and crossed his arms with a smirk. I nodded. "Funny, I've never seen you around." He smiled when he saw my eyes widen.

"What?" I asked awkwardly.

"What?" He raised his brows and stared back. I narrowed my eyes and looked him up and down with suspicion.

Jax had me flustered and was 100 percent messing with me, but there was a good chance that he was also serious. *Don't think about him at a sex club, don't think about him at a sex club, don't*— "So, back to the question of what women in your friend group dress like. I know it's not leather." I moved the conversation away from leather and sex clubs.

"Um…they dress like normal."

"Helpful."

"You're asking a guy how women dress. That's all I got."

"So I'll just have to guess." I nodded and fully faced my displayed clothes, ready for the task.

"I'll help you guess." Jax jumped in ahead of me, and he actually was helpful. I thought it was adorable how he would pull down a top, then bottoms, and hold them up to make an outfit. Sometimes he would smile and show me, but other times he'd frown, shake his head, and put them back.

"What the *fuck?*" When I heard Jax's uncharacteristically high-pitched exclamation, I knew what he'd found. He turned back to me with raised brows and eyes wide, holding a black leather harness.

"What?"

"Where the *hell* have you been wearing this?"

"I told you. I'm a dominatrix," I explained coolly, and I saw him eye me with suspicion, wondering if I were telling the truth.

"Liar."

"I'm very serious."

"What club, because I haven't seen you at Straker's?" He stared at me, and I stared back. I was guessing Straker's was a sex club and that he was actually serious.

"Okay, I'll come clean." I was having so much fun with Jax hanging on my every word. "I'm not a dominatrix."

"So…you're…the…opposite…?" He cocked his head as he continued to stare at me.

"What's the opposite?"

"Okay." He chuckled and snapped out of the intrigue. "This will remain a mystery." He put the harness back and continued helping. Yet another hypomanic purchase, again at four in the morning, through an indie leather artist's website. I'd messaged her my measurements and the style of my liking. It had only been worn one time, but not by me. I styled my sister's Halloween costume one year—a dominatrix. I had no reason to wear it, so I was glad someone could.

I continued to watch Jax sift through the hangers and look through my clothes.

"Oooh la la." He smiled once he pulled down a slinky red dress from the rack. "You have to try this on." I shook my head. "For me?" He pouted. I considered it but still shook my head. "Fine. Then stay there." He held up the dress and extended his arm, holding it away to line up with my body. "Oh, yeah, my imagination is going wild right now."

"Jax." I chuckled and shook my head, insecure, but that subsided as he looked at me.

"Say my name again." Jax smirked as he closed one eye and tilted his head.

"No." I narrowed my eyes and brought my hands to my hips.

"There she is! The seductress. I knew it."

"You caught me." I giggled and fell into his playfulness. I brought my hands up my body and to my hair and ran my fingers through the long strands for a final pose. Jax's smirk fell, and his eyes softened as he watched me move. He took in a deep breath as his gaze followed my hands raking through my hair, then over my features, ending with my mouth. My lips curved into a smile, gaining confidence from how he looked at me, which brought his eyes back to mine. Jax straightened and dropped the dress.

"Okay, turning off my imagination before it gets away from me." He nodded to himself and put away the dress, hooking the hanger over the rack and pushing it further into the mass of clothes. He picked up a sweater and jeans, an outfit he'd already shown me, and held it up again. "Good?"

"Perfect." I nodded, and he held up his hand, making me smile as I brought mine to his for a good high five. "Now go away."

"I can't stay?" he asked with a gasp, like he was hurt.

"Nope."

"Fine. Where's the rest of the leather?"

LITHIUM

"Coatrack in the corner by my bed." Jax scurried out of my closet. I closed the door and locked him out.

"There's no coatrack!" Jax called from the other side of the door. I ignored him and started changing from my arts-and-crafts camp clothes into the outfit he'd put together. I pulled on high-rise skinny jeans and buttoned together a cropped ivory knit sweater, the length hitting a few inches above the jean waistband—a sweater I also had in black, red, and purple. There were four buttons down the center, but I left the top one open. A requirement of my wardrobe, it was wearable sans bra, as they irritated the scar tissue from my spinal fusion surgery.

"Did you get these in Italy at the museum?" I heard him call from the other side of the door as I slid into and zipped up short-heeled black leather boots. *He better not be exploring.* I hurried to get out there so I could monitor him.

"Uffizi, yes," I answered, knowing that he was talking about my posters of *Primavera* and the *Birth of Venus* that I had taped on the wall above my bed.

I smoothed out my outfit and entered my room. I found him leaning down and trying to read the titles of a few books I had stacked on the hardwood floor by my bed.

"Dante, of course." Jax sighed as he straightened, disappointed that he hadn't found anything scandalous.

"What are you doing?"

"Snooping," he admitted. "Trying to find more leather because I'm onto you." His eyes scanned my room and continued the hunt.

"There's no leather." I rolled my eyes and watched him closely, hoping he didn't continue in the direction he was going.

"I dunno. It's always the quiet ones." He looked over to smirk at me, then continued in the direction I didn't want him going, right to my dresser.

"Ha ha. You're funny," I said stiffly as I moved toward him.

"Ohhh, I'm getting warmer." He caught on to my awkwardness and smiled, stepping evener closer to my dresser. "Burning hot?" he teased as he put his hand on the top.

203

"Cold. Ice cold." I crossed my arms and shook my head. "You will not find any leather here, so don't waste your time."

"Yeah, but I know I'll find *something* here. Sexy lingerie drawer?" He smirked and wiggled his eyebrows.

Truth was I had a lingerie drawer. It was just the second one down. Another case of manic spending. I'd order beautiful sets online—the bra, garter, underwear, stockings. Sometimes the package would be delivered before my mood fell, and I got to try them on thinking I was the sexiest woman in the world, a real femme fatale. I would think, *Damn, I'm sexy. Where is a sexy man to share this with? Manic sex drive, but I'm forever alone. What a waste. Woe is me.* I'd sway around as I looked at myself in the mirror, either with a sultry pout or a pleased smile, and run my hands up and down my lace-clad body—it was a wonderful high. I wished that the manic confidence could rub off on the stable me. Other times, the package would come when my mood had already fallen into depression, and I didn't dare try them on at all. My moods altered my perception of myself. Looking into a mirror when manic, I'd see a goddess, and when depressed, I'd see an ogress. It really did fall that far.

"Go find *something* over there," I ordered Jax and pointed to the other side of my room.

"I already snooped over there. What are you trying to keep me away from?"

"Nothing, you're just annoying me, Scooby-Doo."

He arched a brow and put his hand on the top-drawer knob. He maybe was only messing with me and wasn't going to overstep, but I couldn't risk it. Honestly, his discovery of seven hidden prescription bottles would be the end of the world.

"No, no!" I don't think I'd ever moved so fast in my life as I bolted to my dresser and stood between Jax and my secrets.

"I found your secrets!" He smiled, almost giddy, and poked me.

"No..."

"Liar. Stand aside." He snickered, and I stood my ground. He pushed me aside. I was trying not to panic, but my heart was pounding and my stomach tight. I basically threw myself over my dresser. "Really, you're only intriguing me more."

"Please, let it go." My voice came out soft and desperate. *Don't cry, don't cry.* I looked away, too scared to stare into his eyes that were now intense as they studied me closely. He lifted my chin so I had to look at him.

"Okay." He respected that but continued to analyze me.

"Thanks." I felt so awkward and released the deep breath that I didn't realize I was holding and ran an agitated hand through my hair. Jax took a step back but just one. He continued to stare down at me with a frown. I could tell he was trying to figure me out. I continued to calm down and leaned my back against my dresser with another big inhale and exhale.

"It's because you have secrets," he murmured, and I rolled my eyes because he already knew that, "and I almost found out. Is the answer in that drawer?" I didn't reply. "Yeah, and I bet there's more."

"Stop trying to figure me out." My eyes narrowed because even though I was loving having his body so close to me, he always asked too much.

"Why?"

"Because you won't." Hearing that, Jax's brow smoothed out, his jaw clenched, and he took a big inhale before he looked away from me. I immediately felt guilty and wanted to take it back, but I'd meant it. I didn't want him to ever know I was bipolar or what made me so broken. The number of people in my past, from acquaintances to close friends, that disappeared when I showed them who I was on the inside was staggering. There was only so much rejection I could take, so I'd decided to never tell anyone again.

"Okay, Mia." Jax sighed and turned away and went to sit down on my bed. I remained there awkwardly against my dresser for a few more moments, then pushed away. I stood in front of the full-length mirror I had propped against the wall. I took a deep breath and sighed, trying to work my mind back to that playful attitude we'd both had minutes ago as I checked out my outfit.

"Not bad." I nodded, approving of my appearance as I turned side to side to see how I looked at different angles. I was still nervous for the party but felt my confidence grow as I looked at the sophisticated woman in the mirror. I brought my hands to my hips as I turned around and smiled at Jax. "I think I'm ready to party." He was sitting on my bed and looked me up and down.

"I did good." He smirked, trying to take credit. His eyes dropped down again to gaze at my body more slowly. "You're going to get a lot of attention tonight." He sighed but shrugged when he looked back up at me.

"What do you mean?"

"The guys are gonna love you. That's what I mean."

"Then I should change." I chuckled awkwardly and looked in the mirror again, rethinking the inch of skin revealed between my crop top and high-waisted jeans. I brought my hands to the hem of my sweater and tugged down to see if it could cover me more. Of course not. It was a crop top. I sighed and dropped my arms back to my sides.

"No, no, that's not what I meant. I'm not criticizing you. You look good." He hurried to make himself clear, but I knew what he meant. I was reminded that I was going to be at a party, with a cartload of booze and only strangers—I didn't want to think about a bunch of guys getting drunk.

"No, I know." I looked back to my closet and decided to find a sweater with more fabric. The confident woman I wanted to be, who wore what she wanted without giving a fuck, was always challenged by the frightened girl inside me who wanted to hide. I sighed and turned to go back to my closet.

"Mia." Jax caught my hand before I could make it across the room and pulled me closer to him. "Why are you changing?"

"I don't want attention or guys to love me."

"Well, I don't really want that either." I frowned, not understanding. "Never mind. Why?"

"I don't know. I just don't."

"Okay…two more inches of fabric isn't going to make a difference."

"Three more?"

"No." He chuckled and shook his head. "I picked this outfit out, so it'd be rude to change."

"Alright, just to be polite." I sighed and moved away.

"Ready to party?" He clapped his hands as he stood, ready to get going. I nodded. "Okay." Jax put his hands on my shoulders and directed me toward the door and gave me a push so I'd stop overthinking, then followed me through my apartment.

I stopped at the door and turned to Jax. I looked him up and down. "Is that what you're wearing...?"

"Shut up, nuisance." He laughed and led me out the door.

Chapter 21

During the short car ride back to the studio, Jax tried guessing the contents of my secret drawer.

"You're a witch. Dark magic. You have voodoo dolls and…" Jax gasped and looked at me with frightened eyes. "You have a Jax voodoo doll! That explains so much."

"No." I chuckled.

"I don't know if I believe you, but fine. Umm…you really are a spy! And you have, like, ten different passports and wads of foreign currency in there. Weapons too. I bet there's grenades and nunchucks in there. Is there a bazooka under your bed? I should've checked there. How many languages do you know?" I laughed. "Am I *right*?"

"If I told you, I'd have to kill you. It's for your safety, Jax. Give up."

"Fine." He sighed but shot me a side glance with a smirk like he was on to me.

By the time we got to the studio, my nerves were calm, and I felt confident to face the night. Mostly because Jax let me play the music loud.

―――

"Yes! Mia, you look hot!" Nick ran over and made me do a twirl for the sole purpose of checking out my ass, but I didn't care.

Jax did change once we arrived at the studio. He disappeared upstairs to his loft and returned looking way sexy. He swapped his tee for a casual button-down shirt and his messy faded jeans for clean dark ones. The shirt was tucked in the front, so I could see he'd added a belt. I watched him roll up his sleeves, baring his forearms, before helping the guys push all of our stations to the side and protecting them with thick canvas. Since they always called me weak, I had no problem lounging on the couch watching them work—mostly Jax.

"Ahem." Ozzie cleared his throat. I looked over to see him standing next to me with his arms crossed.

"What...?" I frowned at his disapproving expression, eyes narrowed and brow arched, and sat up straight.

"Who are you looking at?"

"Presently, you..."

"Who *were* you looking at?" he clarified. I paused. He'd caught me checking out his other best friend.

"Nick and Jax covering my station with protective sheets. I'm still nervous my work could get damaged." *Damn, that was good.*

"Okay..." He took a second to think it over and decided he believed my lie. "Okay." He sighed and sat down next to me.

"This'll be interesting," I mused, talking loud enough that they all looked at me. "Seeing you guys in a different context."

"What do you expect?" Steven asked.

"I have no idea. That's why it'll be interesting. Do you guys all revert back to your college personas, relive the glory days, or are you classy adults who talk about politics and who's getting married?" I asked seriously, but they all laughed at my examples and didn't answer me.

"You'll see for yourself." Ozzie patted my leg as he got back up to help with the rest of the prep work.

I sighed, giving up, then heard my stomach rumble, so I went to the kitchen to find something decent to call dinner. No luck. I didn't want to have another protein bar as a meal. "Guys. Is there time to get dinner?" I yelled, then went into the studio. "I'm hungry. Jax didn't feed me."

"I was supposed to feed you?" Jax crossed his arms and looked down at me.

"You kidnapped me, dragged me through a liquor store, and intruded on my home. I think a meal is the least you could've done." I waited, a haughty yet joking hand on my hip. The sly curve to his lips told me to prepare for a retort. I narrowed my eyes, wary of his advance as he walked toward me.

"What's the most I could've done?" he said roughly, low enough that only I could hear. He was teasing me, but the heat in his stare was real. I played along. I batted my eyelashes and bit my lip, like his deep voice and dark-blue eyes were affecting me—which they were, but I would never reveal that. His brows knit together slightly with intrigue when he registered my expression and looked at my mouth. Once he met my eyes again, I couldn't hide my knowing, very satisfied smirk. He read me right away. I was messing with him. "You little—"

I smiled and sashayed away, preventing him from making a comeback. I heard him call me a menace as I grabbed my purse from my station and headed for the exit. The boys all called after me, thinking I was bailing. "I'm just going to McDonald's. I'll be back!" I hurried out of the studio before they could ask me to deliver them a haul of chicken nuggets.

———

"Welcome to McDonald's. Can I take your order?" a voice came through from the speaker in the drive-through.

"Hi. I'll have a cheeseburger Happy Meal and a small chocolate shake please." I ordered and pulled through to pay and collect my food. "Stormtrooper. Nice." I smiled when I picked out the little plastic toy and put it in my second cupholder.

I took a very long route back to the studio so I could eat my dinner in peace and buy time before party people started arriving. I wanted to show up and fade into the crowd.

It wasn't long until I maneuvered through the streets to pull up to the studio. *I'm nervous.* I put my full-body mask back on—I had no nerves or anxieties, I had no past of darkness that made me distrust all people, I wasn't afraid of a man's touch. I was who I should've been and who I was trying to become—*fake it till you make it.*

I hurried up the stairs, not wanting to give my insecure mind any time to bring me down. The party had just started, and everyone was in the kitchen pouring drinks. I heard all of the boys' elevated voices and some new ones. I peeked my head through the doorway to check it out. Most of them had their back to me, standing around the center island, but one was sitting near the kitchen table and locked eyes with me. He frowned, obviously not recognizing me, so I smiled and waved.

"And who is this?" the stranger asked the room, looking at me with a tilt of his head, which got everyone's attention. They all turned around as I stepped into view.

"Mia!" Ozzie and Nick yelled out.

"Hi." I smiled brightly in response to their enthusiastic welcome. I scooted across the room to stand by Ozzie.

"Guys, this is Mia. She's our new artist and good friend." He proceeded to introduce me to the three men across the island counter from us.

"Well, hello, stunner. Welcome to the family. I'm Kyle." He grabbed my hand for a shake.

"Thanks…" I murmured and looked away from his eyes to the next guy. "Nice to meet you." I smiled politely as I shook the hands of the two men next to him, Graham and Ryan.

"Hey, I saw her first." The man I first met eyes with rose from a kitchen chair to stand with us. "I'm Patrick. Nice to meet you." He smiled and grabbed my hand for a shake. He was the tallest of the four of them and obviously knew he was charming, with his beaming white smile and sparkling green eyes. I nodded and pulled my hand back. "What are you having, Mia?" he asked with raised brows and motioned to the mountain of booze on the center island.

"Um, I'm just having water first," I said awkwardly and sidestepped around him.

"Alright, but we won't stay tame for long. Be ready to catch up." He winked, and I turned away to get to the refrigerator.

I fished out a water bottle, and when I closed the door, Jax was on the other side, which made me jump. "God." My fright made him chuckle, and he leaned against the counter. I did the same next to him and unscrewed the cap.

"See." He motioned toward the group of guys. "You aren't getting any attention and they all hate you."

"Yeah." I chuckled and rolled my eyes before taking a sip of water.

"They're good guys." *They're always good guys.* "We've known them a long time." *Even if it was since childhood, it doesn't matter.* I really wasn't paranoid and judging their friends. It was just that my memories never left my head. I didn't realize that I was zoning out until Jax's hand came into my vision as he waved it in front of my absent face.

"Hm?" I met his eyes again.

"You know you're safe here…" He stared at me with a small frown.

"Of course I do." I smiled and shrugged off whatever he saw in my expression. I looked over the faces of Patrick, Graham, Kyle, and Ryan and sensed that they would be nice and safe party people, so I decided not to be skittish. I was in a comfortable environment and surrounded by my friends. I shook it off, ready to have fun. I held up my bottled water and decided I needed something stronger. "Okay, time for a drink." I set it down, and Jax pointed out where my tequila was in the assortment of bottles and cans. "Oh, no! Jax, it looks like they forgot to bag the pink Kinky vodka you really wanted. Shoot," I announced at a decibel loud enough for everyone to hear. They all knew I was making fun and laughed along. Jax just rolled his eyes and pushed me to the side to confiscate the tequila bottle. I reached for it, but he kept it from me and walked around the island to the cupboards, where he proceeded to place it on the very top shelf.

"The night is young, and you've already started trying to annoy me. No drinks for you," he declared and crossed his arms.

"You think I won't get to that?" I raised my brows and glanced from the top shelf back to him.

"You can try. Good luck climbing in those tight-ass jeans."

"You think I have a tight ass?" I smiled, full on shifting into a fun attitude. He narrowed his eyes as his jaw moved back and forth, and he looked me up and down, stifling a smile of his own.

"Mm-hmm. I do. Which is why I always think about bending you over every time you try to annoy me. Which, as you know, is a lot." His words and teasing smile momentarily paralyzed me. My eyes widened, and I felt my cheeks turn pink. "Don't look at me like that." He stared into my eyes, then mouth, and took a big side step away.

Don't picture it. Do not picture it. Do not picture Jax bending me over. Too late. Shit.

I blinked my eyes, trying to get the image out of my head, and had to recover quickly so as not to give him the satisfaction of seeing me flustered. I cleared my throat and looked around. He had moved to the other side of the room, and I glanced up at the bottle he'd stuck on the top shelf. I was surrounded by men—someone could get it down for me.

"Um, any tall, strong men in the room who can reach the top shelf for me?" I smiled sweetly. The four men offered at the same time, and I saw Jax roll his eyes. Patrick stepped through his friends to be the hero and retrieved the bottle for me. I thanked him kindly but didn't want to hold eye contact for too long. Out of all of the guys, he'd be the one to catch my eye—if it weren't for the blond, blue-eyed beast that dominated all of my thoughts. Patrick was almost as tall as Jax, strong but not as strong as Jax... No one compared to Jax. It wasn't fair for them, really.

"Let's get you a drink." He smiled, and I felt a buzz of anxiety from his touch but looked past it, figuring I'd have to conquer that sooner or later. He picked up a Solo cup.

"It's okay. I got it," I said casually as I ignored the cup in his hand and reached for a new one. I poured in a splash of the liquid gold tequila for myself.

"Alright, then." He nodded and waited until my drink was in my hand. "So..."

Patrick chatted me up a bit, and I went along with it. He had that classic charmer personality but was still very nice. More people kept flowing into the studio, and there were more guys and a fair amount of girls mingling around.

Jax and I didn't interact much after that, as we were both busy. There was always a line of female friends wanting to catch up with him. I would watch them saunter up and wrap their arms around his neck, pushing their bodies close to his along with a friendly: "Hey! How are you? It's been so long!" *I'm not jealous.* Sometimes he would glance over and catch me staring, which was fine with me, since I sometimes caught him doing the same thing. He was right. I did get a lot of attention as the only new girl at a party. I always felt his eyes on me when a guy put his hand on my arm or back, when a guy tried to play with a long strand of my hair, when they would try to refill my drink or drag their eyes up and down my body.

Ozzie did a good job with checking on me, making me feel comfortable, but I could tell he wanted to cover a lot of ground and catch up with people, taking advantage of one of the few occasions they were all together. So I drifted off into the kitchen to have a quiet moment. I took a deep breath, soaking in strength from the solitude. Just as I was wondering where Jax was, he came into the kitchen. I turned to face him. He circled around the counter to the sink, and the whole time, I kept my front to him. He eyed me, taking a minute before realizing that I was hiding my tight ass from him.

"Fuck off." He chuckled and drank a glass of water, then poured me one. I accepted the offering and took a long sip. "I see you've been thinking about it," he said.

"N-no." I brushed it off and took a few steps away, putting distance between us.

"Mm-hmm. I bet you're thinking about it right now." He stared me down with amusement, as I had backed away to the other end of the counter.

"*You* are thinking about it."

"I know," he countered with a smirk. He loved getting me flustered.

"What are we thinking about?" Nick asked, interrupting our weird moment, and I welcomed it. He didn't expect an answer as he bounced around the kitchen until he found more beer.

The quiet of the kitchen was broken as more people filtered in. Some of my favorite songs started to play, so I just leaned against the counter and sipped my drink, swaying to the music.

"It looks like you're having fun," Jax murmured as he leaned against the counter next to me.

"I actually am." I smiled.

"I'm glad you came," he said quietly as he inched closer, creating a degree of privacy around us in the crowded and noisy room.

"Pretty sure you didn't want me to come." I glanced at him with an arched brow as I sipped my drink.

"Of course I wanted you to come." He smiled brightly and turned to lean his hip against the counter to fully face me. "You fell victim to reverse psychology. I'm so smart."

"Why?"

"I knew nothing the guys said would get you to come."

My lips quirked up at the thought of him knowing me well. "How would you know that?"

"I may have you figured out a little more than you think."

"Oh, really?"

"Just not those secrets." He shrugged.

"Hey." We both looked across the kitchen island when Ozzie raised his voice to get our attention. "You two look awfully close." He narrowed his eyes as he looked between us.

"No, we're not," Jax said casually and pushed me aside to put several feet between us. "I just met her."

"Yeah, I don't know this guy." I raised my brows and pointed at Jax with my thumb.

"Liars." Ozzie rolled his eyes, then walked out of the kitchen, which continued to get noisier and filled with more bodies.

"What's going on over there?" I asked Jax as I tilted my head, trying to see what the crowd of people was doing around the counter island. I spotted Patrick slicing lime wedges.

"Tequila shots," Jax explained once he got a glimpse of the lime, salt, and clear liquid in shot glasses. "You've taken tequila shots before…"

"I sip tequila…"

"Ah, that's right. You don't like parties."

"Where's Mia?" I heard Patrick call my name and look around the kitchen until he found me. "Come here." He motioned me over with an inviting smile. I glanced at Jax, who was staring at his friend, and I hesitantly moved through the group of tequila-shot takers. "You're my tequila girl." Patrick pulled me next to him and poured from the Jose Cuervo bottle into the mini glass. "Time for a shot. I told you you'll need to catch up." He smiled, and I watched him cut another wedge from the lime.

"So, I just toss it back…" I glanced from the shot to him.

"C'mon, girl." He laughed like I was kidding and squeezed juice onto my hand, then sprinkled on some salt. I watched a couple girls beside me do it first so I didn't embarrass myself by asking for the steps, then took my first tequila shot. I licked the salt, tossed back the alcohol, and sucked on the lime. I really enjoyed the taste, and I smiled when I made eye contact with Patrick. "You're so cute," he said. I blushed from the attention and awkwardly glanced back to Jax. His arms were crossed as he continued to watch me and Patrick. "My turn." I was too focused on Jax's heated gaze that I wasn't expecting Patrick to push my hair over my shoulder and place a lime wedge on my neck.

"What are you doing?" I flinched away with wide eyes just as he was smearing the juice over my skin.

"You haven't done a body shot before?" he asked with raised brows and a little laugh. I stared and shook my head. "This is the fun part." Patrick put his hand on my waist and pulled me closer. I felt his entire hand on my skin. I stopped breathing and leaned away when his body got too close. I honestly felt bad for having such a reaction to a guy simply putting a hand on my hip, but there it was.

"Excuse me." Jax's deep voice interrupted, and his long arm chopped between me and Patrick. "Mia, you have a phone call." I frowned and stared at him. "It's urgent." He pulled me away from Patrick and back to our quiet corner.

"Alright, I'll be waiting!" Patrick called after me, then went back to being the bartender. My interaction with him had been pleasant, but I appreciated Jax's interruption, as I didn't have to push away from Patrick myself when he got too close.

"Who's calling me?" I crossed my arms with raised brows.

"It's the CIA. They want a progress report on your secret mission."

"Oh, yeah, that's very urgent." I nodded slowly. "Maybe you just didn't want me and Patrick doing a body shot."

"True. Maybe you didn't want that either..." he hedged and waited to gauge my reaction but straightened and turned to look at someone who called his name.

"Jax! Hey! How are you? It's been so long!" A woman approached and put her arms around his neck, not caring that he was in the middle of a conversation.

"Claire, hey." Jax smiled but pushed her away a few feet so she wasn't on top of him. "All good here."

"I'm great." She beamed. She looked nice and was obviously very excited to see him, so I started inching away. *I'm not jealous.* "Last time I saw you, we were upstairs." She was all playful and cute, and I went from inching away to taking long steps. *I'm a little jealous.*

Chapter 22

I fled the kitchen and entered the studio, where most of the party was. The music was louder and the room was more crowded. I weaved through the bodies and strange faces, searching for a familiar one. The first person I found was Nick, as I spotted his shaggy blond head bobbing around in the crowd. When I finally reached him, I could see he was already engaged in a conversation.

"So I stayed at Hannah's place last night, and guess what I found this morning?" a man named Jared said to the three guys around him. I didn't want to interrupt, so I hung back, waiting for their conversation to be over to jump in. "There were, like, ten pill bottles in her bathroom. The girl's *bipolar.*" I felt my heart sink when he said the word like it was so repelling—*bipolar.*

"Oh, shit." One guy gasped with a laugh, like it was funny.

"What'd you do?" another guy asked.

"Ran out of there, didn't want to get killed in my sleep," Jared answered seriously but also laughed at the situation.

"Good call, man, those girls are crazy," the other guy said. I stopped breathing, hoping Nick wouldn't join in on the commentary.

"Hey! Mia," Nick cheered, pausing the boys' conversation when he noticed me standing off to the side. "Guys, this is Mia," Nick proudly introduced me to his friends. They all looked at me, ready to include me in their huddle, but all I could manage was a slight head nod as my chest twisted the longer I stood in front of them.

I didn't want to stay within earshot in case Nick had something to say, so I backed away and fled again, this time to the bathroom.

Once I got to my destination, I closed the bathroom door and leaned against it. "Shit." I sighed and raked my hands through my hair. I moved to face the mirror and placed my hands on the counter so I could calm down. With every inhale and exhale, I was trying to hold back the insecurities and fears that threatened to break through after Jared's little breakup story. I'd heard everything those men had said before—I just wasn't expecting to hear it at my colleagues' party. I was sure that everyone with bipolar had experiences with the stigma, like I did.

You're my friend, but you being bipolar is too much for me to deal with. Bye.

Oh my God, that girl is such a bitch. She's bipolar.

If a mother is bipolar, you should call child services.

You're bipolar? Don't kill me.

The stigma hurt me. It perpetuated me having to hide who I was because who I was would be rejected. I'd learned that society saw people with bipolar as people who you didn't want as a friend, a partner, a parent, a coworker, or anywhere in your life.

The insecurities and fears I was trying to hold back came pouring out when I remembered my colleagues. What if Steven, Jax, and Nick found out? Would they see me differently? Would they treat me differently? Would they have even hired me? Would they reject me like everyone else had? They were good people with good hearts, but the stigma could overpower that. *They must never know.*

———

It was later in the night and time for me to leave the safety of the bathroom and rejoin the party. I looked myself in the mirror as I straightened my posture, deciding that Jared's comments had no effect on me. After a good deep breath, I was ready to go and had my hand on the doorknob when I heard Jax talking in the hallway. I lingered behind the door when I heard my name—*because eavesdropping is always a good idea…*

"You want to what?" His voice was deep and I waited for the response.

"Take Mia home. She's single, right?" It was Patrick.

"Why?"

"Why?" Patrick chuckled. "Because she's hot and fun." I held my breath, afraid that I knew where the conversation was going.

"Well, I wouldn't if I were you."

"Seriously? Why not?"

"She's not really your type. I don't think you'd be satisfied."

"Well, I guess we'll find out."

"Nah, man, there's plenty of other women here to choose from."

"Oooh, do you want her for yourself?"

"No…I'm just looking out for you."

"Well, thanks, man, but I'm going for it."

Tears pricked my eyes as I listened. All day, I had been excited to be around Jax, happy that we were getting closer. Well, that had just been destroyed in one short overheard conversation. I sucked in a shaky breath and locked down my emotions, then opened the door and exited the bathroom.

"Excuse me," I said casually as I shifted my shoulders to slide between the two men clogging the narrow hallway. I didn't look at them as I breezed past and didn't look back. I hurried back to the party and retrieved my purse from the kitchen and beelined for the exit.

"You're leaving?" Ozzie stopped me, confused by my sudden departure. I had about two minutes before the tears broke through and needed to get to a safe area. I nodded and moved past him. Jax was still in the hallway when I made it to the stairs.

"Mia?" he said tentatively, but I ignored him. I descended the stairs, then heard his footsteps behind me. He was following me. Asshole. I hit the elevator button. "Hey," he said. I turned my back to him. He touched my arm, but I flinched away. "You don't have to leave." He came closer again, and thankfully, the elevator doors opened.

I glanced at him, meeting his eyes, which was a mistake because he definitely saw the broken pieces in mine. I stepped into the elevator and hit the down button. Once the doors closed, I filled my lungs with a deep breath and held the railing, finally alone. *That hurt.*

I got home and went straight to bed, allowing myself to cry. I fell asleep with Jax and Patrick's overheard conversation on repeat.

———

I woke up relieved it was the weekend and that I had two days away from Jax. I felt around the covers for my phone until it slid into my palm from under my pillow. The screen brightened, and I saw the notification of three missed calls from Jax. I used my finger to swipe all the way to the left, erasing it from my view. I sighed and stared at the ceiling until my phone started to buzz with an incoming call from Ozzie.

"Hey, Oz," I answered sleepily.

"Can I come over?"

"Ugh, it's so early. I just woke up."

"Brunch and mimosas."

"I'll be ready in five." I pushed myself upright, energy already filling me.

"Great. I'll be outside your building."

"Actually, ready in ten is realistic."

"You're being timed."

"Okay, okay, I'm getting going, bye!" I hopped out of bed and scurried around my room to get ready for a social outing that just got stressful, as I took Ozzie's timing somewhat seriously—like when we were younger, and he'd timed me running up and down the stairs to get him a soda from the kitchen because he didn't want to get up from his beanbag chair in the basement.

I splashed my face with water in the bathroom, brushed my teeth and hair, and dabbed on lip stain. My outfit was next, and I just grabbed the first combination I saw. I wanted to make it downstairs in less than ten minutes, which would be a record, so I not-so-gracefully buttoned myself into vintage high-rise Levi's and pulled on a gauzy lavender sweater. It took a couple tries to get my head through the right hole, as I was unnecessarily going too fast for my motor skills.

"Keys, phone, purse, ready! Seven minutes," I congratulated myself but realized that I only had socks on when I got to the door. My maroon Doc Marten boots were on the mat, so I grabbed them and went.

Ozzie started laughing once I exited my building and bounced onto the sidewalk he stood on. "You did not just run through your apartment building in only socks."

"I did, yeah." I smiled and bent down to pull one boot onto my foot.

"Ten minutes. Record time." He nodded but continued to laugh as I took a long time fumbling with the laces with shaky hands. "You're technically not ready."

"Yes, I am." I pulled my pant legs over each boot and straightened. "Ta-da." Ozzie just shook his head as his eyes looked over my head.

"Your hair is going crazy with static. Blonde everywhere." He waved his hand over my hair to get it to settle. "I give up. Let's go."

"Let's." I fell into step beside him and followed his directions.

"But did you remember to take your vitamins?" Ozzie glanced down at me with a smirk. He called my pills "vitamins."

"Ahhh." I dropped my head back with a groan, then rolled my eyes at myself.

"You literally have been taking them every morning and every night for four years. How do you still forget?"

"I was caught up with my race against time," I defended myself but didn't worry. My morning medications weren't too strict on timing, so I could take them a little later than usual and be okay.

"Okay, that's fair." He nodded as his eyes followed our feet. "You have two different shoelaces on. One black, one yellow."

"That is an accurate observation, Oswald."

"Blah, blah, why?"

"I was starting to change the black laces to the yellow ones, but after I did one boot, I didn't feel like doing the other since tremors make everything so damn annoying and my hands cramped. I think it looks cool, so I never changed the other one."

"Okay, makes sense." Ozzie chuckled. "How have your hands been, by the way?"

"Same as always. Sometimes obnoxious and sometimes not that noticeable. Then the in between." I shrugged and held up my hand to gauge the tremors. "Still there, but I can use utensils easily."

"And when you're using a pencil?" He glanced at me with a frown. It was a good question.

"I manage. It just takes me longer than it used to, pre-bipolar. I do a lot of erasing. When I bring a project from my easel to the table, that's so my hand can rest easier on the paper and I can aim better, getting the pencil to touch without so many poke marks on the paper when I miss."

"Jesus, Mia. That's so messed up." I shrugged again, since, yeah, I knew that. "If it's a side effect, then you can maybe get something to replace the medication that's causing them, right?"

"It's an option. I spent four years trying to find the right combination of medications that work. They are all intermixed together; if I stop taking one, the others might not work as well. I'd have to cut out lithium, and that's my favorite."

"You have a favorite?" Ozzie chuckled.

"Yep. I love lithium." I nodded seriously and smiled thinking about it.

"You're smiling over a medication."

"Ha ha, yeah." I laughed at myself and shrugged.

"You're crazy." Ozzie smirked, knowing that I didn't mind him calling me crazy because I did too. He wasn't wrong.

"Really, though, it's the drug that saved me, so, yeah, lithium is my favorite, and I love it."

"Fair enough." Ozzie patted me on my back and looked forward to the restaurant we were approaching. "Well, this was a great leisurely morning walk. Riveting conversation."

"Now mimosas!" Ozzie held the door open for me, and I walked through.

We followed the hostess further into the restaurant and weaved between tables until we got to our booth. Once we'd settled into our seats, Ozzie sat forward and placed his folded hands on the table. "So." He smirked when I gave him a suspicious stare, knowing he had an agenda. "Let's talk about last night."

"What was last night?" I frowned. Honestly, I had temporarily forgotten after our walk and talk. "Oh." I nodded. "It was a fun party."

"If it was so fun, then why did you suddenly leave without saying goodbye?"

"It was fun up until that point." I shrugged, quickly trying to decide if I should tell him everything.

"Can you tell me what happened? I was worried about you."

"Well." I slumped into the booth cushion. "I just overheard a conversation…" I explained to him Jareds's bipolar breakup story.

"Oh, Mia." Ozzie sighed and shook his head. "Jared's an asshole. I'm sorry."

"It's okay. I hear that shit all the time."

"No, it's not, and I'm so sorry you had to hear shit like that at our party," he said kindly.

"Thanks, Oswald." I used his full name and smiled, appreciating his concern.

"Then what?" Ozzie was quick to move on to another topic. I shrugged. "I know something else happened." I shrugged again but knew he was on to me. "Why did Jax disappear after you left?"

"Disappear?" I frowned.

"He went to his loft and never came back down. Did you have a fight?"

"Oh." I put my elbows on the table and buried my face in my hands. "It's stupid," I muttered as I straightened again. "I overheard Patrick asking

Jax about me. He wanted to take me home, I guess. Jax told him not to because I wouldn't be good enough or something like that."

"Why would he say that?"

"Because he thinks I wouldn't be good enough. I told you—I'm not his type. He's not interested in me."

"I'm sorry…" I could tell Ozzie was trying to think of something nice to say.

"It's fine. It was just disappointing to hear that said about me. No matter who was saying it. So…"

"Do you want me to talk to Patrick? He was asking about you."

"No."

"He seemed to really like you."

"He doesn't know me. He just wanted to *take me home*."

"Mia, you're always yourself, and everyone liked you. Anyway, Patrick's not really like that. Like…take you home, yeah, but not just to ditch you. He'd understand, too, if you told him…" Ozzie looked into the distance and squinted, searching for the right way to phrase something.

"That I'm bipolar?" I frowned, doubting it.

"Oh, no, don't do that." Ozzie shook his head, not knowing that even his tiny reaction had a tiny effect on me—making me want to hide. "Inexperienced."

"I don't want you to talk to him," I said, dismissing the topic altogether.

"Alright." Ozzie nodded and sat back. We looked at each other for a little longer, mostly Ozzie waiting for me to say more, but I didn't. "What's going on with you and Jax?"

"Ozzzzzz." I groaned and dropped my head back against the booth. "Nothing."

"I'm just protective over you, okay?"

"He's not interested in me. That negates all danger, so you don't have to protect me from anything."

"Yeah, well, I see you together a lot so I'm not making this up. You guys are bitching, then you're all whispery. It's confusing." *Tell me about it.* "How do you feel about him?" *Well, this is embarrassing.*

"Um." I looked away and tried to think of something. A lot had developed between the two of us but nothing I was confident in sharing, especially since I only knew my feelings, not his. But I could guess. "He's kinda an asshole…and he thinks I'm annoying so we just don't get along." *And I get butterflies whenever he looks at me.* "Sometimes our mutual interests bring us together in a friendly conversation…then he says I'm not satisfactory and other women are better, soooo…." *So I wish he wanted me, but some things cannot be. Suppress, suppress, suppress.* "Nothing new."

"Yeah, okay." Ozzie nodded, agreeing with me about Jax's attitude. I wished he had a different response—something like, *plot twist, Jax actually wants you even though he thinks you're not satisfactory and other women are better!*

"So, where's our mimosas?" I looked around the restaurant for a waitress.

"We haven't ordered yet." Ozzie started to laugh at the amount of disappointment on my face, but then a server appeared at our booth.

"Hi." I smiled and ordered a mimosa and waffles.

"And I'll have the Healthy Start." Ozzie smiled, and it looked like he was done.

"And a mimosa," I interjected, which made the server smile and look to Ozzie, who didn't correct me. "Healthy Start." I rolled my eyes once the server was on her way to the kitchen. "You always get the Healthy Start, then eat my waffles. You can't have the best of both worlds."

"Actually, I can. You eat like a chipmunk, and I haven't seen you eat more than half an entrée since you've been here and probably ever. So, I order the healthy thing and get to take bites of the good thing."

"Great system. Well, this time, I'm getting the leftovers to-go."

"Nah, I'm going to eat that second waffle."

"Fine." I sighed because he was right.

"Speaking of diet…are you eating enough? I'm not, like, saying I see weight loss, just a concerned friend knowing that you have, like, other side effect issues."

"Uh…" I thought about his question since I often lost track of what I ate, which was probably not a great sign. "My diet isn't better or worse." I shrugged.

"Which means…?"

"A side effect is daily nausea, but it varies. I don't think I remember what it's like not to be nauseous. Mostly, I ignore it. Ignoring it makes it more comfortable to live but also shuts off hunger cues. Being on seven medications for four years causes big digestive issues. Basically, I never have an appetite, and it hurts to eat," I explained, and he nodded along, waiting for me to continue. "Nutritionists may say I don't eat enough. But I haven't lost weight, so that's good."

"What the hell do you eat, though?"

"During the day, I can eat an energy bar or cereal or sometimes half portions of bagels or waffles. I drink a lot of Boost—they have a juice one now, which is good. I eat whatever I want for dinner because it's easiest to stomach at that time so I just get whatever sounds good enough to eat, like fried things are good right now. I eat cookies or mix protein powder into ice cream to pack in more calories."

"Okay…" Ozzie nodded and stared at nothing. He was trying to reel in a lecture. I knew it was coming when he sighed and rubbed his fingers over his brows. "That's not ideal."

"Yeah, well, bipolar isn't ideal. I do the best I can." He eyed me like he was going to challenge that. "That's a non-arguable point."

"Okay, okay. Just, you've always been slim, right? I don't want to see you fade away. How will you know if you're malnourished?"

"Seriously, I'm not malnourished. When my hair falls out or my nails flake off or I drop below a certain number on the scale, I'll know…I don't want that," I explained, and he nodded, his brow creased. "See?" I tugged on the lock of hair hanging over my shoulder. It was a dumb gesture that held no meaning, but I knew it'd make him smile.

"Alright." He smiled and sat back in his seat, and I smiled when our mimosas arrived. "So, if you have no appetite, why not eat healthy dinners?"

"Doesn't sound good and I don't feel like cooking."

"There are healthy things that are easy to make and taste good." I shrugged. "Okay, I'm coming over tonight and we're going to cook a healthy dinner." I agreed as our food arrived. We enjoyed our meal, and Ozzie also enjoyed taking one of my waffles.

Chapter 23

Saturday night, Ozzie showed up at my apartment with a grocery bag full of vegetables, rice, and chicken.

"Ah-ah." I stopped him before he could get further into my apartment.

"Wow. Never been held up at my own apartment, which it basically still looks like." He chuckled as he looked around. We usually spent time at his new place since it was nicer. I ignored him as I pulled down a side of the brown bag he carried and peeked inside.

"Okay, you may enter." I pulled out the bottle of Chianti that I made a requirement for our night of cooking and went to the kitchen.

"So, we are making a healthy version of chicken fried rice," Ozzie explained while I poured two glasses of wine. "You're helping me." He arched a brow as he watched me rest my elbows on the center island counter.

"Sure." I nodded as I took a sip of wine, but I definitely wasn't helping. He knew that, too, but liked to be sassy.

"I also brought Tupperware since I knew you wouldn't have any."

"Why...?"

"We're going to make a big batch and portion it out so you can have dinner ready for the next few days. See, healthy can be easy."

"Nice." I nodded along with his plan and pushed myself up to sit on the counter.

"I'm doubling the vegetables because you're very behind."

"Thanks, Mom," I teased as I watched him prepare the ingredients.

"Okay." He put his hands on his hips to glare at me. "Both you and Jax have always said that, and it's annoying."

"You know we're just teasing." I smiled and swayed my legs back and forth, not commenting on his sassy-mom pose.

"Because I'm the most mature and responsible."

"That is true," I agreed immediately with a formal nod.

"That's probably why you like each other so much." He chuckled and pulled out a cutting board.

"*Like* each other?" My legs stopped swaying, and I stared at him.

"I mean dislike each other." He rolled his eyes and started slicing a red pepper. "You seriously need to get stools or something in here," he commented as he glanced around the barren kitchen and me sitting on the countertop.

"Okay, Mom." I snickered and hopped down from the counter, seized my wineglass, and retreated to the other side of the kitchen.

"Seriously?" Ozzie rolled his eyes again and stopped slicing. "Jax did the same thing earlier this week. I swear you're Jax in a dress."

"How dare you!" I gasped, offended. "I am not Jax in a dress. If anything, he is Mia in a dress. Wait, Mia in…pants?" I frowned and looked off into the distance, trying to figure out what I was trying to say. "But neither! We aren't alike. You're just…the same with us."

"You're being so awkward, it's funny. Just like Jax when I said the same thing to him."

"'Jax' is now a banned word in this apartment. So is 'Jackson.'" I pushed myself up onto the side counter to sit again, just farther away.

"What about Mr. Caine?" Ozzie teased, and I actually blushed. That was embarrassing.

"He said it first!"

"Whatever." Ozzie started to laugh. "He outlawed your name, too, but we were at my apartment, so it was invalid."

"Well, this is my apartment." Ozzie just smirked and went back to slicing. "Reminder what I heard him say about me last night. Stop bringing him up."

"Yeah, okay." He sighed. "It's just such a funny topic." I didn't have anything to say after that and just enjoyed the smooth slicing sounds as Ozzie cut the peppers while my eyes fogged over. *It's not funny to me.*

"Mia...you okay?"

"Yeah." I immediately snapped out of it to reassure Ozzie that I was okay.

"He's been better, right? The banned name hasn't been as much of an asshole? To your face, at least."

"I guess." I shrugged and started to sway my feet again.

"I've talked to him about it a lot." Ozzie nodded and grabbed an onion while I drank wine. "I think he's over whatever it was that made him like that."

"Which was...?"

"I told you about his family issues."

"Yeah, his brother is getting divorced." I knew there was more.

"That and something else from his past came up. He grew up in London."

"Wait, what?" I hopped down from my perch to return to the counter-top closer to him. He arched a brow and handed me a carrot, and I rolled my eyes. I pretended to start slicing the carrot but focused on listening to everything he was saying.

"His mom is British. I don't know why, but Jax lived with his mom in London for a year while his dad and brothers lived here. He was just a kid, and I think something happened to his mom that fucked him up a bit."

"I have so many questions."

"Honestly, I don't have answers." He shrugged and continued. "So when he was with his family and that shit went down with his brother's divorce, something else happened that was linked to...whatever happened before. I really don't know. But, anyways, from there, he came to the studio, where he met you. I *know* that's why he was an asshole to you. I also know that when you fired back, he actually did aim the asshole at you. So that whatever dynamic continued with both of you. Which is why I think it's because you're so similar. You're stubborn idiots together."

"Wow, okay."

"And I think he's over it. Are you?"

"Um…I don't know what you're asking, so I'm just going to say yes."

"Are you done being resentful and retaliating?"

"Oh. Yeah, definitely. For a while, honestly."

"Then why do you still fight?"

"Now that is a different story." I smiled when I saw Ozzie's arched brow and the way he froze his cutting movements. "I'm past him being an asshole when we met and the hostile attitude that followed. That doesn't mean I'm going to immediately get past everything else that keeps happening. We fought because of what happened at the mansion, not because of our rocky introduction. Same with last night. *We just don't get along…* for the most part."

"Yeah, alright." Ozzie sighed and continued his cooking, then glanced at my still-whole carrot. "You're not helping."

I picked up a knife and held it up over the carrot. My hand shook. "Oh, no, my tremors. This is a safety concern. I should not be holding a knife." It was a valid point. Ozzie knew it, too, but still rolled his eyes as he snatched the carrot back and placed it in front of him.

When dinner was ready, it actually looked good and tasted even better.

"You've had superb attendance at work, Mia," Ozzie mused. He looked like he was teasing, but I still shot him a questioning look.

"Thanks, Parole Officer Ozzie…"

"You just always used to grumble about having to tell your boss that you couldn't go to work two mornings a week."

"Ohhhh." I chuckled because I wasn't expecting him to bring that up. Which reminded me… "Ah, shit. Ow." I face-palmed too hard.

"Did you forget you have doctors?" Ozzie chuckled as he continued to eat and waited to hear what I had to say.

"Basically." I sighed. There was a pit in my stomach because I hadn't yet set up therapy sessions with my psychologist. I had been distracted and let myself overlook it. "Dr. J is going to be so disappointed in me for being an irresponsible bipolar-an."

"Well, I'm glad I just reminded you."

"I'm not," I grumbled. "It's annoying. Always having to report to a psychiatry check-in or dip out for a therapy session or ditch for a blood-draw appointment." I pushed my fork around the rice in my bowl.

"But...don't you have to?"

"Yeah, that's the point."

"I'm sorry."

"It's fine. I'm just not going to do it."

"But you have to." Ozzie frowned, concerned about my reluctance.

"I'll call when I feel like it." Ozzie was about to argue. "I'm doing really well right now, so that's what matters. I'll schedule an appointment when I feel I need to. Now I just want to focus on my new life." Still, Ozzie looked like he was going to argue. "Non-arguable point."

"Fine." He looked at my bowl. I had picked out all of the chicken. "But you have to finish your dinner."

"I'm done." I just smiled and pushed my bowl away. He rolled his eyes. Ever since we were kids, whenever he told me what to do, I wanted to do the opposite. Now we were adults, and I could still be immature like that.

"I'm just a concerned best friend, okay?" Ozzie stood, picking up both of our bowls to bring them to the sink.

"You can be concerned, but know that I'll tell you if I start to not do so well, okay?" I followed behind him, hoping he trusted me. Unfortunately, he knew not to. I'd been known to hide my mood disorder until it was too late. But that was before. This was different.

"Yeah, okay." Ozzie sighed and then pulled me into a big hug. "Love you, crazy girl."

"Love you too, neurotypical man." I smiled and hugged him back.

After our cute embrace, Ozzie dished out the leftovers into Tupperware containers and put them in my fridge so I had something healthy to eat for several more nights. It warmed my heart that he was taking care of me and to know that he wanted to.

The night was still young, and we decided to watch a movie.

"*Monty Python and the Holy Grail*?" I asked eagerly as I settled onto one side of the couch and pulled up my legs.

"Nope. You just quote the entire movie," Ozzie vetoed from the kitchen. "Might as well put on your one-woman play."

"*Anchorman*?"

"Same issue!"

"Fine, I'll let the television decide," I huffed and picked up the remote to start browsing the channels.

"*James Bond* marathon!" Ozzie cheered and hopped over the back of the couch, wine bottle and glasses in hand.

"Deal." I smiled and snatched my glass from him and waited for him to fill it up with red.

————

Ozzie left after *Casino Royale*. While I was getting into bed, our conversation about the banned name replayed in my head. Ozzie had asked me if I was over whatever feud Jax and I had going after our messy introduction. For both of us, the answer was yes. However, I knew that a new thing between us was just starting—one-sided or not. It was true: we did rub each other the wrong way, and I didn't see that magically changing, but the hostility had subsided, and something warmer crept in. There had been moments when we'd rubbed each other in the right way. Metaphorically—there had never been any rubbing. I grew more drawn to him every day as I learned more about him, observed his personality, and discovered his quirks, and the frequency of his gaze locking with mine continued to increase. I felt things escalating, and I didn't know what to do about it because he obviously felt differently. I'd heard him say it myself.

————

I spent Sunday enjoying my own company—I needed to take care of my introverted and defective self. I thought a lot about what Jax said. I thought I already knew his opinion of me, but it hurt to hear that confirmed by the man himself, and it hurt that I hoped it'd be different.

Monday morning, I walked into the studio, and only Jax was there.

"Since when am I ever the first one here?" I groaned and went straight to my station.

"Mia."

"Yeah?" I turned to see Jax standing right in front of me. Looking up at his face, the emotions of the party resurfaced. When I stared into his eyes, I heard him talking to Patrick all over again. I felt the hurt I'd felt in that bathroom. I'd wallowed enough over the weekend, and now I had to get over it. I just wanted the conversation to be over before it started.

"Um...I don't know how much you heard—"

"All of it." I remained neutral. *I just heard the truth, and that's okay. I don't care. The truth hurts sometimes, but not this time because I don't care.* I was good at lying to myself.

"Oh. I really didn't mean it..." Jax spoke gently, hands in his pockets and guilt written all over his face. I didn't believe that he hadn't meant it, but I did believe that he felt bad that I'd overheard the insult.

"Okay." I shrugged, suppressing my emotions.

"Okay? You left really upset."

"I left because I just felt like leaving. Not because of you, so calm down."

Jax was surprised by my neutral reaction, and my impassive responses were clearly making him uncomfortable, since he just stared at me, not knowing how to continue. After a very awkward moment and a few uncertain blinks, he added to his excuse: "Well...it's really not what you think. It probably sounded worse."

"You told Patrick that you wouldn't take me home if you were him, that I would be unsatisfying and most women would be better. Can you make it sound better?" I recited his anti-Mia comments with, I think, a successfully impassive expression.

"No, Mia, you're wrong."

"You were speaking in code?"

"No, I didn't mean any of that."

"So you want to take me home, I'd be satisfying, and I'm better than the rest of the women?"

"I…" He stared at me, and his brow twisted in a very conflicted frown. "I just…um…I didn't mean what I said, and…just don't think I'm an asshole, okay? I—"

"As opposed to what I already thought of you?" I asked with a head tilt but knew it wasn't fair.

"Wow. That's so not fair."

"Prove me wrong, then." Still, I stuck to it.

"Considering your attitude, that'd take a while. How long do we have?"

"Until the rest of the guys show up."

"Fine." He sighed but agreed to make the effort. The elevator dinged. I looked at him with a smirk. "You're not so much better, you know." He glared at me, and I just shrugged.

"Good morning! I pulled a sweetheart Mia and got us all breakfast!" Nick announced as he ran into the studio.

"More like I got us all breakfast and Nick is taking credit," Steven clarified as he held a paper bag of bagels.

"Thank you, Steven, for breakfast and, Nick, for the announcement." I smiled as I approached the two boys at the table. I glanced over my shoulder to see that Jax was still staring at me from my station. Just another day.

We spent the rest of the day stuck in the same tense and awkward energy.

Chapter 24

On Monday, Jax presented us with a new commission. The client was very religious and spoke with each of us on what the subject of our work would be, listening to our suggestions.

The drawing we decided upon was a scene of the archangel Michael slaying Satan. I recognized many of the paintings depicting the biblical moment and was excited to do my own rendition.

By Wednesday, I was almost done with the main figure but was getting frustrated and, honestly, disheartened. My tremors were worse than usual, and the more I drew, the angrier I got over the impediment. All I had to do was draw the leg, but I couldn't even manage an outline.

I was bent over my table, arm resting on top to anchor my hand that held my HB pencil. I tried to look past the harsh markings from too many errors and focus on my drawing. The pencil bounced as my hand shook, and I couldn't avoid the sharp stabs of graphite on the paper, leaving dark indents spattered over my drawing. *Inhale.* I focused completely on getting the point of the pencil to connect steadily to the paper and finally got the graphite to mark where I'd aimed. *Exhale.* With one slight jolt of a tremor, my pencil slashed across the paper. "Fuck." I felt the wood crack as my fist clenched around the pencil in frustration. I dropped it and stepped away. *I just want to make art, goddamn it!* I sucked in a deep breath, trying not to get emotional, and when I looked up, I saw that all the boys were staring at me. I guess I cursed louder than I'd thought.

"Uh…hand cramp," I explained with a shrug, not looking anyone in the eye. I moved my drawing from the table to my easel and stepped back to analyze my work. The archangel figure was stunning, and I felt my lips quirk up, impressed with myself, but then my eyes zeroed in on a major fault. Where the left leg should be, the paper was damaged. With the many sharp pencil pokes and harsh scrapes, I had erased too many times, and the paper was noticeably thinned and fraying. I felt a lump in my throat as I stared, feeling like I would have to start over.

"Mia." I was surprised when I heard my name so close to my ear and looked over my shoulder to see Jax standing behind me. "What's wrong?" He came up beside me and followed my eyes to the part of my drawing that was causing so much frustration.

"Um." I didn't want to talk to *the* Jackson Caine, professionally trained, talented, and accomplished artist, about my problems. "Nothing."

"You don't like it?" He frowned, and I just shrugged. "Why? It looks awesome."

"I know. Until I butchered the paper there."

"You know you can just draw over that…"

"No, I can't. It's destroyed. Look." I ran my finger down the roughened paper, then quickly dropped my hand before he could see it shaking.

"I'd say you've got one more shot."

"I don't. Every new pencil mark blends in with the hundred erased ones."

"Why are you pressing so hard there? Is it like a dimension thing?" he inquired as he noticed the shitty pencil strokes that cut into the paper and could barely be erased. I sighed and shook my head.

Jax looked at me, then glanced at my table, where I had laid out the rest of my graphite pencils and tools. "May I?" he politely asked, and I reluctantly nodded. He went to my table and looked over what I had been working with. I watched his fingers run over the different pencils, trying to find a certain degree of hardness. Then I watched him leave to retrieve something from his station and return.

"What are you doing?" I frowned when I saw that he'd brought with him an X-ACTO knife and then picked up a 4B pencil.

"I will show you." He rolled my chair over and took a seat, then pulled a small bin from under my table and set it in front of him. "It's not hopeless, but you're right. The paper is thinning, and any more runs with the eraser could ruin the drawing's integrity. So, we'll prevent that from happening." Jax held the pencil in one hand and used the knife to act as a sharpener. "You can create a softer point for the pencil so it doesn't make such harsh strokes and use a softer degree so the lines aren't so defined and just glide on top." With his thumb, he put pressure on the blade against the wooden pencil length and carved around it, letting wood shavings fall into the bin.

"That looks strange," I said when he held up the newly adjusted 4B pencil. He had scraped away the wood all the way around to lengthen the tip, and continued until the tip of graphite was exposed and protruding about an inch from the wooden pencil.

"Yeah." He nodded, then pushed his feet against the concrete to roll closer to my easel. He held up the pencil to an untouched space, holding it almost parallel to the paper, and made soft markings that wouldn't need to be erased. "Use that until you find what you want. Then you can go over it with the HB you used with the rest of the body without disrupting the paper any further."

"Huh."

"Mm-hmm." Jax held up the pencil for me to take and stood. "I hope it helps." Then he walked back to his station.

I brought the paper back to my table to try again. The pencil was easier to hold with the long, slanted angle, my hand lying softly on the paper. My tremors remained, and it was still difficult, but it worked, and I didn't have to start over. I appreciated Jax's help but was also really embarrassed that he'd seen the mess I'd made of my drawing. What he'd showed me was a simple thing that I should've already known as a professional artist, but I'd never had any training. I put my AirPods in to block everything out and focus on my drawing. I listened to Queen's *A Night at the Odeon*, my appointed project album, on repeat and didn't look up from my drawing until Ozzie waved his hand into my vision hours later.

"Hm?" I straightened and took out my AirPods.

"It's almost seven o'clock," he informed me, which surprised me, since it meant I had been in the zone for six hours. "We're going to go to Floyd's but didn't want to leave without you, so we kept working, but now we're really thirsty." I looked around and saw the boys smiling and nodding. They all sensed I was having a hard day with my project, and my mood lifted when I realized they were waiting for me.

"Well, let's go." I took off my glasses and abandoned my station to follow the boys downstairs. The elevator doors opened, and Nick, Steven, and Ozzie stepped in, but before I could join them, Jax pulled me back.

"We'll take the next one," Jax informed the boys as the doors closed. My heart started beating faster. I looked up into Jax's stormy eyes and waited for him to say something. "I hate when you're mad at me."

"Okay," was my only response. Feeling awkward, I turned away from him.

"No." His voice was deep and firm as he grabbed my arm to make me face him and held me with both hands circling my biceps. "You're going to talk to me."

"What do you want me to say, Jax?"

"Anything. You haven't talked to me in three days."

"I don't have anything to say."

"Since when?" He arched a brow and stared me down. He had a point. "Mia." He sighed and looked at me with softer eyes. "I'm *sorry*, okay?"

"You don't have to be sorry."

"Really…?"

"Really. You don't have to apologize for your own opinions. Just don't put them on other people, and we're good."

"Those aren't my opinions." His grip on my arms tightened as he spoke slowly, bending down to look more directly into my eyes. "Why don't you believe me?"

"Because you said it," I replied softly and looked away, feeling vulnerable with him so close to me.

"I didn't mean it! I just didn't want him hitting on you."

"Why?" I frowned and brought my eyes back to his. He blinked a few times, then sighed as he straightened to his full height and dropped his hands.

"Just forgive me." He was intense as he stared down at me.

"Okay, I forgive you." I nodded and meant it. Even though we worked in the same room, I had missed him. The days were dull without laughing with him or at him. I hadn't even looked at him, so I missed the little moments of excitement when I caught him looking at me. It was only three days, but I'd noticed it.

"Thank you." He exhaled with a nod, then smiled and held his arms out. I shook my head and leaned back. "This nice moment needs to be punctuated with a hug. Let it happen," he said.

His arms wrapped around me and pulled me against him in an embrace. I hesitated for only a second before wrapping my arms around his middle, and my eyes momentarily fluttered closed when I felt my cheek press against his chest. It was sensory overload—the feel of his hard body against mine, his smell, his long arms holding me, and that adorable smile I'd seen as he'd moved in. *Did he just smell my hair?* I didn't want it to end. Neither of us let go until we realized we were past the time of a usual friendly hug and backed away.

"Okay, nice moment punctuated," Jax said, and we both nodded. "We should probably catch up with the guys."

"Probably." I pushed the button for the elevator doors to open, and down we went to rejoin our friends.

———

The next day, we continued working on our projects, and I was happy to see that my tremors weren't as bad as the day before. It was still a struggle, but Jax's guidance had made it easier. There was always a fear in the back of my mind and in the pit in my stomach that someday my tremors would worsen and stay that way.

I'm an artist—how the hell will I make art if I can't control a pencil? Or even a brush? Someday, I may not be able to rely on my hands, but, maybe, I could use the rest of my body…

That wouldn't be too hard…have a vision, paint a canvas, maybe blue, then paint my body, maybe red, and put them together. Art.

Chapter 25

For our religious project, the client had insisted on a strict deadline. Our artwork felt hurried, and we were stressed toward the end. The next Wednesday, we'd finally achieved the perfection we demanded from ourselves and got our work to the client. A weight lifted from all of our shoulders, and we collectively sighed. Finally, we could relax around the studio. We started our post-project ritual of cleaning and reorganizing our stations.

"Hey, guys!" Nick got all of our attention as he rushed into the studio from the kitchen. "We still got a ton of booze left over from the party! Who wants to day drink?"

"What we got?" I asked, already having an idea for what to do with the leftovers.

"Like, a couple cases of beer and seltzer…then a few bottles, like Captain Morgan—" Nick rattled off.

"Ah!" I interrupted with an excited hop in place at my station.

"You're not thinking…" Ozzie eyed me with a smirk from his station. He knew the mention of the spiced rum bottle excited me.

"Ship of fools!" I announced, which made Ozzie laugh and the rest of the boys stare, confused.

"Ship of what?" Nick asked with a frown.

"Fools," I answered, getting excited about the idea of playing my favorite game.

"Okay…still what?" Nick asked me again.

"It's a game Ozzie and I made up as kids," I explained. "It's like life-size Candy Land."

"Then we modified it into an adult version, which just adds in booze," Ozzie added.

"Is there a rules sheet?" Steven asked, intrigued.

"Who cares! Let's play!" Nick clapped, then hurried across the studio to stand with me at my station. Steven shrugged and followed, along with Ozzie.

"Jax, this game calls for participation from everyone," I called out to him. Jax was still standing by his station. I could tell that he was hiding his interest, but I knew he was intrigued.

"Alright. I'm in." Jax swaggered over to stand with the rest of the boys crowded around me.

"Okay. This is Planet Neptune," I said, diving into the directions. I pulled out a blank sheet of paper and set it up on my easel. "And the floor is ocean lava." I started drawing a map of the game to turn our studio into Planet Neptune—pointing out the routes and the different zones as I went. "And there are four zones—zone one is Jaws, zone two is the Bermuda Triangle, zone three is Mermaid Lagoon, and zone four is Venus's Shell." I explained the rules for each zone.

"Dear God, your imagination." Jax laughed once I'd finished my little presentation. I noticed that all of the boys were listening intently, following along with the rules of the game as I drew on the map. We all decided to put off our cleanup duties until the next day.

Ozzie and I then ran around the studio to set up Planet Neptune while the others watched with impatient excitement. I scurried around the room, placing chairs, tables, pillows, and cushions on the floor to create a path through the zones to get to the ship. Ozzie set up the ship and captain's chair, which was just a table in the middle of the room with a chair on top of which sat a bottle of Captain Morgan. As we set up the layout, we told everyone else to gather the booze. Ozzie and I finished up by arranging the beer and seltzer cans in lines around the chair on the table.

"Okay!" I raised my voice to get everyone's attention so we could commence ship of fools. "One, two, three!"

"A pirate's life for me!" Ozzie and I called together.

Ozzie set us up for the next verse: "Three, two, one!"

"Find the rum!" we all chanted together and took a shot of Captain Morgan, grabbed a can of beer or seltzer from the table, then dispersed to the different chairs, pillows, and tables that were scattered around the studio.

"I abolish the zone-four rule! I'm not taking off my shirt," I announced as I stepped on a pillow in Venus's Shell.

"Since when are you shy?" Jax teased, then smiled when he saw me blush.

"What the hell does that mean?" Ozzie asked with narrowed eyes.

"Nothing! Jax is just being a dick," I hurriedly answered before Jax could say anything else about the time I'd flashed him in the bathroom.

"Sure." Jax smiled and winked at me. Thankfully, Ozzie believed that Jax was just being a dick. We then all agreed that the zone-four rule would be optional.

Basically, the game was just running around like idiots, trying not to touch the floor, and drinking the entire liquor cabinet. Everyone figured out the routes while Ozzie and I shouted directions and rules. Still, we paced our drinking so we'd be able to drive home at the end of the day.

The game gained momentum as we followed the zones' rules. Nick was standing on a pillow in Jaws, wobbling on one leg. Steven was in Mermaid Lagoon, trying to sing along with "Walk This Way" playing through the speakers. Ozzie was in Venus's Shell, shirtless, as he wanted to show off his abs. Meanwhile, Jax and I finished our drinks in the Bermuda Triangle, opting out of the zone's "truth or dare" rule. I temporarily forgot about my lack of coordination and balance, and my spinal fusion. I tried to hop from a small table to a chair, but I lost my balance, and my fused spine tipped me over—I fell to the ground. "Ah...! Ow." Luckily, I didn't face-plant and landed on my hands and knees. "It's okay, guys! Don't come running all at once!" I yelled sarcastically after everyone winced but remained in their spots.

"I got you." Jax smiled and left his cushion to stand in front of me. I raised up onto my knees and was surprised when I felt his hands circle my waist, then lift me into the air. Once I found my footing on my chair, he hesitated. Jax's hands flexed around me and held on longer than needed.

"Thank you," I murmured awkwardly. I loved the feel of his touch, warm and electrifying, and when I looked into his dark-blue eyes, I could tell he liked it too. I sensed the rest of the boys watching us and brought my mind back to the game. "Ha! You're in ocean lava. You have to start over." I snickered as Jax stood on the floor in front of me.

"That's fair. Even though ocean lava makes no sense." He dropped his hands from my waist. The boys watched our little exchange with curious looks, but we ignored them. We waited for Jax to start over by returning to the ship, taking a shot of rum, picking up a can of beer, then finding the space we chose for him.

Soon, we had finished all of the booze and Nick was the first one to get to the table. I started playing "Ship of Fools" by the Doors over the speakers.

"Aha!" Nick cheered as he climbed onto the table and sat on the chair. "I'm Captain Morgan!" He took a swig from the bottle of rum, and we all applauded his achievement.

"Alright. Time to sober up," Jax announced, and we all started converting the room from Planet Neptune back into our art studio—cushions and pillows returned to the couch, chairs and coffee table were staged in the sitting area, and the side tables and roller chairs went back to our stations.

"That was a good game," Jax said to me as we all gathered in the kitchen.

"Best game ever!" Nick announced with an excited hop. I went to the fridge and started handing out bottles of water to the boys. "We gotta play this again sometime."

"Post-project ritual?" Steven suggested, and we all agreed.

We ordered pizza and relaxed for the rest of the day. I was pleased that Ozzie and my game could offer all of us a well-deserved day off. I was even happier knowing that we'd play it again.

Chapter 26

The fun energy from our recreational break carried over to the next day. Even though our cleanup duties were dull, we were all joking around and helping each other. Jax plugged into the speakers and played Metallica. I didn't even try to stop myself from headbanging, and neither did Jax, which entertained the other three boys. I was standing on my stepstool adjusting my easel when Ozzie's voice broke through the loud music.

"Jax!" he yelled over the song. "Wherever I May Roam" was playing. Jax held up a remote and clicked a button to lower the volume, then looked at Ozzie, giving him his attention. "Have you talked to Chanel?" I paused what I was doing and listened.

"Yep," Jax answered and went back to his work.

"And?" Nick chimed in. Ozzie, Steven, and Nick all looked at Jax now. *Who the hell is Chanel?*

"Memorial Day is on, and she's excited to see all of you."

"Uhh. Who's Chanel?" I raised my hand and asked whoever would answer.

"My mom," Jax answered.

"O-kay."

"We've been going to his parents' beach house almost every year for Memorial Day," Steven kindly informed me. The guys started interrogating Jax about who would be there.

"Joe?" Ozzie asked, and Jax nodded. "His crew?" Jax shrugged.

"Ugh, will those bitches be there again? Like…Naomi or Haley?" Nick grimaced.

"Natalie and Hannah?" Jax frowned and waited for confirmation.

"Yeah, and there's another one. The Monterey bitches," Ozzie offered, as he apparently shared the same opinion of the women as Nick.

"If you mean Natalie, Hannah, and Whitney, I don't know."

"What about Connor?" Steven asked.

"Not this year." Jax shook his head and continued answering questions about people I didn't need to know about. I wondered what kind of family he had and shrugged to myself. I turned back to my cleanup and let them discuss their plans.

"Mia." Jax called my name, and I looked over my shoulder. "You'll come with." I spun around, surprised, and faced him.

"Why?"

"Because everyone is invited."

"Oh…well, thank you, but—" I was going to decline, but Jax didn't let me.

"You'll come? Great. We're leaving Friday."

"That's tomorrow…"

"Very good." Jax praised me for knowing the days of the week. *I guess I'm going.*

"Wait, where are we going?" I asked Jax, but he was already walking away. All of us then focused on prepping our stations for the next job for the rest of the day. I was able to dig up more information on our weekend away. Like…where we were going. Jax's parents had a beach house in Monterey. Memorial Day weekend, their family and neighbors got together to party. That's all the information I had.

———

"Oz! I shouldn't come, right…?" I asked Ozzie nervously when I called him later that night.

"Why not?"

"Because he doesn't want me to." I sat on my bed and looked out my window. I was excited to go but stressed out that I shouldn't.

"I can tell you want me to convince you... Jax invited you. That means he wants you to come. How's that?"

"No, that's scary...no." Ozzie sighed and tried a new tactic.

"You like annoying Jax."

"That's a good start."

"So does his brother."

"Oooooh." I felt myself light up at such a prime opportunity of antagonizing Jax with the aid of his brother—double the force and double the ammunition.

"Really, I've known his family for a long time," Ozzie said. "They are very nice and will love you."

"Okay."

"You're coming?"

"Yes."

"We are all happy you're coming."

I hung up and let out a heavy sigh. I'd been holding my breath for the entire conversation. *Now, what do I bring? Oh, hell.* I dialed Ozzie again.

"I don't know what you should wear!" Ozzie yelled at me when he answered, as he anticipated my question.

"But you doooo," I sang back, and he chuckled. "I just need to know if there is an accessible body of water and what the vibe is..." I spoke quickly, and bless Ozzie for answering me.

"There is a pool and an ocean. They always have a Memorial Day party with the community, which is kinda fancy. Other than that, the vibe is...I don't know, casual...but *not* like your cabin casual...like beach-house casual."

I rolled my eyes at his reference to my cabin in small-town Minnesota. "That's why I'm asking, Ozzie. I don't know beach-house casual."

"Okay, bring casual summer dresses, leggings, nice sweaters, a pair of jeans and shorts, a bathing suit..." Ozzie started rambling, so I just smiled and kept listening. He was a good friend, and the knowledge he had gained from growing up with two sisters was a plus. He also ended up listing every type of clothing, so it wasn't a lot of help.

"Okay, okay, got it. Thanks, Ozzie. See you tomorrow." I hung up on him and faced my closet. I spent two hours packing and fit everything into a duffel. I included a few outfits, my basic toiletries, and some makeup. Of course, I remembered all of my medications and made sure that I had enough to cover my long weekend. I put out my nightly and morning pills on my dresser and sealed the rest up in my duffel. I decided to take my night meds earlier than usual and got a good night's sleep.

———

In the morning, I went all out with self-care pampering, which wasn't much, mostly just the usual but at a leisurely pace, and extra moisturizer. I wanted to look my best as I prepared to meet Jax's rich and sophisticated family—an assumption I made from their connection with Ozzie's family, the Bishops. I studied myself in the mirror and felt confident about how I looked and—*oh my God...Jax is going to see me in a bathing suit...in a bikini.* I hadn't thought of that and felt butterflies in my stomach because I was going to see *him* in a bathing suit too. I applied more moisturizer. *Okay. I think I'm ready.* I took my charger from the wall and a bag of Twizzlers from the cupboard for our drive. Wearing my usual outfit combination of a baby tee and high-waisted ankle-cropped leggings, I gathered my things and went out the door.

I was the last one to arrive at the studio, and Ozzie, Steven, Nick, and I waited on the sidewalk for Jax to pull his truck around.

"Shotgun!" Ozzie shouted before I could, and I felt my heart sink with disappointment. I stood there awkwardly on the sidewalk, staring at the front seat with longing. I looked away, and my eyes connected with Jax's as he got into the driver's seat. I wondered if he'd hoped I would sit next to him. We both looked away, and I climbed into the back seat, stuck sitting between Nick and Steven. *I'm the front-seat attendant. Damn you, Oswald Bishop.*

I tapped my feet in excitement—or anxiety—as Jax pulled away from the curb and we began our road trip to Monterey. Five minutes went by, and everyone was on their phones, and it was too quiet. I leaned forward and poked Jax's shoulder. I got momentarily distracted when my gaze ran down his arm and to his hand, which gripped the steering wheel. His voice snapped me back to my intentions.

"Yes, Mia?" Jax glanced at me with a smirk.

"Are you gonna kick out the jams?" *Motherfucka.* I finished the lyric in my head and smiled sweetly at him.

"Do you have any requests?"

"Nope," I said to be flexible but knew I would definitely intervene if he played something stupid. He fiddled with his phone for a moment, tapped play, and set it down. Music began blasting through the truck.

"*Kick out the jams, mothahfuckahs!*" MC5.

I started laughing in glee—he knew my song reference! "*I'm gonna kick them out!*" I shouted along with the song's next lyric. Funnily enough, Jax did too. We both turned to each other in surprise and laughed.

Ozzie looked between the two of us. "You two are so weird." He sighed and turned down the music.

Thankfully, it was a short song, as I had hit my headbanging limit.

We were all having fun, and I had to take most of the credit for it. The boys would've been content not to utter a word the whole two hours, but that would've been so boring. I would've worked myself up into a ball of nerves before meeting Jax's family. Which I was doing anyway, but still, the road trip was a good distraction. I handed out Twizzlers as we played car word games, but we ran through them quickly.

"Oz, text my mom and say we'll be there in twenty," Jax instructed as he handed Ozzie his phone. I was hit with a small wave of anxiety. After Ozzie sent the text and before he could hand the phone back to Jax, I took it out of his hand.

"Excuse you?" Jax looked at me, confused as I rested my elbows on the middle console between the two front seats and fiddled on his music app. I found my pump-up song on whatever playlist that was on the screen.

"*Is this the real life? Is this just fantasy?*"

"Bohemian Rhapsody" boomed through the speakers, and Ozzie sent me a knowing glance. Freddie's voice crooned through the car, soothing me. We all joined in on the "mama" but let Freddie finish off the ballad.

"*I sometimes wish I'd never been born at all!*"

"Here we go..." Ozzie chuckled, and I launched into the operatic section. The surround sound in Jax's pickup was a brilliant feature, and I freaked out over the back and forth between the speakers. The boys helped me with some "Galileos," and I got ready for the big riff. *Boom...*

"*So, you think you can love me and spit in my eye!*"

I didn't go all out like I would have at home but still danced despite the restriction of my seat belt.

"*Any way the wind blows...*"

I did my terrible imitation of a gong, and the song was over. "Bohemian Rhapsody" could cure and excite anything and everything that stirred in my heart, no matter what it was. The six minutes of bliss were comforting and energizing, but when the music stopped, I realized we were almost at our destination.

"Oh!" I remembered that I knew basically nothing about the Caine family. "I need to be briefed on Jax's family!"

"Let's not." Jax tried to shut me down, but Ozzie, Nick, and Steven were eager to fill me in.

"Well, they're rich, but seriously, don't get intimidated because they're super nice. They have this summer beach house in Monterey that's awesome, and I think we've all been there together five times?" Ozzie looked to Nick and Steven for confirmation, and they nodded.

"Jax has two brothers," Steven informed me, but Ozzie took over again.

"Conor is the oldest. He has a family in North Carolina so he won't be there. Joe is next. He's going through a divorce but might be—Jax, is Joe single?" Ozzie turned to Jax.

"That's hardly pertinent information. I think he's bringing someone," Jax mumbled back, and Ozzie just shrugged.

"And he's an attorney in LA. He's a lot of fun. I think you'll like him."

"He'll definitely like you!" Nick teased and elbowed me. That comment almost made me nervous, but then I saw how it upset Jax, and I got excited instead.

"Can we be done?" Jax sighed but was ignored as Ozzie continued his description of the Caine family.

"Chanel is an angel. Jax beat me up once for calling her hot," Ozzie said. Jax muttered something under his breath but let Ozzie continue with his informational session. "Jax's dad is a self-made commercial real estate mogul but retired and still makes money—I don't know. He's a business genius."

"Yeah, don't imitate Chanel's accent. She doesn't like that," Steven informed me with a side glare at Nick, who I assumed had been inappropriate in the past.

"We are here," Jax said. I looked through the window and saw rocks. Jax shot me a weird glance before he got out of the truck. I jumped down from the pickup and rounded to the bed to get my duffel and then followed the boys up the stairs toward the house.

We didn't stop when we got to the house, and I followed along a path to a smaller house. We got to the entryway, and Ozzie, Nick, and Steven walked in, but Jax stopped and stepped aside. I hesitated, and he looked annoyed as he motioned for me to go ahead of him.

"Ladies first? Aren't you a gentleman." I smirked at him and took a step, but Jax shot his arm in front of me.

"Courtesy revoked." He gently pushed me back and passed through the threshold.

"You are no gentlemen." I feigned outrage as I walked into the house after him. Jax turned and caught my arm to pull me closer.

"I never claimed to be, darlin'," he murmured so only I could hear him. He gave my arm a quick squeeze before releasing me and then joined the rest of the boys. *He does not affect me whatsoever. I do not get goose bumps every time he talks all hot and rough to me. My arm isn't tingling from his touch...and I'm not thinking any of this!*

I followed the boys up the stairs that opened to a loft, one big room with four beds. They each threw their bag on a bed.

"Well...I feel awkward," I announced with my duffel dangling from my arm, and the guys all looked cluelessly at me before it clicked.

"Oh, shit!" Ozzie shot up from his bed once he realized that there was no place for me to sleep. "How did we not think of this?"

"Mia, you can have my bed," Steven kindly offered.

"Or mine, I don't mind sleeping on the floor," Ozzie offered as well.

"Same!" Nick joined in, too. They were so sweet. We all looked at Jax, who was lounging on his bed comfortably.

"Those are great options." He nodded and smirked at me. I rolled my eyes.

"Thanks, guys." I pointed my appreciation away from Jax. "But I'll be just fine on a couch. I don't care." I shrugged and went downstairs to locate a good couch or, even better, a futon, but the boys came quickly behind me and pulled me back outside. As we walked the short distance to the big house, I looked ahead at the beach house we were approaching. It looked virtually the same as the guest house, just larger. They both had a pale-gray wood exterior with white trimming, each covered in tall windows. Traditional coastal but modest in size.

I was at the back of the group as we filed into the big house and into the kitchen. Jax's parents greeted us with open arms and affection. His mom hurried to give Jax a big hug, and he looked so happy to see her. She was beautiful—an obviously classy woman in a flattering white sheath dress with sunflowers painted on. She then turned to us.

"The boys are back!" She clapped her hands, then froze when she saw me. "I didn't know a woman was coming!" She seemed ecstatic to see me and rushed over to hug me. I smiled politely back but didn't get a chance to speak. "Oh, how wonderful."

"Mom—" Jax tried getting her attention but was cut off.

"Jackson! How dare you not tell me you were bringing a girlfriend!" She playfully hit him on the shoulder. My eyes widened in horror and shot to Jax, who looked visibly uncomfortable. Ozzie, Nick, and Steven burst out laughing, while I stood there, awkward as ever.

"No, no." Jax softly chuckled along with the boys and addressed his mother. "She's not my girlfriend. That's just Mia." I glared at him. *Just Mia?* Nice. His mom withered at the correction.

"I'm sorry for the confusion." I smiled politely. "I'm not *just* Mia, though. I'm new to their artist group." I shot Jax a quick glance. "It's very nice to meet you. I'm sorry. I feel like I'm crashing the party." She studied me closely as his dad came over to me.

"Don't mind our rude son. Welcome to our home, dear." He smiled kindly, and I shook his hand.

"Thank you, sir."

"Call me Caine."

"Thank you, Caine."

"And call me Chanel." I smiled and nodded at his parents. Their warmth and welcome made me feel comfortable, and I needed that. I'd also enjoyed Jax's dad's jab at his son. Chanel's accent was soft and melodic, and I could only imagine Nick trying to imitate it. Their kitchen was what I expected—nautical and fancy. The house was open, spacious, and brightened by natural light from the massive windows that stretched the length of the walls to the high coffered ceiling. It was minimalist but felt warm and cozy in the presence of the husband and wife. White, shades of blue, and dark wood were mostly the only colors except for the bright arrangements of flowers on every table.

"Well, go on outside and relax. Jackson, your brother will be here any minute." Chanel shooed us out a sliding glass door and onto a deck that ran the length of the house—a lavish outdoor dining set on one end and an expansive lounge patio set on the other. A pool was located just off the deck, several stairs closer to the beach. Some elevation and a lot of rocks separated the deck and pool from the ocean, and I spotted a long pathway down the rocks to the water.

"Hey, 'just Mia,'" Ozzie said as he sat on a big, plush couch. "Come sit." I gladly sat next to him. Nick and Steven laughed as they sat on the couch across from us. A long table separated us, and by the looks of the pebbles and lighters, it had an electric fire feature.

"Thanks for the introduction, Jackson." I turned my attention to Jax as he rolled his eyes and sat on a massive wicker chair to the side. I noticed that the furniture was all oversized. I felt like I was going to be swallowed by the cushions but remembered it was a household full of men. Jax made his seat look almost small, and I tried not to stare at his body as he kicked up his feet to rest on the long table.

"Whatever. Don't call me that." He brushed it off but then solidified that I was going to call him by his full name again during our stay.

"Mia, do you like beer?" I heard Caine call from the door, and I declined politely. Caine matched Jax's tall stature and looked just like him, only twenty to thirty years older with long, striking silver hair pushed back, much like Jax's. With his short beard and tortoiseshell glasses, jeans, and knit sweater…he was my old-man type. I stealthily studied Jax's features and knew he'd end up looking just as good as he aged. Jax caught me looking at him and smirked, so I obviously pretended that I was looking at the sky.

"Okay! Beer for the lads." Caine joined us and handed the boys bottles of beer, then took a seat on another massive wicker chair.

"Mia…" Chanel called from the sliding doorway, then asked if I wanted lemonade. I hesitated with my response. "I'll put vodka in it…?" she added.

"I would love some."

She came walking out of the kitchen with two vodka lemonades, and I took my glass eagerly. "Thank you very much." She clinked her glass with mine, and I knew I already really liked her.

"So lovely to have you all here," she said brightly and took a seat on the ottoman in front of Caine. "How was—" She shot her husband a playful glare when he extended his long legs on the ottoman and gave her a little nudge as if to knock her off. She was about to carry on when he nudged her again with more intention. "You bugger," she huffed and shoved his legs off the cushion, trying to hide her adoring smile. I smiled, admiring their connection. "Anyways! How was the car ride?" she asked all of us.

"It went by quicker than usual, having Mia with us." Ozzie chuckled, and I felt embarrassed by the attention turning to me. I turned to look at him and waited for further explanation, but Jax cut in.

"She treated us to a one-woman performance of 'Bohemian Rhapsody.'" He looked at me like I was annoying, but his soft smile couldn't mask it.

"The opera part?" Caine asked Jax, who replied with a yes.

"Okay, it wasn't *just* me. These guys were my backup vocalists." I was quick to get the focus off of me and my terrible singing. "Except for *Jackson*." I smirked when I called him by his full name, and he glared at me.

"He didn't?" Chanel asked, apparently surprised. "But you're such a good singer." I wanted to focus on that subject, but Chanel quickly excused herself to go back inside. The guys offered more anecdotes about our road trip, making Caine laugh, while I just sat back and accepted the teasing.

Chapter 27

"Where's Jax's girlfriend?" A booming voice came from inside the house. A man who could only be Jax's brother appeared and joined us on the deck. He looked so much like Jax, athletic and impressive. Same blond hair but short and clean-shaven. Within the first second of seeing him, before he advanced, I could see the physical differences between the two brothers. Joe was shorter than Jax, but not by much, and he was just as fit, but with more bulging, bulkier muscles. His eyes landed on me, and he smiled and immediately bounded over to where I sat and took a place between me and Ozzie on the couch.

"Joseph, leave her alone." Chanel spoke sternly as she followed him out of the house. By her obvious exasperation aimed at her middle son, I figured that she must have already warned him about me inside. Joe didn't listen and put an arm around me.

"You must be the girlfriend." He was either trying to piss off Jax or make me uncomfortable, but either way, I played along.

"What gave me away?" I asked. Joe looked at me, surprised, and everyone laughed. "But I'm not a girlfriend. I'm just Mia." I smirked, knowing that the boys and his parents would catch the joke.

He leaned toward me and spoke under his breath, knowing everyone could hear: "Not a girlfriend. That's even better."

"Joe," Jax said roughly, irritated. "Aren't we expecting Brianna?" I remembered Jax saying that Joe was bringing a girl.

"Who?" Joe shot a confused look at Jax, and I couldn't tell if it were real or fake. "Oh! Bri. We broke up." Joe then winked at me.

"Oh, that's too bad," Caine commented, but Joe just shrugged, obviously not bothered by the separation.

"Well, this has been fun. Joe, there's a chair for you right there." Jax was losing his patience.

"I'm comfortable." Joe stayed put, but I really wanted him to not be nearly sitting on me.

"I'm not!" Ozzie shouted to break the weird tension.

"Oz! Hey." Joe did the man handshake, then left to claim his own seat, acknowledging the other two boys. "Nick, Steven."

"Okay! Where were we before Joe made a scene?" Chanel tried to turn the mood fun again after another glare at Joe.

Thankfully, the attention dispersed to Ozzie, Nick, and Steven. It was fun listening to Jax's family being so attentive and comfortable with the boys, and I learned a few new things about them.

"Mia." Joe raised his voice and got my attention in front of everyone. "Have you gotten a tour yet?"

"Um. No," I responded neutrally, and he rose to his feet.

"Well, then, let's go. I'll be your guide." He raised his eyebrows at me, and I didn't know what to do.

"No." Jax shook his head, his irritation spiked again by his brother.

"Joseph, sit down," Papa Caine scolded his obnoxious son, saving me from an awkward situation. Then he refocused on me. "Mia, would you like a tour?"

"Yeah, sure."

"Good. Jax will take you." Papa Caine had betrayed me.

"What?" Jax sat up straight in his chair. He looked at his dad, obviously caught off guard, then at me. "Let's go." He stood up and saw that I was still sitting on the couch. *Mia.*

"Okay." I sighed and avoided all eye contact with the others as I followed Jax inside. He slid the screen door open and ushered me inside with a push. "Ow."

"That didn't hurt." Jax rolled his eyes, and I looked over my shoulder to give him a look and noticed that his family and the boys were watching us and snickering—awkward. I ignored them and let Jax steer me ahead of him into the entryway.

"*Are you kicking me out?*" I abruptly turned around and ran right into Jax's massive hard body. "Oh." I stepped back and looked up at his smirking face.

"No, I'm not kicking you out. I probably should, though."

"Probably." I shrugged, then looked around, deciding to momentarily be his grateful and enthusiastic guest. "What a beautiful entryway! High ceilings...fancy." I put my hand on the dark wood banister that swooped to the end of the staircase. "Even fancier." I turned with a little hair flip, trying to act fancy, and climbed the steps.

"There's nothing up there," he called from a few steps below me.

"You're a terrible tour guide," I scoffed but kept walking up the stairs.

"Probably because I was drafted." He followed me onto the second floor.

"Joe would've been a better tour guide, for sure," I taunted as I peeked into open rooms from the hallway.

"You're right. Let's go get him." Jax turned and started walking away. I stared after him for a second, considering how to play it. I decided to call his bluff.

"Great idea." I nodded, passed him, and descended the stairs ahead of him.

"Mia…" Jax called after me, and I hoped he'd stop me before I got to the sliding glass door. I didn't want Joe. I wanted Jax.

"Time to be relieved of your duties," I said as I made my way through the kitchen. I opened the sliding glass door and shot him a smile over my shoulder.

"No." Jax stopped me by pulling me away and sliding the door shut. "I changed my mind."

"You don't want Joe to replace you?" I asked. He shook his head. "And why not?"

"I want to be the one to show you around," he said simply, his voice genuine.

"I want you to be the one to show me around too," I said just as simply, looking into his eyes.

"Then let's go."

"You'll be a good tour guide now?" I teased with an arched brow.

"The best." He made the promise with a serious head nod. "This is the kitchen."

"Wow. Impressive."

"Just keep walking." He chuckled and pushed me farther into the house. "That's the living room—it has the nice furniture and fragile things… you shouldn't go in there. That's a fireplace—we use it to make fires. There's a clock. It's not digital, so you should just look at the kitchen one. It's on the microwave, but it does more than show time. It heats things up, but not tinfoil. I made that mistake once. That's a dining room. People eat there. But not just Pop-Tarts and Twizzlers, real meals with substantial food. Nutrition is important—something to think about. Here's a den. It has the TV, but I suggest trying the books. You can keep up that vocabulary. That's a rocking chair, which is a chair that rocks—you probably shouldn't use it. You're a safety concern. If you do, make sure you have a spotter. A picture of a bird…" I soon followed him out of the house through a side door. We walked down a path across rocks to get to the beach.

"This is the ocean. It's like a lake but a lot bigger. See, you can't see across it." Jax was being annoying and referencing my home state of 10,000 lakes.

"I'm learning so much today! First a microwave, now a massive lake. Thanks, Jax!" I expressed my gratitude in a mocking tone but actually had enjoyed the impromptu tour. Instead of turning back, I paused to absorb the soothing but exhilarating effects of the salt water. "This feels amazing, though." I flexed my toes in the sand, then softly smiled at Jax, who stood next to me and was watching me. "I am happy to be here," I murmured and looked back to the horizon.

"I'm happy that you're here. I wasn't expecting it."

"Expecting what? Being happy I'm here or that I am here?"

"I don't know." He took in a deep breath of the salt air and looked to the horizon with me, exhaling. "Both. You."

"You weren't expecting me?" I looked up at him and frowned and watched him shake his head, still staring at the ocean.

"Nope." He glanced down at me with a small smile and shrugged. "Now, if you'll follow to your right, the tour will continue." Jax took my shoulders and guided me down the shoreline so we kept moving. "The guest house is there." Jax pointed to the house we'd left our stuff in. Then to the structure between that and the water. "A gazebo, but we never use it. That's about it."

"It's beautiful." I nodded as my eyes scanned wherever he pointed. "Thank you, tour guide."

"You're very welcome, guest." We both bowed our heads toward each other like professionals, but in a silly way, then moved from the beach to the wooden walkway and the stairs to the main house. We made it back to find that the scene hadn't changed—except for a greater amount of beer and a picked-over cheese platter on the table. We rejoined the group and took our previous seats.

"You have a beautiful home," I complimented Jax's parents.

"Made it through the tour, okay?" Caine asked me, and I nodded.

"We started to worry after Mia tried to escape," Joe teased us both, and it was clear they had all witnessed my in and out with the sliding glass door. Everyone laughed, but Jax and I just looked at each other and shrugged, not knowing how to respond.

"They usually figure it out," Ozzie assured the group and tried steering everyone's attention elsewhere.

"Where has the time gone?" Chanel suddenly rose to her feet. "I need to get started on dinner. You kids get settled in. I'll let you know when dinner is ready." The older couple went inside.

Hunger hit me hard. I'd hardly eaten anything during the day, and I was annoyed at myself for forgetting to eat. I discreetly held up my hand to see if the shaking had, in fact, amplified, then gently nudged Ozzie.

"Will you cut me a hunk of cheese? Please," I murmured to him, knowing that my tremors were bad enough for everyone to notice if I tried holding a knife. I quickly lifted my hand to show him, and he nodded. He was about to slice, but I nudged him to go bigger. "Thank you." I took the cheese gratefully—a delicious nutty gouda was my guess—and nibbled on it as I followed the boys back to the guest house.

Unlike the main house, the interior was styled more like a cabin, with its rich wooded walls that matched the furniture. It was minimal and rustic, and I sucked in a calming breath, as it reminded me a little of home. Even though I knew it wouldn't last long, the stress in my shoulders loosened as I felt more comfortable in a strange place. I looked around the first floor a little more and discovered it was just a kitchen and a family room with an open floor plan and high vaulted ceilings—no bed for me. I sighed and sat on the lumpy couch. It was big enough to double as a bed but definitely uneven enough to aggravate my back.

"Well, I guess this is it." I took a seat on a hard cushion, dropped my duffel at my feet, and looked around for blankets.

"No way. Take my bed," Ozzie offered again.

"No, it's fine. Really. I'm not overly excited about sharing a bedroom with a bunch of boys anyway." I chuckled lightly, but Ozzie looked at me, unsure if he should insist.

"We can figure it out later," he told me, and I shrugged.

"Beer!" Nick squealed from across the room. We all turned to see him in the kitchen area with his head in the fridge. "Oh, Chanel, I love you!" He took out a handful of bottles and put them on the table, and we all joined him around the center island—the island had two levels, one counter level and one bar level. The boys took theirs, so I peeked into the fridge and grabbed a water bottle.

"Your parents are lovely, Jax," I told him as I twisted off the cap and they popped open their bottles.

"Well, they certainly like you." He took a swig of beer.

"I know." I smiled and went to stand by Ozzie. "In Ozzie's defense, your mom *is* hot, Jax."

"Thank you!" Ozzie put an arm around my shoulders and smirked at Jax. It was true. Chanel was beautiful and held herself so confidently and gracefully. In response to my weird comment, Jax just rolled his eyes and took another drink. I went to the sliding glass door and looked outside. There was a small deck, then a sandy wooden walkway down to the ocean with the gazebo Jax had pointed out to the side.

I excused myself to the lower-level bathroom, which I'd claimed as my own—a barrier between me and the heathens upstairs. I heard the boys' thundering steps up to the loft to get ready for dinner, so I did the same. I relished having a solitary moment to take my time freshening up. I sprayed rose water on my face and hair, filled in my lipstick, re-curled my lashes, and flipped my hair around for renewed body, making sure my wispy bangs hit my cheekbones. Final touch, a spritz of perfume at the back of my neck. I changed into full-length leggings and switched my tee for an oversized seafoam-green sweater with a deep-cut V that flattered my collarbone and neck but didn't show off cleavage. It was warm enough for the night temperature but cool enough for the exposed skin and was appropriate to wear without a bra—I felt classy. To show off the V-neck, I pushed all of my hair to fall down my back and left the bathroom. I saw that the boys were already waiting for me at the door, so I followed them out.

———

As we walked to the main house for dinner, I kept hoping my stomach wouldn't embarrass me with an obnoxious grumble. Caine, Chanel, Joe, Jax, Ozzie, Nick, Steven, and I gathered around a long dinner table. I sat down first, which was always a mistake, because then I couldn't control who sat by me—this time, it was Jax's brother, Joe. Jax came in with the breadbasket and visibly stiffened when he saw me sitting next to his brother. He set the basket down in the middle of the table, then sat down in the chair across from me.

It was a lovely salmon dinner, and I accepted a glass of delicious sangria. The conversation was mostly about our work, which was a very welcome topic, until that subject was exhausted and the focus landed on me, the newcomer.

"So, Mia." Joe raised his voice and turned in his chair to face me. "Tell us about yourself."

"Oh. Um...okay." I smiled nervously. I hated navigating what to tell people as they watched. It was never simple, and I often edited down my answers or even lied.

"Start with where you're from and your family," Joe nudged me, and I was grateful for the prompt.

"Well, I'm from Minnesota—" I began.

"You're from Minnes-OO-da?" Jax cut me off with a little smirk as he imitated and exaggerated my voice. My Midwestern accent always appeared when I said the name of my home state. The boys all snickered with him, and I pursed my lips, stifling a smile.

"Interrupting is very rude, Jackson," I said sternly, and his eyes narrowed, but he stopped himself from making a comeback in front of his parents. I'd forgotten I was in the presence of his family and became very self-conscious about if they'd think *I* was being rude for calling out their son. I glanced over to where they sat and saw Caine and Chanel smiling as they looked between us.

"Excuse him. Mia, please continue," Joe urged me.

"Okay. My family lives there—"

"So, tell us, Mia, what do you do for fun in Minnesota?" Jax interrupted again and crossed his arms. He stared at me and raised his brows, and it was my turn to narrow my eyes. He was definitely setting me up for a comeback, and mine just fell out.

"Oh, fer fun? Dontcha know we gO on the bOat?" I answered his question with stereotypical Minnesotan phrases. Jax's eyes lit up with humor, and he burst out laughing, and so did the rest of the table. I felt a little shy from the attention but brushed it off.

The laughter died down, and I looked across the table at Jax and smirked. He smiled back and shook his head as he chuckled again. Nick and Steven were asking for more "hick talk," which was not correct, but Caine reeled everyone in.

"Okay, okay. Now we all know that Mia is from Minnesota," Jax's dad announced, then gazed at me through his tortoiseshell glasses and nodded his head. "Please continue."

Damn, I thought I'd gotten myself out of this.

"Sure. My family still lives there, and I have two sisters—the older one is a nurse, and the younger is studying to be one."

"Middle child," Joe interjected and held up a hand, making me laugh. I nodded and accepted his high five. "Where did you go to college?" Joe asked, and it instantly became harder to breathe, as we were cruising into dangerous waters. I just hoped I didn't have to jump ship.

"University of Minnesota," I answered smoothly even though my chest tightened. I thought that was the best answer I could offer—telling them about Washington or the all-girls school would lead to more questions. Any further down the education road, I'd have a heart attack.

"How'd you like it there?" Joe asked, and everyone's eyes were on me. I couldn't answer, and my throat started to twist as I felt the pressure to respond while ugly memories flashed inside my head.

Oh, God, I'm going to have a panic attack right in front of Jax and his family, oh, shit.

"Hey, Mia." Ozzie got my attention, and I looked down the table to where he was sitting. "Tell them about Zeus!" Ozzie was my savior, jumping in to redirect the topic to something easier for me to talk about. I finally let out the breath I was holding and blinked away the memories. I replaced the dread with comforting thoughts of my dog.

"Good idea." I smiled at Ozzie. I turned back to the rest of the table and made eye contact with Jax. He was watching me closely with a slight crease in his brow as if he were suspicious or even concerned. I quickly looked away and told them about my young mastiff dog waiting in Minnesota for me to bring him to live with me in San Francisco.

The attention on me continued but didn't touch on anything too personal or close to my traumas or secrets. Once the attention left me to focus on Steven and Nick, I looked down the table at Ozzie and mouthed, "Thank you." I knew that if he hadn't interrupted during the college conversation, I would've stuttered while my hands shook more severely, at the very least. I was discreet about showing my gratitude to my best friend, but when I straightened in my chair and looked back to the rest of the table, my eyes locked with Jax's. He was the only one watching me, and I immediately looked away, avoiding his eyes for the rest of the meal. Soon, we finished eating, cleared the table, and took time to help stack plates at the sink.

"Chanel, what's for pudding?" Nick asked her in a butchered posh British accent. She turned from the sink to glare at him.

"You get no pudding. Get out of my sight." She pointed outside, and Nick actually giggled before running away. "Twit." She shook her head. "How do you stand them?" Chanel asked me seriously, and I thought it was a pretty good question.

"I really don't know. Probably just because I have to." I shrugged and we had a nice little laugh. All of the boys were outside by then, and it was just me, Chanel, and Caine in the kitchen. "I'd love to help with cleanup if I can," I said softly so the boys didn't overhear and call me a kiss-ass.

"Oh, no, no, darling. Go join the fun. We can handle this." Chanel smiled warmly, and I thanked them for dinner again and went outside. I noticed Channel calling me, and others, "darling"—more like, "d-ah-ling"—and wondered if that was why Jax so frequently used that term of endearment.

"What are we doing tonight?" Ozzie asked the group. "Fire? Games? Bar?"

"How about we gO on the bOat." Jax smirked as he mimicked my Minnesota accent again. He got the guys to laugh, and I actually did find it funny.

"You betcha," I responded, using another stereotypical Midwestern phrase, adding to the fun.

"The sky looks weird," Nick announced.

"Great observation, weatherman," Joe called back but didn't even look up. I did. It was green.

"I agree with Nick...are we getting a storm?" I looked around and everyone shrugged. I already noticed the wind picking up.

Chapter 28

A half hour later, it was pouring. We got rained on as we ran back to the guest house, and the boys changed into sweats while I traded my sodden sweater for another baby tee. The rain dampened everyone's mood, and I was bored. Ozzie was throwing a mini basketball against the wall—playing catch with himself. Nick was on his phone playing a game. Steven was on his phone talking to his girlfriend. I didn't know where Jax was.

"Ozzie! I'm open." I got his attention so he'd toss me the ball, but he didn't. Just then, the door opened, and Jax walked in. He was soaking wet from the rain, his thin sweater clung to his muscles, and some of his long hair fell into his face. He looked into the house, and I was the only one looking back.

"Mia, give me a hand." He held up arms full of paper bags. I went over and collected the bags and placed them on the counter. When I turned back, he was still standing on the mat. "Thanks. Can you grab me a towel?" He ran his hands through his dripping hair to push it out of his face.

"I don't know where they are." I stared at him, wanting the visual to last.

"Cabinet in the bathroom."

"I don't know where that is." I kept looking at him, pretending to be confused. He stared at me, annoyed.

"Fine. I'll get it myself, even though I'm literally drenched and will make a mess..." He sighed but quickly perked up. "You look like you need a hug," he said and smiled.

"What?" I didn't catch on until it was too late. He pulled me toward him and wrapped his long arms around me and squeezed.

"Ah!" I squealed at the sudden sensation of cold water being transferred onto me. I tried to push or wiggle away from his embrace, but he didn't let go.

"Mia, you really need this hug. I can tell."

"No, I don't!"

"Don't fight it."

"Go away, you giant!" Jax started laughing and let go. I pushed away, breathing heavily.

"You liked it," Jax teased but suddenly stopped laughing. I was wearing a light-blue T-shirt, and he'd just made it X-rated. "You should go change," he ordered me.

"Why?" I challenged him, my hands on my hips. It was his fault, and I knew I looked pretty *irresistible* to him right then.

"Your shirt is ruined." His eyes darkened, and I tried not to smirk. He had already looked—I might as well make him uncomfortable.

"It'll dry." I shrugged. "Thanks for the hug. I'll get you that towel now." I turned around, knowing he wouldn't let me walk past the other guys. He grabbed my arm and pulled me back. "I thought you wanted a towel?"

"Stop," he growled.

"You made me wet!" I scolded him, but he just smiled.

"Did I?" Jax spoke seductively and pulled me closer. I aggressively shoved him away.

"You know what I meant. You got my *shirt* wet, then order me to change? Too bad."

"You're going to stay in a wet shirt looking like a Playboy Bunny until it dries?" I just nodded. "Then you leave me no choice." He looked dangerous, which worried me, so I tried to step away. He grabbed my arm again and pulled me into the coat closet. My body started to heat up, thinking he was going to come in with me, but he didn't. "Until your shirt dries. Have fun." He closed the door.

"Jax! Don't you dare lock me in here!" I pushed past the coats and searched for the knob but only felt wood, no knob. "This is illegal!" I banged on the door. "There's poor ventilation in here!" I listened but didn't hear any of the guys or movement. "I'm getting lightheaded! I could die!" Nothing. "Since I'm going to die in a coat closet, alone...I should get my affairs in order. I'd like it to be documented that 'In My Time of Dying' by Led Zeppelin must play at the funeral. Definitely open casket. More dramatic that way, so people can see how young I was and shake their heads, saying how tragic it is—she had so much more to give! Gone too soon!"

"Oh my God, shut up!" I heard someone yell, but I couldn't tell who. I just giggled.

"Then let me out!" A few seconds later, Jax opened the door. "Thank you." I tried to step out, but he held me back.

"No, no." He held out a sweatshirt. "Put it on, then I'll let you out."

"But my shirt is already dry." He frowned and glanced down to see my still-wet shirt. He looked back up at me and narrowed his eyes. I started laughing, and he threw the sweatshirt at me, then closed the door again. I rolled my eyes, took off the offensive shirt, and put on the sweatshirt. He let me out finally, and I was freed from the closet. I went straight to the bathroom to wring out my shirt and then draped it on the shower rod. I left the bathroom and walked further into the main room to see the four boys playing catch. It was actually really cute.

"No one pass to Mia," Ozzie said, focusing on catching the ball.

"Hey!"

"You always drop it." He looked at me. I knew it was true. "We are seeing how long we can go." He turned and passed the ball to Nick, who sat on the couch—his phone still in one hand.

"Very exciting." I nodded. Nick then tossed the ball for Jax to catch, but I stepped in and caught it. "Ha." I then reached out to Jax and dropped the ball in his hands. "I didn't want to play anyway, so." I walked back into the kitchen. "I need a drink," I said out loud.

"Look in the bags... Reverse!" Jax told me as he passed back to Nick, changing the direction. I looked into the bags Jax brought in and found Jameson and Tito's, along with ginger ale, soda, and tonic.

"Anyone want a Jamo-ginger?" I called to the guys as I made myself one. Jax was the only one who said yes, as the others were still finishing their beers. I made two and walked over to Jax. I took a sip from one and handed him the other. He looked between the two drinks, then at me, and took the one I'd sipped from.

"When I kill you, it won't be with poison." I smirked and took a big sip from the denied drink. Jax chuckled and refocused on the game but then shot a suspicious look at me, frowning once he realized I'd said "when." Steven threw the ball, and Jax didn't catch it.

"*No!*" Ozzie held his head in despair.

"*Damn it, Jax!*" Steven yelled at him, while Nick just laughed.

"Jax is out," Ozzie announced definitively.

"Oh, come on," Jax groaned.

"Does that mean *I* get to take his place?" I picked up the ball.

"No!" yelled all three boys, and I threw the ball back into the game.

"You're a menace." Jax shook his head at me.

"Who, me?" I smiled sweetly, then found a bookcase and started browsing through it. It was mostly just games, so I grabbed one and turned to Jax. "Wanna play Scrabble?" He nodded eagerly. The boys playing ball all groaned, and I stared at them, confused.

"Jax and his brothers are psycho with that game. We don't play it anymore," Ozzie said gravely and shook his head. I wondered if there was a good story since I couldn't see anyone reaching psycho level while playing a word game.

"Okay, that's an exaggeration." Jax rolled his eyes, defending himself.

"You guys call it Death Scrabble," Steven reminded him, and Jax didn't deny it.

"Death Scrabble. Now I really want to play." I smiled and did a little hop of excitement.

"Of course you do, dark witch with nunchucks," Jax teased, and I didn't deny that either as I let Jax take the box from my hands. He sat down at the end of the table and started setting up the board and tiles. "I'm kinda a big deal in the Death Scrabble world, so play at your own risk," he warned me and looked me up and down as if I couldn't survive Death Scrabble. I smiled, nodded, then skidded a kitchen chair down the table and sat at the corner edge next to him, ready to play.

"So…what happened? With your brothers and this game," I asked out of curiosity as I dug letter tiles from the black pouch and set them on my rack.

"Let's just say no one won and someone ended up with a pencil through their hand."

"What?" I stared at him, knowing he was serious. "Say more!"

"It's not to be spoken of ever again." He shook his head. I grabbed both of his hands and inspected each side but found no signs of pencil penetrations.

"So, it wasn't you," I stated, happy to have found an excuse to touch his hands. "Oh! Were you the perpetrator?" He just chuckled and shook his head.

"Joe's not here…it should be safe," Steven reasoned to Ozzie, as if we were waiting for their approval.

"Joe, in the billiard room, with the pencil!?" I asked Jax as I put the info together like in the game Clue. He shrugged. "Let's get Joe." I smiled at him with a faux-menacing look.

"No!" Jax yelled like a little boy in protest, and it was adorable.

"Fine, if you're gonna be a baby about it." I sighed, giving up, and started studying my tiles. We played an uneventful round of Scrabble since Jax refused to keep score once I started beating him.

"Do you want to go mess up their game as much as I do?" Jax whispered, and I nodded. "It's nice being just with you, though."

"Yeah, kind of a rare moment," I commented and he nodded.

"So, University of Minnesota is college number three?" I didn't respond. "What happened?" he asked, clearly remembering how I'd gotten uncomfortable when we'd talked about my college education at the Sinclair mansion.

I forgot that he knew I'd gone to several colleges. Number four was my state community college, where I'd dropped out of ten classes as I tried to make progress on getting a degree while struggling with bipolar disorder.

"Nothing." I stared back at him, wordlessly communicating that he shouldn't go there.

"Okay…then why did you only say one school?"

"Easier." I shrugged.

"Because stating more than one college is difficult to vocalize and understand…" He looked at me like he didn't buy it.

"I forgot about the others." I shrugged again, hoping he'd back off. He rolled his eyes at my lame responses but knew I wasn't going to give anything up. He shifted in his seat and faced me squarely.

"You seem to get uncomfortable when there's attention on you. You're articulate and interesting, so what is it?" *Content, Jax.* I knew I could answer a question intelligently but not if the content was my life. This man saw right through me, and it was truly unsettling.

"I don't know how to answer that."

"Honestly."

"Then I respectfully withhold my answer," I told him, and my voice sounded weak, so I turned away from his eye contact and sat back in my chair. I glanced back at him, and he was studying me closely…again. I wondered how much he could see.

"Refill?" I stood and took both our cups into the kitchen, even though they were half empty. I picked up the Jameson and poured, but the weight of the full bottle exaggerated my tremors—the bottle shook violently in my hand, gushing an excessive amount of whiskey into my cup. Jax had joined me in the kitchen and took the bottle out of my hold and set it down on the counter. I took a deep breath and lowered my hands to the counter and looked out the windows to the ocean. My senses were ultra-sensitive, and I jumped when Jax took my hand. It must have still been shaking. How could I explain that? As usual…I just didn't.

"Mia, I'm sorry, I didn't mean anything—" Jax still held my hand, standing close to me.

"No." I cut him off and shook my head. I pulled back my hand from his, and with a heavy sigh, I turned to face him. "You—um. That was—um...not you." I flitted my other hand away to show it was no big deal and should promptly be dismissed. I finally looked up at Jax. His eyebrows were knit together with confusion and concern.

"So, what just happened?"

"Depends... What did you see...?" I looked around awkwardly.

"I asked you why you get weird talking about yourself, and you got weird. Then you came in here, and your hand went crazy." He tried to keep it light but was still staring intensely at me. I took a step back.

"Huh...I see it differently. Um. You asked me a deep question, and I didn't want to talk about it—"

"Because you don't like talking about yourself." I rolled my eyes.

"I came in here to pour a drink, but the bottle was crazy heavy, and my weak little arm couldn't handle it." I spoke clearly and Jax nodded.

"Then go write something on the board." He pointed to the dry-erase board on the fridge and found a marker.

"No."

"So you're lying." He wanted me to admit it, and I didn't appreciate it.

"I'm not." He held the marker out to me. *Okay...I just ate a big meal, which helps ease the tremors. I managed the Scrabble tiles well enough. The Jameson bottle really was heavy.* I really thought I could do it since I knew what angles of my wrist were more controlled. I rolled my eyes, sighed heavily, and took the marker. Standing in front of the fridge, I held up my hand and tried to draw. But, of course! My hand was still shaking, and I couldn't even get it to land on the board except for two dots. I instantly set the marker down. "That marker is really heavy." I folded my arms to hide my hands. Jax picked up the marker and just raised his eyebrows.

"It's a dry-erase marker." I actually chuckled at how stupid it was, but Jax didn't think it was funny. His eyes went to the two dots on the board, then shot back to me. "Is that what happened to your drawing? All of the erasing?" I stopped breathing. *Don't cry, don't cry, don't cry.* "Is it?"

"No." He looked at me like he didn't believe me and was going to continue the interrogation. "*No.*"

Jax stared into my eyes as if he'd find the answer there if I wouldn't speak it. I looked away. "Are you okay? Just answer that honestly, and I'll drop it," he said. He had no idea how complicated that one question really was. *No, I'm not okay!*

"I'm okay." My delivery of the lie was confident but not convincing. All I wanted was to finally answer him truthfully, but I knew that I couldn't.

"Then okay." Jax took a few steps away but looked like he didn't believe me. I nodded and reached for my cup. "That's going to be a very strong drink," he warned me with obvious concern. I had accidentally poured a lot of Jameson. I just shrugged and splashed in ginger ale, fast enough that the tremors weren't as noticeable. "Do you want to pour some out...?"

"No, I'm good." I smiled and walked away. The guys were about to find out just how well I could hold my liquor. I approached the boys, who were *still* throwing that damn ball. I looked back at Jax and smirked. He nodded. It was time to ruin their game. It didn't even look like they were having fun. Nick had just thrown the ball toward Steven, but I intercepted it, tossed it to Jax in the kitchen, and he hid it in the nearest cupboard.

"You two are sore losers!" Ozzie yelled at us, but Nick and Steven sighed in relief.

"Thank God," Steven muttered

Nick bashed the game too. "That was prison." Ozzie got intense with games sometimes. They must have been throwing for an hour.

"Inclusivity, Ozzie!" I put a hands on my hips. "We're all playing a game together, and we're gonna like it!" I commanded the boys as thunder rumbled from the sky. "That was great timing." We all laughed and went through the bookcase of games together.

"Twister!" Nick screamed and grabbed the box. *Oh, God. I'd rather not.* Thankfully, the other guys felt the same.

"That would be so wrong." Ozzie looked at him, concerned by his choice, and Steven just shook his head.

"Oh, come on!" Nick whined, then looked to Jax.

"Sorry, man. That's a no for me." Jax laughed and shook his head. "Actually...I'd play." We all looked at him, weirded out. "If Mia plays." I scoffed, but the three boys supported him.

"That's a no for me," I mocked Jax but was very serious.

"That's fine. We'll ask you again after you finish that drink." Jax smiled and picked up a deck of cards.

We played BS, but I didn't really care. I called bullshit on everyone almost every turn, just for fun, and had the biggest deck of cards—yes, I was that person. Early in the game, Jax went to the kitchen and back, then wordlessly plopped a straw in my drink. He could tell I was self-conscious about my shaking and had seen that the one time I'd picked up the cup, I'd nearly slammed it down in silent irritation at my tremors.

"Mia, would you like a refill?" Nick asked me from across the table, and I looked into my cup and saw that it was empty.

"Sure." I shrugged.

"Aha!" Nick jumped up from his chair.

"Finally. I hate this game." Steven pushed away his cards.

"She's not going to do it." Ozzie rolled his eyes and collected the cards to put them away.

"Mia, wanna play Twister?" Jax leaned in and asked me with a smirk. They actually thought I was going to say yes. I cleared my throat and leaned toward Jax.

"No." I smiled, then sat back in my chair. The boys all groaned.

"Oh, come on, Mia. Be a bro! We wanna play!" Nick whined and hopped up and down to show his enthusiasm like a toddler.

"Then play, bro." I laughed comfortably from my chair.

"We can't play with just men," Ozzie reasoned.

"Guys. Leave her alone. Mia doesn't want to play because she's nervous." Jax patted me on the head, and my eyes narrowed.

"No, I'm not." I looked at him, utterly confused.

"You are, though." He walked away and into the kitchen.

"Why would I be nervous?" I stood up, ready to dispute his argument, and the other guys backed up.

"It's obvious, darlin'," Jax said.

"Do tell, darlin'." I folded my arms. He just smirked and walked closer to me, but I took a step back and watched him skeptically.

"You're nervous that you won't be able to resist me."

"Excuse me?" I hissed.

"You don't want to play because you wouldn't be able to handle my body being so close to yours." He shrugged. "We understand."

"Someone's conceited."

"Someone's nervous."

"I'm not."

"Prove it."

"Fine." I really had no other choice. I glared at Jax as he just smiled, very pleased with his reverse psychology.

"Yay!" Nick cheered and retrieved the game. I left them to set the thing up and went to my bathroom. I took off the massive sweatshirt Jax made me wear, planning to switch back to the shirt he'd gotten wet. I took it down from the shower rod and smoothed it out. It was dry and not wrinkled, so I put it on over my leggings. The combination was comfortable and flattering but not too dramatic since only a glimpse of my waist showed as I moved, and the leggings made my legs look damn good. I rejoined the group and saw that the mat was down and Nick held the spinning wheel. I groaned. *I don't want to do this, but, oh, well, I'll make it fun.*

"Why is there no music playing in here? Ozzie, can you hook up to the speakers?" I asked. He nodded and got his phone. "But! I get to dictate what to play." They agreed as a thank-you to me for playing Twister with the men children. Ozzie announced that he'd connected to the speakers. "Classic rock station, please. Heavy on the Queen." I nodded my approval at Ozzie when "We Will Rock You" started playing throughout the house. I went to the kitchen for another drink as I sang along to the song.

"I made you one." Jax handed me my cup. I knew he'd poured my drink because of the shaking incident, and the small gesture made me incredibly happy.

"Thank you." We made eye contact, but I quickly averted my gaze from his intense dark-blue eyes, still embarrassed that he'd seen that.

"You're welcome," he murmured.

"Mia! Hurry up," I heard Ozzie call.

"Resist Jax and let's play," Nick added, and I glared at Jax.

"I had to." He made a lame excuse and chuckled. I ignored him, and we rejoined the guys. I sat my drink on the table and lifted my arms to tie my hair back with a scrunchie. Jax stared at my shirt and clenched his jaw. He was definitely thinking about the wet T-shirt contest I'd won before shoving me in a closet, and I loved it.

"Game one! Steven versus Mia," Nick announced.

"Shouldn't there be more than two?" I asked him, but he just shook his head and told me to play. "So, I have to play this game four times just for you guys?" He nodded along with his goofy Goldilocks giggle. I sighed and accepted it. As always with Steven, our game was calm and easy.

"Okay, Mia—one point." Steven rolled away from where he fell on the mat, and Ozzie hopped in.

"Watch out, Bell," he taunted and stood in a ready position, which was very unnecessary.

"Bring it, Bishop." I softly laughed at his competitiveness over a game of Twister.

"Mimi, left foot—blue!" We started off steady and strategically. I was pretty sure we were playing it wrong, as we alternated turns. Ozzie was hit with a "right hand green." Then I got a "left hand red." We both struggled to keep our balance.

"That's impossible. I have a fused spine!" I complained as Nick shouted my move and Ozzie snickered.

"Gonna fall already?" Ozzie teased, and I made the attempt but fell.

"Men—one point." Nick clapped, then handed the spinner to Ozzie. "My turn!"

My game with Nick was the longest so far, mostly because he took so long to make each move. I held a bridge position over Nick while he was crouched under me. The following moves caused us to tangle together, and my legs extended to the opposite ends of the mat.

"How is that even possible?" Nick watched my body, impressed by my in-the-air splits.

"I'm flexible. You're not." I smirked, and Ozzie shouted his next move. Nick had to rotate his body to reach his spot, which lead him to be faceup under me. I then had to stretch one leg to the same row as my hand, resulting in a deep-lunge situation. Ozzie shouted a move for Nick.

"Hmm. Where is a yellow..."

"Right next to you."

"Where? I'm color blind." Nick continued to stall.

"Hurry up!" I groaned, my limbs tiring. He then "accidentally" hit the inside of my elbow, making me fall on top of him. Ozzie, Steven, and Nick all started laughing. Jax just rolled his eyes. "Nick!" I yelled at him but started laughing, too, and rolled off.

"I win!" He jumped up from the mat.

"You do not!" I stood up and looked at Ozzie, who was still laughing but nodded.

"Mia—two. Men—one-point-five," he announced and I scoffed.

"Nick gets half a point for cheating?"

"He gets a half point for making you fall, which was hilarious." I glared at the two boys but ended up laughing with them. It was a good point. I went over to the cup that I'd left on the table and bent over to suck from the straw without picking it up, then plopped down into a chair.

"Oh, no. You're not done," Jax said dangerously, standing in front of me.

"Actually, I hurt my arm when I fell... I don't think I can play anymore." I shrugged. Ozzie, Nick, and Steven all booed me. Jax grabbed my arm and pulled me to my feet.

"Ow," I whined at the contact, but Jax just rolled his eyes and dragged me to the mat.

"You're nervous," he whispered in my ear, and it pissed me off.

"*I'm not.*" I glared at him.

"I feel like we should take bets," Ozzie said to the other boys, the three of them lined up in chairs to watch us.

"On who wins?" Steven asked.

"If Mia can resist Jax or not!" Nick cheered.

"What the hell do you think I'll *do*?" I growled. Really, did they expect me to take my clothes off and jump him?

"Fine, fine. We'll bet on who wins," Ozzie assured me. Nick and Steven bet on Jax, and Ozzie bet on me, which he probably did out of pity. The game, as usual, started off slow.

"I'm proud of you, Mia," Jax said condescendingly.

"Fuck off," I mumbled, and he just laughed. The moves were surprisingly and thankfully easy, since playing against him was a lot more of a challenge because he took up the entire mat. I tried to clear my head and not think about his large, strong body. That proved impossible, so I focused on annoying him rather than resisting him.

Jax rolled his eyes when I used a move to return to a standing position and bent over with straight legs to the spot right by my feet, discreetly showing off my flexibility—but still physically necessary with my spine.

It took only a few moves for us to get into a compromising position. I was hovering above the mat on my hands and feet, facing up like I was doing a crab walk. Jax then stretched an arm across me to plant his hand on the circle next to my head, and was then hovering over me.

"Hi." He smiled, and I rolled my eyes. Nick called my move, which made me transfer my foot to a farther spot, forcing my legs farther apart. Jax noticed, and I smirked. Ozzie then called the next move for Jax. We tangled together more and more, but we couldn't get out of a position with him on top of me.

"You two Muppets with the spinner! You better not be making this up." I tilted my head back to scold them, upside down.

"They are." Steven laughed from the sidelines.

"This is *rigged?*" I yelled at them. The boys were taking turns at the spinner, and I knew they were playing their own game to see who could get us the most entangled.

"If you can't handle it..." Jax taunted from above me.

"Shut up," I growled, annoyed, but he only smiled. "Steven, don't let them do it anymore!" Steven just shrugged. I glared up at Jax. *Game on.* It seemed like it was going on forever. We were back to making small moves, and I was able to shift out of my vulnerable position. I let out a sigh of relief. I realized that the guys were giving us directions to reverse our positions, and I was soon doing a bridge over Jax. Both of my hands were on either side of him, and so were my legs, extended behind me. My limbs were almost half the length of Jax's, which made it so that I was a lot closer to him on top than he'd been to me—our bodies were only inches apart.

"Hi," I said with a smirk as he looked up at me, amused. "You know...I think this whole thing was a ploy so you could get close to *me.*"

"You think so?" he responded playfully, and I nodded.

"I think it's *you* who can't resist me."

"You wish." He smirked, and I continued to focus on annoying him. For my next move, I had to bring my right leg closer to my right hand. As I made the move, I bit my lip in concentration, then looked back at him with an innocent expression. Jax narrowed his eyes but took his turn. We were still in the same compromising position. That's when my scrunchie fell out, and my hair came tumbling down. I tilted my head so it was all on one side. *What timing.*

"You did that on purpose," he accused me, and I couldn't help but giggle.

"How could I have done that on purpose?"

"You're a witch." I started to laugh harder and dropped my head a little to hide my face cracking up. I regained my composure and looked back to Jax under me. Then he pushed me so I tumbled to the side onto the mat.

"Ow!" I gave him a kick so he fell too. We both glared at each other, and I was prepared to run away, but our game was interrupted by a new guest.

Chapter 29

"Looks like I came at the right time!" Joe walked in from outside and threw down his soaked raincoat and kicked off his boots. He put something on the kitchen counter and came further inside. Jax stood up, and I could tell he wasn't as happy as Ozzie, Nick, and Steven were to see Joe.

"This is perfect! You can be our tiebreaker. Mia—two, men—two." Nick cheered. I didn't know how they got that score, but I did not want to play against Joe.

"No, it's two to three. I win." I pushed myself up into a sitting position and eyed the scorekeepers.

"Jax won with half a point," Nick explained. "He maintained the upper hand during the match."

"He pushed me, so I win!"

"True, but then you kicked him after the game was over, and that's a penalty." Ozzie shook his head at me with disapproval, and I rolled my eyes.

"In retaliation!" Bastards always ganged up on me. "I call for an investigation."

"Violence is never the answer," Jax said gravely as he stood over me.

"Fuck off," I grumbled and stood up.

"I like you." Joe was laughing and pointed at me. "But don't worry about it. I'm too old to play a silly children's game." I didn't like his condescending comment. He wasn't that much older than Jax.

"Oh. I see. Well, I was excited to play you, but if that's how you really feel...I understand." I shrugged and looked over at Ozzie, who was now smirking at me.

"Hey, now. I don't mean to disappoint you. I'd love to play." He walked closer to me, ready to take back his jab.

"Don't worry about it." I smiled sweetly at the corporate Jax lookalike. "I don't want to play with someone who thinks it's silly."

"I don't think it's *that* silly. I just meant, like...I'm an adult, so I don't usually play kids' games, but if it's against you, then..."

"Joe. It's okay." I patted him on the shoulder and went back to the mat, where Jax was still watching me. I bet he thought I was going to try make him jealous by flirting with Joe—I considered it, but ultimately, I wanted to be closer to Jax. "Ready for a rematch?" I looked up at him and smiled.

"You're on." He smiled back genuinely as I did some quick stretches. I was having a lot of fun, and we stepped onto the mat with something more than friendly competition in our eyes. I had my hands on my hips and swayed a bit back and forth to the sound of "Sweet Emotion" playing from the speakers.

"Joe, you have to make sure Ozzie and Nick don't mess with the directions. Please," I told Joe, who had sat down at the kitchen table with the scorekeepers.

"Sure." He sighed as he cracked open a beer, and Ozzie told him he was an idiot.

The game was on and progressed much like the first round. Slow and steady until the boys manipulated the moves to twist us into compromising positions. This time, it was me holding myself up like a crab and Jax hovering over me.

"No, don't go there!" I yelled at Jax before he set his hand down. "Then I can't get through."

"You know we are playing against each other." Jax chuckled as he put his hand down on a yellow circle. I had accepted that the boys were making up the directions as my next move had me bend my leg so my inner thigh was against Jax's leg. He rolled his eyes. If the game continued like this, one of us was sure to call it, as our positions became more tantalizing the longer we had to hold it. Then the song changed, and I started laughing. "What's so funny?" Jax eyed me, since the lyrics hadn't started yet, and I just smiled. "I don't trust you."

"*Get down make loooove,*" I sang with the Queen song, and our audience started hollering and laughing.

"For fuck's sake," Jax groaned. "Don't get weird." He glared at me.

"What's weird?" I tilted my head to the side in question. Jax was instructed to move his foot over one color so we kept holding the damn position. I knew that Ozzie and Nick calling the moves would make it go on forever. I knew how to speed things up. "*You say you hungraaay. I give you meat,*" I sang with Freddie, and the crowd went wild. "*I suck your mind. You blow my head.*" Jax clamped one hand over my mouth, and my eyes widened in surprise as he held himself up with one arm. *Damn...okay....*

"Shut. Up," he scolded me, and I started to shake with laughter. "Can she be disqualified?" He looked up at Ozzie and Nick, who must have shaken their heads because they then called the next move. They told me to move my hand over one color, and I did, but Jax didn't move his hand away from my mouth—so I licked it and he yanked it away. "Did you just lick my hand?" I shook my head.

"Are they always like this?" I heard Joe ask the other boys, and they said yes.

"Sing again and it's game over," Jax scolded me, but I kept smirking. "I mean it." I just nodded and looked into his fiery eyes with mischief that veiled my desire for him. Ozzie gave him his next move, and Jax lifted his hand.

"*Come on, so heavy...when you take me.*" Of course, I had to sing again. Jax brought his hand to my chest and pushed, making me fall to the floor, and I started laughing.

"So, who wins...?" Joe asked the judges.

"This is a tough one." Nick rubbed his hands together.

"Judges need to deliberate in private," Ozzie announced and whispered with Nick. "Jax wins. Penalty on Mia for foul play."

"That's fair." I caught my breath, still on the floor. Jax stood over me, shaking his head but smiling.

"Good game." I held up my hand, and he rolled his eyes but took it and pulled me to my feet.

"Mia, how did you get so bendy?" Joe mused from his seat at the table as he eyed me.

"I'm just flexible." I shrugged and picked up my drink. My flexibility was limited to my legs but helped compensate for my fused back. "What have you been up to?" I asked Joe, genuinely curious, since we hadn't seen him since it started raining.

"With the parents. Legal stuff." He looked at Jax as if his brother knew what the legal stuff was, and I figured that it was divorce-related. I searched the back of my mind, trying to remember what Ozzie said when I was eavesdropping at Floyd's. He was questioning Jax about why he was so pissed off the day he met me. All I could remember was that Joe's apparently nasty wife was named *Britney* and that it was fucked up. "Mom baked cookies." He motioned to the plate he'd brought with him.

"Oooh!" Cookies sounded so good, and I rushed into the kitchen. I brought the plate of cookies over to the boys and laughed when I heard Joe remind Nick that he didn't get any pudding. I took time to tidy up the counter, getting rid of all of the empty beer bottles and cups, as the guys talked at the table.

"You always surprise me." I jumped when Jax spoke beside me. I hadn't even noticed him joining me.

"How's that?" I turned to him, curious.

"I dunno." He shrugged. "I expected you to try to piss me off with Joe."

I smiled. *I knew it.* "Mm-hmm. I did too." I folded my arms and leaned my hip against the counter.

"And that song." He smirked and took a step closer to me. I took a step back. "Oh, don't get shy now."

"I'm not," I said defensively. I hated when he called me shy. "You are the one who quit."

"So?"

"Why did you?"

"Because you're annoying."

"How was I annoying?"

"You have a terrible singing voice. My ears were about to start bleeding." I started laughing at that ridiculous excuse.

"If that makes you feel better." I smirked.

"It's true."

"Had nothing to do with the lyrics or that I was under you? Did your whole plan backfire, Jax?"

"Nope."

"*I can squeeeeeeeze! You can shake me. I can feeeeel when you break me,*" I sang more of the lyrics, exaggerating them to be silly and to avoid embarrassing myself because, yes, I had a terrible singing voice. I couldn't go into the next verse because Jax's face was priceless, and I started laughing. He didn't think it was funny and grabbed my arm and pulled me out of the kitchen. I stopped laughing when he opened the closet door.

"Don't you dare!" I tried getting away, but there was no hope. He pushed me in and shut the door. "Jax!" I pushed on the door with no inside knob. "Someone let me out!"

"Did you just lock her in the closet?" I heard Joe ask, but I didn't hear the response.

"Joe! Be the good guy and let me out, please!" I didn't hear anything for a little bit.

"I'm going to let her out…" I heard Joe say, and soon the door opened, and Joe stood aside to let me walk out, looking very confused. *He's new here.* I stormed past the guys and went into my bathroom on the opposite end of the great room. I wanted a minute alone. I did a little freshening up, then saw the sweatshirt Jax had given me earlier, so I took off my shirt and put it on for comfort—by the size and smell, I knew it was one of his. *Okay...I'm good.* I walked back into the room and took a seat at the kitchen table with the rest of the guys. I leaned back in my chair and glared at Jax.

"What?" he asked casually from his spot at the head of the table.

"Stop locking me in the closet."

"It was an accident." He was acting so innocent, and I rolled my eyes.

"I think I missed something..." Joe sat between us and continued to look confused.

"You've missed a lot. Don't even ask." Ozzie chuckled and shook his head.

"Let's play ten fingers!" Nick shouted—I don't think he had an inside voice—and looked to everyone for approval. All the guys were into it, but I wasn't familiar. "Okay, everyone, make sure you have a full drink." My cup was empty, but all the guys went to the kitchen for refills. Jax saw me look over to the crowded kitchen, and he stood up, picked up his cup, then mine, and went over.

"What's ten fingers?" I asked the room as they got situated around the table.

"You hold up ten fingers, and everyone takes turns saying something they've never done. If you've done it, you have to put down a finger and drink," Ozzie explained to me, and I nodded my understanding. Jax returned and put my drink down beside me, then took his seat.

"Well, Mia is obviously going to win," Jax said to everyone.

"What's that supposed to mean?" I narrowed my eyes at him.

"Whoever is the last one still holding up fingers wins," Ozzie informed me. I thought about it for a second and realized Jax meant that I was inexperienced, and I rolled my eyes.

"I start! Ummm, never have I ever—wait...I did that—ummm..." Nick paused for too long.

"Time's up. Never have I ever walked in on my parents doing it," Steven said, taking the first turn.

"That's weird but okay," Nick grumbled, then put a finger down. The only other person to put a finger down was Joe.

"*What?*" Jax stared at his brother, horrified. "No. Don't tell me. Never have I ever smuggled drugs across state lines."

"That was one time!" Joe got defensive and was the only one who put a finger down. "Never have I ever...skipped school. Not including college." Joe looked around as Jax and Nick lowered a finger. Thank God I could put a finger down too.

"*You* skipped school?" Nick singled me out. I nodded. "For what?"

"None of your business," I replied sassily and took a drink. I wasn't about to tell them that I skipped school to get away from bullies and would sit at the closest Caribou Coffee reading Jane Austen. "Oh, right, it's my turn. Um...never have I ever been bitten by a shark." They all stared at me, and no one put down a finger.

"Mia, that's not really how it works..." Ozzie chuckled, and I just stared. "No, yeah...great turn. Um. Never have I ever participated in an orgy." Joe was the only one to put down a finger. All the guys called out Jax.

"I haven't! Well, define an orgy," Jax asked Ozzie.

Ozzie laid the definition down: "Interactive sex with more than three people."

"More than three? Nope." He smirked. I wondered what they were talking about.

"Never have I ever hooked up with an older woman..." Nick announced, then looked at me, "or man."

"What's older? There's a wide age range here," Steven asked.

"At least fifteen years older than you."

"When you say hook up..." I looked to Nick to specify because I never knew what people meant by that. *Is it sex? Is it just making out? Who knows?*

"At *least* making out." I put down a finger and took a sip of my whiskey ginger ale. To my horror, no one else did.

"*Whoa*, Mia!" was the collective response, and the boys started laughing...except for Jax.

"I don't believe you." Jax crossed his arms and narrowed his eyes. I just shrugged and kept my finger down. "Who?"

"You obviously don't know them."

"*Them?*" He looked shocked, and I smirked but really hadn't meant to give that away.

"Do I know about this?" Ozzie leaned in and asked quietly even though everyone could hear.

"Remember when the cops were called on me?" Ozzie nodded. "I was with Phil." Ozzie started giggling since he had the insider details, and the other guys freaked out when I mentioned the cops. I had told Ozzie the story with a more humorous angle so he didn't know it was a painful memory.

"What about the other one?" Ozzie asked through laughs.

"Jim."

"Oh, right." Ozzie kept laughing over the other men's confusion.

Really, that situation had been altogether terrible—I just laughed about it instead of feeling even more shame than I already did. It was one of my past experiences that didn't qualify as assault but was still traumatic. Newly diagnosed with bipolar and living with my parents, I got a job at the town bar. I made friends with the locals and would join them for drinks after my shift. I thought they saw me as a friend too. Bipolar mania made me vulnerable—reckless behavior, impaired judgment, blind trust, and no sense of danger were the harmful effects of mania—and when you mixed that with alcohol… I drank one Jameson and ginger ale past my high tolerance, and the seven drinks I'd had before hit me all at once. I was surrounded by men ready to take advantage of me. Me, a twenty-two-year-old girl, making out with two different older men in one night and my dad calling the cops on me for staying out too late? You see, it could go either way based on delivery—tragic incident or funny anecdote. I decided to lean on humor rather than humiliation when I told the story in order to live with it. I knew if it weren't for my bipolar mania, I would never have trusted them, I would have never gotten into their car, and I would have one less bad memory.

"Story time!" Nick clapped.

"Um. No." I laughed and shook my head.

"How old are you?" Joe asked and looked at me and squinted his eyes.

"Twenty-four." I was not about to offer up that the men were fifty years old.

"I'm so confused!" Nick held his head in his hands.

"Yeah, I'm going to take this back." I put my finger back up. They all booed me. "Fine." I put it back down. Jax started to say something, but I pointed at him. "No."

"Never have I ever"—Steven yelled out of turn just to keep the game going—"gotten into a physical fight. Brothers don't count." Jax, Joe, and Ozzie put down a finger and drank.

"Never have I ever had the cops called on me." Jax smirked at me. "And parties don't count."

"You got me. Good for you." I lowered a finger and drank, but no one else did. "I'm the only one? How boring, guys."

"I bet that'll be the last finger you put down," Jax said.

"I bet you're very right. Like you said, I'll win."

"Never have I ever been involved in a schoolgirl fantasy," Joe said while trying not to laugh. Only Steven put down a finger, and we all laughed. "Dude." Joe glared at Jax.

"*Dude,* I never did that."

"I thought with Kelly?"

"That was you!" Jax started laughing, and Joe shrugged, then put down a finger on his own turn.

"Steven...were you the schoolgirl?" I whispered across the table, which made everyone laugh.

"Never have I ever bribed a teacher or boss," Ozzie said. I shrugged at that, not having done such a thing, but Nick and Joe put down a finger.

Next, Nick said he'd never been to the ER for a sex-related injury, and only Steven put down a finger, but he wouldn't explain further. Steven said something about jellyfish; then it was Jax's turn.

"Never have I ever...had a sugar daddy...or mama." He stared at me, and I rolled my eyes.

"Nice try." I didn't put down a finger because I really hadn't…although I'd had offers.

"So, you did those old guys for free?"

"I didn't *do* them." I glared back at him.

"Never have I ever…corrupted a virgin." Joe put that out there, and I felt my body tense. Nothing against Joe, but I was just uncomfortable whenever virginity was on the table. Steven and Nick put a finger down. "Seriously?" Joe laughed, and I just stared at my drink in front of me. That's when Ozzie and Jax also put a finger down. "Wait, seriously?"

"Yeah, it's not that weird." Jax shrugged and sat back in his chair. I glanced over at Ozzie, and he just nodded his agreement. I knew Nick and Steven were the only two who'd put a finger down, but then Ozzie and Jax put a finger down for me and that warmed my heart.

"Well, okay, then." Joe chuckled, then noticed my hands. "Mia and I are the only ones who didn't put a finger down, I guess." He nudged me and winked, like we had something in common.

"Should I?" I looked over to Ozzie, and he and Jax nodded. "Okay. Never have I ever had sex," I said casually and sat back in my chair, waiting for everyone to put a finger down. Joe was laughing but soon caught on that it wasn't a joke.

"Wait…you're serious?"

"Yep."

"Aren't you twenty-four…"

"That's my age." I nodded.

"Mia…I'm sorry…I really didn't mean anything bad about it…"

"You really hurt my feelings. I want to go home now." I looked away, hiding my not-hurt feelings.

"No, no, no, no, I didn't mean to hurt your feelings!" Joe's eyes were wide, and he sat up straighter, looking a little frantic.

"Okay, I'll stay." I smiled and sipped my drink while the rest of the boys started to crack up. Joe stared at me, not knowing how to react. "Joe, I'm messing with you." I looked him in the eye. "I am a virgin, though,"

I added. Ozzie and Jax already knew about my virginal status, and for the sake of messing with Joe, I really didn't care that the rest of the boys learned that private information.

"Oh my God." Joe scrubbed his hands over his face, then shook his head, letting himself laugh. "Okay, I deserved that."

"I had to." I shrugged and laughed too.

"I really didn't mean anything bad by it, okay?"

"Okay, thank you." I looked around the room, seeing where everyone was at in the game. I reached over to put one of Joe's fingers down since he hadn't yet, which made him smile. "Alright, boys," I said, "let's keep playing so I can win."

That's exactly what we did. Joe, Nick, and Ozzie were all drunk. Steven was mild as ever and already up the stairs to bed. Jax was in control as usual. I was just chilling and celebrating my win with a final chug of whiskey.

"How the hell is she not wasted?" Joe yelled to the whole room.

"That's actually a really good question." Jax eyed me, and I shrugged.

"Go Mia and her high tolerance," Ozzie cheered and patted me on the back.

"Why?" Jax asked and leaned forward. Obviously, he'd wondered this before and wanted to get an answer out of an inebriated best friend.

"She's weird." Ozzie sighed and reclined in his chair, closing his eyes. I chuckled, appreciating his response.

"Alright. I'm going to bed. Good night, you crazy kids." Joe stood up and turned to me. "Mia." He held his arms out to me, and I eyed him. He wanted a hug. I leaned against my chair, like it would be too much of an effort to stand for a hug, and extended my hand. He just chuckled and accepted the formal farewell. "See ya tomorrow." It had stopped raining outside, and he walked back to the main house.

"We are going to bed." Ozzie hit the table and stood up with Nick. "Wait, Mia, you don't have a bed!"

"I do! Don't worry about me," I assured him. "Good night." He nodded and went upstairs, pulling a half-asleep Nick with him.

"How is it that you can consistently outdrink a group of men?" Jax asked. It was now just the two of us at the table.

"I don't drink as much as them."

"Hardly," Jax said. "You know why." I shrugged. "Why?" he asked like I'd finally answer him honestly. Of course, I couldn't.

"I'm a robot." He stared at me, not amused. That was something about Jax that made him so different—he noticed, cared, and asked, wanting a true answer. Still, I couldn't give him an answer. "Okay, I have this condition." That got him to perk up and lean closer. I almost felt bad for messing with him. "It's called sober-itis." He rolled his eyes and sat back in his chair. "It's a thing."

"Whatever." Jax sighed with disappointment. He stood, then remembered our insufficient sleeping arrangements. "You don't have a bed."

"I have a couch." I shrugged, and Jax tried to convince me to take his bed upstairs, saying he'd sleep on the couch. "No, no, no. All my stuff is down here, and Ozzie snores really loudly. I'll be fine." He hesitated a bit but knew I wouldn't change my mind.

It was really creepy down there by myself, and the couch sucked. I kept thinking about Jax—it drove me crazy knowing that he was just upstairs. I took my night meds and drifted off to sleep.

Chapter 30

I woke up with the sunrise since I was surrounded by windows. I took the opportunity to shower before the boys woke up and was relieved to find a hair dryer underneath the sink. I got ready for the day in peace, thankful for the time alone. I opened the windows to let in fresh air after the storm and checked my weather app—the forecast was a high of seventy-two and sunny. I put on a tank top and shorts since I didn't know what the plan was for the day, and the boys were probably going to sleep for another hour. I cleaned up the mess we'd made the night before and searched the kitchen for coffee. I had a full pot ready by the time the boys came bounding down the stairs.

"Chanel says brunch at eleven!" Ozzie announced through a yawn and went for the coffee.

"How do you know?" Jax asked with a little frown.

"She texted me."

"Why would she text you?"

"Because I text *her*." Ozzie smirked, teasing.

"That stops now." Jax was serious.

"Okay, man, no problem." Ozzie nodded but then shook his head when Jax couldn't see him, laughing silently.

I changed out of my tank and shorts and into a casual sundress. It was a soft red with a yellow floral pattern, sleeveless, silky, and buttoned down the front. I stepped into my sandals and grabbed a vintage cardigan to wear if it got chilly. We went to the main house at ten to hang out on the deck. I stepped into the kitchen and found Chanel preparing the food.

"Good morning," I greeted her, and she looked up and smiled at me.

"Good morning, dear. You look lovely." She complimented my dress, and I was happy to see she was wearing a sundress too. She refused my offer to help and told me to go relax with the guys.

"They're just talking about sports, and I gave up pretending to be interested in that a long time ago." She laughed at that, nodding in agreement.

"Me too. Ugh. American sports." She grimaced, making me smile and feel comfortable with her. "Let's see...you can get the table settings ready. We have eight people. Plates are there, silverware there, and glasses over there." She pointed around the kitchen, and I got to work. I placed everything on the end of the counter for people to help themselves when the food was ready. "Should we have mimosas?" Chanel stopped her stirring.

"Yes!" I then took that on as my next task.

"Did you have fun last night?" Chanel asked kindly while I lined up wineglasses for the mimosas. "I felt bad when the weather turned on us."

"Oh, yes. I always have fun with the guys—well, most of the time. And thank you for the cookies."

"You're very welcome. I think it's wonderful they have a woman on the team. They really respect you, Mia. Joe thinks you're a riot." She chuckled as she mentioned Joe.

"Oh…" I didn't mean to sound awkward, but I did.

"He meant it in the best way, darling." She smiled warmly, then paused and set down her spatula. "I'm sorry I made you so uncomfortable yesterday. I just jumped to the conclusion that you were Jackson's girlfriend, and I shouldn't have."

"Don't be sorry. I understand. I just was caught off guard. I assumed he told you…"

"He should have." Chanel tsk-ed and shook her head. "I should have known better. He never brings women home. Anyways, you seem to handle him just fine." She giggled but didn't elaborate. "Brunch is ready! Call in the men." We all grabbed a plate and shuffled through the line of food Chanel and I laid out on the counters, then went to the dining set on the deck.

————

"Joe said you guys were entertaining last night," Caine commented as we all sat back in our chairs, finished with the delicious brunch.

"We played Twister." Ozzie laughed and shook his head. "It's a lot harder now than when we were ten."

"You guys played Twister together?" Caine asked for clarification.

"No, we all played against Mia." Nick giggled. Caine and Chanel both laughed.

"You poor thing!" Caine looked at me with sympathy, and I just smiled. "But you're such a tiny thing. I'm sure you had fun beating them."

"You'd think so." Ozzie chuckled. Caine and Chanel looked surprised and turned to me.

"The game was rigged," I defended myself. Jax scoffed and my eyes narrowed at him. "I would've won if you hadn't pushed me. Twice."

"Jackson!" Chanel gasped.

"Son, we taught you not to hit girls." Caine rebuked him but still chuckled.

"First of all, I didn't hit her. Second of all, she deserved it."

"Oh, that's not right." Chanel shook her head and picked up some plates to bring inside.

"Not right," I scolded Jax, echoing his mom.

"Do you want to start this, darlin'?" Jax stared me down with a smirk from the end of the table. I was sitting in the middle, so I leaned forward to rest an elbow on the table and stare back at him.

"You already started it, *darlin'.*" I smirked and sat back in my chair. Caine and Joe started laughing.

"You're right," I heard Caine murmur to Joe. I knew Jax's family must have been talking about us. I didn't know what their perspective or opinions were, so I tried to not overthink it.

"I'm gonna see if Chanel needs help..." I stood and cleared the table of some empty glasses and made my way inside. When I passed Jax, I skirted the edge of the deck to keep my distance. He noticed and shot me a very knowing and dangerous smirk, which excited me. Unfortunately, when I looked away, I noticed Joe and Caine watching us. I felt very self-conscious but acted oblivious and went on to the kitchen.

"I'm here to help," I sang to Chanel when I joined her in the kitchen. She started telling me no, but I said, "Please?" She seemed to understand why I wanted to hide out at the dishwasher and let me help her for longer than necessary with the cleanup. Even when the job was done, she sat at the counter and had another mimosa with me.

"Okay. Looks like the boys are ready to swim." Chanel motioned to the window, and I saw the guys in their swim trunks around the pool. "I hope you brought a bikini," she whispered, and I nodded with a small smile. "Well, get going, darling!"

I got going. I went to the guest house and changed into my bikini. I wore a red set that was simple yet extremely flattering on my body. It was perfect. The bottoms were cut to hit higher on my hips, accentuating my legs and minimal curves and showing some cheek. The top was a straight-across bandeau type but with thin straps holding it up and lifting my breasts. I curled my lashes, and the only makeup I wore was lip stain. I put my sundress back on as a cover-up and headed over to the main house with my sunglasses. When I got to the pool, the boys were playing volleyball in the water. It was Nick and Steven versus Ozzie and Jax. I sat on one of the fancy cushioned lounge chairs and watched. The ball was hit out of Ozzie's reach and almost knocked me in the head, but I caught it and they all turned to see that I'd joined them. I was welcomed with a lot of splashing and enthusiastic encouragement to get in the pool.

"Mia! Be on our team!" Ozzie swam to the ledge, and I threw him the ball.

"No, thanks." I chuckled. Playing volleyball with men was the worst.

"Come on! You're good!" Ozzie bobbed up and down in the water. I had played in high school and I was pretty good—but that was eight years and a spinal fusion ago. I shook my head and they went back to their game.

"Would you like sunscreen? UV is six right now." Chanel came up behind me and handed me SPF 30 lotion. I thanked her, and she went back into the house. I looked around and saw Caine reading on the deck and Joe coming toward me.

"Need a hand?" He smiled and sat on the chair next to me.

"With what? Oh. No, thank you," I said, rejecting his offer to help spread sunscreen on my body, and he reclined in his chair. I unbuttoned the top of my dress, just far enough to shrug off the straps and let it gather at my waist. I covered almost all of my body but couldn't get my back. "Um, Joe? I need a hand."

"My pleasure." He smirked, but I ignored it as I held my hair up for him to access my back. Of course, I glanced over and made eye contact with Jax. I looked away quickly so I didn't get a read on his facial expression, but I was guessing it was not pleasant.

"Thank you." I smiled. I peeled my sundress off over my head and repositioned myself on my chair to face the sun. I laid my head at the foot of the lounge chair and extended my legs to the opposite end. I figured I could tan for a little while and relax. I wasn't planning on chatting with Joe the whole time, but I didn't mind his conversation—he actually was good company. I kept the focus on him so he did most of the talking. I just nodded along with my eyes closed, losing track of the dialogue while enjoying the warmth from the sun. Suddenly, I was lifted from my chair and into strong arms. *Jax.* I gasped in surprise, and he laughed.

"You're going to throw me in the pool?" He just smiled. "Don't throw—" I was in the air, then hit the water. The bastard had thrown me in the pool. I surfaced and glared at Jax. He looked very pleased with himself, and the other boys were laughing at the side of the pool with him.

"*Why?*" I growled as I shoved all my hair out of my face and wiped my eyes from the chlorine, then swam to the ledge.

"You looked hot... I figured you'd want to cool off." He shrugged and looked down at me, holding on to the edge of the deep end. I scoffed and rolled my eyes. I put my hands on the concrete and pulled myself out of the pool. "I was being nice. How about a thank...you." His delivery faltered when I got out of the water. I stood in front of him, soaked, with water droplets sliding down my skin and my wet bikini clinging to my body. I knew from the cold water that my nipples were noticeable through the material. I rubbed the water from my face, then raised my hands behind my head to gather my hair and squeezed out the excess water, knowing that the posture arched my back and pushed up my breasts. I lowered my arms with a sigh and looked up at him. His hot gaze roamed my body, then fixated on my mouth, and when he saw my saucy smirk, his eyes met mine and narrowed.

"You're right. I was hot, and that felt *so* good, thank you. Now, excuse me, I'm going to resume my conversation with Joe, which you so rudely interrupted." We glared at each other, and I was about to make a move to get past him when he smirked. He pushed me back into the pool. I was even less prepared and resurfaced sputtering and mad. "What the *hell*?"

"Sorry, I just felt like it." He smiled, and the guys laughed again. I groaned and swam to the edge again and got out.

"Stop throwing me in the pool," I demanded.

"That's up to you." He smiled and crossed his arms as I raised my brows. "If you're annoying, you'll go in the pool."

"I was literally not doing anything, just minding my own business!"

"I know. It was very annoying."

"Your judgment on annoyance is greatly skewed."

"It is, yeah. I'd be careful if I were you." He nodded and spoke casually, but I knew better. He walked a few steps away to the chairs the guys were gathered around with beers. I neared their group to pick up my towel from my lounge chair and started drying off. I felt that weird pressure down my ear and bent to try to get it out.

"You okay, Mia?" Ozzie chuckled when he saw me.

"Water in my ear." One more head shake, and it was out.

"Are you going to stop being annoying so you don't get thrown in again?" Ozzie asked, obviously setting me up.

"Oh, yes. Jax is so intimidating. I'm going to behave myself now, according to his arbitrary standards that I discern through telepathy." I rolled my eyes and ran the towel down my hair. Joe started laughing, and Jax glowered. "Am I being annoying right now?" I smiled at Jax, and he nodded. "Use this as an exercise in self-control."

"I can't not..." Jax looked around at the guys, and they all nodded.

"Or be the bigger person, Jax." I stated seriously.

"Mmm. I don't think so." He flashed me a dangerous smile and stood up. I could either just be thrown into the pool right then, or I could run and have more fun.

"Run, Mia!" The guys all laughed, and I did too. Then I ran. I rounded the pool, and instead of going in a circle, I ran down the walkway to the beach. The sand slowed me down, and Jax was already twice as fast as me. His strong arms wrapped around my waist and took me down. Jax landed on his back, bringing me with him. I was on top of him as we caught our breaths. Once we made eye contact, we both started laughing. He still held my waist, and I didn't make any move to get off him.

"You really can't help yourself, can you?" he murmured. I shook my head and smiled.

"You started it!"

"*You* started it."

"You threw me in the pool, and I didn't even do anything."

"But you did."

"I didn't."

"You just so needed that sunscreen on your back that you asked Joe?" He narrowed his eyes.

"He was the only one there!" I defended myself, but he didn't care. "I take sun protection very seriously," I said with an upturned nose. I watched him stare at me as his lips twisted, and he didn't even try to hold back his smile and chuckle at my point. "Ha ha, sorry I didn't want to get sunburnt." He rolled so I was on my back, and he hovered over me.

"You look fine." His eyes dropped to my body, and I felt his eyes touch every inch of my skin. "So, why the hell would you need Joe?"

"He offered."

"And you always say yes to offers." His eyes narrowed, sarcasm lacing every word.

"What?" I frowned and stared up at him. His eyes were fixed on mine. I watched his gaze shift from one pupil to the other, and I couldn't tell if he were withholding something or trying to come up with more to say. His jaw ticked, and he swallowed before he spoke.

"You don't want anyone to touch you!" he blurted out, and my eyes widened, not at all expecting his proclamation. I sucked in a deep breath. I didn't know what he'd observed of my behavior—I couldn't figure out how he could see parts of me I always kept hidden. "And you let Joe."

"I…" I stared up into his dark-blue eyes, at a loss for words. There was so much emotion that swirled in his irises that I could tell had been there for some time. I wondered if he could see the same emotion as he stared down into mine. I didn't know what to say, so I went with denial. "I don't know what you mean."

"Considering you stopped breathing, I think you do know what I mean."

"So?"

"So, I look over and my brother has his hands on you, rubbing lotion all over you."

"Well, I would've preferred your hands on me, but you weren't there."

"You would've?" He paused and look down at me like he hadn't expected me to admit it. I felt like I was breathing heavily, and I became hyperaware of him on top of me.

"Yeah," I said quietly, reminding myself to breathe. "You know because…with the options…you have the biggest hands to…cover more area…efficiency, and…"

"I should stop you now before you get weirder," he murmured with a small smile, and I nodded. "Do you always have to be so goddamn complicated, Mia?" Jax asked softly. I nodded again. Jax just sighed, twisted around, then easily sat up in the sand, taking me with him. I slid into a very intimate position, straddling his lap face-to-face. "Serious question." He looked into my eyes and sat up straighter, which tilted my body. I gasped and had to lace my hands around his neck so I wouldn't fall backward. "Will you ever let me get to know you?"

"Jax." I sighed and looked away from his face. I thought about everything he'd ever said and done leading up to this question. I didn't understand why, but I knew the answer. My eyes reconnected with his. "Someday."

"That's enough for me." He smiled and stood, then wrapped his hands around my waist so I could find my footing in the sand and stand. "Alright, let's go. There's a pool you need to be thrown into."

"Jax, do *not* throw me into the pool a third time. I swear—"

"You'll do nothing?"

"It's not fair. You're twice as big as me and ten times stronger and faster," I complained, and he laughed.

"I think you like that I'm twice as big as you and ten times stronger and faster." He spoke the truth, but I just narrowed my eyes at him in an ambiguous response. "You have your own strengths, darlin'."

"Like what?"

"I'm not telling you. You'd then use the knowledge for mischief."

"You're right." I smiled and skipped ahead of him.

"Now *that's* not fair," Jax said from behind me, so I stopped just when I got to the walkway for the house and turned to look at him.

"What?" I frowned and watched him approach me. Once he got closer, I could see his eyes raking up and down my bikini-clad body. I couldn't help my bright smile and brought my hands to my hips. "I don't know what you're talking about," I teased, and his eyes finally met mine again. He smirked and shook his head, then bent to grab my legs and threw me over his shoulder. "Jax!"

"Oh, shut up." He laughed as we neared the pool.

"Ugh, you're such a caveman!" Then he threw me in.

When I surfaced, I just heard the boys laughing.

"I think *you* are annoying," I said once I got to the edge of the pool and bobbed in the water, glaring up at Jax as he looked down at me.

"What are you going to do about it?" he taunted me with a big smile, his hands on his hips. I was ready with a good comeback, but suddenly, those words fell out of my head as my mind only registered Jax in a swimsuit. Since I'd been thrown in the pool three damn times, I hadn't gotten a moment to notice his bare torso, which looked exactly how I'd imagined. His strong chest; cut abs; hard, lean muscles; and the way he looked standing over me was just too much to handle.

On the beach, I was mesmerized by his eyes. In the pool, my eyes were glued to his body. I'd never seen a man like that in the flesh. I felt like I was in a cologne commercial—he would dive over me, into the pool, and once he came for air, our eyes would lock, and he'd take long strokes to close the distance between the two of us. I would be the passive model, helplessly subdued by his scent, and let him push me against the pool wall. My head would tilt back so I could hold eye contact, but my lids would be heavy and my lips already parting. His head would dip down to bring his mouth to mine and—

"Mia." I snapped out of the daydream and dragged my eyes up to his. He arched a brow, still waiting for my comeback.

Without a word, I dipped underwater and swam away until I was in the middle of the pool. "I'll just stay in here for the rest of the day," I announced.

"Very wise decision." Jax smirked. I rolled my eyes and floated on my back.

I stayed in the pool for probably two hours—until my fingers got all wrinkly. The boys joined me for some of the time but only to play keep-away from me since I couldn't catch the ball to save my life. They started doing flips off of the diving board to see who could get the most rotations. I had fun appointing myself as the judge until refreshments arrived.

"Who wants margaritas?" Chanel announced as she carried a pitcher filled with lime-green liquid in one hand and a tray balanced over the other.

"Oh, thank you!" I hopped up from where I had been sitting on the concrete with my legs in the pool and pulled over a table for her to more easily set down the tray filled with cups.

"Come on, boys! I brought refreshments!" she called to the guys in the water. Ozzie, Nick, Jax, Steven, and Joe joined me around the pool furniture.

I'd air-dried for the most part and was raking my hands through my hair to get it to dry faster. I looked around the seats for a fresh towel but stopped when I felt one being draped over me. I glanced up to look at Jax standing behind me and enjoyed the feeling of his hands on my shoulders, holding it in place a few moments longer before backing away.

"Thanks," I murmured, and my lips quirked up when we made eye contact. My hands clung to the towel edges to wrap it tighter around me, and my focus went back to pouring myself a margarita.

I had a lot of fun chilling poolside with them but eventually made an excuse to go back to the guest house. It was almost four o'clock, and I needed alone time. I peeled off my suit and took a shower. I kept my towel around me as I got ready for the evening. Jax made me feel so good, and it was killing me. *He'll make me fall in love with him, then reject me, and I'll be even worse off than before. Which is pretty fucking bad.* Suddenly, I was exhausted and lay down on the couch to relax and center myself for the rest of the trip.

Chapter 31

"Mia!" I was startled awake by Jax's rough voice. I had fallen asleep on the couch. I was lying on my side and looked up to see Jax down on one knee to meet my eyes. Unfortunately, I was still wearing a towel. Fortunately, it was still secure around my body. "Mia. Get up. It's ten o'clock!"

"*What?*" I bolted upright with alarm, and Jax started laughing. My towel came open with my sudden movement. Everything was still covered except for obvious side boob and hip. Jax had stopped laughing, and I quickly hugged the towel tightly around me.

"It's only six!" I heard Nick yell from the kitchen before he ran upstairs.

"Dinner soon." Jax looked at my towel. "Is that what you're wearing? A bit scandalous, but I respect your choice." He winked, then walked away and went up to the loft.

It took me a good minute to shake off my sleepiness from the nap before I could change into something not scandalous. I put on my high-waisted Levi jean shorts and a light-blue sweater that was held together by pearl buttons down the middle. I always left the bottom few unbuttoned so it wouldn't bunch, and it looked way more fun that way. I slipped on my sandals and was ready to go.

"Dinner's ready…come get it!" Caine called to us on the deck, and we all huddled around him at the grill as he dished up hot dogs, brats, and burgers.

Everyone was already seated when I got to the patio dining table. The only free seat was right at the end, next to Jax, who sat at the head. I tried to not let my excitement for another dinner where I got to sit next to him show.

The conversation went to Caine and Chanel's plans for the holiday party. I was about to take a bite of my food when I felt Jax's eyes on me, and I froze. I looked over to meet his gaze, and he just smiled even though I'd caught him staring. "Are you going to watch me eat this hot dog?" He nodded his head, and that was fine with me. "Enjoy." I proceeded to put the phallic-shaped meat into my mouth and take a bite. I chewed my food and made a small hum of pleasure. There was a drop of ketchup on my finger—*ha ha, perfect*—so I brought my finger to my mouth and casually sucked on it. I made eye contact with Jax as I pulled it out. His scowl was a mixture of lust and anger that was boiling over in front of a table full of friends and family. Really, all I was doing was eating my dinner—he didn't have to watch.

"Do you want to go for a swim?" he growled at me, and my eyes widened with alarm. He *would* throw me into the pool, fully clothed and during dinner. I shook my head. "Then behave." I glared at him, and he smirked. I truly despised it when he said shit like that, like I was a little girl. I was trying to hold back what I wanted to say so bad, but...I couldn't. Jax had pointed his attention back to the table, so I leaned in closer to speak in his ear so no one else could hear.

"Okay...Daddy," I purred. It was the first time I'd called Jax "daddy." I watched his profile for his reaction. Obviously, he wasn't expecting it, as he just blinked and clenched his jaw before turning his head and pinning me with a hot gaze. I leaned back in my chair.

"What did you just say?" I was instantly intimidated by how sexy he looked, blue eyes even darker and smoldering. I shook my head and had to look away, but my eyes snapped back to his when I felt my chair move. He had his hand on my seat and pulled me closer. "Say it again, Mia." His voice became more teasing and intimidating as he spoke in my ear and dared me. "See what happens."

"No..."

"Then be careful," he warned, and I nodded. From the look in his eye, I knew to take him seriously. I was careful for the rest of dinner.

"Should we go out tonight?" Joe asked whoever was listening as he stretched his arms and sat back in his chair with a belly full of burgers—having only sisters, I was always astounded by how much food men could eat. Slight disappointment followed after his suggestion. I so did not want to go to a bar. Thankfully, everyone was feeling the same.

"Come on, I want to see my friends." Joe had moved seats to sit next to me. "It'll be fun!" He nudged me with a wink, but I had no idea what that wink meant.

"Your friends suck," I heard Jax say bluntly.

"Yeah, I'm backing up Jax on that." Ozzie chuckled, and so did Nick and Steven from down the table.

"You just don't want to go because my friends will hit on Mia," Joe whined, and I took a sip of my drink and looked away.

"True." Jax nodded.

"Well, don't stop everyone else's fun because you're jealous."

"It's not about me. I doubt Mia will want to be in a crowded bar with all of your scummy friends." Jax sounded irritated with Joe and genuinely concerned for me. He knew that I got uncomfortable in those situations, and I was grateful to him for defending me. I smiled at Jax, then turned back to Joe.

"True."

"Fine." Joe sighed and gave up. "I didn't know you hated my friends. They're coming tomorrow, anyway—ha ha." He dropped that underwhelming information and left.

I looked around to see that Ozzie, Nick, Steven, Jax, and I were the only ones still at the table.

"I'm glad you guys didn't want to go out," I acknowledged them all.

"Ah, it sounded boring, and Joe's friends really do suck," Ozzie offered.

"They're coming tomorrow?" I asked, and they all groaned at my reminder.

"Rich frat boys, but grown men," Steven explained, and the other guys agreed. I nodded, understanding the type.

"They won't be a problem. It's a holiday, and they'll bring their wives and act like decent human beings," Jax said, then finished off his beer. In slow motion, I watched his hand flex as he raised the bottle to his mouth and took a long swig of beer, tilting his head up to catch the last drops. I could watch his strong jaw work for days. He wore a plaid shirt with rolled-up sleeves to display his strong forearms and hands. I snapped myself out of my trance before anyone could notice—except Ozzie. Once he caught my eye, he flashed a knowing smirk my way. I dragged my eyes away from Jax and around to anything else, pretending like my best friend hadn't just caught me checking out his other best friend.

"Game time!" Joe hollered from inside, clearly having decided to stay home as well. We all made our way inside to go to the basement game room.

The room was big, and I noticed there was a weird assortment of movie and sports posters on the walls. It was cozy with a wraparound couch in front of a big-screen TV and a loaded bar. I looked around the room to see the entertainment options—ping-pong table, billiard table, retro pinball machine, dartboard, and a poker table. Caine and Chanel were at the bar fixing another pitcher of margaritas, which got me excited. Ozzie, Joe, Steven, and Nick were at the far end of the room playing with the basketball hoop games.

Jax then held something with a black handle out to me, and I took it. He walked over to one end of the air hockey table.

"I haven't played this in ten years." I smiled at the old memories.

"That's impressive dexterity for a toddler."

"Ha!" I laughed genuinely since that was a pretty good shot, I admit.

"Scared you'll lose?"

"Terrified. Please go easy on me." I was clearly being sarcastic, and went to the other end of the table.

"Say 'please' again." He smirked and looked me up and down.

"No." I scowled and tried not to let him affect me. He just chuckled and put down the puck. We started playing.

"You suck at this." Jax laughed, and I rolled my eyes since I was only one point behind.

"*You* suck at this." I scored, making us tie.

"Care to make it interesting?" He flashed a devilish smile and waited for my response. My eyes narrowed at him as I tried to decipher his motive. I hesitated and pursed my lips but shrugged in agreement. He walked to the side of the table, and I joined him. He bent down to speak softly in my ear so only I could hear. "If I win, you sleep in my bed." My eyes widened in surprise and horror, and he started laughing. "Calm down. I won't touch you." That's not what scared me. It was that I'd want him to touch me.

"Fine. If I win, you have to sleep on the couch, and I get your bed," I said. Jax nodded with a smirk, and we shook on it.

"First one to ten wins?" Jax suggested, and I agreed. We both played pretty well with our new motivators and stayed tied most of the time. I was seriously considering throwing the game, my eyes glued to his hand on the paddle, flexing as he shot the puck. The wager intimidated me, though, so I focused on making Jax sleep on the couch. It was nine to nine when I scored and won the game. *Thank God.*

"Good game." Jax sighed.

"Couch." I smiled, and he rolled his eyes.

I skipped my way over to a margarita, and Jax and I joined the other boys for a ping-pong tournament. Like the flip contest, I couldn't hit the ball if my life depended on it and had to be scorekeeper. The ball bounced back and forth, and I let my mind wander. I thought back to the potential of sharing a bed with Jax. I pictured the bed in the loft, and that thing was not big. I couldn't even imagine Jax's large body fitting comfortably on the mattress, so where would I have gone? There would definitely have been overlap, and images of the different positions our bodies could be in to fit together streamed through my mind. I wouldn't have minded being draped over him, feeling his hard muscles beneath me. I had an eyeful of his bare torso at the pool, strong and smooth, and I wanted to touch him. I knew none of that would happen, and that it shouldn't, but I already felt myself developing feelings for him at high speed. I didn't need to set myself up for disappointment or even rejection in the future by getting a taste of what it would feel like to fall asleep and wake up beside him.

Pretty soon, we called it a night so we weren't wrecked for the party. We went back to the guest house and wasted no time getting ready for bed. Thankfully, the boys had their own bathroom, and I had mine. I went through my bedtime routine and took my nightly medications. I put on my PJs and went to take my place in Jax's bed upstairs. I turned the corner and saw Jax lying on the couch.

Chapter 32

"Oh, here she comes. The victor," Jax announced as I exited the bathroom. "Nice PJs." He smirked as his eyes raked up and down my cotton tank and shorts.

"Hey, loser. Enjoy the couch." I smiled down at him. His eyes narrowed and he grabbed my wrist, then pulled me down on the couch next to him. He wore only sweatpants, his strong chest on display, and lay on his side against the couch, supporting himself with an elbow to face me better.

"Now, was that necessary?" he questioned, his face close to mine as I sat sideways on the center cushion, facing him. I just nodded.

"Well, I have a bed to claim." I smirked my satisfaction at winning our little bet but didn't make a move to stand. My body felt drawn to his, and I didn't want to leave. I then noticed that Jax hadn't let go of his strong grasp on my wrist.

"Yes, but you can still stay here with me a little longer?" His suggestion and hold on my wrist made me smile. It wasn't until I nodded that he released me. "Good." I was mesmerized by his dark-blue eyes as he ran his finger down my clean cheek. "You look younger," he murmured, and I frowned. He then brought his long finger from my cheek to poke the wrinkly spot between my furrowed brows. "It's not an insult." He looked into my eyes. A scowl was my only response. "You don't look like a child, Mia. You just look...natural...and fresh and..."

"Innocent." I finished his sentence, knowing that's what he was thinking. He nodded, and I rolled my eyes.

"It's not bad! You wear hardly any makeup and still stand out as the most beautiful woman in the room." He sounded so candid and sweet that the compliment hit me hard, especially coming from him. It shook me, as I knew that couldn't be true. I didn't know what to say but couldn't look away from his eyes. "Good game earlier," he said.

"I beat you." I smiled, grateful for the change in topic.

"You did. Glad we didn't hit the bars?"

"Very. It was nice what you said to Joe... Are his friends really like that?"

"Joe's a good guy. His friends, not great. They would've made you uncomfortable."

"Grabby and don't back off when a girl says no?"

"I wouldn't have let that happen. That must suck, how women have to deal with that." Jax spoke gently, and even though his words made me feel better, they also made me feel uncomfortable. I didn't like the subject and looked away.

"You have no idea," I murmured, not meaning to say it out loud.

"Why do you say that?" I looked back at Jax and realized that he had been watching me closely, looking for something that he knew I wouldn't say out loud. I wasn't prepared to explain, so I just didn't.

"I dunno." I shrugged and moved to lie down on my stomach next to him. I propped myself up on my elbows so I could face him.

"I'm sorry about my brother," Jax offered softly, and I cocked my head to the side, not sure what he meant. "Ten fingers...the virgin thing..."

"Oh. It's okay." I shrugged it off. "I understand."

"What do you understand...?"

"It's weird...being a virgin."

"No, it's not," he said warmly, but I just shot him a questioning look. "Maybe some people think so."

"So, um..." I awkwardly looked away, too insecure to look at him while I asked the question. "Do you think so?"

"Of course not," he said kindly. "Well…it's unusual, but that doesn't make it weird." I nodded. "I don't think you're weird, Mia."

"That's reassuring," I said with a sarcastic smile, teasing him. His scowl was adorable, and I almost felt bad for ruining a nice moment.

"Fine," he said with a huff and sat up straight on the cushion. "Here I am trying to be a nice guy, and this is what I get." He swung his legs over me so he could stand from the couch and put his hands on his hips. "Good night, weird virgin."

"Jax." I giggled at his dramatics. "Come back."

"I'll think about it." He turned away and walked to the kitchen. I missed the warmth of having his body next to mine but didn't have to miss it for long as he returned to the couch with a box of Oreos. He handed me one, then got comfortable on the couch with me again. He sat up on the cushion, so I shifted from lying down to sitting up next to him. "So I have to ask."

"But do you?" I said with a weary expression. He nodded. "But do you really…?" He nodded again. Jax was the last person I wanted to talk to about virginity. "Fine."

"So, as I've said, it's unusual to be a virgin at your age"—he paused when I rolled my eyes—"but not weird, and I'm not judging, I promise. But…is there a reason why it's never happened for you?" I didn't say anything. "So there is," he guessed correctly, and I knew I had to decide what and how much I would reveal to him.

"You have one guess."

"Oh, easy." He teased and rubbed his hands. "Of course, you're Saint Mia." I started to laugh. "What? There's a special place in heaven for you."

"True." I giggled.

"Okay, honest guess, though…are you, you know, like, saving yourself for marriage?" I shook my head. "God…?"

"No. But I do feel like…I've made it this far."

"What do you mean?" Jax placed his hands together with a slight tilt of his head and engaged eye contact. He cared.

"If I wanted to have sex, I would've had sex."

"So, why haven't you?"

"I've had plenty of options, okay?" He smiled and nodded. "But there's never been someone that's made me want it…"

"In your twenty-four years, you've never wanted it?" He looked surprised.

"A guy has never made me feel like bow-chicka-wow-wow." I smirked and shimmied my shoulders, making Jax laugh.

"That's a crime."

"Right?" He smiled and nodded. "People have tried to convince me, like, oh, just do it and get it over with."

"Because…it's not like you're scared of it?" he asked, and I froze, his question a painful one that would make me shut down. But, sitting with him and looking into his eyes, I felt like I could keep talking.

"I'm not going to have sex just to not be a virgin."

"I see what you mean. You know what you want, and you won't settle for less?" I nodded. I knew what I wanted, and I wouldn't settle for less than the man in front of me. "That boggles my mind, though. Twenty-four years, and *no* guy has made you want it?" he asked me with genuine disbelief and interest.

"It's mind-boggling," I agreed.

"There's more, though." I frowned and waited for him to clarify. He always could see more than I wanted him to. "You say you haven't felt like it. Why not?"

"There's no why. It's out of my control, purely physiological. My body has never felt like…" I trailed off as I suddenly became embarrassed by the topic. A certain memory of Jax and me in the kitchen at the mansion came to mind.

"Arousal?"

"I don't want to talk about this anymore." I felt my cheeks heat and looked away from him, anticipating being teased, but he was quiet. I glanced back at him and was surprised to look into sad eyes. "What?" I asked quietly, feeling self-conscious when he stared so closely at me.

LITHIUM

"You deserve everything you want, Mia." Jax spoke seriously, which warmed my heart. If only he knew. Jax continued to gaze at my face, and I saw his eyes shift around to my different features. "I can see your freckles better." He smiled as he poked at my speckled skin.

"Yeah, they go crazy when I'm in the sun," I said, relieved that he'd changed the topic.

"They make you look even younger." He laughed, knowing I wouldn't appreciate his comment.

"I can easily start pointing out how *old* you are." I frowned at him, and he stopped laughing.

"I'm not old," he scoffed.

"Yes, you are," I sang in a teasing way. "Aren't you, like, forty? That's old." I was exaggerating, of course—he didn't look older than thirty. He looked perfect.

"You know I'm not, nuisance," he grumbled and I just giggled. He then poked at my waist, threatening to tickle me.

"I'm sorry! You don't look older than your age. But considering my perspective...that's six years older than me. That's a lot," I stated even though it wasn't a big age gap in my perspective.

"So thirty and up, you're not interested, hm?"

"*Actually*, younger than thirty-five, I'm not interested. Call me in five years."

"You're kidding."

"I'm not. Sorry," I said seriously, then smiled. "Isn't Joe thirty-five?" Jax narrowed his eyes, and I saw his jaw tic. It was so easy to piss him off—it was impossible not to. He slowly shook his head. "Are you sure? I think he is..."

"No," he said darkly, and my smile widened.

"Yes," I teased, and he paid me back by tickling me.

"Take it back," he growled as I laughed and struggled against him.

"Okay!" I gasped, and he stopped his torment and raised his brows, waiting for me to take it back. "Isn't he single now?" I knew I was asking for it then, but I couldn't resist. He started tickling me even harder, his fingers digging into my sides, making me squirm. I slid off the couch and onto the ground to get away from his evil hands.

"Nice try." He laughed and joined me on the floor. Kneeling over me, he kept tickling until I was almost out of air.

"Okay! You win!" I cried beneath him.

"Do you mean it?" He kept up the tickling, and I pretended to pass out, making him stop and laugh. "Okay, drama queen, let's hear it."

"I'm dead. You killed me," I mumbled with my eyes closed, remaining on the floor.

"Death by tickling?" Jax chuckled, and I felt two fingers press against my neck. "I got a pulse!" he announced like someone on a cop show, and I giggled. "You're very lucky, Ms. Bell. You'll live to see another day." I opened my eyes and took a deep breath, recovering from the almost-fatal tickling attack and the striking visual of Jax above me. "Now take it back!" Jax said like an evil villain.

"I take it back. You're not old. I don't exclude men under thirty-five, lucky you, and I'm so not interested in Joe!"

"Good." He smiled sweetly.

"You can get off me now."

"I'm comfortable right here. Aren't you?" he asked me with a smirk. I shook my head. "Liar," he accused me, and it was true—I was very comfortable. He still knelt over me with his hands on either side of me, and I liked it too much. "Oooh, I understand now. This is just like the Twister situation." He smirked at me, and I rolled my eyes. "Face your fears, Mia."

"*I suck your mind. You blow my head. Make love! Inside your bed!*" I sang in a ridiculously seductive voice until Jax covered my mouth with his hand.

"I thought I told you to be careful." He looked down at me with an arched brow. I smiled and nodded. "I wonder how many warnings I'll give you," he mused with his hand still over my mouth, and I rolled my eyes. His eyes scanned my body, then met mine again, and he smirked before taking his hand away and standing. He offered me his hand, and

I took it, letting him pull me up. I returned to the couch and plopped myself down on a cushion.

"Speaking of warnings." He stalked closer and sat down next to me. We both faced each other, sitting pretzel-style on the lumpy cushions. He held out the Oreo box, and I grabbed a cookie while keeping my eyes on his. "What did you call me earlier?" Jax placed his elbow on the back of the couch and rested his chin on his fisted hand. I copied the position.

"Jax." I smiled, knowing that was not what he was thinking about.

"No."

"Jackson."

"No." He rolled his eyes.

"Caveman?"

"No."

"Mr. Caine?"

"Closer."

"I'm all out. Maybe you're thinking of someone else."

"Oh, I'm certain it was you. Who else would call me 'daddy?'" He smirked, and I blushed a little.

"What's your point?"

"I wanted to make you blush." Him saying that made my cheeks heat up even more, and I covered them with my hands.

"I only said that because you were being condescending! That's what you get for telling me to behave, mark my words. And your face was priceless."

"Because you push my limits," Jax nearly growled. "You're lucky I haven't lost my control."

"What would happen?"

"You'll find out. I'm sure you will go too far someday. It's just a matter of time." He looked at me in that dangerous way he did. His eyes were dark and stormy and made me tingle. "You'll think about this conversation a lot. I can tell."

"W-why?" I asked, a little too breathlessly.

"You will imagine what would happen. I do. I wonder how many warnings you have left." He looked at me with such wicked intent that I wanted that to happen right then. I licked my lips and averted my gaze. I couldn't, though. I let out a small sigh.

"Can I have another Oreo, please?" I asked clearly, having broken the spell. The box was behind him, and he nodded but didn't give me one.

"Come get it." He smirked, and we both started to laugh at how lame that statement was. "But really, though, you have to come get it." He looked at me seriously but with a hint of humor. I stood up, walked the border of the room, maintaining maximum distance from Jax, and rounded behind him to grab the box of Oreos, then backtracked to my spot on the couch. I took a bite of my cookie as I maintained eye contact with Jax, who was trying not to laugh.

"Happy with yourself?" I nodded as I ate the rest of my cookie. "You're funny," he said casually, but I savored the compliment. "Why do you like classic rock so much?"

"Oh." That was a conversation shift. "Uh…I don't know." I shrugged, but he stared at me until I gave an answer. "We already talked about it."

"Yeah, your alternate universe of dead rock legends, but not why you like it *so* much." He watched me closely, waiting to see if it was a question I'd answer or evade. I sighed and gave in.

"Well… I was thirteen. 'Sympathy for the Devil' was the first classic rock song I ever heard—well, really listened to. The drums and Mick's vocals, then the lyrics, oh my God, it was amazing. I've listened to it a million times thinking through the words. It made me just feel, which was wonderful. So…I like how it makes me feel."

"What do you think the song means?" Jax asked with pure interest that made me feel comfortable to keep talking.

"Well, at first listen, it's all cool and edgy that the devil was talking about the bad shit of mankind, but then it's like…why is the devil being so polite, you know? He tries to charm and seduce you into embracing and acting on your dark desires, which leads you to sympathize with him. It's not the devil's ideas. It's people's. The devil doesn't do all the bad shit. People do. That's his game—his seduction and temptations, how far can he get someone to go." I gave my answer and instantly felt self-conscious. Jax was staring, and I felt like I'd given too much of myself away. "Um…what?"

"You're just…" Jax smiled and looked into my eyes. "People don't really talk like you do. They don't really think like you either, do they?"

"Oh. Shit. I talked too much," I mumbled and looked away. I felt Jax's long finger on my chin as he tilted my head back to face him.

"Mia. Stop," he said gently, and I reluctantly looked into his eyes. I felt vulnerable anytime I shared information about myself, no matter how simple or small. "I like listening to you talk. It's not too much." I nodded but remained quiet. "Mia…it made you feel… Why was that new?" That question was too complex to answer and impossible to put into words.

It was the time of my life when I was diagnosed with depression, which led to bipolar. I hadn't really felt since then. Jax could tell I was closing myself off. He traded his earnest look for a more lighthearted affect. "Maybe another time. Excellent song review, by the way. You would've made a great music journalist if we were the 1970s."

"I was more thinking groupie." My comment caught him off guard and made him laugh.

"Of course. So, you were a headbanger back then, and you're a headbanger now."

"I guess so." I shrugged with a proud little smile.

"I have a hard time picturing a thirteen-year-old Mia rocking out to the Stones. Did you dress the part too?" He smiled when he could tell my answer was yes. I sure did, but not in the way he might be picturing. I once made a necklace out of real raccoon teeth to replicate Steven Tyler's—but I was definitely not telling him that.

"I got sent home from school when I wore an AC/DC shirt to class with Angus on it."

"Your school was against rock music…?"

"Well, his guitar was impaling his abdomen, and there was blood everywhere."

"That's an important detail." Jax chuckled, and I shrugged.

"It was a Catholic school—I don't know." I rolled my eyes, and he laughed harder. I asked him about his musical journey. He'd already shared that it had started with his dad, so he told me about all of his dad's vinyl records. "I need to talk to your dad."

"Mia. He's a happily married man. That would be wrong." He held my shoulders and spoke sternly, making me laugh. "Tell me more about you." He sat back and showed more of his interest.

"Jax..." I sighed, and he tilted his head.

"*Why* do you get so uncomfortable when you're asked about yourself?"

"I don't know." I shrugged.

"You do know. We both know you know."

"I know that you know that I know and that we know that we both know."

"And then you get weird and try deflecting." I just nodded, and he sighed. "You're not going to give anything away, are you?" he asked. I fidgeted and slowly shook my head.

"Okay. Tell me anything. It can be stupid, boring, serious, funny... anything." I figured that I could share something with him, especially since he was so interested and that was a novelty to me.

"Okay..." I tried to think of something. *What do I even say?* "Steven Tyler was my first sex dream." I blurted out the first thing that came to my mind and regretted it immediately. Jax burst out laughing—like, crying laughing. I patiently waited for him to get ahold of himself.

"Ahhhh. Ha ha. Okay. I'm done. Sorry but"—he started to chuckle again—"how old were you?"

"Sixteen." I shrugged.

"Your first sex dream at sixteen? No wonder you—" He stopped himself from finishing that sentence—sometimes he was a smart guy.

"I regret telling you that. Rock was on my mind, and it just—that was terrible judgment on my part." I shook my head with disappointment in myself. "Shame on me."

"No! Don't. You know it's funny," he pointed out, and I gave in and laughed with him.

"Now you tell me something embarrassing."

"Oh, no, no. That's your fault you made it embarrassing. But let me think... I wanted to be in *Star Wars*."

"That was my favorite movie growing up! I've seen it twenty times!"

"I've seen it twenty-one times," he one-upped me.

"Luke or Han?"

"Vader." He nodded his head, completely serious, and I laughed at him.

"Little Jackson wanting to be the villain. It all makes sense."

"I'm just kidding. Han Solo."

"Antihero. That makes so much more sense."

"Shut up, he has the *Falcon* and Luke is weak."

"That's very fair. He's also arrogant, selfish, temperamental, a loner, stubborn—"

"With a heart of gold!"

"He comes around," I conceded and shrugged even though I loved Han Solo too.

"That leaves you with Princess Leia."

"I did identify with Leia." I smiled, remembering my elation when I found out Carrie Fisher had bipolar.

"Mm-hmm. Makes sense. Stubborn, self-righteous, sarcastic..."

"More like charming and witty," I countered.

"Beautiful. Hot body." He winked at me, and I rolled my eyes. He just wanted to make me blush, so I moved the conversation along.

"Except that bedsheet she wore...and those cinnamon rolls on the sides of her head."

"How about the gold bikini?"

"I approve of the gold bikini."

"You know who else does? Han."

"Of course. Han was obsessed with her." I smirked, and he smirked back.

"Leia was obsessed with Han. Let's be real."

"No, he relentlessly harassed her until she gave in!"

"And it was the best thing that ever happened to her. She was on a fast track to be a space spinster and die a virgin."

"Not in that bikini." I winked at him, making him laugh and agree with me.

"Oreo please." He nodded his head to the Oreo box behind me.

"Come get it," I mimicked him from earlier.

"Okay." He shrugged and leaned forward. That was stupid of me. "Excuse me." He smirked as he reached behind me, and I tried backing up as much as possible but just ended up slipping, and my back hit the cushions. "Mia, you're sending signals...!" Jax playfully taunted me as he was reaching above me to get a cookie.

"Just get your cookie and return to your side of the couch, Mr. Caine."

"And when you say 'cookie'..." He smirked again, still above me, and bit off half of the Oreo. *Why did that have to be so sexy? Why?*

"I mean Oreo." I rolled my eyes. "Now get off me, please and thank you."

"Now, when you say 'please'...it's quite vague. I assume it's open to interpretation." He was having a lot of fun messing with me, and I was having fun too. No matter the situation, I had fun with him. I tried not to smile, but, of course, I couldn't stop the corners of my mouth from lifting. I tried pushing him back, but he didn't move. Not even an inch. I basically pushed myself deeper into the cushion.

"That was cute." He chuckled at my weakness.

"See what I mean. It's not fair." I pouted, referencing our earlier conversation.

"I think you like it." He looked at me and raised an eyebrow. Busted. But I'd never admit that—never, ever. If I tried to reply, I would say something I'd regret, so I just shook my head. "You don't have to admit it. I know," he said. His face was close to mine now, and I couldn't stand it anymore. I rolled myself off the couch and onto the floor.

"Come back," Jax ordered, amused.

"No. I'm rather comfortable," I lied and settled into the rough carpet.

"Well, I'm not."

"Too bad for you," I sassed back but then rolled out of the way when Jax joined me on the floor.

"We should get some sleep," he murmured beside me. I nodded, suddenly tired at the mention of sleep and the effects of my nighttime pills dragging me down. "Come on, then, you have my bed to take over." He poked me, as my eyelids were fluttering. I shook my head. I didn't want to get up—I was so tired—but I also didn't want to leave him.

"Here's fine."

"You're not sleeping on the floor." I just nodded my head with my eyes closed. "Well, you hit a wall." He chuckled. "Couch it is." He picked me up and brought me to the couch. To my surprise, he lay down with me. "Is this okay?" I heard him murmur in my ear as he draped a blanket over just me, respectfully providing a bit of separation.

"Yes," I murmured back. He didn't start hardcore cuddling, which I appreciated. We were barely even touching, and I just enjoyed his presence until I quickly fell asleep. We didn't go to sleep cuddling, but we sure woke up that way.

Chapter 33

"*What?*" Our alarm was Nick screeching and Ozzie and Steven rushing over to see what he was looking at, which was Jax's arm around my middle and me curled into his side with our legs entwined on the couch.

"Am I seeing things or is that Mia and Jax sleeping together?" Steven thought out loud, and I wasn't wild about his choice of words. *We didn't sleep together. We just slept next to each other... Yeah, this is weird.* I looked over to Jax. Once we made eye contact, we both started laughing.

"I think we just woke up in a weird alternate universe..." Ozzie whispered to the other two.

"Good morning." I sat up and acknowledged the onlookers. They just stared at me and Jax. "Nothing happened."

"Why are you two *sleeping* together?" Nick asked and crossed his arms.

"We didn't." I rolled my eyes. They couldn't actually think that we'd done anything.

"Then what happened?" Ozzie demanded, and I was a little surprised by his intensity. I looked over to Jax, who had sat up as well.

"I...don't know. Last thing I remember is Mia handing me a drink..." Jax looked at me in horror, but I wasn't amused. I crossed my arms while the other boys laughed.

"That's a lie," I stated matter-of-factly. No one actually believed I drugged him.

"So what *happened?*" Ozzie demanded again, even more intensely than before.

"Okay. I'll tell you guys. They won't make fun of you, Mia." Jax sighed heavily, and I looked at him, horrified of what he was about to say. "Mia thought she saw a ghost and was too scared to sleep alone. I was the only one awake," Jax explained to the guys, and they actually bought it.

"Mia...ghosts aren't real." Steven broke the news to me, and I found it hard not to laugh. I looked over to Jax, who just shrugged and smiled. It was kind of funny. I shook my head with amusement, then left the guys to shower.

After the shower, I went through my morning routine just like any day. I put on leggings and a baby tee, and we made our way to the main house. The kitchen table was full of cereal boxes. I took a seat on the end in front of a bowl and spoon as everyone else joined. A box of Cocoa Puffs was in front of me—my favorite. I went to grab them, but so did someone else. Jax was sitting across from me—and we both had a hold on the cereal box.

"Unhand the Cocoa Puffs." I tried pulling the box closer, but Jax had a firm grip.

"We both know I'm getting them first," he said confidently, but I wasn't going to give in.

"Not without a fight," I promised, and Jax started chuckling.

"I'll *let* you have them." He let go.

"Yeah, you will," I said with some sass, and he kept chuckling and shook his head. I noticed Chanel and Caine looking at us from the kitchen island, but I ignored it and poured some cereal into my bowl.

"Someone pass the Cocoa Puffs!" I heard Nick yell from down the table. I looked at Jax.

"Don't do it." He shook his head gravely. With a smirk, I extended my arm past Joe and Ozzie to hand the box to Nick. "After all I've done for you!" Jax looked at me, taking dramatic offense to my betrayal. I shrugged and poured almond milk in my bowl. I took a big, crunchy bite and smiled with my mouth closed.

———

"Surprise!" I heard an unfamiliar voice yell once everyone was gathered outside after breakfast. A man showed up on the deck, and Chanel and Caine freaked out.

"Conor!" They both jumped up to greet their eldest son.

"Conor, you can't surprise me like this!" Chanel scolded him for messing up her hostess calculations, but she was clearly happy to see him.

After greetings, Conor looked around and found me where I'd hung back to let the family hug.

"Jax's new girlfriend!" Conor smiled, and my stomach dropped again. I quickly looked behind myself, then back at him, as Jax's girlfriend wasn't me. They thought it was funny, and I smiled.

"Hi. I'm Mia, not Jax's girlfriend." I shook his hand, and he nodded with a smile. I was pretty sure Joe was the one who'd told him the false information.

"Mia is our new artist," Jax offered warmly, unlike the first introduction.

"Very nice to meet you." Conor was handsome and had darker hair than his brothers and looked more like Chanel with a longer face and not the strong masculine jaw that Jax, Joe, and Caine had. He was shorter than his younger brothers, but not by much, and I could tell he was just as athletic. "I'm gonna keep bringing stuff in. Margaret is just getting the kids out of the car. They're still watching *Finding Nemo*." Conor went back to help Margaret—it was a safe assumption that she was his wife. Margaret showed up with two adorable little kids. Leo and Lucy looked around three and one. Leo looked like the Caine boys, and Lucy just looked like a baby but clearly had Margaret's near-black hair. Joe picked up Leo and was making him giggle—he whispered something to him, and the boy didn't seem to understand but nodded anyway. Since I was the new girl, attention came back to me. Margaret smiled and shook my hand and formally introduced me to the children.

"Hi, Leo. Hi, Lucy." I waved a little hello to them. Lucy seemed shy, naturally, as she wobbled on her one-year-old legs and held her mom's hand, but Leo didn't as he took a little toddler step toward me.

"Uncle Jax girlfriend," he said in a strong but squeaky little voice, pointing at me.

"Oh! How nice!" Margaret did a little clap and focused on us. Everyone started laughing, and Leo looked around, confused. My title was quickly corrected, and Margaret seemed disappointed.

"Uncle Joe!" Leo whined and turned to the man behind it all.

"Good job, buddy," Joe said, laughing, and everyone scolded him for being an instigator. Well, now everyone knew me, so hopefully, that was the last of that. It was sweet seeing everyone so comfortable and connected with each other. Even Ozzie, Steven, and Nick felt like part of the family.

————

The party was later in the afternoon and catered so we didn't have to worry about any prep work. It was fancy...very unlike Memorial Day at my family cabin. So we just relaxed around the pool after breakfast, and I kept an eye on Jax for any sly sneak attacks. I wore another bikini, this one lavender with underwire cups. It was very European and, as always, classy. I clipped half of my hair back and out of my face and put on my sunglasses as I sat peacefully on my lounge chair.

"Mia!" the boys yelled from the pool.

"No," I responded without looking up from my iPad.

"Come in!" Ozzie called from the water.

"No."

"You're boring," Nick whined.

"I'm staying dry, so no one bother me."

"Why would you think we'd bother you?" I heard Jax closer to me and lowered my iPad. He had his elbows on the ledge of the pool, and he looked so enticing, but I kept up my disinterested affect. "Okay, I promise that I won't bother you."

"Get on this floaty—you won't get wet!" Ozzie pushed a blow-up chair across the water. I put down my iPad on my lap and sat up straighter. I looked at Jax and flipped up the shades on my prescription glasses.

"I don't trust you. Any of you."

"Those are *flip shades*?" Jax laughed. I flipped them back down and picked up my iPad. "Fine. Guys, Mia's busy reading *Fifty Shades of Grey*," Jax yelled to the whole pool.

"Not true!"

"I don't know...it wouldn't surprise me," Jax said, and the other guys agreed. "*Why?*"

"It's always the quiet ones." Ozzie started to laugh.

"You're getting very defensive, Mia..." Jax teased.

"You're bothering me," I growled and decided to start ignoring him. I forgot that Caine was right next to me and was quietly chuckling through our entire exchange. I sighed and showed him my iPad, displaying Mick Jagger's memoir, to prove that I wasn't reading erotica. He nodded and smiled. "I lost my concentration." I looked at Caine and set down my iPad, hoping he'd want to chat.

"Wanna play a game?" he asked me with a smile, and I nodded happily. "Chess or Scrabble?"

"Hmm...chess!" He nodded and reached next to him for a large travel chess set. "Where did that come from?" I laughed in surprise, as I hadn't noticed it before. He dragged a side table between our lounge chairs, and we set up the game.

He let me be white, and we were a few moves in when he sat up straight and eyed me. "Are you going for the *four-move kill*?" I nodded a little sheepishly. "You think you can take down an old man that fast, huh?"

"No! That's how I set up my game. I like the arrangement." I hurried through my explanation, hoping he wasn't actually offended.

"Okay, Bobby Fischer."

"I feel more like a Kasparov," I responded with a shy shrug. Caine's brows lifted, no doubt surprised by my knowledge of the game. I loved that he seemed impressed, and I wanted his approval.

"Why is that?" Caine inquired, regarding me more closely.

"I've said too much already." I shook my head, not wanting to readily give up my method. I wasn't that impressive of a player, but I knew I could keep up. My dad taught me how to play when I was younger along with his deeper knowledge of the game. I was familiar with some of the chess grandmasters, and my favorite was Kasparov—he was most creative and liked the attack.

"Well, then, bring it on." Caine smiled, and we were halfway through the game when he gave me the greatest compliment I could've asked for. "You might be better than Jackson," he whispered like it was a secret.

"Could you say that louder?" I whispered back, and he laughed.

"Jackson! Mia might be better than you!" he shouted toward the boys in the pool behind me, and I looked over my shoulder to see Jax's confused, then irritated, look once he saw the chessboard. I turned back to Caine and smiled with appreciation.

"You don't have to flatter her, Dad," I heard Jax say behind me, disgruntled, and Caine shook his head.

"I always mean what I say." Caine was talking only to me now. "It's nice seeing my son having fun," he said casually. His comment surprised me and made me smile. I glanced over my shoulder to the boys in the water, and my eyes instantly found Jax. He was sitting on the edge of the pool and gave a goofy head nod when he noticed me looking at him. I looked back at the chess set before he could make me blush. Too late, as I remembered his dad was sitting in front of me. "I wonder why that is," Caine commented, his voice still casual, but he was looking at me more closely.

"Does he not often have fun?" I asked curiously, since I thought of Jax as a fun-loving man.

"He does, he does." Caine nodded. "But not like this." I frowned and cocked my head to the side, not understanding. He just chuckled and shook his head, not explaining further. "Your play."

I forgot about his vague comments and looked down to the board. I scanned over the pieces and focused on my next move. I was very thankful to my dad for teaching me, as it was a good game. We didn't take it too seriously or spend long thinking about moves.

Toward the end, Caine kept getting my king in check, but I evaded. It was impossible to get a checkmate, and I knew I was done.

"You win." I let out a sigh and tipped over my king, but I was happy with how well I'd played.

"Good game." Caine smiled and shook my hand. "Really, Mia. I wasn't expecting such an exciting match."

"Am I better than him?" I asked curiously. Caine thought about it and rubbed his chin.

"I think you're about even." He nodded, and I accepted that answer. "Does he bother you a lot?" Caine asked me.

"Umm..." I wasn't sure what to say to the man's dad.

"Be honest, dear, you won't upset me."

"He does...a lot." I chuckled to myself. "But I give it right back." I couldn't help but softly smile.

"I've noticed." He smiled warmly at me, and I felt more comfortable. "Maybe because you two are so similar."

"Similar?" I was shocked. "I don't think so..." I laughed at how absurd that sounded, and Caine gave me a skeptical look.

"It's obvious. You're even as dense as he is about your connection. Oh, well. With time." He stood and patted me on the shoulder, then walked away. I sat there for another minute, blinking and feeling nothing but confusion. *Dense...did Papa Caine take a shot at me?* I let out a sigh and decided not to overthink it.

"You clearly lost." Jax plopped down on the end of my lounge chair and studied the board. I swiped my hand across it, collecting the pieces to put away. "Are you better than me?" he asked with a smirk.

"Your dad said we are even." I glanced at him and folded the board closed.

"He didn't," he said with disbelief.

"He did," I said, mimicking his deep, shocked voice.

"Let's settle it, then." Jax sat back up.

"Another time." I rolled my eyes and set the travel game aside. My conversation with Caine had scattered my mind. I wouldn't play well against Jax now.

"What'd my dad say?" He looked at me more closely now, and I couldn't decide if I wanted to tell him.

"He said that we are similar." I smirked at him, and he recoiled in exaggerated offense to the comparison.

"How dare he," he whispered, and I giggled. "We really are nothing alike, though. That's weird."

"That's what I said." We both had a laugh, then moved on. I tried to keep myself from thinking up ways we were alike. Then I had a thought about the battery concept. *Opposites attract and the same ones repel each other? Oh, whatever.*

"What's happening in your book?" He raised an eyebrow, and I rolled my eyes. Truth was I had read the entire Fifty Shades trilogy.

"Well"—I sat up straighter and leaned forward so only he could hear—"Anastasia's wrists and ankles are tied to a bed, and she's completely naked, and Christian has this flogger—" Jax covered my mouth with his large hand, and I started laughing.

"Okay! You're done now." He spoke roughly, but I was still smiling. "Mia...*final warning.*" My eyes widened at his threat, which I took seriously, and I nodded. Jax smiled with satisfaction and lowered his hand. "Good girl," he said with a wink, then ran away. I gasped and glared after him. He didn't play fair.

Jax had jumped into the pool to rejoin the rest of the boys, so I just sighed and settled into my lounge chair, lying on my stomach and facing the pool. I looked over the top of my sunglasses and watched Jax move around the water and sighed to myself before lighting up my iPad again. I continued my pleasant afternoon reading about Mick Jagger.

"Hey, girl!" Joe called to me as he jogged into the pool area from the beach.

"Hi." I looked at him and pushed off my elbows and sat back on my heels to face him better.

"I'm making a run to the liquor store. Want to join?"

"Oh. Um..." I asked what time it was—two o'clock. "Really? I should start getting ready for the party. Thanks for the invite, though." I smiled and got up.

"Alright, see ya later." Joe ran off.

I stood from my chair and stretched, masking a yawn, as the sun had made me sleepy. I looked out at the rest of the pool to see where everyone else was. Steven and Nick were in the water, Ozzie bounced on the diving board, and Jax stood at the edge of the pool. Jax's back was to me as the four boys tossed around a ball. *To try to push Jax into the pool or to not try to push Jax into the pool...* I caught Ozzie's eye, and he smiled, knowing my intent, and nodded. I was going to push Jax into the pool. His attention was on Steven, the one with the ball, as he awaited the throw. I casually waltzed over, and when Jax was leaning over the water, I pushed him into the pool. I only stayed long enough for the satisfaction of seeing him hit the water and then resurface.

At first, Jax was shocked when he saw me standing at the edge of the pool. Then he laughed. "Oooh, you're in trouble!"

"Bye, guys!" I smiled and waved before fleeing the scene. I left the pool right as Conor's family arrived and made it back to the guest cabin. I had just the right amount of time before the party to shower and enjoy my victory and alone time.

Chapter 34

I finished getting ready in the safety of the bathroom. I did my usual makeup and hair routine, then added my favorite, and only, earrings that dangled with small jade teardrop stones that I got in a vintage shop in Florence.

I brought a couple different options with me for the Memorial Day party in Monterey. Usually, I'd be spending it at my cabin with only one outfit for the entire weekend—swimsuit, sweatshirt, and sweatpants. I chose a light-blue-and-white floral-print dress with a bustier-inspired top, with a fitted silhouette and slender shoulder straps. It was the perfect thing to wear to a Monterey Memorial Day party. The bustier, waist, and flirty mini length made it sexy but most of all…classy. I thanked myself for packing plain-white low-sandal heels—the height and posture gave me more confidence in certain situations where I felt inadequate. I started to get a little nervous for the party. I was still the only stranger, and I got anxious talking to new people. I checked my hands to see how badly they were shaking that afternoon—noticeable but not debilitating. Deep breath, spritz of perfume, a little extra lip stain to exaggerate my pout, and I was ready.

I peeked out of the bathroom to make sure the coast was clear. It wasn't. I pushed my long blonde hair off my shoulders to tumble down my back but let my wispy bangs drape over my cheeks. One more deep breath, and I made my exit. Jax was leaning over something at the kitchen table, so I went to see what he was looking at. He sensed my approach and looked up.

"Well, look who it is." Jax sat back and crossed his arms. "The hit-and-run. You're in for it now." He tilted his head back and stared at me, and I just smiled. I stood in front of him, and my smile widened when he straightened in his chair and took in my appearance. "Okay." He sighed and looked into my eyes again. "You're not in trouble anymore."

"What a relief," I said. He rolled his eyes at my sarcasm, then held a finger up and twirled it around.

"Go on. Do a little spin." I shook my head, and he groaned, irritated. "Just spin."

"What's the magic word?"

"You'll spin if I say 'please?'"

"It wouldn't hurt." I shrugged, and he shook his head.

"Please," he said with annoyance, but at least he still said it. I smiled and did as he asked. He sighed and continued to stare at me. "You're very beautiful."

"Thank you," I mumbled and blushed under his intense attention.

"Come here." He waved me over. I looked at him suspiciously, not knowing his intentions, and he rolled his eyes. "Please." I softly giggled because that wasn't why I was hesitating, but I accepted and walked over and saw that he was working on a crossword puzzle. "There's one that I don't know, but you definitely will."

"That's cheating."

"No, using your phone is cheating. I'm phoning a friend."

"Aw. We're friends?" My teasing sentimental tone made it sound like I was kidding, but he had never referred to me as a friend before.

"Yes, now pay attention. Guitarist for Queen. Eight letters."

"*You don't know this?*" I was genuinely surprised.

"I can't remember! Joey Something?"

"*Joey?* I'm disappointed." I shook my head.

"I'm very sorry. Now tell me the answer."

"Mmm. No. You'll remember it."

"John?"

"That's the bassist."

"I know Freddie."

"I would hope so."

"Whatever, just tell me! This is going to drive me crazy until I finish it." I just smiled at his pain and didn't help him.

"Ready to go!" Ozzie announced as he descended the stairs with the rest of the boys, and we all went on our way to the main house.

It was beautiful. The outdoors were decorated with flags and flowers, and the grounds were littered with places to sit and eat, drink and converse. Servers dressed in white shirts and black ties carried around food, and there was a bar set up on the deck, which we flocked to.

"Oz," I whispered to my best friend and Monterey Memorial Day veteran as I pulled him aside while we waited for alcohol. "Do you guys, like, stick together or disperse?"

"Uh. Both?" He looked at me, a little unsure, then patted my back. "Don't be nervous. You always feel awkward, but no one can tell."

"But—"

"Trust me. Don't overthink it," he whispered and gave me a small squeeze around my shoulders.

"Mia." Hearing Jax behind me, I turned. He handed me my drink.

"Thank you." I took it, and the weight of the full glass made my hand shake. I quickly used my other hand to anchor it by holding the bottom. I looked up and saw that Jax was watching me. *Great.* We made eye contact, and he gave me that concerned, questioning look—an expression that was becoming very frequent. I offered a weak smile back and turned away.

Apparently, Joe had been telling guests that I was Jax's girlfriend, which turned out to be a good icebreaker. I met some family members—aunt, uncle, and cousins, but mostly friends from the community. Basically, a crowd of rich people. I got temporarily disconnected from my friends and surveyed the land. Jax was talking to a group of people I didn't know, and Ozzie, Nick, Steven, and Joe were with a crowd of men by the pool. I wondered if any of Joe's notorious friends were around. I started making my way to them but was cut off by three girls. They looked older than me but couldn't have been older than thirty. They were dressed expensively but didn't look as classy as I'd expect. They were flashy, covered in iconic Louis Vuitton and Gucci logos.

"I'm Natalie." The middle one stuck her hand out, and I shook it. I eyed the petite brunette and her backup blondes, sensing hostility.

"Hi…I'm Mia." I had a feeling they weren't going to be welcoming and glanced at the group of boys I had been headed for. The other two girls introduced themselves as Hannah and Whitney, and I nodded politely, putting together that they were the Monterey bitches the boys had asked Jax about.

"Rumor has it that you are Jax's girlfriend." Natalie looked me up and down with obvious distaste.

"I'm not."

"Yeah, I knew that didn't fit." She pursed her lips, and I knew it was time to leave them.

"Yeah…nice to meet you." I tried to sidestep away, but they did too.

"So, then, what are you doing here?" Natalie crossed her arms and popped her hip.

"I work with Jax, and I'm here as a guest." I fidgeted with my drink a little, getting nervous that they were going to say something offensive.

"Mm-hmm. Well, I'm just warning you now—he's unavailable."

"I didn't know he had a girlfriend, but okay." I tried walking away again, but Natalie took another step and kept going.

"That's not what I meant. He's unavailable to *you*."

"Aw, look at the poor thing. She's shaking." Hannah pointed out my tremors, and the other two laughed. They had no idea how deeply they shook my confidence—more than what they'd intended. I cursed bipolar and my medications and stood there with wide eyes, shocked that someone would use that against me.

"Well, that's none of your business." I tried to speak confidently but really didn't pull off the delivery, as my cheeks reddened.

"Oh, sweetie. This is us helping you. I've seen you looking at him, and maybe he'd be interested in you as the shiny new object, but he gets bored fast and would break your little heart." Natalie gave me a faux-sympathetic look.

"You don't know me." I took even breaths so I didn't lose my temper. When I said "lose my temper," I meant cry.

"And no one here cares to. You obviously don't belong here and *definitely* not next to Jax."

"You're not his type, and he's way out of your league." Whitney added the lame insult like it was right out of a *Lizzie McGuire* episode. Natalie elbowed her so she'd shut up.

"Exactly. You'd maybe get a pity fuck. Trust me, he'd never take someone like you seriously." She snickered, and I flinched at her crass insult. My cheeks calmed, and I rallied my confidence so I could stand up to that bitch who attacked my worth as a woman and human being.

"Thank you girls so much for looking out for me. I'll be sure to stay far away from him so I don't interfere with your clearly one-sided infatuation plan to trap him into a relationship. An 'accidental pregnancy' seems like your style. Good luck." That last part was bad—I wasn't proud of it, but she deserved it.

"You little bitch." Natalie turned red and slapped me across the face. I had *not* seen that coming. The shock of the blow and my weakened grip caused me to drop my glass, but thankfully, I didn't fall. It shattered on the ground, and within seconds, Jax was beside me.

"Mia." He put his hands on my shoulders and turned me to face him. His eyes widened in horror when he saw me—Natalie had probably left a red mark. "What the fuck?" Jax turned to look at the Monterey bitches and pulled me back. Natalie actually seemed a little scared. "Did you do this?" He spoke roughly, trying to rein in the rage I felt emanating from him.

"That girl is a snake, Jax. Don't defend her," Natalie verbally spat on me, regaining her bitchy control.

"Leave." He spoke low and sounded scary. Natalie tried to say something, but Jax cut her off. "I'm bringing Mia inside. You better not be here when I come back," he growled and held on to my arm with painful tightness. He adjusted his hold on me to take my hand in his. In a daze, I followed him into the house.

He led me past the kitchen filled with workers and into the main-floor bathroom. He looked over my face and took a deep breath, then picked me up around my waist and set me on the counter. He rested his hands on the counter on either side of me and looked me levelly in the eyes. His gaze was a mix of anger, concern, and maybe guilt.

"What happened?" He spoke softly, and I felt myself snap out of the daze and welcomed the strength I took from his presence.

"They, um...confronted me and wanted to know who I was. I tried to walk away, but they basically harassed me... I'm pretty sure Natalie is crazy-girl obsessed with you, so watch out for that." I chuckled weakly at just how nuts she was. "They were being really cruel and laughed at my, um...hands." I glanced at him to make sure he knew what I meant. He gently held up my hands and saw them shaking, and I quickly pulled them back and clasped them both in my lap.

"What did they say?" he asked me, and I hesitated. "Mia, please tell me."

"It was all about you... Natalie thought I was a threat, I guess, and tried to shame me away? Said I don't belong here." I paused and tried to think through what she'd said. Jax nudged me to go on. I considered not telling him but was too hurt and needed his comfort. "She said you're unavailable to me and you'd only be interested because I'm a new object, or something—um, you're out of my league and I'm not your type...a-and, um...you'd only fuck me out of pity—her words...I don't know. You'll break my little heart." My voice hitched on the last sentence, not because of Natalie but because I thought it was true but so badly hoped that it wasn't. I sighed and shrugged, running an anxious and shaking hand through my hair. I didn't look at him during my ramble and was proud that I didn't shed any tears, so I nervously looked up at him. He was silent, and I could tell was trying to suppress his anger in front of me, but I knew.

"Mia...I am so sorry."

"It's not your fault."

"Why did she hit you?" He frowned, and I realized I hadn't explained that part.

"Oh. I said something very...sarcastic. She didn't like it," I said casually, and he smiled.

"Of course you did." He softly chuckled. "What did you say?"

"Well...I kinda feel bad about it... I'm not proud of it," I admitted and looked away. Jax placed a gentle hand on my chin and tilted my head up to look at him.

"Go on," he urged with a small smile.

"She kept saying she was helping me or looking out for me, so...I thanked her for her concern and assured her that I won't interfere with her plan to trap you into a relationship and...yeah." Jax started cracking up, and I joined in.

"And?"

"That's it."

"No, you said 'and.'" He waited for my answer, but I didn't want to tell him. "You're blushing. What did you say?" I hated my traitorous cheeks.

"I don't want to tell you. It was mean, and I feel bad."

"She deserved it. Tell me."

"I said...something like she seems like the kind of girl to get pregnant on *accident* to trap you, and I wished her luck."

"You're adorable." Jax was really laughing then, and I felt a little better that he wasn't judging me.

"It's true, isn't it?"

"Yes, I think so too. That's when she hit you?"

"Yeah. I really didn't see it coming."

"I'm sorry." He looked crushed, and I felt bad to have been the reason that he seemed so sad, even though I was the one with the handprint on my face. He lifted his hand and lightly touched my cheekbone. I winced, only a little, at the surprise of the sting. He pushed my hair behind my ear to see my face better. He took a washcloth and ran it under hot water to dab over my skin. I noticed the white towel had tiny red spots.

"I'm bleeding?" I raised my hand to feel the broken skin.

"Yeah, she was definitely wearing a ring."

"Am I going to be scarred for life?" I asked him with faux-dramatic panic, and he chuckled.

"I doubt it. You'd still be gorgeous with a scar, though. Ooooh, your nickname could be Pacino!" I rolled my eyes, but his comment did make me laugh.

"Mia! You in there?" It was Ozzie, and Jax opened the door to let him in as well as Nick and Steven, who crowded in after him. "Oh, shit! Joe said to come check on you. I had no idea this happened."

"Did he—" Jax started, but Ozzie cut him off.

"Kick out the Monterey bitches? Yes. What the hell happened?" Ozzie asked, and Nick and Steven joined in with expressing their concern.

"Natalie is obsessed with Jax and is creepily possessive...thought I was a threat and went on the offensive." I sighed, not wanting to tell the whole story again.

"Do you want to go back to the guest house for the rest of the party?" Jax asked me kindly, but I shook my head.

"I want a drink," I said. Jax nodded and picked me up by the waist again and lowered me to the floor.

Chapter 35

We all went back outside to rejoin the party. Jax got me another drink and stayed by my side. We snatched food from the different servers and hung out. Caine and Chanel both checked on me, and I assured them that I was fine. I could tell there were people wanting time with Jax, so I started to drift away, but he caught my hand.

"Jax, I'm fine." I smiled to assure him that I was okay. "I'm going to visit with the kids." He nodded, and I walked toward the pool area to where Margaret and the two children were sitting on a couple lounge chairs. "Mind if I join?" I asked, and Margaret looked at me as if I were her savior as I sat on one of the chairs.

"Mia, *thank you*. I'll be back." She transferred the baby from her arms to my lap, then ran off, leaving me alone with Leo and Lucy. I was not expecting that, but okay. Leo was very interactive and liked to talk. He told me a lot of stories, so I gasped and laughed at the right times. Lucy was content playing with my hair while I watched Leo put on a show for us. I think he was being a dinosaur or King Kong…maybe a Transformer, I really couldn't tell by his movements or squeaky voice. Conor came over and thanked me for watching them.

"No problem. They're fun."

"Okay, kiddos. Time to go inside." Conor clapped, and I transferred Lucy from my arms to his.

"Nooooo, stay." Leo pouted.

"Come on, we'll watch more *Nemo*."

"Can Mimi come?" he whined and ran over to me. He pulled on my hand, and my heart exploded. The little boy only called me "Mimi," and I thought it was adorable.

"Mia has to stay with the adults. Right, Mia?" Conor looked to me for confirmation. I honestly wanted to watch *Nemo* with them but didn't want to overstep. I stood up on my short heels and smoothed out my dress, which had wrinkled from Leo climbing on me.

"Your dad's right, Leo. But do you want to play again tomorrow?" I bent down to face him. He nodded enthusiastically and hugged my legs. Conor took his hand and brought the kids inside.

"I love him, but that kid is a pill." I looked up and saw Jax waving me over to the deck.

"Really? I think he's delightful."

"I think he has a crush on you." Jax chuckled.

"Oh, stop, I was just playing with him."

"I don't get it either." Jax looked me up and down, so I hit him. "I'm kidding!"

"Sure." I rolled my eyes.

"Now will you tell me his name? Queen?" Jax asked as we stood on the deck, but I shook my head. "Give me a hint."

"His guitar was made out of his fireplace."

"That gives me nothing."

"He wrote '39.'"

"I hate that song."

"Me too!"

"I don't care!"

"What are you two arguing about?" Caine stepped in, looking amused.

"Your son doesn't know the name of the guitarist of Queen, and I'm refusing to tell him," I filled him in. Jax rolled his eyes.

"Jackson! I'm disappointed." Caine shook his head.

"That's what I said." I looked at Jax and shook my head.

"Just tell me!" Jax groaned with frustration, and I giggled. I looked at Caine, who nodded.

"Okay. It's Brian May."

"Oooooh. I knew that."

"Sure you did." I laughed, and his dad joined in. Jax left to join the guys around the pool, and I stayed on the deck with Caine.

"The party is winding down. Did you have fun?" he asked me genuinely.

"I did! Thank you so much for having me." I smiled gratefully.

"Just that minor hiccup." He winced as he looked at my cheek.

"No big deal," I assured him, being honest. The party guests were almost all gone, and the sun was setting. Conor came out of the house with a great sigh. Apparently, the children were giving their dad a hard time.

"Oh, man," Conor said to me, "I wish you lived in North Carolina to be our babysitter." He shook his head with exhaustion.

"You have a babysitter," his dad reminded him.

"Leo said he loves Mia—AKA Mimi," Conor said, and the two men chuckled.

Suddenly, Joe hopped onto the deck from the side of the house, carrying water guns. He tossed one to Conor. *Oh, this is too good.*

"Hey, Joe," I called over to get his attention.

"Hi, Mia." Joe straightened from his stealth position and smiled at me.

"Where you going with that gun in your hand?" I asked him, amused.

"Ambushing your boys." Joe snickered.

I turned to his brother and dad and clarified for them: "He meant to say—going down to shoot my old lady..." Caine and Conor both started to laugh, and I was relieved they understood that I was quoting "Hey Joe" by Jimi Hendrix. Conor stepped next to his brother, getting in on the ambush. I looked back at Joe and saw that he carried guns in both hands. "You want help?"

"Hell yeah!" Joe laughed, and I hurried over to them. I slipped off my heels and followed the two men down the deck steps and toward *my boys* hanging out around the pool. They both ran in, water guns blazing, and

I couldn't stop laughing at the sight of grown men acting like little boys. Ozzie, Nick, and Steven dispersed and were running away but somehow also fighting back. They looked like maniacs.

"And what do you think you're doing with that?" I stopped laughing when I heard Jax call me out, and I looked over to see him still in his chair. He hadn't reacted when Joe and Conor attacked, but something told me that he would when I did.

"With what?" I hid the gun behind my back and started stepping backward to keep an eye on him.

"With that toy behind your back." He smirked and folded his arms.

"Ooh. You mean this?" I held up the water gun, a Super Soaker.

"Don't do it," he warned me, and I smiled.

"Do what?" I asked innocently and continued backing away, gaining good distance.

"Don't do it..." he sang, taunting me further.

"Don't do...this?" I sprayed him with water, and he scrunched up his face to avoid getting shot in the eye. He looked adorable, and I almost forgot that I was in immediate danger. I continued to step backward as he stood up slowly and sighed. That's when I ran.

Toward the beach, getting far away from the pool. Like last time, I didn't get very far. He caught up to me and picked me up by wrapping an arm around my waist. I squealed in surprise but mostly from the excitement of being in his arms. He spun me around a few times, then set me back down on my feet. The world moved around me, and I struggled to keep my balance—the bastard made me dizzy! Then the bastard pushed me! Not roughly, of course, just enough for me to stumble onto the sand.

"That was cute." Jax laughed, confiscating the gun during the takedown.

"Don't you dare! I'm a defenseless woman!" I sat up and pointed at him from the sand.

"Ah. You're right. I can't spray a defenseless woman with a harmless water gun even though she has it coming."

"So glad you understand." I stared up at him. He smiled and sprayed me anyway. I held up a hand to shield my face. The spray stopped, so I lowered my hand only to bring it back up as he sprayed me down again. I couldn't stop laughing but got ahold of myself and collapsed to the sand.

"Oh, no. I killed Mia." Jax laughed at my dramatic trick. I felt his fingers press on my neck. "Aw, bummer. You're dead." He sighed and picked me up with ease. "Amelia Bell. Gone too soon. Buried at sea." I heard the waves getting closer, and my eyes shot open.

"No!" I squirmed to get down, but he walked into the ocean, so I held on. "Jackson!"

"Is that the best thing to be calling me right now?" He eyed me, and I slowly smirked. "Call me Daddy and you will go in the ocean," he scolded me quickly.

"Jax, please put me down," I asked sweetly, then made an important specification: "On land!" He chuckled but brought me back safely to the sand and set me on my feet. I folded my arms and glared at him. "Soon, you won't have pools or oceans to throw me into."

"So, I should take advantage of the luxury while I still can." He smirked, and I backed away.

The horizon then caught my full attention. The sunset was breathtaking, and I immediately sank down to enjoy it. Jax followed and sat beside me on the sand. I breathed in the salt air deeply and savored the fresh wind. I lost track of time, but we sat there until the sun melted into the horizon and it was dusk. Content, I sighed deeply and blinked away from the sky, catching Jax watching me. I had pulled my feet toward me and hugged my legs. I turned my head to rest on my knees and met his eyes.

"What?" I murmured.

"Nothing Natalie said was true." I felt my gaze soften at his words and smiled. "Believe me," he almost whispered, and I nodded.

"I do."

"Come closer," he ordered.

"You come closer." I smirked, and he rolled his eyes but couldn't stifle a smile. He turned and reached his arms around me and pulled me close. He didn't make a move, and the sky got darker. I didn't want to leave that rare special moment with nothing. He pushed an errant lock of hair out of my face and hooked it behind my ear. "Jax," I said quietly, and he brought his attention from my mouth to my eyes, which made me nervous. I'd never seen his eyes so clear and bright, and even in the dark, it distracted me.

"Hm?"

"Kiss me." I spoke softly and was unsure if he even heard me, but then his face brightened. He brought his hand to tenderly hold the side of my face and leaned in. I'd thought about what it would feel like to have his lips on mine so many times. When our hands touched for the first time, the tingle and zap made me feel a pull to him ever since. I tried ignoring it, but the pull just grew stronger until it became too much. I needed more. The kiss started soft and sweet but turned passionate within seconds. His tongue licked, and I parted my lips, letting him deepen the kiss. Soon our hands were on each other, and I softly moaned into his mouth, making his movements more forceful. We were a second away from being horizontal when we heard our names being called by Ozzie. We broke away and moved apart.

"Come in, guys! Don't want you getting lost!" Ozzie yelled, then disappeared back onto their property. It was dark enough that he couldn't have seen anything. Jax and I both looked at each other again and softly laughed. I was disappointed when Jax rose to his feet but knew we had to get back. He offered me his hand and pulled me up. I tilted my head back to look up into his eyes, and his sparkled as he looked down into mine. His gaze dropped to my mouth, and he sighed before those sparkling eyes lifted to connect with mine once again.

"Let's go. Before I change my mind and keep you out here."

"That would be fine with me." I shrugged and followed in his large footsteps in the sand.

"Mm-hmm." He chuckled and grabbed my hand to pull me forward so I was walking next to him.

We got back to the house, and everyone dispersed to change out of our fancy outfits and into bonfire clothes.

"Can we make *s'mores*?" I did a little excited hop as we walked down the path.

"Of course," Jax assured me with an affectionate smile.

———

Back at the guest house, I went straight to my bathroom and flinched when I saw my reflection in the mirror. "Oh, shit!" I looked closer. The guys hurried over and stood in the doorway. My cheekbone had a raised cut, and a bruise was forming. I'd never been hit before and hadn't been expecting such a harsh visual. "No one told me I looked this bad!"

"Because you don't," Jax assured me.

"Mia, you were still the hottest girl at the party, even with a messed-up face." Nick patted my shoulder, and I stared back at him. Everyone was old at the party, so that wasn't a big feat, and he said I looked messed up. "Since when do you have freckles?"

"You, go away." I rolled my eyes and shooed Nick out. I made the others leave, too, and washed my face. I walked out into the big room, and all the guys were waiting for me.

"Thanks for waiting but go on without me." They hesitated. "I have missed calls from my mom, so I'm going to call her back. I'll meet you on the beach. I won't be long. Bye." I smiled with a wave and waited for them to leave before falling onto the couch. *What the fuck just happened? I asked Jax to kiss me. Oh my God, I'm an idiot.* I'd loved it, but I shouldn't have done that. Now that I'd had a small taste, I knew how good it could be. I wasn't calling my mom. I was trying to get my head straight even though it hadn't been straight to begin with. I tried to never get my hopes up, but I just did. I had no idea what he wanted but would bet it wasn't what I wanted. I was afraid he would expect more of me, but at the same time, I wanted to give him all of me. He'd be my first and last, while I'd just be the virgin he corrupted. My mind rerouted from its default negativity to all of the reasons that would lead me to hope—every thoughtful gesture, affectionate look, how much we laughed together, and the magical way he always made me feel when I was with him. My body was still buzzing and my mind reeling from that one kiss. *That* was greater than my fear of the future. I was thinking too much, so I went with the only other way my mind operated: not thinking at all. I sighed and got on with my evening. Ultimately, I wanted him. That was an existential novelty, and I knew he would be the only one.

I finished getting ready for the beach bonfire, putting on my cozy knit leggings and an oversized crew sweatshirt. Already jittery with excitement, I hurried out the door, eager to see Jax again. I walked down the path toward the beach to join the others, my excitement building with each step. I realized that I had to use the bathroom and stopped at the main house. I was walking down the hall when I heard Jax and Joe talking in the kitchen and I heard my name. I stopped and listened—eavesdropping, a very bad habit.

"What?" Jax's clipped voice sounded so close to me, just on the other side of the wall, and I held my breath.

"You heard me. Why aren't you and Mia together?" Joe asked him—for a second time, apparently.

"Why?"

"Because you've been all over each other since you got here," Joe explained with a chuckle, and I felt my cheeks heat, thinking of Joe watching us.

"What? No, we haven't."

"And you can't keep your eyes off her for more than a minute."

"That's an exaggeration."

"Fine. Two minutes."

"That doesn't mean anything."

"Of course it does. Mom and Dad think so too," Joe said, and I felt even more awkward as I thought of Chanel, Caine, and Joe talking about me and Jax.

"Why the hell are Mom and Dad involved?"

"Jax, it's so obvious. That girl is—"

"Perfect. I know."

"So, then, what's the problem?" There was a long pause. "Ohh. She rejected you."

"I don't want to talk about Mia. Just let me pour my drink and we can go back to the fire." Jax spoke slowly and calmly, and I could just picture him on the other side of the wall holding a bottle of Jameson, trying to pour himself a drink, but pausing with all of Joe's interruptions.

"Fine. At least I can actually admit that *I* like Mia." My eyes widened in surprise at Joe's admission. *Joe likes me?*

"*What?*" I heard the thud of the bottle on the countertop. Jax may have been as surprised as I was. He reengaged fully with his brother with a stern voice. "No, you don't."

"Of course I do. She's awesome. But she can't keep her eyes off of you either. If you like her, do something about it."

"I don't need a pep talk, Joe."

"You obviously do."

"She's complicated, okay? She's different from anyone else I've ever met. And—and she's difficult." *Different. He's called me different before. Complicated. Why does it sound like a bad thing? Difficult—of course.*

"That's why you aren't together?"

"I don't know! Mia and I aren't together. The end. Now can we please go back to the fire?"

"Fine," Joe said, and I heard the swoosh of the sliding glass doors open, then close.

I remained leaning against the wall, frozen. I thought through everything Jax had just said to his brother and felt a lump form in my throat and my stomach twist. I thought our kiss had meant something to both of us, but I was obviously wrong. I was ready to throw myself at him. I was ready to give everything to him. I felt my heart crack and splinter, a few pieces falling to the floor. I wrapped my arms around myself to keep it from breaking completely.

My body started to tremble as I stood in the empty hallway. I turned and fled back into the bathroom. I pushed the door closed and leaned against it for support. I sucked in deep breaths, willing myself not to shed a single tear. Of course I did. He'd denied me so fervently. I felt like an idiot. I tried to think of the sweet moments we had together, but it was all tarnished by his denial. Everything that happened between us didn't mean anything to him. He'd said so. But it meant everything to me. *We had only one stupid kiss, and I thought it meant so much more than he did. God, I'm stupid.*

I dabbed at the tears on my cheeks, then wiped away the ones that clung to my jaw. Jax thought that I was different, difficult and complicated, and that's why we weren't together. Then he'd said "the end." We were "the end" before we'd even started.

I cried for just the right amount of time—my eyes brightened but didn't get red or puffy. I didn't know what to expect once I joined the boys at the bonfire. As far as Jax knew, we'd just shared a kiss at sunset. As far as I knew, Jax and I weren't together, but his brother Joe liked me. I already decided not to think and stuck to my plan. I promised myself one thing before I left the bathroom to find the flames at the beach—Jackson Caine would not break my little heart.

To be continued…

Ship of Fools
On Planet Neptune

Game Instructions

Object of the game: drink all of the fools, become captain of the ship and sail away.

What you'll need: Alcohol
Fun playlist
A good attitude

Set up: Put a table in the middle of the room to be the "ship" and gather your drinks (beer, seltzer, drink of your choice) on the surface to be the "fools." Put a chair on top of the table and place a bottle of Captain Morgan on top to be the "Captain." Divide the room into four areas to be the zones. Place pillows, tables, chairs, etc. around the room, making a path around the table. There must be one space on each corner of the table (see map).

Start:
"1, 2, 3, a pirate's life for me!"
"3, 2, 1, find the rum!"

Players take a shot of rum, grab a "fool" from the "ship" and run to a space in one of the four zones. Choose who starts.

Spaces: pillows, chairs, couch, tables, etc. set up as a path around the table

Floor: ocean lava

Zones: four chosen areas of the room. Each zone will have a rule.

Moves: Each player takes a turn to move one space while other players have a chance to win a move.

Win moves:

Player whose turn it is choses one of the three-

1. **Forehead fingers:** player whose turn it is counts 1, 2, 3, and everyone puts a number to their foreheads. Anyone with a number no one else has wins one space.

2. **Quote:** player whose turn it is starts a quote; those who complete the quote wins two spaces.

3. **Common ground:** player whose turn it is can say two people/places/thing; those who respond what is in common wins three spaces.

Every time you win a space—drink.

Zone rules:

Zone 1. Jaws: players must stand on one leg throughout the zone.

Zone 2. Bermuda Triangle: truth or dare. This applies to each player once per game.

Zone 3. Mermaid Lagoon: steal a turn by singing along to the song playing.

Zone 4. Venus's Shell: no shirts allowed while you're in the zone.

If player doesn't follow Zone rules, player must finish their drink.

Throughout the game, players move from space to space on the path around the room, taking turns and winning moves. Players take one can from the table when they move into the next zone (the spaces on the map that are on each corner of the table). Once the beverages are all gone, the next person to a table space wins by getting on the chair to become "Captain" and "Sail away" by drinking from the Captain Morgan bottle.

If player steps in ocean lava, player must go back to the table for another shot, and the rest of the players choose what space they start on.

Empty cans get thrown into Davy Jones's locker—a trash bin.

Map:

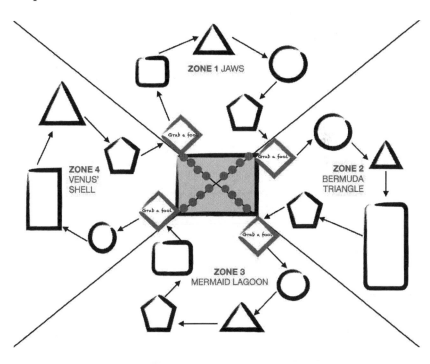